GOOD TO GRAVE

WHY SOME HUMAN HOSTS SUCCEED ... AND OTHERS BURN

Michael Park

FOX POINT BOOKS

Good to Grave: Why Some Human Hosts Succeed and Others Burn

Paperback print edition ISBN: 9780999771549

Published by Fox Point Books; foxpointbooks.com

ALSO BY MICHAEL PARK

Kentucky Dragon
The Glass-Face Man

For Michael

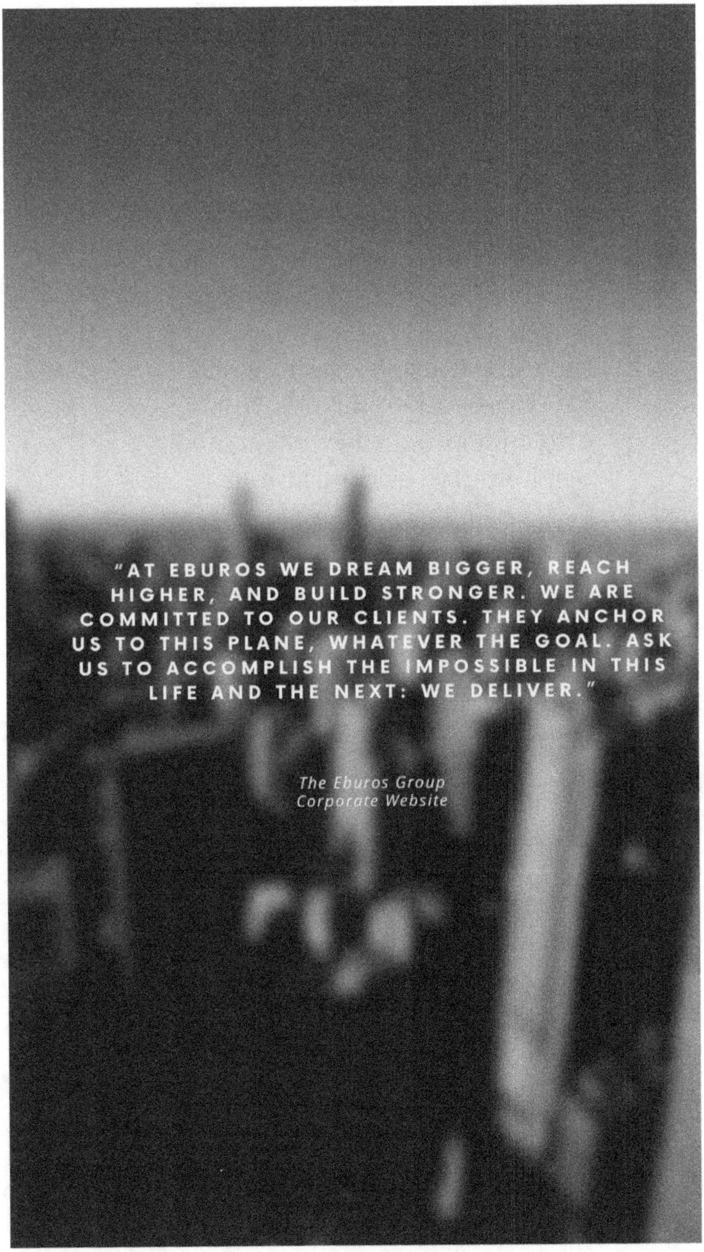

"AT EBUROS WE DREAM BIGGER, REACH HIGHER, AND BUILD STRONGER. WE ARE COMMITTED TO OUR CLIENTS. THEY ANCHOR US TO THIS PLANE, WHATEVER THE GOAL. ASK US TO ACCOMPLISH THE IMPOSSIBLE IN THIS LIFE AND THE NEXT: WE DELIVER."

The Eburos Group
Corporate Website

Reminder !

The refrigerator in the common kitchen area on the 20th floor will be cleaned out at 5 PM on Friday. Please be sure to remove any food, preserved tissues, fluids, and specimens, as well as any disciplinary residual limbs.

Questions or concerns should be directed to Office Services

PLEASE NOTE THAT ALL HUMAN BLOOD SHOULD BE PROPERLY LABELED AND STORED IN THE FREEZERS ON FLOORS 8-9, 16, AND 32.

THE EBUROS GROUP
NYC - ALL STAFF

Chapter One

Something was wrong with her shadow. Josie noticed right away, when Angela approached across the marble-hardwood lobby of The Eburos Group office tower. Thin and dark skinned, with a taut, no-nonsense smile, Angela shook Josie's hand as if she were handing out a business card. And the practiced way she assessed Josie's blue blazer, skirt, and blouse drummed in Mom's words: 'Everything is a test in the interview—*everything.*'

"Do you go by 'Josephina' or 'Josie'?" Angela asked, already leading Josie toward a line of security turnstiles.

So she knew Josie's full name.

"Josie," Josie said. "Thank you."

'Thank you?' Why am I thanking her?

Angela swiped them through with a plastic ID card. Past the turnstiles, a wall of ivy flanked two elevators, with a waterfall in the center, rushing over the golden swell of The Eburos Group tree logo. Not an immense redwood or classic oak tree, no, Eburos used a squat trunk-and-fronds image. *A yew tree, chosen for the symbolism of longevity, and probably because it fits on a landscape business card.*

On the first elevator, a screen displayed a day-trading stock market show. Angela used her card again and hit the top floor: 45.

"You're not from New York?" Angela asked. Her English was fast and clean, almost too practiced, as if she'd learned it professionally, maybe outside the U.S.

Josie adjusted the fake leather portfolio under her left arm, loaded with her resume and reference letters. "No, but I went to high school and college in the city." The elevator hit 5, 6, 7—rising, quickly, but not fast enough. Plenty of time for Josie to screw up this casual-critical small talk. *No. I've got this.* In this close, mahogany box, she smelled Angela's cinnamon-and-ginger perfume.

Angela watched her more closely, still smiling. "And how do you want to add value for Mr. Dean?"

Straight out with it. Fine. Josie prepped this.

"I want to learn," she said. "He's a visionary, and at NYU I majored in business—love new challenges ..."

Shit, coming out like gobbledygook. Josie clenched her hand on the corner of the portfolio until the pressure drained anxiety from her chest into her fingers.

The elevator dinged and stopped at the 22nd floor. The door opened to let on a big man in a dark suit, with a shaved head, tired eyes, and expensive-looking, heavy cufflinks. He stank of sour coffee through a musky cologne.

"Angela," he said, then noticed Josie.

"Tommy, this is Josie Morris. She's interviewing today at the top."

"Great." He straightened to face Angela, as the elevator continued up. "There's an issue there now."

When Tommy adjusted his coat, Josie noticed the thick bulge in his chest and shoulders, as if he were wearing heavy padding under his collared shirt. *And is that the lump of a gun holster on his left side?* Josie didn't have a good view, but either way, he was built like a squarish athlete. A rugby player, maybe.

"I hadn't heard," Angela told him, eyes flicking to Josie, then back. "Let's take this conversation off-line."

He started to answer, then nodded. The elevator opened to a small reception lobby on 45, backed by wraparound glass overlooking a balcony and the close press of downturn Manhattan, all the way to the sun-streaked curl of the East River separating them from Brooklyn. From here, the irregular crush of glass towers blocked out all but narrow slices of the view. Posed against the windows, a large, taxidermy grizzly bear stood on its hind legs, teeth bared and claws up, facing the hunched, bleach-white skeleton of a bull. The bull poised in mid-step, front hoof and leg bones up, its horns angled at the bear's gut. Vines and lush ivy dangled from the wood of the inner walls, just like the lobby, giving the place an almost-woodland smell.

"One moment," Angela told Josie, and she went with Tommy down a short hall with some kind of mural to a single door at the end.

Josie tracked Angela's shadow on the wall, until Angela and Tommy stopped at the end to knock. *What is it? Something about the shadow is off. No. It's normal. Anything else is delusional.*

A young female receptionist wearing EarPods smiled from a nearby desk. "Get you anything? Water, tea, or CSF?"

Josie's portfolio vibrated. "Shit," she said. Somehow, she forgot to switch off her cellphone in the lobby downstairs. "Sorry, CSF?"

"Cerebrospi ..." the receptionist started, and the phone went off again.

Josie apologized and crouched on a sofa at a coffee table arrayed with today's newspapers—*The New York Times, Wall Street Journal,* and two others printed in dense foreign symbols Josie didn't recognize—to find her phone. Who would be calling? Mom and Dani both knew how important this was—*should* know. And no way Everett would bother her now ...

The phone screen lit up with a missed call from Mom, and a text message bubble:

> *Mom: Call when you can. It's important.*

Mom set this up. Her relationship with Mr. Dean from Yale was the reason Josie had even gotten a foot in the door, which meant the only explanation for a cryptic message was if something terrible ...

"Josie?" Josie looked up: Angela waited at the hall entrance, arms crossed. "He's ready for you." Josie turned off her phone as she stood, fighting to contain the uncertain swirl in the back of her mind. *Mom knows I'm here. Something happened. Something bad.*

Josie followed Angela past wall panels depicting a cosmic timeline that began in darkness, before exploding into erupting stars and space nebulas that finally coalesced into ringed planets, asteroids, and a tiny blue blip, labeled *'Now,'* alongside a heavy black door.

Inside, pigs were flying. Hanging from the ceiling by iron hooks, taxidermy pigs—*real pigs, Jesus*—were suspended in mid-air with white-feathered wings glued to their backs. A short man in a rumpled suit stood behind an overstuffed desk, smoking. *Mr. Dean, that's him.* Past Mr. Dean, wraparound windows looked down on the city, except for a back wall of crammed floor-to-ceiling bookshelves, with a strange empty space of plaster between them. On that space, someone had drawn a crude mock-up of blue pillars, a brownish sky, and a pale chalk man. Almost a stick figure, the chalk man looked completely out of place, as if he'd been added by a child.

Josie forced herself to look away. At the desk, Tommy-from-the-elevator faced Mr. Dean and a young, dark-haired woman, who was probably in her early twenties—Josie's age.

"... and what if I did?" the woman asked Mr. Dean. Her voice shook, as if she were fighting tears, cheeks flushed bright red. The woman pointed at Mr. Dean. "How would you stop me?"

Mr. Dean noticed Josie and Angela and signaled with a cigarette between his fingers. The room stank of cigarettes and old coffee.

The woman spun, following Mr. Dean's stare back to Josie. She was pretty—not Josie's type, really—but with wide, honest eyes and hot in a Renaissance portrait kind of way. The knees of the woman's suit pants were flecked with dirt, and when she stabbed a finger at Josie, Josie saw dark crust in her nails, as if she'd been crawling in soil.

"Who is *she*?" the woman said. "Another one? Is she the new me?" Tommy reached for the woman's arm, and she jerked away. "Don't touch me." Then, to Josie, "You're not in yet, are you? Run. Turn around and go."

When the woman locked eyes with her, Josie's mouth tasted dry, and her stomach lurched. *She believes this, whatever it is. She is genuine.*

"That's enough, Grace," Mr. Dean said and raised his eyebrows at Tommy, who caught Grace's shoulder. "To be continued."

"Don't," Grace said, but she couldn't slip free as Tommy walked her to the door. "You," Grace called again to Josie. "Don't talk to him ..." She winced and tried to pull away from Tommy.

"This way," Tommy said.

"No," Grace said, and she grabbed the slippery window glass. "I'm not me anymore, but I won't belong to him."

Tommy took her out, and Angela followed, shutting the door behind her. Josie was alone with Mr. Dean.

"Hysteria—a common sign of genius—is sometimes just hysteria," he said quickly, and paced to a bookshelf, positioning his back against the edge, like a bear with an itch. He didn't stop moving, fidgeting and bouncing back to the desk again. Like a static charge, his manic energy tensed the air. "Tell me what you know about derivatives markets."

"I'm not ..." Josie hesitated.

"You're no expert, I understand. But leverage is an innovation every bit as significant as a super-computer. More, possibly. Value created where none existed. Making one into many by force of will. The Eburos Group is a ship, Josie, and I am its captain. Our name, 'Eburos,' what's the derivation?"

She prepped for this. *Of course I know. Everyone knows.*

"Yes," she said, "it comes from an old Celtic word for 'yew tree.'" And when he didn't answer, Josie continued, "The yew tree, they can live for thousands of years, but there aren't many left ..."

"They survive on our logo." Mr. Dean watched her reaction, didn't smile. *What am I supposed to say?* "A Gaulish-Germanic tribe living in what is today part of the Netherlands, Belgium, and Germany were called the *Eburones* by Julius Caesar, who, of course, annihilated them entirely. The name '*Eburones*'? Chosen by Caesar, after the king of the tribe, Catuvolcus, killed himself by drinking yew sap, which contains taxines. He was too old to run. *Eburones-Eburos.*"

What is this history lesson? So random Josie felt like she should smile, waiting for him to wink. But not a joke.

He tapped out cigarette ash across the carpet and pushed off the desk to pace along the windows, like a tiger at the bars of a cage. "Permanence is a curious target. You're aware that the Fortingall yew in Perthshire, Scotland is perhaps 9,000 years old? A place the Romans never truly conquered. Better to identify the delta, *before* the slaughter, isn't it? Dear old Catuvolcus faced a one-in-a-generation intrapreneur and 40,000 best-of-breed Roman legionaries. Generational aptitude is tested most in the face of the unexpected. What do you expect?"

What do I expect? What kind of question is that? "I expect ..."

Mr. Dean continued, "There are three classic generational arche-types: fighter, merchant, and artist. Study war so your children can study commerce, so *their* children can study poetry—thank you, John Adams. My predecessor was a fighter, obviously. Which are you?"

Mr. Dean squinted out the window, and Josie followed his stare. Through a horizontal gap in the skyscrapers, the speckled water of New York Harbor curved away, and she could just make out the shape of Liberty Island and the darker rut of Governor's Island on the left. Out the Bay, past Staten Island, Josie knew Dutch Island might even be visible from this height. Not clear enough now, though. The horizon was a hazy screen, hiding the island's famous hilltop windmills. Mr. Dean frowned, as if disappointed with the view.

I'm not intimidated. I studied hard. I deserve to be here. So which am I? "I'm a fighter," she said.

He snuffed a cloud of cigarette smoke, as if that were the wrong answer. "I would have thought artist. Nomadic much of your young life, fears of social dislocation until NYU. How many cities before you arrived here for high school? Six, seven? Not better or worse, you understand, but very different. Not really a fighter."

What was he saying? That she wasn't strong—or that her past was frivolous? *Or just flexing with background check bullet points.*

"Maybe," she said.

"What's your impression of this?" He swept his cigarette around to encompass the room.

'This' meaning his office? Does he want a specific answer? As if she'd been meant to gather clues on the elevator ride up to solve this puzzle. *The art, maybe?*

"The pigs," Josie said, glancing at the dangling, airborne pigs along the ceiling. "And the bear and the bull in the lobby—it's all very literal, isn't it?"

"Yes, our culture is direct," Mr. Dean said. "No silos here. Do you know their provenance?"

"The bear and the bull?" *Another quiz.* "A bear market trends down," Josie said slowly. Too basic, she tried to remember freshman econ. She'd spent an entire semester in class with Everett, listening to lectures about the fundamentals of market movements, pounded a half-dozen textbooks and a thick course packet. *Where is that info now?* Standing in this office, when it actually mattered, why was her mind blank? *Calm down.* "The term 'bear market' is old. It comes from 'bearskin jobber,' doesn't it? A trader of bear pelts, who sold the furs, before catching the animals."

His face blank, unreadable, Mr. Dean nodded. "Go on."

"It was about selling something that doesn't exist yet," Josie said. "The bears hadn't been caught."

"Trading away the corpse of someone who is still alive and walking around," Mr. Dean said, watching Josie's reaction. "Leverage."

He said 'someone.' Not an animal, *someone.* She clenched her right hand tight, until she felt prickles of fingernail pain that cleared her head. *Don't show him that you have no clue where this is going.*

"And the bull?" he asked.

Josie knew this one. An essay she'd written sharpened in her mind, until she could almost see the print-out pages. "The old Dutch stock market," she said. "There's a theory the term 'bull market' is related to the notices they used to put up—*bull*-etins on the board." When he didn't respond, Josie continued, "There's also a school of thought that the terms are simpler. They may come from the animals themselves. Their style of attack. The bull stabs *up* with its horns, and a bear swipes *down* with its claws."

"And what do you believe?"

What do I 'believe'?

Her brief confidence puddled again. "I don't know," Josie said.

"Hm," Mr. Dean said. "That phrase is a problem here. 'I don't know,' 'I don't understand'—we don't use those words. You *do* know." He waited, as if she were supposed to agree with him.

The chalk wall painting caught her eye, and she looked without meaning to. *Did it just—no.* The stick man was unchanged.

Mr. Dean followed her line of sight and raised his bushy eyebrows. "Do you see something?"

"No," she said. *Just your amateur wall art.* Why was the bizarre image even there? Inherently unsettling, but also not. The fuzzy, searching position of the chalk man looked vulnerable, as if he were staring into the office for help.

Mr. Dean waited, the room quiet. "You are sure you don't see anything?"

"Like what?"

"I'm not sure there's a role for you here."

Josie adjusted her portfolio. "What?"

"Angela has 1,200 resumes for the position," he said, matter-of-fact. He wasn't trying to intimidate her, just stating the obvious. "Pre-screened. Your mother is a good friend—please tell Caitlyn how nice it was to meet you. Thank you, Josie."

It's over. Just like that.

He went back to the desk, already lighting a new cigarette. As she turned to the door, a numb lump formed in her stomach. *What did I do wrong?*

Behind the desk, he said into a phone earpiece, "Hello? Yes, it's Solomon Dean. Patch me through to him ..."

"What was I supposed to say?" Josie asked, and she looked back at him. "Whatever this job is, I can learn to do it. Just give me a chance."

He blinked at her, said into the earpiece, "Hi Walter, one second ..." Then pressed a button to mute it, and to Josie, "Angela will take you back down."

"Your art is garbage."

Did I just say that?

A smile flicked at the corner of his mouth. "Really?" "The wall timeline is beyond pretentious, just like ..." She caught herself. *No job, but he's still powerful. And Mom's friend, too—don't do it.* "It's bullshit," she said.

I did it. Yep.

Mr. Dean rummaged through the desk papers, then into the drawers and found a small pink rubber ball. He tossed it to Josie.

"An everyman memento of our meeting today. No ivory tower here," he said and waved her away, the cigarette streaking smoke trails.

Like I'm a fly. A nuisance. Josie turned the ball in one hand. A stress bouncy ball, with no label or stamp, and nothing odd about it, except that it was here. *A child's toy? Is this a joke?* She went to the door, and as he launched into his earpiece conversation, the wall painting caught her eye again. The chalk man was gone.

Wait.

The door opened, and Angela pulled her back out. Returning to the elevators, the bright receptionist caught Josie's eye again. *What did she say before? Water, tea, or ..?*

"Hi," Josie said to the receptionist, as Angela tapped to call the first elevator. "Earlier, when I came in, you asked me if I wanted—what was it, 'C-S-F' ..?"

A terrified flicker-check: the receptionist glanced at Angela—impassive—then smiled at Josie again, totally normal. "No, I'm sorry. I must have misspoken. I'm new. This is my first ..."

The elevator opened, and Angela nudged Josie in. On the ride down, she told Josie they would be in touch. A polite 'don't call us, we'll call you'—but they wouldn't. *I blew it.*

I misheard the receptionist ... but the chalk man. She'd glimpsed columns on the wall. Except no, it happened fast. *I must not have noticed the chalk figure somehow.* The thought felt limp and unconvincing even as Josie tried to make it click. Back through the security turnstiles in the ground floor lobby, she decided that Mr. Dean could have wiped the image off without her noticing. Maybe the dusty smudge really was chalk, and he'd swiped it away with his back.

Angela stopped in the lobby. "Thank you for coming in ..." And Josie realized what was wrong with Angela's shadow, why it bothered her. When Angela spun to go, her shadow turned first.

It's leading her.

"The job of a leader is to understand and bleed competition. Often, however, managers define competition too narrowly, focusing only on direct human competitors. Yet competition for profits goes beyond living rivals to include four other competitive curses as well: the active dead, harvesters, potential succubi, and substitute products. The extended rivalry between these five curses defines an industry's structure and its competitive environment. "

SOLOMON DEAN

SOLOMON DEAN, CEO
THE EBUROS GROUP

"THE FIVE CURSES"
AUGUST 2008

Chapter Two

Numb and squinting in the sun glare, Josie mixed with the sidewalk crowd outside. Passing corner food trucks and homeless people, she found her cellphone, texted Dani:

Done

Then called Mom.

"And?" Mom asked, barely one ring in.

Josie continued past a massive, photo-realistic mural of a humpback whale exploding out of the East River, easily ten meters tall, on the side of a skyscraper. "Crashed and burned," Josie said. "Why did you ..."

"Oh no, what happened?"

Across a busy intersection, Josie neared the statues of a memorial outside a church, then stepped into shadowy scaffolding alongside a construction site.

"It was weird," Josie said. Angela's shadow and the disappearing chalk man weren't real, of course. Stress illusions, like the receptionist asking about 'CSF.' *Or something.* Josie had promised not to hide these things from Mom, since Dad died more than eight years ago. All this time, Mom's mantra had hardened into truisms for Josie: *No one remembers everything. Everyone's version of the past is wrong. We rewrite our lives in our minds every day, and so what if the trauma of losing Dad wrecked me for awhile? It would wreck anyone.* After Dad's death, Josie made it through high school by ignoring the blotchy holes in her memories. Like slivers of glass in her mind that twinged if she focused too hard. And only one little flare up before college, weeks of anxiety that had long-since faded into dream after-images. *Everyone is scarred, my pain isn't special. So why fixate on this now?* "I'll tell you later, promise," Josie said. "What was that text? Did something happen?"

"I'm so sorry, did it throw you off? I knew you were at Eburos today, but I thought maybe I'd catch you before ..."

"No, Mom, it's fine. What happened?"

"It's Uncle Don. I hate to have to ... but I'll just say it. He had a heart attack."

"Shit." Josie caught a metal scaffolding pole, and a dude in a suit clipped her from behind, grumbling. People flowed by her fast, like a stream current around a fallen tree. *I'm a broken branch.* "Is he okay?"

"He's in the hospital here. I think Saturday is cancelled, Josie."

Dad's older brother, Don, moved south-south, to Miami, after Dad's car accident. 'I've earned palm trees and sun. And don't talk to me about hurricanes.' Even at a distance, Mom insisted they keep Uncle Don in their lives. *Because he remembers Dad the way we do, even if we never talk about it.* Now, though, Uncle Don was visiting Mom in Connecticut, and all of them—Mom, Uncle Don, Josie, and Dani—had planned a night out in the city on Saturday. A too-optimistic celebration of the future transformed into a toast to failure. *Because I bombed that interview. Just as well we're ditching it.*

"It just happened," Mom said. "There's nothing you can do. We were driving around, looking at the early fall leaves when it happened. The first time I went leaf peeping, since ..."

Since we were living in Hartford? Or maybe Boston even? All the places Dad moved us to escape himself. Coming to theaters this fall: Escape From Your Own Brain Chemistry! 'Schizo,' from the Greek 'skhizein,' meaning 'split' ... and 'phrenia,' derived from 'phren' or 'mind.' Taken together, schizophrenia translates into the wholesale disruption of your daughter's childhood, followed by your early death on a highway in Kentucky. Even today, whole sections of her experiences, mini-lifetimes in Josie's past from city-to-city, still felt unreal. Other parts were gone completely, slashed out because a part of her didn't want to dwell. *Repression, suppression, blocking: also known as waking up each morning. Move on.*

"Mom, I should be there with Uncle Don," Josie said. A wave of car exhaust hit her, and she walked faster toward the subway. Just another block.

Dani texted:

> *What's the verdict?*

That was her thing now: practicing lawyer-speak. Dani tried to play it as a half-joke, but Josie suspected there was more insecurity in it than that. This week, Dani's first-year law school classes started up at Columbia. The plan was for Dani to commute from their Brooklyn apartment, at least at first, and then think about a move to Morningside Heights, if and when she lost her mind on the grind of the M, L, and 1 trains. Josie texted back:

> *Guilty*

> *Contempt of court*

"I'll update you about your uncle as soon as I see him," Mom said.

I should be there. He's my family, the only one left besides Mom. But Josie said she understood, ended the call, and ducked into the Canal Street subway station. As she continued down to the platform, her phone buzzed.

Dani texted:

> *So sorry*

> *We'll find the right fit*

The right fit. She sounded like a soulless LinkedIn quiz, as if a job were a pair of skinny jeans. 'Oh, does that pinch at the waist? We have a larger size right here.'

Dani:

> *You're too good for them anyway. My Josie sees things other people miss*

Uh huh.

Back in Bushwick, she followed Myrtle Avenue past coffee shops, hole-in-the-wall burrito restaurants, and new chain clothing and bric-a-brac stores, until the street bled into apartment complexes and a public high school that had seen better days at the corner of their block. Josie mounted a short flight of steps to a nondescript four-story apartment building wrapped in vinyl siding. They lived on the second floor.

What was she going to tell Dani? *I failed, because I didn't have an opinion about derivatives markets? Oh, and there was a disappearing chalk man and a woman who followed her shadow ...*

Reaching for the front doorknob, Josie lost her grip on the rubber ball—still holding it for some reason—and it bounced away down the steps. *Shit. Totally forgot I had that.* Josie started for it ... and at the bottom of the stairs, Dani caught the ball in one hand, a cloth bag of groceries in the other.

"Almost lost this!" she said, smiling. Dressed in a white t-shirt that she knew was too small over a dark bra, Dani looked lanky-sheik, with short black hair, her muscular torso accented from the way she held the bag and now raised the bouncy ball. "You drop this?"

"Keep it," Josie said, and they kissed quickly on the stoop, before heading in.

Through the first floor hall and up two flights, their little one-bedroom looked more pathetic than it should have, with cheap arthouse photos of birds and abandoned factories in the kitchen that opened to their second-hand couch and dated TV living room on the right, complete with sagging, overstuffed bookshelves all the way to the street windows. After two years in this place—since junior year at NYU—it wasn't aging well.

Did Mr. Dean sense that this is where I come from? A fragile, striving platform, just a whisper above first-world poverty, only really sustainable because of the holiday and birthday checks from Mom and Dani's parents' in Virginia.

Josie tossed her portfolio on the chipped kitchen table and went back past their bedroom on the left, into the bathroom.

"You all right?" Dani called from the other side of the door.

No. I crashed and burned, and Uncle Don is in the hospital. Josie stared at herself in the sink mirror. The shower dripped behind her, toilet gurgling off to her left. "Fine." She'd looked professional and polished this morning, hair flat and shaped to her shoulders, lips sharp red but not aggressive, her brown eyes full and smart. Now, though? Hair frizzed from the subway and with crinkles around her eyes and tight jaw, she looked dazed. Like she'd spun in circles too many times. Like a child. Josie cried. Hunched forward, both hands tight on the sink, she felt a shudder knock through her chest and shoulders. *They rejected me, because I don't deserve that job.* Dani should know about Uncle Don. *And I shouldn't hide the rest, either, even if it isn't real. Tell someone.* Why was this shaking her? Because after the summer blur of graduation celebrations, Dani and Mom cheering her on, and now ... nothing. Josie applied to a hundred jobs, at least, and not one interview, except the pity meeting at Eburos. And that only happened, because Mom knew Mr. Dean from Yale a lifetime ago, before Dad even. The $950.47 in her checking account would last until next month, maybe a little longer, if Mom helped. *Then what?* This apartment lease was up for renewal. No real discussion of it with Dani yet, and Josie had just assumed they would make things work.

She splashed her face. Eburos was a failure, no more worrying about Mr. Dean or anything else she saw. *Maybe that's good. Move on.*

As the tear-flush faded from her cheeks and nose, the front door buzzed, and Josie heard Dani laugh. A moment later, when Josie went back into the kitchen, tall, broad-shouldered Everett strode over to pick her up in a quick twirl and place her beside Dani. "Happy days are here again! The birds are singing, the sun is shining, and you look marvelous." In freshman orientation, four years ago, she'd bristled at Everett's pompous, attention-seeking acrobatics. Now, though? She knew better. Everett just *was.* Not an insecure act or performance, he couldn't help his outsized personality, even if it made them extras on 'The Everett Show' whenever he was around.

"I was told not to bring it up," Everett said, "but are you okay, Josie? That *New York Magazine* profile on Dean made the guy sound like a real maniac. You know he's never been seen outside the building. He lives there, and everyone who works for him—all around the world—they have to pay homage, like a Mughal King."

"It's done," Josie said. "I didn't get the job. Thank you, though."

"She's over it," Dani said.

"All right, all right," Everett said. "No more downer talk. I'm buying tonight. Drinks on me, okay?"

After a brief back-and-forth, they agreed that the microwave clock hitting 6:30 meant time to go out. On the front stoop, Everett called to a passing couple, "Merry Christmas!"

How has he survived in this city? Not even mid-September, and it was still way too early in the evening for Everett's shenanigans, but as they walked, as he and Dani talked music and politics, the failure-weight began to drain out of Josie's system. At a high-top table at a corner bar called *Spats*, Josie imagined that life wasn't changing. They would all start classes again soon. She would moan about tests and papers, and tease Dani for calling soccer 'football.' On weekends, they'd see Mom for brunch or Sunday dinner at her new place in Fairfield. There would be holidays and arguments about trivial pop culture, and always the looming stress of money, but the plod of Josie's life would continue just like it had.

Josie sipped her gin and tonic and focused on Dani and Everett again, both cradling half-empty beers.

"... America runs on law, not privilege," Dani was saying. "It's what differentiates us from Europe."

Dani's half-joking rationale for becoming a lawyer, Josie had heard a version of this speech at least a dozen times. How many beers had Dani downed already, though? Josie hadn't been counting.

"And because we don't have inherited nobility, anyone can win in the courts," Dani said, her words slurring. "Anybody can become noble.""Our nobility advertises on highway billboards and bus stops is what you're saying?" Everett asked. He traded a quick eye roll with Josie.

"Law is *the* noble profession," Dani said.

"It's also parasitic," Josie muttered. Mr. Dean was a lawyer, just like Mom. Josie knew that from the bios she'd read the last few days. But a very different kind of lawyer. The kind who wielded the law like someone interrupting the flow of a board game to rob the bank on a technicality.

Everett clapped and started to respond with a joke, when Dani frowned at her. "What is? Going into law? Are you serious?""I don't know," Josie said, watching her half-eaten garden burger. "Seems like it's about making money, not high ideals."

"Did you forget your mom's a lawyer, Josie?""And?" Josie stared back at her. *Mom's a lawyer, so that proves all lawyers don't get rich? Because she struggled for nonprofits all her life and now frets about bills the same as us?*

Dani snorted—she looked ugly when she did that. "Well, you would know, I guess.""What does that mean?""It means you don't have a job or any plans," Dani said. "It's easy to criticize other professions when you don't have one."

Josie felt the air go out of the room, like she'd been punched in the gut. She looked down, fingers trembling on her glass.

Everett leaned in, waving a hand to distract Dani. "Danger! Dani: eyes up. Let's talk happy things. Karaoke tonight?"

Dani brightened. "Abso-fucking-lutely. How early you want to go?"

The two of them started talking quickly again about the evening. Dani pounded her beer and stood to order another.

I don't have a job or plans? What the hell? My plan is to be with you. Be a team, together.

When they finished, Dani wandered to the restroom, and Everett said, "She's drunk, Josie. That's all. Too early, but it happens.""I know." *But so what if she is? She meant it, didn't she?*"I'm not apologizing for her," Everett said more quietly. "But I wouldn't read into it tonight."

This was new. When Dani drank, she got philosophical and sweet, not like this. *The stress of today maybe, or something else.* Back outside, the street darkened, and after another bar, they rode the subway to the East Village. No escape from karaoke. Past a stretch of outdoor restaurants adjacent to a courtyard where a blanket crowd watched a black-and-white movie on the side of a building, Dani led them into *The Boombox.* A single-room karaoke bar already crowded under the shimmery lights of a mirror ball. While Everett waited at the bar, Dani and Josie found a U-shaped couch facing the central singing area and screen. A tattooed girl in tights swayed and rasp-sang Lou Reed, giggling after each verse.

"You should be happy for me," Dani shouted over the music.

"What?"

"Happy," Dani said. "Have you ever tried just being happy? And not so ..." She shrugged, watching the singer, not Josie.

"Not so me?" Josie said.

"Yeah, maybe."

Walk out. Josie's left arm trembled where it rested on her leg. But too many people jammed in here. She couldn't even see the dark exit door anymore. *Why is this happening? I told Dani what happened. She's supposed to ... She's breaking up with me.*

Everett appeared with an armful of oversized Sapporo beer cans, shouting over the music that he put in songs for all of them.

No, we're not breaking up.

"What song?" Josie asked, but neither of them heard. The Lou Reed girl finished, and the bar erupted in applause. Josie didn't touch her beer, not even when her name was called for 'Total Eclipse of the Heart.' With her eyes closed, she blocked out the room and let the familiar lyrics flow, just like in the shower—until finally, mercifully, it ended.

After 3:00 AM on the walk out, Dani draped an arm over Josie's shoulder, as Everett guided them in a loop past quiet office towers and bass-pounding bars, until he froze.

"Wait, wait—Josie," Everett said. "That's where you interviewed today, right?"

Across the street, they'd somehow arrived at the dark Eburos building, the windows still and black, except for the top floor. *Is Mr. Dean smoking and grumbling up there right now? Is the chalk man back?*

"We need the subway or a taxi," Josie said.

"We do," Everett said. "But first ..." He trotted across the street, and Dani jerked away to follow, calling for Everett to slow down.

"You're our lookout!" Everett shouted back to Josie.

"What are you doing?"

Everett dashed to the main entrance with his head low, as if he were planning a break-in. Josie started into the street, and a taxi honked and swerved, its headlights bright in her face. She stumbled back. Across the street, Dani waited behind Everett, as he lined up with the lobby doors. A spurt of liquid splashed the glass at a low angle in front of him.

Damn it. 'No!' she wanted to shout. 'Stop!' There must be cameras, security.

More cars passed, but no one on the sidewalk, and when Everett finished pissing, he adjusted his pants and high-fived Dani. Then they both came back, panting and laughing.

"Your honor is redeemed," Everett said.

"You see?" Dani said. "Everett stood up for you."

"I can't believe you did that," she said.

"I covered my face," Everett said. "Nobody will know ..."

"What were you thinking?" Josie asked.

Dani shook her head, smirking "He was thinking about *you*. They insulted you today. Fuck that place. You don't need them."

"Also ten beers," Everett said, patting his gut. "I was thinking about that."

Josie led them away faster, checking the dark lobby again for any movement. Nothing.

"That was really fucking stupid," she said. "Both of you ..."

Dani grunted. "Jesus, can we go one minute, without you telling me how dumb I am?"

Before Josie could answer, Dani swayed into the street and waved down a cab. Josie climbed in the back, unspeaking beside Dani, while Everett chatted with the driver up front. Not just drunk, Dani was acting wrong. Like she wanted to fight. Josie felt hot emotion—anger or tears—tug at the edge of her vision and bobbing nausea in her stomach. *I'm not drunk, not really, so what is this? Pain. Just disorienting pain, that's all.*

They dropped off Everett first, and back at their apartment, Josie followed Dani into their dark bedroom, collapsed on her side of the bed. *Are we going to talk about it?*

TONK.

She looked over: Dani bounced the rubber ball off the ceiling, caught it in one hand—and again. The condolence prize from Mr. Dean. *Fuck him, too.*

TONK.

"Talk in the morning?" Josie asked.

Dani started to respond, then heaved up and rushed out. The bathroom door slammed. Josie heard the toilet seat and cough-gagging. She draped an arm over her face. *It'll be better tomorrow.*

But it wasn't. Not in the morning, when Josie woke with dry mouth and Dani still snoring beside her. Josie climbed out of bed and started into the kitchen—stopped. She heard movement on the living room couch. Someone was here.

MEET ANGELA MASSADO

ANGELA MASSADO: People ask me all the time what it's like to work there [at The Eburos Group], and my honest answer: amazing. Every day, I am thrilled to do what I love. Are there long hours? Yes. Is it hard work? Of course. And sure, sometimes, well, the firm takes its 'pound of flesh,' so to speak, but it's such an honor to participate in true disruptive immolation.

INTERVIEWER: Innovation.

ANGELA MASSADO: Sorry?

INTERVIEWER: 'Innovation,' you mean.

ANGELA MASSADO: Ha, of course. Absolutely. Mr. Dean is literally innovative as Hell.

Chapter Three

"Hello?" Josie said.

Nothing.

She crept closer along the wall for a better view: Everett. He sprawled on his back, face line-streaked and eyes squinty as he smiled up at her. It looked forced. *He can't be here. We dropped him off first.*

"Top of the morning," Everett said.

"I didn't know you were here."

"Sorry, yes—your door was open, and I came by, because I left my hat."

Weird. He hadn't worn a hat yesterday, and the reflexive explanation sounded so obviously wrong. Why sneak in and lie about it?

"Want coffee?" Josie asked, as she went back to the kitchen.

"No, thanks. I just ..."

Josie rinsed the countertop coffee maker, let the sink run to fill it. She glanced back, expecting Everett to be up. But no, he still slouched in there, only half visible. "You just what?" Josie called.

"I don't know," Everett said quietly.

What is wrong with him?

Josie poured water into the back of the coffee maker, found a filter, and scooped in grounds, then returned to the living room doorway, as the machine gurgled. Everett still hadn't moved.

"What's wrong?" Josie asked.

He blinked up at her and stretched off the couch, with a ripple of pops and cracks from his joints and the bones in his back. "It sounds worse than it feels," he said and staggered toward the door.

As he passed, Josie caught a whiff of old sweat and the curdled, almost rotten stench of alcohol on his breath. "You drank too much," she said.

He leaned hard on the door. "I had a really bad dream."

And probably still drunk—that's all.

"Are you okay to get home?"

Everett turned his fingers on the doorknob, but loose, so it didn't twist. "I've never had a dream like that before."

Not him either. Everett's voice dropped to a whisper, as if he were apologizing. Ashamed of what he was trying to say.

"Let me get you coffee for the road."

As Josie started back to the sink, he caught her arm, his eyes red with tears. Not crying, but his lip bobbed open, as if he might.

"Everett ..."

"I was on the wall," he said, searching her face, as if she were supposed to know what that meant.

"Stop," Josie said. "Let go of me."

Everett noticed his hand on her and let go. "Shit, I'm sorry. Is Dani okay? She was outside, collapsed in the street. It wasn't just me."

"I don't understand what you're talking about," Josie said slowly. She felt a coiled calm, as if this were happening to someone else. Watching herself ease away to the coffee maker, eyes on her cellphone, charging at the wall socket on the kitchen table. *Call the police? No, this is Everett. Just drunk. He's never done this before, though. Not even close.*

"Dani was hurt," Everett said again. "Not moving."

Josie took a cat mug out of the cabinet and poured herself a cup. "Where?"

"The place," he said. "Your office."

Josie forced herself to neatly slide the coffee pot back, so it could continue to fill, then leaned back on the counter to face him. If she kept a routine now—*I am not rattled, I am calm*—he would leave. Her phone was an arm's length away to her left. *What if he grabs me again?*

"I think you need to sleep it off," Josie said, her voice deliberate. *I am in control.* "Whatever this is."

"I didn't mean to ..." Everett shook his head, massaging his forehead with one hand. "Jesus, what is he? The little chalk man ..."

Josie blew on the coffee, took a sip that singed her tongue. *Don't ask. He doesn't know. That's impossible. This isn't about Mr. Dean's office. Just a nonsense hangover delusion. Someone slipped him something at the karaoke bar. He shouldn't even be here.*

"Please," she said and forced a weak smile. "For my sake, go get some rest."

Everett nodded, murmured something, and opened the door. "Josie, can you apologize for me? Please? Tell him I made a mistake. I didn't know."

"Sure," Josie said. "No problem."

Everett relaxed a little, forehead glistening with sweat. He started to thank her, and Josie crossed to close the door. She clicked the lock.

What the actual fuck? He'd never done that before, randomly sneaking in to ramble about a bad dream and a chalk man. The chalk man in Mr. Dean's office, of course. *No. Bullshit.*

Josie drank more coffee and went to shower. Under the warm spray, she told herself that people did this kind of thing. Just because Everett hadn't in the past, didn't mean—*enough.* Back in the bedroom, dressing in sweatpants and a t-shirt, Josie heard Dani stir and cough on the bed.

"Something strange ..." Josie hesitated. "Everett was here."

When Dani perched up, confused, Josie told her, and Dani sank back again, already tossing the rubber ball overhead.

"Okay," Dani said at last. "What's your point?"

"He's never done that. And he didn't sound like himself." Dani didn't answer, just caught the ball, then flicked it up for another catch. And again. "Nevermind," Josie said. "Can we talk today?"

Dani concentrated on the ball, not her. "I have orientation."

"What? You didn't tell me that."

"Well, I do." Dani palmed the ball and flopped on her side to face Josie. She looked older, her cheeks sunken with hungover dehydration, dark bags under both eyes. "It's not like you tell me everything."

Josie stiffened, finished dressing. *She's already picking another fight. Why? She wants an excuse to argue, to make this the rhythm of the day or maybe a reason she can stalk out and justify flirting with a new girl at Columbia. Stop it.* Josie hadn't told her about Eburos, not really. Or Uncle Don.

"You're right," Josie said. "I forgot to mention yesterday—my uncle is in the hospital. He had a heart attack."

Dani swiveled her legs off the bed and slouched forward to study Josie. "Your dad's brother? When?"

"It just happened."

"I mean when are you going."

That's what she cares about. Not 'how is he' or 'what can we do,' but 'how soon is Josie leaving.'

"I don't know," Josie said. She felt cold, suddenly alone, as if Dani weren't even here. A hologram of a person occupying the room, not

Josie's living, breathing girlfriend. "Before I go, we should talk about the lease."

Dani pulled herself up and stumbled out. "I feel like shit," she called back. "Not right now."

Josie heard the bathroom door slam, then the shower. *How did this happen so quickly?* Yesterday and all the days before were fine, good even, until Josie got home from the interview. Not perfect, but they were happy. *We were, weren't we? I'm not imagining that?* In Josie's frantic job interview prep and Dani's law school planning, Josie must have missed the signals.

Don't fixate on her. Do something physical. Move. She headed out without calling to Dani and walked two blocks to a squat building with the dark forms of people on treadmills and stationary bikes half-hidden past sheer, tinted windows. Inside, '80s music played over loudspeakers in an open room of exposed, brightly-painted pipes and concrete wall bricks. Glass filled the walls, and the familiar smell of rubber, nylon, and sweat hit Josie as she flashed a membership card at the welcome desk and walked past a row of lockers and a closed office door, straight back, just like always. *Losing this membership, too.* When they first moved to the neighborhood, Josie fought with NYU for three months to convince the student affairs office to subsidize this local gym membership for her mental health. A long shot, but it worked. *Now, though? Now, I'm not even technically allowed to be here.*

Alice, a short-haired trainer in her late thirties, spotted Josie from a row of weight machines, and waved. Not a friend, though. A year ago, Alice had gotten weird when Josie started to invite her to Josie's twenty-second birthday dinner. Back then, they spent hours together, and Josie opened up. 'I hate exercise,' she'd said, as Alice coached her through the motions on different equipment. 'It's because you haven't found the right movements,' Alice said. Josie had rolled her eyes and struggled with a squat thrust and butterfly arm movements, before finally letting the weights drop and pointing at a line of three empty rowing machines along the far wall. 'What about that?' Alice had whistled. 'Rowing is hard—a full body workout, really. We may want to build to that ...' But Josie had smiled, already headed to the first Concept 2 rower, just like now. 'But you get to sit down,' Josie said.

Now, Josie lowered herself to a rowing machine. She saw Alice approaching out of the corner of her vision but still planted both feet in the stirrups and adjusted the difficulty setting on the black wheel ahead of her, tapped to activate the touchscreen workout display.

"Hey, Josie," Alice called. She stopped alongside the rower, arms crossed and cheeks still flushed from whatever machine she'd just been on. "Didn't expect to see you today."

"Well, I'm here," Josie said. *Dick way to answer. Stop.* She forced herself to pause and smile up from the rowing display. "Sorry. I'm just ... today isn't great."

"Exercise will help."

No hidden agenda in that reply, Alice meant it. She worshipped at the altar of interval training and cardio, really and truly believed an elevated heart rate could solve all. Two weeks ago, Josie had listened to Alice's mini-lecture on oxygen health over lemony-orange ice water.

"Hope so," Josie said. "I was fighting with Dani, and ... it's stupid."

"I'm sure it isn't." But Alice stepped back, with a solemn 'you've got this' smile. "Just focus on the water in front of you."

That was her saying, and she probably cribbed it from a bumper sticker—Josie never asked—but it stuck. And it worked. When Josie first tried the rowing machine, with Alice crouched beside her, counseling her on form—'Try to keep your back straight ... fingers loose—good, way to pull your knees up ...'—that phrase helped Josie push through an extra two intervals. *The water in front of you.* Now, she leaned in, both hands out on the handle of the rower, and then pulled in, so it slid up to her chest on a chain, her seat gliding back and legs extending in one fluid motion.

No water here, of course, just cushioned floor mats, wall-length mirrors, and Duran Duran in the air. Josie had never rowed on the water, only ever done this. For the past year, she'd learned to appreciate rowing, hard and steady movements, until sweat beaded her brow, then matted her hair and armpits, until gradually, her torso was shaking and wet, her mind narrowed to one thought: *the water in front of you.*

Her phone chimed from the floor beside her.

Without slowing her pace, Josie checked the screen: Mom. Probably calling about Uncle Don, of course she was. Talk to her after. Here, now, on the rower, each handle-pull channeled the taut frustration in her chest. She unclenched her jaw, exhaled loud fucking anger. *What is wrong with you, Dani? Is it me?*

No, stop it. I need to talk. Someone else to say I'm not imagining this. Pick up on something I missed. A clue in Dani's behavior or something I did.

When Josie finished, she wiped down the rowing machine and hustled back into the daylight without making eye contact with anyone. Back at the empty apartment—no Dani—another shower focused Josie's thoughts: *who can I turn to?* She couldn't talk to Everett about this, of course. Maybe Mom or one of Josie's flighty political friends from her freshman dorm? No, none of them were close enough anymore. *I'm not alone, but almost.*

Dressing, her phone flashed again: another missed call from Mom. *Alone-ish.* And what else was she supposed to do? Growing up, she moved so often that it was only in high school here in New York City that she'd finally found an actual friend, her first girlfriend, Clara. And that didn't work out. No idea where Clara even lived now, not since that last summer. *Or why we broke up.* Another pinprick, foggy gap in her memory. *Which means trauma. Which means don't stare at it and move on.*

Josie called Mom. "How is he?"

"You don't sound good," Mom said. "Late night?"

A gravely pull in the back of Josie's throat, Mom locked onto it like no one else. *My voice going off the rails with stress, so I don't even sound like me. Or like the calm version of me, anyway. Well, fuck it, I'm not.*

"Too late," Josie said. "Uncle Don—is he still ..?"

"Yes," Mom said. "Out of surgery, but in intensive care. He's in critical condition, they said. And they may try another surgery today or tomorrow ..."

Something else she wasn't saying.

"What?" Josie asked.

"Nothing," Mom said. "It's the insurance. They're giving me a hard time. He's my age, not old enough for Medicare, and Uncle Don wasn't exactly frugal ..."

Josie stared out the kitchen windows at the bricks of an adjacent apartment complex and fire escape, tried to let her mind relax. Now, at midday, the sun only hit the top part of the wall. *Is this about money? Is everything?*

"I shouldn't worry you with this," Mom said. "I'm sorry. It'll be fine."

"Please tell me what's going on."

"You know he's been out of work ..."

He doesn't have insurance. Josie kept the phone to her cheek and felt a tangled frustration, like strings twisting from her belly up to her chest. Her pulse hurt. *Great, next I'll be in the ER. Calm down.*

"Is he going to be okay?" Josie asked.

"They don't know," Mom said. "I haven't been able to see him yet."

"How much money does he need?"

"Josie, it's not something you need to ..."

"I'm not a child," she snapped, too loud.

A sudden silence on the line, and Mom said, "It's a lot. I don't know how much, but more than ... He may be able to declare bankruptcy, if it comes to that. They want to do another surgery ..." Mom's voice cracked in an attempt to hide the strain in her voice. But Josie heard. "They're talking about moving him to another facility. That's why you shouldn't ..."

"What can I do?" Josie asked.

"Nothing, sweetheart. I'll tell you, when it changes. Just keep being you, okay? Send good thoughts his way."

They talked a little more, but Josie barely heard and ended the call. Across the room, the door lock clicked, and Dani stepped in, with a paper coffee cup.

"I made coffee this morning," Josie said.

Dani sipped, continued toward the bedroom. "Yeah. Going to lay down for a minute."

"Can I get in bed with you?" Josie asked.

Without turning, Dani laughed. "I don't think so."

Josie heard the rubber ball bounce in there and the rustle of clothes. Normally, Josie's ask should have been a cute lead-in to sex or cuddles, laying together and dishing about family or planning the day. Now, though?

A half hour later, Dani dressed, finished her store-bought coffee, kissed Josie quick on the cheek, and said she didn't know how long Columbia's orientation would last. No suggestion that Josie join, and Josie didn't ask.

That night, Dani returned after dark—"I already ate, they had a reception"—and Mom texted:

No updates

After Dani left again the next morning, Josie's quiet keyboard taps and clicking on the laptop tracking pad filled the apartment. The job search continued: she scanned online listings, customized and re-customized her resume and cover letter, breaking up the day with another call to Mom, a neighborhood walk and another gym workout, until, by the evening, still no Dani. *Still no direction to any of this, like she said at the bar. And I'm running out of time. My bank account is bleeding: drip, drip, drip.* A new message dinged on her phone, with the headline, *'Important Information About Your Student Loan Repayment Options.'* She didn't open it. *That, too. Hide from the debt somehow. Wait for it to magically disappear.*

What if something happens? Uncle Don is in the hospital. If I get sick—no, don't think about that. Josie hadn't confessed to Mom or Dani that she didn't have health insurance, had let it lapse after graduation, because the cost, even for a shitty plan, would bankrupt her in a matter of months. *And that's if nothing goes wrong. I can't afford my half of the rent much longer, even now, when my body is humming along the way it's supposed to. If I had to visit the doctor or a fucking hospital, like Uncle Don ...*

Mom texted that Uncle Don hadn't come out of recovery yet. But he might finally be up for visitors soon:

Fingers crossed

Staring at a boxed package of Mac N' Cheese, Josie told herself that submitting new job applications counted as progress. The landlord—a sweet woman who lived upstate—called, and Josie made the mistake of answering, explaining that no, she still wasn't sure if they would stay. Yes, she understood their lease expired soon.

"This is important," the landlord said. "I know things are busy." A pause on the line. "Dear, if you can't confirm by tomorrow, I'll have to start showing the apartment ..."

The thought of strangers touring their space felt alien, like a documentary of a crisis happening somewhere else. *No, this is our home. If someone else moves in, then what? Where am I supposed to go?*

"I know," Josie said. "Thank you."

"Do what you need to do," the landlord said. "But please let me know."

When the call ended, Josie put water on to boil and swiped aimlessly on her phone. *Settle down. We still live here now. Things aren't ruined with Dani. It's always better than you think. This won't become another episode I try to forget. I won't let it. Just eat and rest, and when Dani gets home, we'll figure it out.*

Josie called Everett. He saw everything the other night, which made him a sounding board for the Dani situation. Over-the-top and non-serious, but nevermind his core personality, Everett would still give an honest perspective. *And I need to talk to someone. Listen to me. Tell me I'm not crazy.*

A woman answered, "Hello, who is calling please?"

The phone on speaker, Josie stared at the ongoing call display. She hadn't misdialed, this was Everett's contact info.

"I think I may have called ... sorry, is Everett there?" Josie asked.

"Who's calling?" the woman asked again.

"This is Josie. I'm a friend of his." *Because whoever this is, she has his phone, can probably see my contact info anyway, right? Maybe it was stolen. Somebody randomly answered, while trying to break into Everett's bank account?*

"Josie, this is Officer Taylor. I'm with the Jersey City Department of Public Safety. I'm sitting right now with Everett's parents at their home. You caught us at a fortunate time. We were just discussing possibilities to gather more information, and I should tell you, you're on speaker. Mr. and Mrs. Fisher can hear you, too."

A muffled voice: "Hi, Josie." Mrs. Fisher—Everett's mom, who Josie barely knew and last saw at graduation, back in May.

"What's ..." Josie stopped, tried to process what 'Officer Taylor' had just said. "Where is Everett?"

"That's our question," Officer Taylor said. "Josie, while I've got you, would you mind if I asked when you last heard from him?"

"Yesterday," Josie said. "We went out the night before, and he slept on the couch. I saw him in the morning." The pot started to boil, steam frothing on the stove in front of her, but Josie hadn't opened the macaroni box. "Is he missing?"

"Everett's parents are concerned. As you probably know, he lived alone in a studio in Brooklyn owned by his parents. It's still early. We're not jumping to any conclusions, but how out of character would it be for him to leave?"

"Leave?" Josie said. The word didn't register.

Another voice—Everett's dad—cut in: "I stopped by today, and he left his phone and wallet—everything. Even his keys. All in his apartment. That's not normal."

If Everett's phone made it back to his studio, then so did he, after his hungover rambling. Which meant he vanished after. *After he told me about his dream of a little chalk man. No, not 'vanished.' That was only yesterday.*

Josie shivered, rubbed her arms. "I don't understand. I just saw him yesterday morning right here."

"Makes no sense!" Everett's dad said.

"You said you were with him the night before, as well?" Officer Taylor asked. "Did anything unusual happen that evening or in the morning?"

"Unusual?"

"Did he get into a fight with someone? Was he followed or acting out of the ordinary? Anything you remember?"

Yes. He picked a fight with The Eburos Group and dreamt about it. What did he say, that he was 'on the wall,' something like that? And Dani was 'on the street, hurt'? What the fuck does that mean?

Nothing.

"I don't know," Josie said. "I don't think so."

"And nothing since?"

"No," Josie said. "Do you have any—I don't know—any-anything yet?"

"A neighbor suggested he may have gotten in a black sedan," Officer Taylor said. "But honestly, we'll need more help. If he contacts you or you hear from anyone ..."

Josie watched the water boil over, spilling across the gas stove in fizzing snaps around the blue flame of the burner.

"It's very likely that there is nothing to worry about," Officer Taylor said. "But we want to be sure ..."

Josie reached mechanically to turn it off and promised she would let them know, if she heard anything. When the call ended, Josie sank into a kitchen chair and called Mom.

"I'm coming to see him," she said.

Mom started to argue, then said, "Yes, okay. It'll be good to have you here. You know, in all this, I haven't had a chance to ask: how's Dani?"

The Eburos Group
EMPLOYMENT
BASICS

Full-time living employees are expected to work at least 40 hours per week or 160 hours per month on average throughout the term of their standard human lifespan (SHL); they are expected to work at least 80 hours per week or 320 hours per month on average as a post-life advisor (PLA). Please note that firm policy strictly prohibits use of the terms 'slave' or 'thrall' in any context. Part-time employees are those who have committed less than 50 percent of their corporeal energy or 'soul' to Eburos and are therefore not entitled to the full benefits package.

COMPANY HANDBOOK

CHAPTER FOUR

That night, washing the dishes after a late dinner alone, Josie heard Dani clomping in the hall, then the bounce of the ball in the corridor. Dani's return signal. *That's her sound now. That stupid fucking ball.*

TONK.

A child's toy, it's probably cursed. That's why Mr. Dean gave it to me, right after I insulted his artwork. It was *pretentious. Screw him.*

As Dani came in, she said, "I know what you're going to say. It's late—I *know.* But these events are required for all first-year law students."

Josie finished the dishes, her fingers puckered into raisins from the soapy hot water, body drained. She watched Dani head into the bedroom, already avoiding her.

"How was it?" Josie asked.

"Fine."

Josie went to stand in the bedroom doorway, as Dani stripped off her shirt and bra quickly, yanking on a stretched t-shit, with her back turned. Nothing sexy about this, like watching a stranger's routine at the gym. Functional and rushed.

"Are there good people?" Josie asked. "I mean are any of the other students—do you think we'll be friends with them?"

Dani threw the ball at the ceiling—TONK—caught it again, as she changed into pajama pants. "Maybe, who knows?"

"Just so I know, though," Josie said, "who are some of the people you've met?"

Dani glanced back at her, cheeks splotchy. *Is she drunk again?* "It's not actually all about you, Josie." She snapped the ball hard into the wall to the left of Josie's head and caught the bounce-back.

"Can you not do that right now?"

"Do what?"

"The ball, can you not—"

Dani threw it again. *TONK.* "*That,* you mean?" She grinned, arms hard and tense. Dani *had* been drinking. Now Josie tasted the faint, sweet stink of beer. She hadn't noticed right away.

"There was alcohol? I thought you were at orientation."

Dani started past her and tossed the ball—*TONK*—caught it. "Yeah."

"Please, can we talk for a second?"

"We are talking." Dani went toward the bathroom.

Josie watched her wind up to throw the ball across the kitchen—*TONK* into the far wall—and Josie stepped in fast to catch it.

Dani's hand was still raised, fingers open and ready for the ball. She stared at Josie, confused. "Don't fuck with me. Give it back." Dani's voice dropped low, with an unpredictable tilt Josie didn't recognize, like a dog growling, ready to bite.

Josie squeezed the ball and felt its solid core, like a nugget of hard plastic in the center.

"Everett is missing," Josie said.

Dani's expression loosened, caught off guard. "What? No, he isn't. We just saw him."

"He's gone," Josie said. "I talked to the police at his parents' ..."

"He's not *gone*." Dani reached for the ball, and Josie backed away, keeping it out of reach. "Are you trying to be funny?" Dani said. "Taking your failure out on me, like a child?"

Josie relaxed her fingers on the ball. "My failure?" She felt a wave of shaky blood up both arms, tingling in her legs. Nausea lurched up her throat, and Josie blinked away from Dani, let the ball drop. "Take it."

Dani grabbed it on the first bounce.

"I thought you'd want to know," Josie said.

"Stop being so dramatic," Dani said.

Still looking away, Josie let her vision blur on the living room couch. *Where I last saw Everett.* She heard Dani walk away, bouncing the ball again. "I'm going to see my uncle," Josie said.

Dani slammed the bathroom door, without answering. But Josie didn't cry. The hot press behind her eyes was like a wave that would hobble her, if she let it. And it would, eventually. But not now. Now, she packed a bag quickly—the shower loud through the walls—scrawled a note, and left.

Ignored on the sidewalk and subway, Josie took an Amtrak train from Penn Station and dialed Mom after she cleared the lights of the city. Alone in a shabby seat, watching the dark landscape of Connecticut out the window, Josie told Mom about Dani. *Tell her everything. Everything except Everett, the ball, the woman's shadow, and the chalk man. That version of everything. The 'everything' that doesn't cause her to panic about my sanity.*

Still, somehow Mom knew. She sensed more.

"Did something happen at Eburos?" she asked.

"What? No, I told you, I just bombed the interview is all."

"Solomon or one of his flunkies, they didn't do anything that made you uncomfortable?" Mom still called Mr. Dean 'Solomon,' of course she did.

"The whole interview made me uncomfortable," Josie said. "It's okay. I just hoped that would work out."

"Something will," Mom said.

Josie rested her head against the glass of the train window, watching light pass in the suburban black outside. "It's late."

And it was: after 2:30 AM by the time Mom met her on the empty train platform, with a tight, lavender-shampoo-and-flesh-scent hug. *Really here.* The night air on the open-air landing smelled like fall leaves and distant wood smoke. Josie let herself go limp, head bowed against Mom's shoulder. On the walk to the parking lot, Mom told Josie that this middle-of-the-night pickup gave her something to do. She hadn't been sleeping much.

Semi-retired, Mom taught as an adjunct at a nearby college to pay the bills, but really, once Josie started college four years ago, Mom had withdrawn from the world. She left Brooklyn, retreated to the too-quiet suburban sprawl of Connecticut, and stopped going out. At first, Josie worried Mom was giving up. Maybe sliding into isolated depression. But in the last few years, she'd decided that Mom knew what she needed and could decide not to get attached to new people, and instead 'just live,' as she'd once put it. Turning sixty in December, she'd earned that, right?

At Mom's apartment, she led Josie into a high-ceiled living room that flowed back to a dining area-kitchen and bright greenhouse space along the rear porch, crammed with dangling ferns, huge-leafed unidentified plants, and vines, mixed in with wooden windchimes, glowy stones, and crystals. There was only one bedroom in the back, so Josie tossed her bag on the living room sofa opposite a dusty TV.

The walls were crowded with framed theater playbills Mom had saved from all the places they'd lived during Josie's childhood: Kentucky, Chicago, Boston, West Hartford—all the way to New York City.

"We can visit at 9:00," Mom called from the kitchen. "Get a little rest, and then I'll make breakfast when you wake up?"

Josie sank onto the couch, her legs twisted sideways to fit. *This is a mistake. I can't stay in Brooklyn with Dani, but I don't live here. I barely fucking fit. Whatever this is, whatever I'm trying to do, it won't last long. Something has to change.*

After a few hours' sleep, they ate eggs and toast with black coffee, as the sky brightened outside. At a small blacktop table in the dining area, Mom talked about the food, Josie's train ride, and Uncle Don, but without focusing on any of it. Pale and distracted, Mom's eyes went glassy when Josie spoke, as if she immediately tuned out. *Worrying about something else.*

When they finished, Mom drove them across town in her rusted blue Toyota, the right rear bumper still duct-taped on from when she'd been sideswiped in the Stop N Shop parking lot a year before. 'Two thousand dollars or two dollars?' Mom had said when it happened. 'I choose tape. Who cares what it looks like.'

Twenty minutes later, they bounced into a hospital parking garage in downtown Fairfield and followed a long track of walking-path arrows to a reception desk inside. A sweet woman told them that yes, Uncle Don could see visitors, but no, they would have to wait until 10:00. A clock in the waiting room read: 9:05. As Josie and Mom found chairs, Mom's phone buzzed. She answered, told Josie it was 'the university.' "I might just take this, if you don't mind ..."

Smiling, the receptionist called over, "No cellphones, ma'am."

They went back outside and split up: Mom to a sidewalk bench flanked by spikey bushes, and Josie started walking to stay distracted, find more coffee. The only thing that might help right now. She didn't know this neighborhood, but it seemed to be laid out in a predictable grid of hotels, low-rise apartments, and office buildings. There: three blocks away, past the wide entrance of a black hotel tower ringed with dragon statues, she spotted a Starbucks, then slowed as she got closer. Inside, the coffee shop was dark and empty. Closed. Squinting, Josie checked the surrounding streets— no sign of more coffee—so she started back, then stopped. A town car pulled up to the dragon hotel entrance, where a uniformed valet opened the front door.

A door that almost certainly had overpriced coffee inside. *Worth it.*

Josie wandered up, and the doorman let her into a blast of cold, floral-scented air. The lobby rose in a swell of black, red-veined marble, set with red dragon couches and expensive-looking tables. A crisp guy at the reception desk noticed her staring. "Checking in?"

"Looking for coffee, actually," Josie said, and he pointed to her right—"Café is that way"—and she froze.

Angela—Angela from Eburos, no-you-didn't-get-the-job-An-gela—sat with her back to Josie at a table across from a man in thick glasses and a pastel blue suit. The glasses man frowned up at Josie. Angela turned. A suspended beat and recognition clicked in Angela's face.

"Josie Morris," she said.

Manilla folders and an elaborate full coffee set, complete with a silver pot, cups, and a milk ladle, were arranged between Angela and the glasses man.

"Hello," Josie said.

"Very nice to see you again," Angela said, her voice light. "This is Mr. Vaughn. Mr. Vaughn, this is Josie, a candidate at Eburos." Angela gave Josie a quick grin, as if that were their private joke.

"Hello, Josie," he said. "Are you joining us?"

Angela's shadow twisted, and Angela turned back around to face him.

Same as before. I didn't imagine it. Josie couldn't look away.

"No," Angela said, "unfortunately, I'm sure Josie has ..." Angela noticed Josie staring at the floor by her chair. "Is something ..?" The shadow flexed out, and Angela followed, leaning back to see. The shadow shrank in again, and Angela did, too. "Are you all right, Josie?" "Your shadow ..." A snap of panic in Angela's eyes, and her jaw hardened, gone again. She smiled, but strained now. "Maybe you should sit for a moment. Would you like some coffee, Josie?"

Josie took a chair beside them, and Angela poured her a steaming cup.

"It's not A-list," the glasses man said.

Josie blew on the coffee and took a quick, hot sip. It was delicious. Roasted and full, maybe the best coffee she'd ever tasted.

Angela squeezed the glasses man's arm. "Mr. Vaughn, perhaps you could give me just a moment with Josie? We have a few items to tie up. They wouldn't be a value add for your time, and I know Singapore is waiting ..."

He gathered the folders in a stack, said, "Of course," and left.

When he was gone, Angela lowered both hands to her coffee cup, as if cradling the head of a small animal. *Ready to snap its neck.* The thought made Josie's arms tense. Her breathing quickened.

"Now," Angela said, "why don't you tell me about my shadow."

JOIN US!

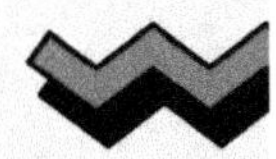

Tuesday's Lunch & Learn on blood topiary best practices has been moved to the John Jay Conference Room on Floor 17. Attendance is for anyone who has either previously completed a harvesting or is now participating in the Q3 soul harvesting program. Green thumbs encouraged! This is a voluntary professional development activity and is not considered paid company time. Employees are encouraged to use their lunch hour for this training.

JOHN JAY CONFERENCE ROOM

12:00 - 2:00 PM

THE EBUROS GROUP

Chapter Five

J osie's phone shook in her pocket, and a waiter approached, with a polite smile. *Ignore the shadow again? Pretend I don't see it? No, she knows. This is real, and she knows.* Still watching Josie, Angela ordered salmon lox and cream cheese on a toasted plain bagel. The food sounded delicious and wrong, like something Josie would enjoy chewing but regret a moment later.

"Anything for you?" the waiter asked her.

"No, thank you," Josie said.

He left, and Josie took another swallow of coffee. Reassuring taste, but it stung in her belly. *What do I do?*

"It's Haitian," Angela said. "The coffee. It's off menu, but they'll bring it, if you know how to order." And then, more quietly, "*And I know how to order.*"

Angela waited, and when Josie didn't respond, Angela's shadow curled to the side. She leaned in, one elbow perched on the table to take up more space in a body language power move.

"You didn't answer me," Angela said at last. "You *were* watching my shadow, weren't you? I saw. What did you see?"

Tell her? No—ask.

"Why?" Josie said. "What do you think I saw?"

Angela tensed, her attention steady, but her poise changed. Under her careful flowered blouse and red skirt, Josie imagined muscles aligning on bone, blood streaming to tighten tendons. Like a cat watching a bird or squirrel out the window. *Except Dani never agreed to get a cat, so how would I know.*

"You don't want to say the wrong thing right now," Angela said slowly. "This is one of the most important conversations of your life. Can you sense the stakes? Even if you have no idea—none—what any of it means?" She rested her chin on her propped fist, a practiced gesture. Angela looked prettier in that pose, vulnerable, like a schoolgirl asking for help. She asked, "What did you see, Josie?"

"Your shadow moves before you do."

Angela's breath stopped, and her face brightened into a smile. She straightened again and found her phone. The waiter brought a plate of bagels and thinly cut salmon, with tiny side cups of cream cheese. As he set it out, Angela tapped her phone, raised it to her cheek. "Hi, it's Angela. It's important. About Grace." She lowered the phone, one hand covering it, to tell Josie, "The C-Suite opens, when I use the magic words." *What words? Grace was the other girl, right? The one who shouted in his office.* When the waiter tried to ask if they needed anything else, Angela ignored him and said into the phone, "Hi, Mr. Dean?" The waiter left. Angela winked at Josie, continued, "I have Josie Morris here with me ... That's right, in Connecticut. She fits. No, I know, but ..." Angela frowned at Josie. "Really? I haven't asked about that ... Okay. I'll let you know. Thank you." She ended the call and put the phone away. Her eyes narrowed. "You are a little sneak, aren't you?"

Josie said, "I don't ..."

"Yes, you do," Angela said. "Don't lie to me, Josie Morris. Mr. Dean says you saw something in his office, too."

"What? I don't know what you're talking about."

"I told you," Angela said, more loudly, and she reached across to clasp Josie's forearm, but not like she had with the glasses man. That had been business-flirty to coax him out. This was harder, less careful. "Do not lie to me. You see my shadow move, and then me—you see me follow it, as if I'm on a leash?" Her fingers tightened, holding Josie's arm against the table. "With Mr. Dean, what did you see? Something on the wall?"

"No," Josie said. "There wasn't anything. Just his office ..." When Angela squeezed, Josie said, "Windows, a desk, books—I don't know. Art, that bizarre chalk man drawing ..."

"That," Angela said, and she let go. She pitched back, smiling and shaking her head. "You. Oh, Josie. You, you, *you*." Angela laughed to herself, then grabbed the phone again. "Talk," she told Josie, "it's okay, I'm not calling him. What did it look like?"

"The chalk man?"

"Yes, the *chalk man*," Angela said, and on the phone again, "Hi, can you get back here? Great. I need the offer papers from the car. Thank you." She ended the call. "Well? Describe it, please." *He disappeared.* "I saw a blue-and-gray landscape, impressionistic, of a platform and ruined columns," Josie said, and the words brought a flash of the empty scene, after she stepped out. "There was a small, white chalk man, sitting there. Rougher than the rest of it ..."

Angela lifted her coffee cup. "And?"

"What?"

"The 'chalk man,' as you call him," Angela said, sipping. "Describe him."

"You've seen him," Josie said.

"I haven't, actually." Angela set her cup back down, noticed the lox bagel. "They're usually pretty good here, but I'm not sure this looks fresh."

This makes no sense.

"You were there with me—you work there. You must have seen the artwork ..?"

"It's not artwork," Angela said simply. "And I can't see him, just like I can't see my shadow. But you can."

"I don't understand," Josie said. "This is a joke? Some kind of test? Mr. Dean told me I wasn't a good fit ..."

"We heard about your past, we know who your father was, but we weren't sure," Angela said. "To be clear, you didn't interview just because your mother knows Mr. Dean. He wouldn't have given you facetime, unless we also knew that there was a chance ..." She shrugged, as if it were obvious and Josie should fill in the rest.

"A chance what?"

"The movie of your life cuts over entire days or months of time, doesn't it? *'Two months later?'* Things you can't remember, because your mind is protecting you from them. Yes?"

She can't know that.

Josie felt heat in her cheeks, adrenaline sweat in her armpits, but she concentrated on her breathing. Right into it. Somehow, Angela knew. They all did. Mom must have told them. Or they learned in a background check—didn't matter.

"Why are you asking about that?" Josie said. "It has nothing to do with this."

"It does, actually," Angela said. "Everything. You've seen things before, Josie. You may have even *interacted* with things before. Things most people can't. That is top talent potential." She turned her coffee mug in a neat circle, her stare totally steady, as if to spot any slip of emotion.

"Why did you mention my dad?" Josie asked. She heard her voice rising, tried to level it out. Her heart swelled in both ears. "Your shadow, a chalk man painting, that has nothing ..."

"Yes, it does," Angela said, leaning closer. "You have unique potential aptitude, Josie. Your father did, too. Even if he died before you were too young to realize it, you still know. Somewhere inside you, you do. Your mother knows. And now ..." She nodded, as if they'd just agreed. "Now Mr. Dean does, too."

The glasses man came back in the front entrance, his brow beaded with sweat. At the table, he gave Angela a manilla folder, and she said quickly, "That's fine, thank you."

He wiped his face with the back of one hand and nodded to Josie. "Congratulations." Then left again, headed outside.

What the hell?

"I *don't* know," Josie said. "About any of this. I just came in here to get a cup of coffee—thank you for that. Now I have to go. My uncle is in the hospital."

Angela pushed the folder toward Josie, suddenly serious. "I apologize, Josie. I didn't realize that. What happened?"

"He had a heart attack," Josie said, and her voice caught. *Shit, this is real. Whatever bullshit Angela is talking about, the hospital is real. What if Uncle Don isn't okay? What if we aren't walking into a recovery room, but another, separate area for bad news? What will that look like?*

"I shouldn't keep you," Angela said. "Family is *the* most important thing."

"Thank you." Josie started to stand.

"Only—before you go ..." Angela opened the folder and shifted two pages out, with a thick blue-tipped pen in-hand. "The one on the left is a nondisclosure agreement. On the right: an employment contract."

Josie held the top of the chair. "I'm sorry?"

"Mr. Dean would like to offer you a full-time position, Josie. And he'd like you to start as soon as possible." Angela's shadow flowed to the left, and when Josie watched her position change to match, Angela smiled. "You knew I was going to do that, didn't you?"

"It moved first, yes," Josie said. *Don't look at the papers. Mom is probably waiting, ready to see Uncle Don, find out how bad it is.* "But I should go."

"Josie, you must realize how selective our recruitment process is at Eburos ..."

"Yes, thank you, but ..."

"... and how active we are. The firm has a strict 'all-in' policy. Our team is enthusiastic from top to bottom. If this is the right fit, I know you'll be eager to seize the opportunity Mr. Dean is offering you right now. You commit to us; we commit to you."

Josie checked the papers, type too small to read without leaning in close. "What is the job?"

"Client Services Advisor. It's right there, Josie."

"No, I mean, what would I do exactly? I don't understand."

Angela tapped the left-hand paper. "I need you to sign these first."

"I appreciate this," Josie said. "I honestly do. This ... I can't tell you how flattering this is." *Strange. Surreal dream logic and not plausible.* "But my uncle ..."

"If there's something we can do, the firm will look into it. Eburos has a private medical network. If you'd like, they can review your uncle's course of treatment. Make sure he gets the care he deserves."

Standing at the edge of the table, Josie felt an unfamiliar swirl of confidence. *Authority, is that it? She needs me? Or this is a game, too?*

"I can't sign without knowing what's going on," Josie said.

"This is a different world than you're accustomed to," Angela said. "I appreciate that. Eburos is trusted by Fortune 500 companies, governments, and ..." She paused, with a half smile. "That man you just met, Mr. Vaughn, you saw him sweating in this weather? He just returned from six months in Dhahran."

She said it like Josie should recognize the name, sit up and exclaim maybe. *Dhahran-what?*

"Saudi Aramco," Angela said slowly. "Dhahran is the company town near the Damman oil fields. Before that, Mr. Vaughn was based in our D.C. office, supporting anchor clients at the Red Cross and DOJ. This is all public information, but we work with presidents, CEOs, and kings, Josie. I'm not saying this to intimidate you, but because ..." She hesitated, as if searching for the most politic phrasing. "I want to make sure you understand why I'm double-clicking on the word 'discretion.' *This* ..." She nodded to the documents. "... this is a ticket to the real reality."

From here, Josie couldn't read the papers. Just a blur of too-tiny lines, with paragraph sections, bullets, and headings in bold. "Can I think about it?"

Angela sat back, her shadow bulbed in, and she crossed her arms. "I'd like a decision by start of business tomorrow morning."

"What time is that?"

"8:00 AM," Angela said. "On the dot. If your answer is 'yes,' bring two forms of ID to the front desk lobby of the Manhattan office, where we met the other day."

Josie reached for the papers. "I can take these?"

Angela nodded, and as Josie shifted the folder and papers under one arm, Angela said, "We will need everything signed before you can move forward."

Josie said she understood—*understand what?*—thanked Angela again, and then went back outside into the sharp, morning sun. Her phone: a missed call from Mom. It was 10:15.

Half-running, her lower back already damp with sweat, she hurried back and called Mom.

"There you are," Mom said. "You said you were just going for coffee. What happened?"

"On my way," Josie said. "I'm running."

"I hear that. How far are you?"

"I was at a hotel for coffee, and I saw ..." She huffed into the phone. "I think I got a job."

"At a hotel?"

"No, *the* job—the one at Eburos that I thought I bombed. A woman from that interview was here."

And? And she wants to hire me, because I saw her shadow move. And the chalk man. Why did she mention Dad? What did Mom tell her?

"A woman you met in New York just happened to be here?" Mom asked, as if Josie were making it up.

"I know, it's weird."

"Coincidences usually aren't," Mom said.

"Well, I didn't say yes ..."

Back at the hospital, Josie met Mom in reception, and they entered a hall partitioned with plastic sheets. Patients were packed into the sheet spaces like cars in a parking lot. A dazed man on an IV watched them pass, beside a hopeful woman with dark spots on her face. The smell of bleach couldn't mask the cramped human smells of body odor, urine, vomit, and a faint musk of sweet rot that made Josie swallow hot stomach acid with a biting coffee aftertaste.

She didn't know what to expect, but not this. None of the patients had their own room.

Further ahead, a woman wheezed and called out in another frantic language, then a second voice shouted back, and someone else yelled at them both to shut up. Like the side yard outside Josie and Dani's Brooklyn apartment in summertime, not a hospital. The tarped mass of patients didn't seem to affect passing nurses and staff, who chatted and laughed, as if people shouting and crying in pain were normal. As if their lives were cheap.

Don't think like that.

They found Uncle Don on a stretcher-bed wedged into a partition on the left. Hooked up to a fluid IV, with oxygen tubes curling out of his nose, he looked ten years older than he had at Josie's graduation. What should have been a shock of dark hair had melted into a thin, gray cap on his head. He squinted at them, his grizzly cheeks and jaw flexing thin.

"We're here," Mom said, stepping in to hold Uncle Don's hand. No pity in her voice or smile, as if they had gathered for a casual photo op.

"I look that bad?" Uncle Don asked and closed his eyes again. "Tell me straight, Josie."

"You look good," Josie said. She glanced at Mom, who met her gaze with a brief, worried flick.

"They haven't taught you to lie yet," Uncle Don said, wincing at the phosphorescent light. "Your mother told me you interviewed with Solomon Dean. It's good you didn't take the job. I never met the man, but Mark used to say that Solomon never saw a dollar he didn't think belonged to him."

Uncle Don still talked about Dad, as if he might walk in at any moment, with a surreal, somehow-plausible explanation for why he wasn't dead. Josie had no difficulty remembering the funeral, though. Dad was long-gone.

A doctor came in. Tall and prematurely gray with a belly, he checked a clipboard without greeting them. "We had a scare, didn't we? Someone needs to take better care of his ticker."

"How serious is it?" Josie asked.

The doctor flipped through the clipboard pages. "It was a heart attack. Emergency bypass surgery. I'd say pretty serious." Still looking at the sheets, not at them, he said, "And I see here you didn't fill out all the insurance information. We'll need that before we can ..."

"What's the prognosis?" Mom asked, her voice taut. She held Uncle Don's hand protectively.

"*Prognosis?*" the doctor said. "Are any of you a medical doctor? No? The *prognosis* is he needs to take his health seriously. I'll be prescribing post-op pain medications, but no refills ..." He watched Mom, as if she were about to argue. "And lifestyle changes. You'll get literature about that." His voice shifted, already wrapping up. "Blood pressure, cholesterol, that'll be up to him.""The surgery," Josie said, "was it—I don't know—did it go well?"He frowned at her, as if she'd asked a question she didn't understand. "Yes."

"I'm fine," Uncle Don said, his voice weak.

"He isn't," the doctor said. "A nurse will be by to talk about the insurance ..."

And when he started to go, Mom asked what caused the heart attack. In a slow tone, as if she were a child, the doctor repeated the word 'lifestyle.' *He blames this on Uncle Don. As if Uncle Don wants to be here like this.*

"Each myocardial infarction makes the next more common," the doctor told Mom. "If he takes responsibility for his health, he should recover, but that's not up to us."

"I'm not a doctor," Mom said. "But I am an attorney."

The doctor tensed. "I'm not sure that's relevant. We are running a CSF analysis to rule out neurological causes and ensure there are no abnormalities ..."

CSF. The letters blinked into focus in Josie's mind. From the receptionist outside Mr. Dean's office.

"... I suggest you complete the insurance paperwork," the doctor said. "Our staff can answer any questions."

"What's CSF?" Josie asked.

The doctor blinked at her, ready to leave. "Cerebrospinal fluid," he said, as if it were obvious, and stepped out.

Cerebrospinal fluid. C-S-F. And didn't the receptionist start to say something like that? Water, tea, or ...

A nurse came to walk Josie and Mom back out, with forms to complete, then reminded Mom that no cellphones were allowed in reception. Josie followed in a daze. *No, obviously I misheard at the Eburos office. Or I'm misremembering. Stress.* Back on a bench on the front drive, Josie checked her texts, while Mom shuffled the hospital paperwork.

Josie texted Dani:

> *Uncle Don is ok. Out of surgery. Weak but he's alert. How r u?*

How are you? She sent it. No reply.

"They're going to bill him hundreds of thousands of dollars," Mom murmured.

"I thought he could declare bankruptcy," Josie said. Suddenly mentioning that as a solution felt wrong. *I thought he had the legal option to destroy his life to appease the hospital.*

"We're not poor," Mom said. Slumped forward, she stared at the documents. "I know that. We're lucky in lots of ways. I chose my work. Probably should have done things differently, but I always hoped things would be easier for you, not harder."

Josie nodded but didn't answer. Mom was only sort of talking to her.

"There could be litigation," Mom said. "They may take everything from him. Uncle Don will never own anything again. I've seen cases of garnished social security, and until he's sixty-five, he'll never ..." Mom let out a long, shaky breath. "God, what if it happens again? I'm sorry, I'm just tired."

Josie put an arm around her. Mom felt flushed, too hot, already sweating where they touched. Stress.

"You said you saw a woman from The Eburos Group?" Mom asked.

Josie handed her the folder, and Mom took out the papers, so they could see.

Halfway down the employment contract, she spotted a figure in bold:

Annual Salary: $230,000.00 USD, plus signing bonus and benefits.'

Mom tapped the page. "Look at that. A *real* salary and full health benefits on day one. I don't want to tell you what to do, Josie ..."

But you are. Even if I didn't need the money, I need the health insurance. Look at what's happening to Uncle Don.

"I told her I would think about it," Josie said.

Mom pushed the papers back into the folder. "You should think seriously about this, Josie. There are moments in my life, when I look back ..."

Tell her. About the real reason they want to hire me.

"We aren't living on the street," Mom said. "But we're being squeezed. Every day. Sorted, either above or below a line. It sounds bad, I know, to complain, sitting where we are. But look at your Uncle. We're one crisis away."

Like if I break my leg or get pneumonia or break up with Dani. This is a way out.

Mom's voice sounded hoarse, confused and deferential even, as if Josie were in charge now. This wasn't like her.

"Tell me about this guy," Josie said. "Who is Solomon Dean?"

The Eburos Group
DISCRIMINATION POLICY

The Eburos Group is an equal opportunity employer.
The firm does not tolerate discrimination against
protected characteristics, alignment, or animated
state. To promote a professional, productive
environment, Eburos is committed to penalizing
every discriminatory, offensive, or inappropriate
behavior to the fullest extent of the law, both human
and other. We ask that you report any discriminatory
action to HR immediately (see 'FAQs: Viscera Clean-
up Best Practices' and 'Progressive Discipline
Process & Termination Methods').

COMPANY HANDBOOK

Chapter Six

"I met him in law school," Mom said.

They watched cars pass. After the frantic, sleep-deprived rush of last night and this morning, Josie felt the tug of droopy exhaustion and an ache in her belly. *Anxious hunger.* But she didn't interrupt. *I have to know what this is, before I tell you what's really going on.*

What's really going on is I have no idea. But it's about a shadow and a chalk man. What if they took Everett, too? What if, what if..?

"Solomon comes from one of those Mayflower New England WASP families, all sailboats and summers in Nantucket, and Harvard. I think there's even a building named for his great-great-whoever in Harvard Yard up in Cambridge. So he was the rebellious one who attended Yale—big family drama." Mom pursed her lips in a tight smile. *The absurdity of the elite.* "But he's not what you would expect. We were friends, pretty close all through law school, until after, when he joined Eburos."

"Should I be—I don't know—worried about him?" Josie asked.

"Worried?" Mom glanced at her. "Why—did something happen?"

"No, he's just very ... not usual."

Mom let out a surprised laugh that relaxed her face. She looked young in that moment, happy, like from back before everything. *In high school, when it was just us.*

"That's the understatement of the year," Mom said. "I probably should have given you more warning. Solomon doesn't behave like other people, because he comes from that world of trust funds and yachts. He's never cared what other people think of him, because he doesn't have to. But he also isn't terrible. I know that sounds strange, but I liked him. We were close."

Josie waited. Mom sounded like she'd dated him or nearly. More here than she admitted. She still cared about this lunatic CEO, didn't she?

"Until after?" Josie asked.

"Right. Until Eburos. And then?" She shrugged. "He went his way, and I was in the city, too, but working constantly. And I met your father."

Dad must have seemed like the anti-Solomon Dean. Josie knew that Dad never locked down a stable career, rejected the entire premise of 'living to work.' As far as Josie knew, and all she remembered growing up, Dad jumped from one electrical contracting project to another each time they swapped cities. He kept their household on the move. In that life-and-death nomadic childhood that Josie never really understood, people like Solomon Dean faded. *We never had enough money, how did Mom and Dad make it work? How did she survive after he was gone?*

"Solomon hosted a couple Yale reunions at the Eburos offices," Mom said. "I attended one with your father. That's when Mark met Solomon." She smiled grimly and watched the road, as if the two men were wrestling in the street, between passing cars. "They did not get along."

"Why not?"

"The usual reasons. I don't remember." A lie, but Josie didn't press. "And anyway," Mom said, "that's ancient history, all before you were born. This ..." She knocked on the folder with a fist, as if asking to open it. "This is now."

"She knew about Dad," Josie said. "The Eburos woman, Angela. She mentioned him."

"I'm sure she did."

She said he was like me. She said he saw unnatural shadows and chalk people, too.

"Should I be worried about any of this?" Josie asked.

Mom turned to face her. "You're not being honest with me. Something else *did* happen, didn't it?"

"*I'm* not being honest? Mom ..."

"What's with that tone?" Mom stiffened. "Go ahead, spit it out."

"She knew about my ... mental blocks, whatever you want to call them." *Years since we talked about this, because we never had to.* "Did you tell them—"

"No," Mom said. "Josie, I didn't tell them anything about you, except that you're my daughter, a bright, promising young graduate who is eager to learn and start her career ..."

"Mom ..."

"I didn't," she said again. "I promise, Josie."

"Okay," Josie said. "A background check or ..." *Or something.* "I did see something, at the Eburos office."

"What?"

"You'll freak."

"Josie ..."

"I saw things they didn't. Things I know weren't there, except that this woman, Angela, seems to know about it."

"What things?"

"Her shadow," Josie said. "This is going to sound ridiculous, but it moves before she does. And on Mr. Dean's wall, there's a chalk drawing ..." Saying it out loud, this description felt forced. Not just absurd, but forced. *As if I'm searching for a reason this can't work.*

"A shadow and a wall drawing," Mom repeated. "I'm sorry, I don't ..."

"Her shadow moves before she does," Josie said again.

"Josie ..." Mom rubbed her jaw, staring at the contract paper again. *Right at the salary number.* "Is it possible you're imagining this ..."

"I'm not, she saw it, too."

"Right, okay," Mom said. "Or, is it possible ..." Mom paused, then asked slowly, "... possible this is a test? What you're describing doesn't sound ... well, it's not normal, but it doesn't sound *that* strange. A trick of the light could explain the shadow, couldn't it? Just to play Devil's advocate."

No.

"I don't know," Josie said. *Could it? Yes, it must. There is an explanation. It didn't really move before she did. Some kind of tech? Angela is wearing something, carrying an FX light. A prototype or something? Stranger things than this attract ten-thousand TikTok views every day. The real test was whether I would mention it, maybe? Gauge how observant I am and whether I am willing to bring up unorthodox topics. Must be.*

And the chalk man? Easy: Mr. Dean scrubbed it out, while I fixated on not bombing the interview. Both elements are psychological. That's all. And the receptionist never said 'CSF.'

"Yes," Josie said at last. "I think it's ..."

"It's possible you're overthinking it," Mom said. "Because there are other things going on in your life."

A part of Josie coiled tighter. The part that was convinced the shadow and disappearing chalk man were real and not an elaborate test or trick. That part made her breathing shaky, until she swallowed and closed her eyes.

When she looked again, Mom tapped the employment contract. "You're going to sign?"

"I'm going to read them," Josie said.

But yes, I'll sign.

The Eburos Group
WORKPLACE POLICIES

Eburos is committed to privacy for our clients,
employees, and partners. As part of our hiring
process, we ask that you sign a non-disclosure
agreement (NDA), in which you confirm that you will
secure confidential information, destroy confidential
documents when no longer needed, and surrender
aspects of your person should they become
compromised (e.g., mouth, eyes, fingers). If you are
unsure about specific circumstances, please consult
your manager immediately (see 'Quick Tips: Seven
signs you may be infested').

COMPANY HANDBOOK

Chapter Seven

"Josephina Morris?" A friendly security guard smiled up behind the lobby front desk, before Josie could even begin the intro she'd mentally prepared on the subway ride in for her first day. The guard pointed to a black bulb camera fixed to the desk, said, "Eyes wide, don't smile. Perfect." He tapped a computer, while a second guard checked in a line of visitors beside her.

Regular employees in suits and smart dresses hustled through the turnstiles and onto the elevators with coffee cups, headphones, and even a few old-school paper newspapers. In the six hours between her arrival back at the Brooklyn apartment and her frantic early-morning shower, Josie closed her eyes in the bed, beside snoring Dani for dream bursts. Micro, nonsensical stories she forgot every hour or so when she woke to check her phone: yes, the alarm was still set. No, she hadn't overslept on her first day. The big day—now.

Not a syllable or text with Dani, and no choice, Josie recycled her only suit jacket from the interview, but wore a different blouse and skirt. Maybe it wouldn't matter, but now, when the security guard plucked a plastic photo ID card from a tiny printer beside his computer, Josie hesitated: frazzled, still-wet hair, too puffy chipmunk cheeks, and a layer of dry skin cut across her chin and lower lip, like an unnatural scrubland on the GPS map of her face.

"Something wrong?" the guard asked but still bright and patient. As if the two people waiting behind her didn't exist and she had all the time in the world.

"No, it's ..." *Not fine.*

It is. You have your ID, complete with name and title and a correct photograph, just like that. So move along.

Exhaustion fear. *The shake in my left hand, as I'm holding the card, the way I'm shifting my weight too much, tremor in my right knee. This is body panic.*

Thinking it should have helped, didn't. *It's a job. Man up. Or whatever.*

"Would you like me to retake it?" the guard asked. "It's no problem."

"No," Josie said. "No, thank you. Where do I ..?"

He passed her a blue-and-red plastic folder, with the gold Eburos Group tree logo embossed in the center. A welcome packet. "Third floor."

She adjusted her portfolio folder—another rehash from the interview, but Josie hadn't wanted to lug in a purse, and she needed her wallet, keys, and IDs. Plus, there would be papers, and a portfolio signaled 'professional,' right?

Through the turnstiles, Josie stepped into a cluster of Eburos employees waiting at the elevators: three young guys listening to EarPods, not much older than her; a gray-haired, Indian man in a country club polo shirt; and a woman in a bright yellow vest, with a clip-on walkie talkie. None carried briefcases or portfolio folders, nothing like that, and as the second elevator opened for them, a pair of middle aged women in Eburos-branded gym clothes stepped out, laughing and talking too loudly, with iced coffees. *I don't know what this is.*

In the elevator, the others tapped higher floors, and when Josie hit '3,' one of the young dudes in a sweater vest popped out an EarPod to say, "First day?"

The door shut, and they rose, everyone else ignoring her.

"Yes," Josie said. "Just now."

"Welcome," he said. "I'm Andy. In comms." No handshake, he gave a mini 'welcome aboard' gesture.

"Josie. I'm in Client Services."

The elevator dinged to open on 3, but at 'client services' everyone tensed, suddenly focused on her, even the gray-haired man, who said, "Good luck, Josie."

And she stepped out into another lobby area, with a huge TV playing muted financial programs. An immense arrangement of flowers surrounded the reception desk by a hall that fed back to frosted-glass offices and conference rooms. Closer to the desk, a card came into view on the flowers: *'With Deepest Sympathies.'* A funeral display.

A round, short-haired woman in a three-dimensional Christmas poodle sweater appearance in the hall. "And you must be Josie Morris! Welcome to the Eburos family, Josie. I'm Maureen!" A quick, surprisingly strong handshake. "Have you had a chance to review the agenda for today?" She nodded to the welcome folder. "No?" She winked and led Josie into the hall. "Welcome to HR. Our little fiefdom within a fiefdom, I call it. Most people don't give us a second thought, except when they need something or miscount their PTO, and then suddenly we become everyone's best friend ..." Maureen paused at an open door on the right.

Inside, a thin, blonde woman talked on a landline speakerphone at a desk crammed with Americana family photos: the woman, her husband, and two boys at Mount Rushmore; at the beach; chasing a golden retriever; and an entire series of festive group dinner table shots with what must be the extended family.

"Beth?" Maureen said. "Knock, knock." And slow knocked on the door, enough to swing it wide—past a guy in a suit and tie, hunched in a corner chair. Head down, he looked young and so bony that his suit poked out awkwardly at the shoulders and elbows.

"That's not enough for fifteen tables," Beth was saying into the phone and broke into a smile for Maureen, mouthed: *'How are you? Love the sweater!'*

On the speaker phone, a male voice with an Eastern European accent, said, "It's what's available in the Long Island warehouse."

"So?" Beth said and shot Maureen a grin and eyeroll, before raising one hand to pantomime a jabbering mouth. "I have *fifteen* tables, and I can't very well only serve ten, can I?"

"No," the phone-man said. A pause. "Let me check on the liver available in Canada."

"You do that, thank you. EOD." She ended the call and brightened.

Still, the boy in the corner didn't move, his arms slack, body prostrate in the chair.

"Wanted to introduce you," Maureen said. "This is Josie. That's her name right now."

Her name right now?

"Hi, Josie," Beth said quickly and started to thank Maureen for stopping by.

"She's in *Client Services*."

Beth froze, still casual, but she clasped her hands together, as if she didn't want to accidentally disturb the desk. "Is that so? Very exciting. Well, you just remember, if we can help out down here, don't be a stranger. Maureen knows where all the bodies are buried."

"Oh you!" Maureen waved Josie on.

Josie stepped out, paused, a sliver of the unmoving boy still visible past the door. "Is he okay?"

Beth shook her head, confused. "Who?" Then followed Josie's stare. "Oh, you mean Martin? Yes, Martin is an *intern*." As if that explained it.

Josie followed Maureen down the hall.

"You said something about my name?" Josie said.

Toward the end of the hall, Maureen stopped to let them into a conference room on the left with a view of the taxi traffic and crowded sidewalks below. Across the street, the outlines of important-looking people moved in offices and meetings rooms just like this one. A bank or a law firm, something like that in the same Eburos world. The real reality, Angela called it.

"Your name?" Maureen said and took a corner seat at the table near a flatscreen wall monitor. "You signed, I take it, everywhere there's an 'X'?"

A deflection, as if she doesn't understand or remember telling Beth that's my name 'right now.'

Josie handed over the employment agreement and nondisclosure agreement. She'd read through quickly on the train back, tried to parse several odd phrases again early this morning, before finally just scribbling her signature.

"Brilliant," Maureen said, and they talked through an agenda in Josie's welcome packet. Everything neatly mapped out, but with an asterisks at the bottom: *'Pending Registration.'* "You are benefits eligible," Maureen was saying, "as of today, so we can walk through the options, if you know what you'd like to select." She showed Josie a website link printed on her welcome folder for the Employee Handbook. "But if you need more time to think it over ..."

A quick knock, and a flustered bald guy leaned in. Over a black suit, he wore a plastic apron, splatter-smeared with red paint, still wet and trickling. His right hand, neck, and chin dripped.

"I am so sorry, Maureen," the paint-man said. "There's a hiccup in one of the mid performance reviews."

Maureen sighed. "Department?"

"Finance."

Maureen popped up, then snatched a remote to turn on the wall monitor. "No worries. We're still in orientation, so I have capacity." Scrolling through an onscreen menu, Maureen gave Josie a 'what can you do' shrug, while the wet-paint man shuffled at the door.

"ASAP," he said. "I was told ..."

"Yes, yes," Maureen said, tapping through the 'Display' options to select 'Cinema Mode,' so the screen blinked to a softer color gradient, when she scrolled down to select, 'New Hire Day One' and pressed play. "Here we are."

A sound like a dog yowling down the hall, and wet-paint man checked the noise, eyes wide. "An internal audit found discrepancies in Quickbooks ..."

Maureen shushed him on her way out, nodded to Josie. "Shout if you need anything. I'll be back in five." And followed him out, shutting the door behind her.

Wet paint. That's all it was.

Onscreen, an animated tree sprouted on a hillside, as an impressionistic red-and-gold sun rose in the backdrop. Upbeat synthetic music pulsed, and when the sun hit the top of the screen over a fully-formed yew tree, the screen flashed to leave the golden, glowing Eburos Group logo.

A grizzled male voice—a famous actor Josie couldn't quite place—said, "Welcome. To The Eburos Group. Family." The video cut through a stock montage of dynamic cityscapes all around the world, then to smiling, corporate people, and flashy stock market tickers. "At Eburos, our people are our most important asset. *You* are Eburos. Respected the world over, The Eburos Group rises from a high-performing legacy of achievement." A quick snapshot of black-and-white New York City, before a cut to more bright montages of attractive people in offices. "You are joining us at an auspicious chapter in the Eburos story. In the past decade, our performance has risen 40 percent year-over-year, with profits surging by a factor of ten. Our leadership is the best in the world." A proud photo of Mr. Dean, smiling at his desk. No cigarette or rumpled suit, and no chalk man behind him, just the skyline of lower Manhattan out sheer glass. "All committed to strategic expansion for the long term, to create an Eburos that will thrive for generations ..."

She said five minutes, how long would this video go on? Josie flipped through her welcome packet, checked her phone, only half listening, until the commercial-looking montages cut to a video of Mr. Dean, still in a sharp suit at his desk. The same photoshoot, must be.

"The lifeblood of our business is our anchor clients," he said, clearly reading a script. "At Eburos, whatever your role, you may encounter an anchor client or someone adjacent to them. It's imperative that we all operate at the highest level, always. That new face at the water cooler?" Mr. Dean paused and cleared his throat, with a slip in his fixed, easy-going expression, as if he couldn't wait to finish. "Or that familiar colleague you've worked with since your first day—*today* ..." A pause, as if waiting for audience laughter, and he continued, "You never know. They may have a relationship with an anchor client, too. No matter who you are or where you are at Eburos, you represent the firm. Treat every individual, living or otherwise, as a potential anchor client by delivering the best results, always."

Wait. What did he say? 'Living or otherwise'?

The video cut to another collection of skyscrapers, then the hustle-and-bustle of cities around the world, like a high-end soda advertisement. The narrator explained that 'innovation' was in the company's veins.

The door opened, and Maureen slipped back in, her cheeks more flushed, as if she'd been running or just ducked in from the cold.

"... pursuit of excellence," the video narrator said. "It doesn't come easy. But for members of The Eburos Group, we commit ..."

Maureen released a shaky breath and switched off the screen, flashed Josie a weak smile. "Sorry. I can keep it running, if you'd like to finish? Otherwise, we can move things along."

"That's fine. Are you all right?"

Maureen straightened her Christmas poodle sweater and leaned close to the monitor to primp her hair in the reflection. "Oh, I must look a state. You're sweet. It's review season." She waved Josie up to the door. "Never a dull moment. But you have your ID, and I explained about benefits—most everything is online. So." She leaned in the doorway, thinking. "What do you say we skip ahead? What's your blood type?"

Josie's legs locked at the edge of the table. Outside, cars honked, and someone whistled over the street noise. The question didn't make sense.

"My ..."

"Yes," Maureen said. "Just to save us a trip to have you tested, if you already know?"

"B negative."

"Oh, that's a good one," Maureen said, and they started back out into the hall, the way they'd come. Midway down, a janitor scrubbed suds into the dark carpet just below a red streak and fresh dent in the wall. Right outside Beth's now-closed office.

"Did something happen?" Josie asked.

"Hmm?" Maureen tracked her stare, said, "Oh, we just like to keep things tidy. So we'll head up to 15 for registration and IT."

"Registration?"

Back at the elevators, Maureen paused by the flower-wrapped reception desk. "Do you want to leave that here? We'll pop right back for it after." She took Josie's welcome folder and portfolio—*My phone, IDs, keys…*—and gave them to the receptionist, who smiled and complimented Maureen's sweater. "Just like coat check," Maureen told Josie. "We like to keep it fancy here!" In the elevator, she pressed to take them up. "Registration is much more interesting than boring old health insurance. I know, I know I'm not allowed to say that."

"Registration for what?" Josie asked.

The elevator arrived at 15 to a jungle room crowded with wall-to-wall trees, ferns, and prickly bushes interspersed with touch-screen kiosks. Only two other people here: a one-armed woman helping a young guy in a tight brown suit make on-screen selections, as if this were a self-service check-in station at the airport.

Maureen walked Josie to a second kiosk wedged into a thick hedge of greenery. "It's routine," Maureen said, "but registration can be … well, see for yourself."

Closer, the kiosk screen came into focus:

Tap to begin.

And at the bottom:

Soul Registration, 0% Complete.

Chapter Eight

"This is a joke ..?" Josie said.

"Hmm?" Maureen sidled alongside her. "Well, we do like to have a good time at Eburos. Employee experience is ..."

"No, I mean *this*." Josie touched the words at the bottom, and the screen blinked to advance to a new prompt:

Alone in a forest, you encounter an injured deer. What do you do?
A – Carry it home.
B – Kill it.
C – Ignore it.
D – Chase it away.
E – None of the above.

"It's a psychological evaluation?" Josie asked.

"There are no right or wrong answers," Maureen said.

So 'soul' is probably an emotive acronym, right? Must be. Clever, and
...

And even as Josie told herself that, a part of her began to scream. A deep, unsettled ridge at the back of her brain spasmed: *all of this is wrong. Leave. Walk out the door now, the way that woman—Grace, was that her name?—urged you to in Mr. Dean's office.*

No. Steadying herself with a slow breath in and out, again, Josie tapped choice '*E—None of the above.*'

"Ooh, interesting," Maureen said, and a new question popped up. At the bottom:

Soul Registration 5% Complete.

Progress.

When you are alone, you feel:
A—Fear
B—Sadness
C—Anger
D—Happiness
E—You don't know.

"Why is that interesting?" Josie asked and read the question a second time. *When I'm alone? What kind of question is that? Alone how? Alone for five minutes or a week? Alone in my apartment or my life?*

"It's unique," Maureen said.

"I know you said there are no right answers ..."

"That's right," she said. "Don't overthink it, Josie. Whatever comes to mind first."

I don't know.

Again, Josie pressed '*E*'—*8% Complete*—and a third question appeared, and then a fourth, and by the time Josie lost track of how many—*88% Complete*—the other kiosk dinged, and the one-armed woman told brown-suit guy, "All right. Right this way." She walked him to a dim gap in the back wall greenery.

He glanced at Josie with a tight smile, pale and with an uncertain quiver in his eyes. "You'll finish in no time," he said.

As if she were afraid or the 'Soul Registration' might meander into an endless loop.

"Come, come," the one-armed woman said, and they both disappeared through the hedge.

"He struggled," Maureen said. "It happens."

Onscreen:

If the world ended tomorrow, you would feel:
A—Regret
B—Relief
C—Shock
D—Nothing
E—All of the above.

Josie sighed. "I don't understand this question ... like, how am I supposed to answer this? How is 'E' even possible? How can someone feel 'shock' and 'nothing' at the same time?"

Maureen squinted closer, as if she hadn't been paying attention, lips moving silently, as she read the kiosk prompt to herself. "Well," she said at last. "You're 88 percent of the way there. That gentleman you saw a moment ago took *years* to reach this point."

Josie watched her expression harden a little in the glass reflection over this new question. *Years, huh?* The suit had looked very dated. *Who wears a brown suit—no, stop it. Focus and finish this silly personality assessment. If the world ended ...*

A brief memory-image of black-metal vines covering buildings. Like the snatch of a dream she'd blurred out, as if the vintage record of her thoughts scratched—*the world* did *end, and somehow came back again, and I've forgotten*—then resumed a steady, ordinary rhythm. She stood in this room at Eburos, smelled the almost primeval musk of plants around them and the faint scent of Maureen's floral deodorant.

What would I feel if the world ended? I wouldn't be surprised. I should be, like anyone, but for some reason, no ...

Josie tapped, '*A—Regret.*'

I'm not done yet. I have too much more to do that I can't even picture today, hopes and dreams and naïve possibilities, probably, but ...

The screen blinked:

Congratulations, your soul is fully registered with The Eburos Group. Please proceed to IT.

"That's it?" Josie asked, Maureen already leading her back to the foliage gap, where the other two had disappeared.

"Yes, indeed." Maureen pressed them through the leaves and into a muted tunnel.

The one-armed woman brushed past them, too close, and brightened when she clocked Josie. "Ah, done already! That's great." And to Maureen, "He wasn't a fit."

"Oh poor thing," Maureen said. "But not everyone is. And for as long as he spent ..."

"I wish I were surprised," the one-armed woman said and started off.

But Josie didn't move. "What do you mean he wasn't a fit?"

"Oh, you don't need to worry," the one-armed woman said. "You finished yours in, what, three days? That's almost record time."

"Three days?"

But the one-armed woman continued back to the kiosk room, and Maureen guided Josie on, the hall widening into a beige passage with motivational posters on either side: *'Teamwork'*—above a team of people rowing crew—on the left; *'Dedication'*—with a mountain climber approaching a snow-capped summit—on the right; and on and on.

"What did she mean 'three days'?" Josie asked.

Maureen frowned, checked a thin, gold watch. "When did we start? Was that Monday?"

"What are you talking about?"

"See? There you are." She showed Josie the tiny display on her wrist. "It's 6:45 PM on the second."

That doesn't make sense. She's confused.

"No, it's the end of August," Josie said.

"It's September 2nd," Maureen said. At the end of the hall, they neared a glass door covered in blinds labelled, *'Information Technology.'*

On the left, a full-maned lion frozen in mid-leap—*'Leadership'*—and on the right, a firefighter illuminated against a maw of orange flame—*'Courage.'*

Maureen gave Josie a sympathetic look, as if she'd seen this before. *And she has. She must have. Whatever this is.*

"Three days—well, technically only 58 hours, so even less—is very good, Josie. That's a good sign."

"A good sign," Josie repeated.

"Yes, that your soul is a value add. Honestly, I can't remember the last time I registered a new hire in less than a month. You should feel very proud. And don't worry, today is still technically your first day, but your hours will all count for PTO. So think of it that way: you can already start planning that trip to St. Bart's over the holidays." She reached for the doorknob.

Don't think about whatever nonsense time slippage Maureen is describing. Just get through the day.

Maureen opened the door to an expanse of cubicles under phosphorescent lighting ... and cages. Just inside, spaced between clusters of wall mail slots and a unisex restroom, sat three huge cages. Curved at the top, the empty cages perched against the walls, like spare equipment someone had forgotten. Chains lumped on the floor of the nearest cage, complete with archaic iron manacles.

Maureen led Josie to a low cubicle in the central aisle, said, "Knock, knock." And a jovial, mustached guy in an Eburos-logo polo swung away from two curved desktop monitors to face them. The mustache screamed hopeful machismo above his slouched shoulders and heavy-set gut.

"Allen here is our resident tech genius," Maureen said.

"Hi Maureen." And he shot Josie a knowing look. "Just turn it off and turn it back on, I always say."

"Ha!" Maureen waved that away. "You're bad. My new best friend, Josie, is new, just finished registration. Fifty-eight hours ..." He raised his eyebrows, and Maureen nodded with pride, as if she'd mentored Josie to speed her through the 'Soul Registration' in *just* 58 hours.

But it wasn't. The kiosk quiz had lasted a half hour, maybe, certainly no more than 45 minutes.

"And now I take it she's here for a laptop?" he asked. "Standard security and encryption?"

"She'll be in Client Services, so ..."

"Ah. So she may not even be in the office much." Back to his monitors, he typed fast—both wrists buckled in strap-on carpal tunnel braces—and said, "Who is her manager?"

"Angela," Josie said. "What do you mean I won't be in the office?"

Allen paused, checked Maureen's expression. Maureen just shrugged. "I only go where I'm told, Allen."

"If you're client-facing," Allen said, "chances are, you'll follow the business. Out and about, wherever they need you."

"What are those cages by the elevators?" Josie asked.

Allen straightened, as if that were irrelevant but wasn't he nice to answer anyway. "The technical term is 'gibbet.' Those are for people who don't install required system updates." A beat, and he chuckled to himself. "Only joking."

"Oh Allen!" Maureen said.

"But we do use Microsoft products," Allen said, "and you'll need to complete the required training modules in the next 30 days. Maureen, have you talked to her about ..."

"Yes, yes," Maureen said, and to Josie, "They're actually kind of fun, you can make a game out of them."

He typed fast again, then paused. "Huh. Okay, I see her in the system. Josephina Morris? Yes, she's scheduled to be a direct liaison with the Friendly Man." He poked at complicated blocks of text onscreen. "See?"

"She's B negative," Maureen said. "So if you can just ..."

"No, no," Allen said. "She'll use shared consoles for now. She's a *direct liaison.*"

"Oh." Understanding clicked in Maureen's face, a brief tension Josie didn't understand, and then Maureen brightened again. "So then you don't need a laptop after all!" And started back for the elevators. "Hungry?"

Josie didn't move. "What's going on? I thought we were here to get my computer."

"Yes," Allen said deliberately, as if she were hard of hearing. "But because you're a *direct liaison,* you'll be using shared work stations for now. Our systems are all arterial, and so if we're anticipating a change, this is our policy." And when she stared back at him, waiting, he sighed. "Ask your manager."

"Who is the Friendly Man?" Josie asked, with a slow, uncomfortable smile. Any second, they would both grin and explain this joke.

But no, Allen just hunched away, tapping on his keyboard, while Maureen squeezed Josie's elbow to nudge her along. "You must be starving. I know I could eat, and you're going to love this, Josie ..." She escorted Josie back through the motivational poster hall and empty greenhouse registration room to the elevators again. "We'll head up to 25. Don't let me spoil the surprise, but oh, I can't help myself: there's a sushi station! And an entire meat counter like you wouldn't believe and ..." The elevator arrived, and Maureen caught herself, one hand to her mouth.

Because so much of this needs to be explained. Finally, she realizes that.

"I am so sorry," Maureen continued and pressed for the 25th floor. On the elevator monitors: talking heads silently debated a corporate merger with close captions above a ticker with commodity prices and ... the time. On the bottom right, it read: 7:12 PM. "I apologize," Maureen said again. "I should have asked first thing, so we could make arrangements ..."

The elevator stopped on 19 to let on an older man in a hipster sport coat and t-shirt combo, holding a black stick, like an AV remote, and as two young people shuffled on after him—a dark-skinned girl in a smart yellow skirt and jacket; and a tall guy in a tight black suit, too-shiny shoes—the hipster old dude clicked a button on the stick. An electronic *buzz* from the young people, who jolted, heads bowed, as they rushed to the back corner of the elevator.

The hipster old dude tapped '41,' frowning at the financial show on the monitors.

"Did he just ..." Josie looked from hipster old dude to Maureen. The doors shut; the elevator rose.

"I know, I should have asked earlier," Maureen repeated, more quietly.

Did I see that? Josie stared back at the two young people, cowering behind them. Both watched the floor, wearing thin, metallic collars. *Like dogs. Exactly like that.*

The elevator opened on 25—a wave of grilling meat smells, tomato sauce, and sharp, Asian spices hit Josie, as Maureen walked her into a high-end, buffet-style cafeteria, ringed with manned serving stations that surrounded busy black tables of people eating in the center. On every side, windows looked out on the twilight glitter of the Manhattan skyline and the near-distant shimmer of the outer boroughs and New Jersey.

"So tell me honestly," Maureen said, tense and suddenly serious. *Here it comes. The reveal. Whatever this is, how much is actual, how much I'm imagining. Am I losing my mind? Tell me.* "Josie ..."

"Yes?"

"I should have asked earlier, and I apologize ..."

"You said that already," Josie said. "It's okay. What's wrong?"

"You don't ..." Maureen surveyed the expanse of sizzling meats, custom sushi, and steaming, premade casseroles, pastas, and soups. "You don't have any dietary restrictions ..." She swallowed, met Josie's eye. "... do you?"

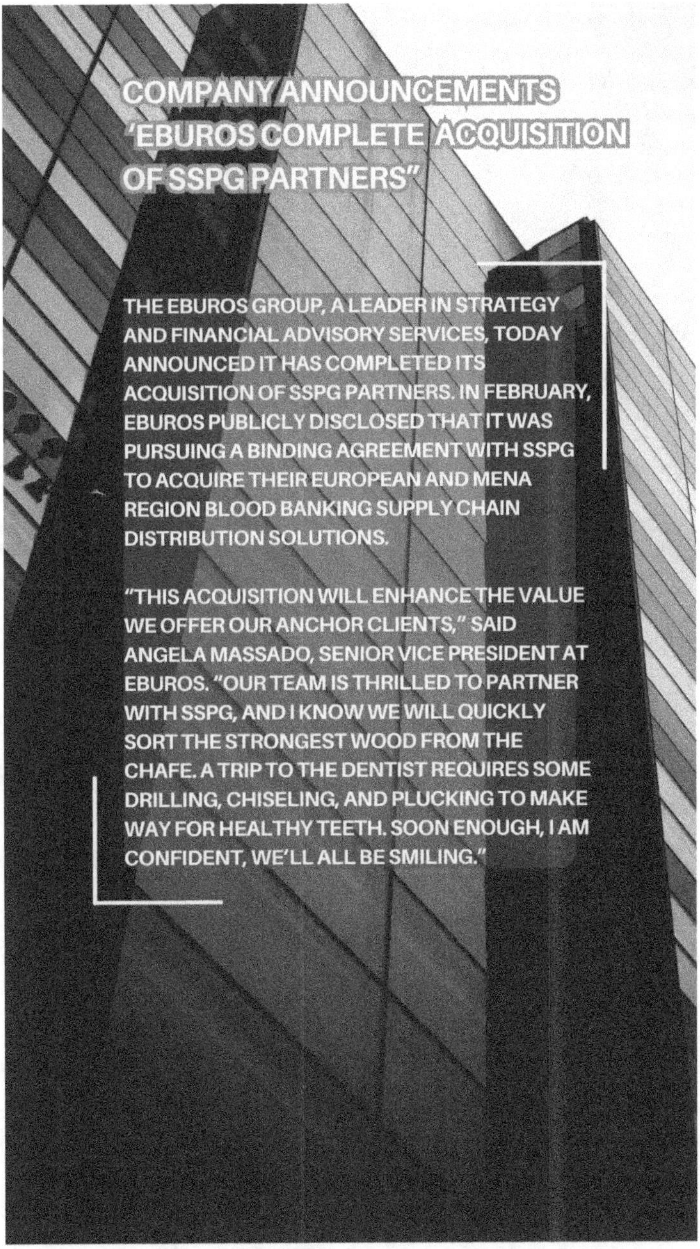

COMPANY ANNOUNCEMENTS "EBUROS COMPLETE ACQUISITION OF SSPG PARTNERS"

THE EBUROS GROUP, A LEADER IN STRATEGY AND FINANCIAL ADVISORY SERVICES, TODAY ANNOUNCED IT HAS COMPLETED ITS ACQUISITION OF SSPG PARTNERS. IN FEBRUARY, EBUROS PUBLICLY DISCLOSED THAT IT WAS PURSUING A BINDING AGREEMENT WITH SSPG TO ACQUIRE THEIR EUROPEAN AND MENA REGION BLOOD BANKING SUPPLY CHAIN DISTRIBUTION SOLUTIONS.

"THIS ACQUISITION WILL ENHANCE THE VALUE WE OFFER OUR ANCHOR CLIENTS," SAID ANGELA MASSADO, SENIOR VICE PRESIDENT AT EBUROS. "OUR TEAM IS THRILLED TO PARTNER WITH SSPG, AND I KNOW WE WILL QUICKLY SORT THE STRONGEST WOOD FROM THE CHAFE. A TRIP TO THE DENTIST REQUIRES SOME DRILLING, CHISELING, AND PLUCKING TO MAKE WAY FOR HEALTHY TEETH. SOON ENOUGH, I AM CONFIDENT, WE'LL ALL BE SMILING."

Chapter Nine

J osie overloaded a tray with samples from almost every station—all choreographed by Maureen: "Oh, and the candied ham makes everyday a holiday!" "I have naughty dreams about these avocado rolls, I swear!" "The burnt cheese crust is the best part, you got a lucky slice!"—until Josie followed Maureen to a table of friendly, business casual people, who welcomed them and resumed a conversation about travel plans.

"Jakarta on Friday," A fast-talking, serious woman was saying. "But if we close in time, I am going to sneak by Bora Bora on the way back."

Knowing smiles from the group, and Josie tested her food: the first bite of ham tingled with a shock of sugary salt that made Josie relax back in her seat.

"What did I tell you?" Maureen said, dipping sushi into a tiny cup of soy sauce.

"You were right." Josie ate faster, suddenly ravenous. Starving, had she ever been this hungry?

"It's the noise as much as the smog," a bright-eyed, bearded man said across the table. "Kathmandu wasn't always so busy, but last month, I swear I didn't sleep for weeks at a time ..."

As the others talked, Maureen leaned closer to Josie. "How are you feeling? Better?"

Josie nodded, mouth full of avocado roll.

"Good," Maureen said. "The shared workstations are very user friendly. But if you need help with them, you let me know."

Josie swallowed and forked a slice of shepherd's pie: ground meat, with mashed potatoes and curled, cheese crust on top. She forced herself to pause for a breath. *Slow down.* "Some of the things today …"

"It's a lot to take in, absolutely."

"Can I get back my phone?"

"Oh, of course, dear!" Maureen snapped her fingers with an 'aw shucks' gesture, as if she should have remembered earlier. "I'm sure it's all set by now."

"All set?"

"Well, yes." Maureen dabbed another sushi roll in her soy sauce, concentrating as she turned it in a arc to evenly soak the rice. "With company software."

"They messed with my phone?"

"Of course." Maureen nibbled half the sushi roll and closed her eyes at the taste. "Mm, today is a good day to be an avocado."

"I don't …" *She forced me to surrender my phone. IDs and keys, too, what could I do?*

"Is something wrong?" Maureen asked. "It's very routine, Josie. Data security and all the rest. Above my pay grade."

From across the table, the bearded man called, "Love the sweater, Maureen. My brother has a Labradoodle just like that."

Maureen beamed, popped the last sushi bite into her mouth. "Thank you! But I'm afraid this little rascal is pure bred Poodle, with a capital 'P.'" She puffed out her chest to make the stitched Christmas dog waggle, and the table laughed.

All but the serious woman, who aimed a glass of iced tea at Josie. "Travel plans?"

"This is Josie," Maureen said. "She's just starting in Client ..."

The serious woman ignored that, asked, "Are you local, Josie?"

Behind Josie, a voice said, "Josie is very local."

Josie spun: Angela approached, dressed in a tight black-and-red zig-zag blouse and crisp dark pants, formal boots. She extended one hand, dark purple nails the same shade as her earrings. All virtual-avatar precise, like in the computer games Dani played, back before she decided to focus all her attention on law school. And back in Brooklyn, if two days really had passed, maybe Dani had spent them with someone else. *I need my phone. But what if she hasn't texted at all? If a relationship falls in the forest and my girlfriend is AWOL, does it still make a sound?* This sudden, slow-moving breakup suddenly flared up, like a low hum in the back of Josie's mind.

Maureen sprang up to shake Angela's hand. "Wonderful to see you, Angela! And so lovely to meet Josie here. I've got my eye on this one!"

Angela's shadow pulled toward the table, then flowed back, before Angela stopped just behind Josie. "Yes, I'm sure." To Josie, "Shall we?"

Josie's stomach gurgled, still hungry, but she nodded and rose to scattered pleasantries around the table, before Maureen rubbed her shoulder, said, "Remember, don't be a stranger. No need to wait for your performance review to give me a shout."

And Josie let Angela walk her back to the elevators.

"How does it feel?" Angela asked.

Josie started to say that she didn't know, how could she with the ordinary-unstable blur that had somehow lasted two and a half days. "I'm tired," she said at last.

"Mm hm, you would be. That's fair," Angela said at the elevators. "I'll show you the nap rooms, right by the new gym."

"Nap rooms?"

"Well, yes." The elevator arrived, and this time, Angela tapped '2.' Back down. "We have an early start tomorrow, and there are still a few details to iron out."

The time ... the elevator monitor read: 7:50 PM.

"It's almost 8:00," Josie said.

Angela stiffened, as if insulted, then shook her head to uncoil again in a quick mental resolution of whatever had almost annoyed her. "We work as needed, Josie," Angela said quietly. "Professional hours are not 9 to 5. It's important you understand that, before things go much further."

"No, I know. I'm not ..."

They arrived on the second floor: a welcoming flow of blue carpet that led down a hall of identical doors on the right, with soothing aquariums set into the walls between them. On the left, tinted glass looked into an elaborate gymnasium, complete with treadmills, weight machines, and ... yes, there at the back, a sweaty guy in short-shorts pulled and thrusted on a Concept 2 rower set in a line with five others. Past the rowing machines, another glass wall looked in on an immense blue-glow swimming pool.

"I'll have an outfit brought down," Angela said. Halfway down the hall, she stopped at a right-hand door, with a green square above the doorknob: unoccupied.

"My phone ..."

"Yes, that, too." Angela studied her, as if searching for the signals of just how impressed Josie was by all this.

I'm too tired. Suddenly beyond fucking exhausted.

"Thank you," Josie murmured. *I should go home.* "But my girlfriend ..."

"Of course," Angela said, then opened one arm to the closed door. "Just a little rest, though. Don't underestimate your need to recharge. Biology is nonnegotiable."

Josie opened the door to a small, windowless pod, complete with a dark, marshmallowy bed and minimalist wall shelves stocked with water bottles, towels, pajamas, and spare pillows. This close to the bed, Josie's legs caved, and she caught her balance on the doorframe, ready to collapse.

"When you wake up, you'll have your phone—all that—and fresh clothing. Showers at the end of the hall."

Josie stepped in. "Okay."

Her forehead throbbed, a dull, weary press behind her eyes. *Lie down. Just for a minute.*

"Rest up," Angela said. "In the morning, we have a plane to catch."

Josie did, the obvious questions—*A plane?*—folding over themselves like shrinking origami thought balloons, as she collapsed onto the bed and slept ... then woke, in total darkness to a soft knock at the door. When Josie sat up, legs and arms heavy but strangely refreshed, soft white light fuzzied on around her. *Motion activated.*

"Yes?" Josie asked.

"Good morning." A hesitant female voice from the other side. "I'm sorry, I need to check if you're up? I have coffee, your outfit, and all your personals here."

Good morning?

Josie opened the door: the dark-skinned, metal-collar girl from the elevator, still wearing the same yellow jacket and skirt. The girl kept her eyes on the ground as she handed Josie a steaming Starbucks cup.

"I didn't add cream or sugar," the girl said. "I hope that's okay." And before Josie could answer, the girl nodded to the hall floor: neat squares of plastic-wrapped clothing and a tidy pile of Josie's registration folder and portfolio.

"Thank you." Josie knelt to sort through it, found her phone. The screen blinked on: 5:10 AM. A string of missed messages from Mom, two from other random friends, but ... nothing from Dani or Everett. *Nothing—really?* And yes, the fucking date had skipped ahead showing today as September 3rd. Two days entirely erased during her registration.

Of my soul.

"Are you okay?" Josie asked, and the girl shied away. "I'm sorry, I saw you on the elevator, and ..."

"I have to go," the girl said and flicked her wrist to check an expensive-looking silver-chain watch. "They need you in the lobby at 5:30."

Josie burned her mouth on the coffee, said, "In twenty minutes?"

A curt nod, still no eye contact, and the girl darted off toward the elevators. Across the hall, people packed the gym, running and lifting and squatting on the machines, most wearing headphones or EarPods and a few clearly talking on the phone.

Twenty minutes to pull myself together and hit the lobby.

Propping the nap room door open with one foot, Josie slipped back into her pod and called Dani. Straight to voicemail. *Like her phone is out of battery or she rejected the call.*

No, it's 5:00 AM, she didn't reject the call. She's asleep, obviously, and her phone must have run out—maybe even broke. She's been too busy with new classes, orientation, whatever to get it fixed. That's why there's no message.

That didn't feel real, no matter how many times Josie repeated it in her mind, but still she tapped a quick message: *'Sorry, I've been incommunicado. New job is crazy. How r u?'*

Good enough.

She took a shaky breath, sipped more coffee. *Get ready. Go to the lobby, this is my job now. Not forever, but right now.* "Okay." She said it aloud, as if the sound would normalize this. *It isn't that strange. It really isn't.*

Josie forced herself up and back out to inspect the clothing piles. Time for a shower—yes, fuck it, she did, and 16 minutes later, she stepped off the lobby elevator in a stiff, gray blouse and dark pants, with curly, still-dripping hair.

At the lobby desk, Angela perked up. She'd swapped into a new, sharp-edged blue suit with purple trim, like a banker from the future. Other employees hurried in around them. "Punctual," Angela said, then noticed the registration folder and portfolio under Josie's arm. "Oh, but you don't need those."

Josie took her phone and keys, but left her IDs—no room for a passport in her pockets—and surrendered the folders to the security guard, before following Angela to a black sedan waiting outside. The bald, solid-looking guy from the interview day elevator—*Tommy?*—held the back door. He wore a Eburos-logo polo shirt and khakis, as if they were off to a country club. *And maybe we are?*

After helping them in, Tommy climbed into the driver's seat. "Air okay?" he asked.

"Fine, Tommy, thanks," Angela said, and to Josie, "Welcome to the party." As they pulled away, Angela continued, "I didn't ask you to bring a bag, because this is a simple day trip. Forty-five minutes in the air each way. No more than four or five hours total, back by tea time."

Downing more coffee filled Josie with a wired with nervous chemical excitement. They turned into the cross-town traffic between the early-morning glow of skyscrapers, accelerating.

"We're going to Dutch Island," Angela said. "A quick flight out of Teterboro this morning." Her shadow flicked up, down—the car bounced, and she did, too. "On the way, Mr. Dean will explain. We have a call scheduled." They made the small New Jersey airport in less than an hour and followed an unmarked road around a long, razor wire-topped fence, past a roundabout, and to a security gate. Tommy typed numbers into a security keypad and told an intercom they were here for Eburos. The gate opened. They pulled in, between hangars and warehouse buildings, then stopped at a network of overlapping runways, labeled neatly with letter-number codes. A small jet waited, with the boarding steps already down. A silver-haired woman in a pilot's uniform waved from the open entry door. *We're flying to Dutch Island on a private jet.* Josie had never been, and certainly never traveled anywhere on a plane like this.

Tommy followed Josie, as Angela hurried up the steps. She hugged the pilot, introduced Josie, and then they all ducked inside. The narrow, wood-paneled cabin fed back to a meeting table and flat screen monitor, like a high-end conference room ... with a woman slumped in a chair at the far corner. *The woman from Mr. Dean's office, who shouted and was escorted out, just as I arrived. Grace.* She sagged against the window, chest rising in a steady, deep-sleep rhythm.

Angela sat, gestured to an empty seat beside her at the table across from the screen. "It's okay," Angela said. "Have a seat, Josie."

Tommy slid into a backward-facing seat directly in front of the sleeping woman.

"What is this?" Josie asked. "Is she okay?"

"She's fine," Angela said.

Behind Josie, the pilot shut the door and tapped Josie's shoulder. "We're nearly ready, if you wouldn't mind taking your seat ..."

"I promise," Angela said, "all this will make sense. Mr. Dean really should be the one to explain."

What am I doing? This is insane. Get off the plane. I am being pulled into a job I don't understand based on craziness I witnessed and then got on a plane with this shadow-woman, a rando security bro, and a girl who may or may not be doped. Or just a deep sleeper. Tommy's choice of seat isn't random either, is it? He picked that spot not only to sit near the sleeping woman, but to block the front exit. I won't be able to run, once I'm in.

Angela found a remote to switch on the monitor, exchanged a quick look with Tommy. The plane engine rumbled.

"Miss?" the pilot said again, behind Josie.

Now. Turn around. Open the door. But what about Uncle Don? And the rent. What about this chance, like Mom said?

Still unmoving, Josie nodded to the sleeping woman. "What's her name again?" She couldn't be much older than Josie, her round face splotchy, as if she were overheated. But she looked calm, totally peacefully, and her body curled slightly sideways, no restraints. Maybe she *was* just asleep.

"That's Grace," Angela said, watching the screen. "I think you met her at the office briefly? She's had a long few weeks. All work, no play. She's crashing—may have even taken an Ambien or two. I wouldn't be surprised, poor thing." Without looking up, Angela asked, "Are you going to sit?"

Decide.

Josie stepped in and let her body settle beside Angela, who patted Josie's arm.

The pilot went into the cockpit, and a moment later, they rumbled forward, the runway slowly scrolling past outside. Josie watched the track turn in a circle as they rounded a corner to line up with the takeoff lanes. The plane stopped.

The screen blipped to a webcam shot of Mr. Dean's office, close up on his leather swivel chair and bookshelf. At the left-hand edge of the frame, the blue-gray column wall painting cropped just into view. *No chalk man.* Their plane lurched forward. Onscreen, Mr. Dean—with the same rumpled suit and wild eyebrows—ducked in from the right. In the chair, he sipped from a 'Eburos'-logo mug and said, "I see you both, great. Josie, my heart jumped when Angela told me she encountered you in Connecticut. Fortuitous." The plane picked up speed. Runway markers shot by quicker out the window past Angela.

"Thank you," Josie said.

"Oh please, thank *you*," Mr. Dean said. "You saw Angela's shadow, and I understand you noticed a figure on the wall of my office?"

"Is it there now?" Angela asked Josie. "Do you see it on the screen?"

Josie shook her head. "No, just the empty landscape columns ..."

The plane pulled up, the runway drifted down, and a layer of trees, rooftops, and streets came into view outside.

"I'm sure Angela has already indicated that you're important, Josie," Mr. Dean said. "You see things we can't. More specifically, you saw the Friendly Man. That's our pet term for him here."

The office towers of New Jersey and the southern curl of Manhattan came into view, and then the glittery gray of the bay. The water streaked with tiny white wave crests. A sailboat cut a foamy wake, then passed out of sight below. They banked away from the city, already over the dense neighborhoods of Staten Island.

"The chalk figure is a person?" Josie asked.

"No," Mr. Dean said. "We don't have a name for what he is. He just *is*."

"Like her shadow?"

"No again. Angela's shadow is an anchor client. And so, in some respects, it can be useful to think of Angela herself as an anchor client."

Anchor client? The phrase itched in Josie's mind, like the sound triggered a tension knot. But no, it didn't mean anything other than … what, a critical customer or client? *Business slang for shadow monster, is that what he's saying?*

He squinted at her, and Angela brushed Josie's arm again. "It's okay," Angela murmured. "You're safe, Josie."

"North American *magicicada*—periodical, brood cicadas," Mr. Dean said. "They lie dormant for intervals of 13 or 17 years. These insects spend the majority of their lives underground, fully alive, but unmoved. Then, at specific intervals, they emerge to procreate. Think of this moment in history as an *active* epoch."

Josie closed her eyes and a took slow, four-second breath in, then released at another count of *one-two-three-four*. She opened her eyes again. *Is this real?*

Mr. Dean poised, waiting. Josie's chest burned. The air was tight, harder to breathe. Angela offered a water bottle, and the cool swallow of liquid helped, but not much. Outside, a broken grid of thin roadways flowed below, as they neared the southern edge of Staten Island.

"I remember cicadas growing up," Josie said quietly.

"Yes, good," Mr. Dean said. "In the contexts of our anchor clients, it can be helpful to think of people as a *resource*. At Eburos, we serve our clients, first and foremost."

Don't think about what that means.

"Where is he?" Josie pointed past Mr. Dean at the empty wall painting. "Did you erase it?"

Mr. Dean barked a sharp laugh that made her jump. "Right to it—I love it! Erase him? Oh my dear, no. He holds the eraser, not the other way around. And he is still here, don't worry. The Friendly Man keeps the lights on, both literally and figuratively."

Josie started to say she didn't understand, stopped. *He hates that phrase, right? Avoid any admission of weakness.*

"That's an *anchor client*, trapped in the wall?" Josie asked.

"No," Mr. Dean said. "As I said, we don't have a name to accurately describe the Friendly Man." Mr. Dean paused for a loud sip from his mug. "He is the heart of the company, our competitive advantage."

Bullshit. A global company like The Eburos Group, with offices all around the world, it didn't profit because Solomon Dean kept a chalk drawing named the Friendly Man company in his office wall. An elaborate hoax, they're waiting for me to pushback.

Unless they aren't.

"If he isn't an anchor client …"

Mr. Dean sloshed his coffee mug, expression distant, as if suddenly bored. "Net-net, he's here. That's the takeaway. How he originally came to be here, why he stays—these are process questions. The Friendly Man has earned his nickname. He is on our side. This is why we place a great deal of faith in the people to whom he chooses to reveal himself."

"Like me," Josie said.

"Yes. And your companion." When Josie looked at Angela, Mr. Dean cleared his throat, impatient. "No. The other one—Grace."

Josie glanced back at the still-sleeping woman. She hadn't budged. The cabin rattled and bounced, and Josie grabbed the armrests. Outside, the clouds muddied in streaks of looping black. They were over the water again, must be closing on Dutch Island by now.

"Are we okay?" Josie asked.

"What's wrong?" Mr. Dean asked.

"Nothing," Angela said. "Yes, Josie, we're perfectly safe. Tommy has it in-hand."

Across the cabin, Tommy snapped out of his seat, and ducked to the back of the plane. Josie heard the *snap-rustle-snap* of panels being opened, as he unhooked a cargo hold along the back wall.

"Have you been to Dutch Island before?" Mr. Dean asked. "No? Well, Angela can talk you through the specifics. The point I'd like to impress is *trust* ..."

A cage. Lifting with both hands, Tommy hauled a cage—a two-foot by two-foot cube, with metal bars and a flat bottom, like a small dog crate—from the rear of the cabin into the aisle behind Josie. Inside, a rooster fluttered and bounced against the sides. It stank of feathers and feces.

"Trust," Josie repeated.

"Yes. Trust that everything we're doing drives value creation. You are part of that team now."

Value creation, but Josie nodded, still watching Tommy at the rooster cage out of the corner of her eye.

Mr. Dean noticed her distraction and asked Angela, "A sacrifice for the Silent Emperor?"

"Yes," Angela said. "I think it's safest to ..."

"Agreed," Mr. Dean snapped, and to Josie, "You see: this, right now, is a deliverable for an anchor client. A precaution to be trusted."

"The Silent Emperor?" Josie asked.

"Our name for him," Angela said.

"So the chicken ..."

"Rooster," Angela said, with a slight smile.

"You'll carry it from here?" Mr. Dean asked Angela.

"Absolutely." Angela switched off the screen.

Tommy opened the cage door and caught the rooster's neck, then jammed it to the floor. Its wings pounded, clawed feet scratching at the shit-streaked metal. *Is this real?* Tommy slipped a knife under its head.

"Oh God ..." Josie looked away. Out the window, they were enveloped by dark clouds, no sign of the ground. In the cabin aisle, wings flapped harder, and she heard a patter of liquid, then a splatter-spray, like a weak hose, and the fluttering slowed. One more burst of noise, and it stopped.

Still, Josie didn't look back. "What the hell is this?"

"He told you, a sacrifice," Angela said simply. "To that." She nodded at the storm clouds outside. "If it improves our odds—well, roosters are comparatively cost-effective. Thank you, Tommy." He took the cage away, and Josie noticed she was squeezing the seat arms again, willed her fingers to loosen. *'Comparatively?' What if it wasn't a bird? What if it was a person? Tommy could do that to me. No. Stop it. Fucking butchered a rooster to ward off the weather.*

The plane bumped and rocked. Tommy swayed, caught his balance, and stowed the cage again.

An overhead speaker crackled. "Sorry about that," the captain said. "Just a touch of turbulence. Should have us through momentarily. Nearly time to begin our descent, so please take a moment ..."

"So?" Angela asked Josie. "Did he answer your questions?"

There's a chalk monster living in the walls of the Eburos office building that somehow helps the company. And I'm on this plane, because I see him and ...

"What about you?" Josie asked.

"Me?"

"Yes. Your shadow. Mr. Dean said you're a ..."

"Anchor client?" Angela shrugged: so obvious. *It is. It almost is.* "Yes," she said. "But not just."

"Just?" Josie said. "What else ..?"

"Do I *look* like a monster?" Angela posed in her seat, one hand teasing at the top of her jacket, legs crossed. "Be honest."

"No," Josie said. "Of course not."

"I *look* like a person," Angela said, "because I am, just like every host."

"*Host?* For one of these things, an anchor client? Like the Silent Emperor?" *Whatever the fuck ...*

"Yes."

As if they're a disease, and she's honored by the infection.

"What are we doing right now?" Josie asked. "Why Dutch Island?"

"Great question," Angela said. She smiled at Tommy, as he returned to his seat. No sign of the knife. "We're here, as Mr. Dean alluded, because of the Friendly Man. He's generous, but can be picky about his terms." She pointed at sleeping Grace. "The Friendly Man chose her, but unfortunately, Grace hasn't always reciprocated. We believe you can help."

"What about him?" Josie pointed at Tommy. "Is he ..?"

"No," Angela said, and when Tommy frowned back, confused. "Our new colleague is just asking if you are *only* you, or also someone else."

"Got it," he said and folded away from them to look out the window.

"How am I supposed to help Grace?" Josie asked. "And the Friendly Man, I still don't understand any of this."

Out the window, the clouds thinned, and a rough green shock of treetops appeared below. About ten miles from New York, Dutch Island wasn't much more than a spit of land. A couple miles wide and maybe twice as long, Josie knew its story in miniature. The last New Netherlands outpost in the Americas, with postcard-famous windmills and an old-timey oceanfront town. The summer ferries were always over-booked, the hotels too expensive for Josie to even consider it. Now, though? *A private fucking jet.*

"Mr. Dean invested in an instrument on the island," Angela said.

"Like a stock or a local company?"

"No. Not financial—the musical kind of instrument. A flute, to be exact."

Josie fought the urge to point out that every word made this *less* comprehensible, not more. *A flute?*

Angela watched the overgrown shoreline of the island below. "It's from Chile, actually. Made by the Mapuche Indians, we think, from the shin bone of a Spanish conquistador. Apparently, the Dutch brought it here. The other instruments the Native people made from that Spaniard didn't survive."

Another joke? Fucking hilarious.

Past a beach, they flew over land. No high rises or bulky highway bridges, the landscape drooped in wide, green fields and hills capped with antique-looking Dutch windmills, long-since turned into photo ops, rather than used for milling or whatever they once did. A small confusion of concrete buildings cropped up along the far shore. Hard to make out in the darkening air. They were flying below the clouds now, but the solid mass of sky cast thick shadows.

A flute made from bones.

"Why, though?" Josie asked.

"Why Dutch Island? We *invested* in the flute, Josie, we don't own it. We're allowed to use it from time to time."

"And the owner is ..." Josie hesitated. "It's not a person, is it? It's ..."

"One of *them? Us?*" Angela met Josie's eyes, still smiling. *Always smiling.* "Well. Yes."

Anchor client music. *Perfect.*

The Eburos Group
WORKPLACE POLICIES

All employees are required to attend mandatory semi-annual training with the IT department on protecting firm information from cyber attack, divination, and possession. Training is typically held the first Tuesday of each quarter. If you cannot attend, you must receive manager approval to complete the training virtually. The training module is not complete until you complete the quiz and print a copy of the certificate, signed by your manager, for HR. Employees are encouraged, but not required, to use PTO for this training.

COMPANY HANDBOOK

CHAPTER TEN

They landed on a small, square-ish airfield, with a ring of charter jets parked around the grassy fenceline like cars circling a drive-thru. As the plane stopped, another black sedan appeared out the window, and the pilot opened the door to drop the landing stairs. A rush of warm, humid air flooded the cabin, mingling with the lingering feather-shit stink.

Tommy jumped up first, but before he reached for her, the other woman—Grace—opened her eyes. She glared up at him. "Don't touch me."

Tommy stopped, looked at Angela, probably for directions. Grace followed his stare, noticed Josie. "Why is she here? Who are you?" she asked Josie.

"She's part of the team now," Angela said.

"The *team*," Grace said and smirked. "Fuck your team."

Tommy tensed, still watching Angela.

"You need to stand up and exit the plane," Angela told Grace. "Please. Let's not ..."

"Yeah." Grace slouched out of her seat and brushed by Tommy, already ducking out to the runway steps.

Angela sighed. "Sorry about that. She's in a mood apparently."

"Why is she here?" Josie asked.

Angela gestured to the door, and as they exited, said, "Like you, she's receptive to the anchor clients. The Friendly Man likes her, so we do, too."

Outside, earth-soaked humidity hit Josie on the steps. The sky clotted gray overhead, and a fuzzy mist drizzled the runway. The damp air clung to Josie, weighing her down, as she descended into a sharp wind gust. It smelled like rain.

"This storm doesn't look great," Josie said.

Tommy and Grace waited at the car.

"Storm?" Angela shrugged. "We'll be fine."

Tommy held the back door for Grace, then Angela and Josie at the far end. He slipped into the passenger seat up front with a thin, dark-skinned driver. Scrawny shoulders poked against the driver's collared shirt, and Josie saw premature gray stubble along his jaw. He couldn't have been much older than her, though.

The driver's deep brown eyes met hers in the rearview mirror, open and curious. As the car turned in a slow circle away from the plane, headed for an exit gate, Angela told Grace, "We spoke to Mr. Dean on the way down. He's anxious for us to complete this today."

Grace let out a flummoxed breath and slapped the driver's seat in front of her. "Fantastic. And what if we don't?"

Through the gate, they bounced out onto a gravel road overlooking a wild expanse of viney shrubs and evergreen trees. They banked left and passed a yellow cab that looked as if it had been transported direct from Times Square.

"That's not an option," Angela said.

"Well, good," Grace said and looked across at Josie. "Does she understand what's about to happen?"

Angela tensed on the middle-seat hump between them. Up front, the driver and Tommy chatted about their route, direct to New Leiden, but back here, the setup suddenly felt overly calculated. As if Angela were a teacher proctoring detention, careful to keep two unruly students apart.

"She knows about the anchor clients," Angela said.

"And?" Grace said. When Angela didn't answer, Grace released a breath, coughing. "Yeah, not so much, huh?" She looked away at the overcast landscape outside.

Rain trickled down the windows, and up front the wipers slashed on. They passed a billboard that read, *'Welcome to Dutch Island! Founded 1617'* above advertisements for local restaurants, whale watching, and the 'Renaissance Hotel.' It overlooked a hillside of bright neon red, orange, and yellow tulips. All transplants, obviously, the flowers wouldn't last much longer, but right now, their colors shone like wet paint. Too sharp and shocking to be real, yet right there—then gone, around a copse of pine-needle trees at the next turn.

The road widened and rose to a cliffside pass above the choppy caps of the Atlantic Ocean. From here, there was no sight of the mainland. They weren't far from the city and Long Island, but Josie knew that Dutch Island prided itself—had built an entire tourism industry—on being cut off.

"First time?" Grace asked Josie.

"She's never been to Dutch Island, no," Angela said, a little too quickly, as if she wanted to jump in front of the question. That wasn't what Grace meant, was it? *What is this?*

"I haven't," Josie said. "I heard about it in school, the same as anyone who grew up in New York."

"And what did they teach you?" Angela asked. Again, blocking Grace from jumping in.

"'The first and the last,'" Josie said. "Isn't that the saying?"

In the front seat, Tommy and the clear-eyed driver fell silent. Rain rapped the windshield in thick bursts, and below, waves exploded against sharp black rocks.

"That's right," Angela said. "The first Dutch settlement in North America. Last to go. They stayed independent up until 1776—and only started teaching English at the primary school here in the 1930s."

"That's not true," the driver said. Hands tight on the wheel, he shifted in his seat awkwardly, as if that had just slipped out. Josie suppressed a smile and tried to meet his eyes in the mirror again. No good, he focused on the road. "Sorry," he said. "It's just that people spoke English here long before—"

"It's obviously a tourist destination now," Angela snapped. She glared at the driver's blurred reflection in the front glass, smiled again. "You should see the rates in the high season. An archaic middle finger, just far enough from shore to be exotic to people from the Hamptons." To the driver again: "How much further?"

"Not far," he said.

Grace said, "She should really ..."

"The anchor client that lives here is old," Angela told Josie. "She's called 'Sandra.'"

Sandra? Not exactly a monster's name. Another joke? When will this fit together into a coherent picture?

Away from the coast, they rolled onto a fenced gulley and around a bend that carried them up a hill of carefully kept farmhouses and windmills. Through the rain, the hilltop overlooked a windy network of estates that fed down to a dense patchwork of checkerboard, colonial buildings at the shoreline. Groves of pine trees made it impossible to take in the entire little port town, but Josie could tell that it filled most—maybe all—of the coast in a blend of tourist sheik and high-end residential neighborhoods.

The car bounced down past athletic fields and a brick school house. Even in the blustery rain, clusters of people jogged along the sidewalk, and as they banked back to an oceanfront drive, more vehicles splashed along the flooded path by a low, concrete seawall. Waves exploded in high, frothy surges that puddled the entire right lane, forcing them into a narrow bend of traffic toward a main drag of skinny Dutch colonials. The bright pastel colors were muted in the storm-dark air. This historically restored wall of storefronts, bed-and-breakfasts, restaurants, bars, and tiny museums was something not-quite-familiar. As if it had been erected by mistake, somehow overlooked for demolition.

They sat in silence, as the car rocked in sharp winds with the traffic. The road was flooded ahead. A policeman in a bright vest waved them onto a cobblestone side street of elaborate graffiti paintings: a woman held a dove beside a robot with red flames curling from his nose. Around a traffic roundabout, they continued by a newer, glass-faced hotel and onto a wide avenue lined with gated villas that fed back, away from the shore. A high stone wall surrounded a dense, above-ground cemetery. They stopped at the entrance.

"Are you serious?" Josie asked.

"She's right, it's fucking raining," Grace said.

Tommy got out to open Josie's door into a wet gust. The air was a thick ocean mist of salt and fishy, animal smells. One hand up against the rain, Josie stepped out, then Angela and Grace followed. As Grace muttered about the storm, Angela leaned in to talk with the driver. Their conversation was swallowed by the sound of slapping rain. Finally, Angela waved them to follow her to the front gate beside a domed building of yellow arches. The grounds beyond were a tight maze of weathered stone monuments. Graves, statues, and mausoleums packed narrow paths, lined by well-kept trees, all on top of the soil, like something out of New Orleans or the Caribbean.

Through the gate, the cemetery expanded as they followed a walking path between low hills. In the pounding rain, Angela guided them by a wall monument decorated with an engraved baseball bat and etched with names, and then a black shrine, inlaid with shallow shelves crowded with flowers, glittery ornaments, jeweled boxes, and glass bottles.

They continued through an intersection between a pair of stone mausoleums with red-and-blue stained glass windows, past a bench covered with the faces of cherubic angels, until Angela finally slowed at a low, stone-brick wall overgrown with weedy bulbs and moss. Everything else here was carefully laid out and preserved in smooth stone lines. Not this, though—or the wooden building beyond. Past the moldering wall, a courtyard opened to a square structure, with a pointed, very Dutch-looking roof.

Angela and Grace stepped over the rocks toward the building, but Josie didn't move. This felt wrong, like discovering a rotten tooth in a mouth of polished ivory. *What is this?*

Tommy joined Angela at the building door, but Grace paused, noticed that Josie hadn't moved from the path.

"They really didn't tell you, did they?" Grace asked.

At the closed door, Angela chatted quietly with Tommy. Neither of them saw Grace slip back closer to Josie.

"This is Hell," Grace said. "The Devil's front door."

Angela waved at them. "We're ready. Come here. I'll go first, but we should talk through the logistics, before heading in ..."

Carefully, Josie climbed over the stone wall, and Grace caught her hand to help.

"... she's not expecting all of us, but that's okay," Angela said, and her voice was lost in a sudden whip of rain. Getting worse. Josie braced against the wind at the edge of the building. "... only need to make sure there's no confusion about the deal. That means," Angela said, "I talk. No one else." She looked pointedly at Grace. "Understand?"

"Of course," Grace said.

"She knows me," Angela said.

"Yeah, yeah," Grace said. "Let's get on with it, and out of this fucking weather."

Because it isn't a tomb—that's why it feels this way. It doesn't fit, because it doesn't look like a mausoleum or grave at all. Someone lives here.

Angela exchanged a quick look with Tommy and knocked three times.

No. It looks like a fucking trap.

The door opened.

THE EBUROS GROUP

WE ARE RECRUITING

GLOBAL INVESTMENT ADVISOR

JOB RESCRIPTION

Across the world, The Eburos Group empowers clients to achieve their financial goals. Our advisor-led investment management businesses shape strategic decision making in a variety of contexts. As client needs evolve, our close relationship allows our team to offer complimentary services and opportunities by leveraging the resources of Eburos and beyond.

HOW YOU WILL FULFILL YOUR POTENTIAL

- Serve as medium and long-term host for clients, including in your traditional lifespan and beyond.
- Partner with strategic groups to manage client needs, such as for caloric intake, karmic exchange, and appendages.
- Facilitate workflow among Eburos teams and third-party service providers to ensure timely deliverables.
- Define success criteria and core metrics, including leading indicators of bloodflow levels, soul degradation, maximal pain threshold (both physical and psychic), and real estate acquisitions.

www.eburosgroup.com

CHAPTER ELEVEN

As the door widened, electric blue light misted out. Josie heard the sound of a TV laugh track, followed by a muffled, sitcom-sounding voice, and then more canned applause. *What the hell?* She followed the others into a tight room, eyes watering at a shock of animal smells, like an unkept zoo habitat.

A wire pen ran the length of the left wall, a blue tarp on the floor in front. The tarp was cluttered with complicated machine parts, rusty gears, and old tools. Lines of electric lights ringed the ceiling, all different shapes—a translucent butterfly, lightbulb, skull—like mismatched sea debris, suspended between long rafters. On the right, a flat screen television perched on concrete cinderblocks shadowed by a network of carefully positioned umbrellas, all staked to the wooden ground with bungie cords. Looping trails of wire and duct tape bloomed behind the TV, like tails, slinking down a hole in the back-center of the room. A pair of empty folding chairs faced the screen. It played an old episode of *'Friends.'* Josie hadn't seen it.

"Sandra?" Angela called. "We're from The Eburos Group. About the flute for Mr. Dean."

"And Grace," Grace muttered.

A small, blonde-haired boy climbed out of the hole, holding a conch shell. Barefoot and dressed in a ragged *'I HEART NY'* t-shirt and cargo shorts. Another burst of audience laughter and applause from the TV.

"We'd like to see her," Angela said.

The boy's face went slack, as he focused on Angela, then the others, and brightened when he saw Grace. "Grace!"

"Hey you," Grace said and tousled the boy's hair. "It's good to see you Samuel."

Samuel? She said it almost like an old friend or little brother, even.

"Are you feeling better?" the boy, Samuel, asked her. "*Tip-top?* When I called you at the baseball place ..."

"Yes," Grace said quickly. Too quickly, maybe trying to quiet whatever this relationship meant to her in front of Angela. "Much better today, thanks, squirt."

Samuel grinned. "I'm not a squirt!"

Angela cleared her throat. "We're here to make a change, Samuel, as part of Mr. Dean's interest here."

Samuel sighed and came closer. As he moved further from the hole, Josie glimpsed a coiled flow of shadow, like inky cloud, attached to his back. He left wet foot streaks on the floor. Her eyes adjusting, Josie noticed darker scratches on the wall and ceiling beams. Tiny writing that looped and curled. Not a good sign. *We shouldn't be here.*

"Her?" Samuel nodded to Josie.

"Yes," Angela said.

"You could stay and watch with me after," Samuel said, his eyes widening again. "I have a new movie about giants that fight robots. I know what happens, but we could watch together."

"I'm sorry, we can't," Angela said. "Is she here?"

"Will he stay with me then?" Samuel pointed at Tommy. Tommy stiffened, a fist at his side. "We can watch whatever he wants."

"No," Angela said. "We have to go after."

"You can see her," Samuel said, and he plopped into a chair to face the TV. The bulbous black line of smoke quivered behind him, like a vapor hose. He motioned to Grace. "I'm glad you feel better. Want me to call your sister?" He held up the oversized conch shell. "So she'll know you're back?"

"My sister?" Grace looked confused. "I don't have a ..."

"Come on," Angela said.

"No," Samuel said. "I want him to stay." He aimed the conch at Tommy. "He has to watch with me, until you come back."

Angela turned to Tommy. "We won't be long ..."

"It's fine," he said.

Samuel didn't look up, as Tommy slowly circled to the second chair, said, "I think I've seen this one. This is the one with the blackout ..."

Grace smiled at Josie. "Having fun yet?"

"What is this place?"

"Keep moving," Angela said, headed for the hole. "Quickly."

"I told you," Grace said and stepped carefully around the flowing dark line behind Samuel. "Nothing good happens here."

Angela led Josie down steep stone steps into a low tunnel.

"No." Josie stopped at the bottom, pulled away. A line of cheap blue lights shimmered along the tunnel roof. Samuel's dark mist-flow shimmered in a rut at the edge of the floor. *This is too much.*

Angela frowned. "Josie ..."

"No." Josie planted back against the steps, ready to bolt back up, knock over Grace on the way if she had to. "I'm not doing this. That boy up there ... I don't need to know everything, but I'm not going in there."

The cavern tunnel was low enough that Angela had to duck as she came back. Grace watched, a step above Josie.

"It's perfectly safe," Angela said. "I know exactly where we're going."

"*I* don't." Josie's pulse droned in her ears, faster, and her left hand trembled against the wall. She couldn't hold still. "No. How do I know ..."

"Josie, listen to me," Angela said. "Mr. Dean chose you, because he believes in you. He wants to trust you. We think you can play a critical role at Eburos. That's not bullshit, it's true." Angela glanced past her at Grace. "Isn't it, Grace?"

"Yes," Grace said softly. "That's ... she's not lying about that."

"See? Even Grace agrees with me. You're in no danger here."

"Then why are we going into—whatever this is—under a cemetery in ..." Josie pressed a hand to shield her face, closed her eyes. *The boy has a Goddamn demon umbilical attached to his back.* Eyes closed, hand still up, Josie asked, "What's in here?"

"Sandra," Angela said. "This is where we find her and use the instrument."

"And why do I have to be here?"

"You're part of the team now, Josie."

Something off. The syllables in that sentence clumped together, like Angela had rehearsed the line.

Josie looked again. Angela smiled, a hand outstretched to help Josie forward. Josie turned to Grace behind her. Whoever Grace was, she didn't seem to believe or trust most of this and had bucked against Angela the whole way. Drugged on the flight, even.

"What do you think?" Josie asked her.

Backlit in blue light, Grace's face was impossible to read. "Angela is right," she said.

The TV laugh track erupted overhead. *Not helpful.*

"Okay?" Angela said, and she took Josie's hand.

Names, dates, and small, crooked words speckled the tunnel walls under bulging curls of rigged electric lights. Hunched in the low passage, Josie tried to focus on Angela and the curve of the rock, but graffiti etchings flashed across her line of sight.

'Christiaan van der Berg, 1868'
'Michael + Sara 54'
'Klaas Jansen – From Barrow to the Edge.'

"How old is this?" Josie asked.

Angela pulled her on, Grace close behind. "Old," Angela said. "There used to be a hot springs on the island. People thought they were healthy—to treat respiratory diseases, that kind of thing."

The tunnel pitched lower. Josie's gut clenched, and she tasted coppery adrenaline, already sweating in her armpits, along her brow.

Angela's shadow pivoted, and she glanced back, probably felt Josie's palm clamming up. "We're nearly there." Ahead, the passage opened into a blue chamber with stalagmites fixed to the floor, reaching up. Strange. Natural or not, this place looked well-worn, with natural formations shaped into a walkable path.

"This next bit," Angela said, "it's nothing to be afraid of, but there are others here."

"Others?"

Grace sighed. "She means other people. Sandra's people." She gestured in. "Can we go already?"

Angela ignored that, studying Josie. "You'll be calm, and the whole process will be over in fifteen minutes, maybe less."

Process? The word sent a cold thrill down Josie's arms, and she rubbed goosebumps away, but Angela didn't let go. *Fucking keep it together. She's right. Fifteen minutes is nothing.*

"The flute," Josie said. "You mean—"

"It's *right there*," Grace said. "After all this time ..."

Angela nodded. "Whatever you see, Josie, remember that we have done this before. You are fully integrated into our strategy now. Nothing bad is going to happen to you."

Josie was breathing too fast. "Okay."

Fifteen minutes.

The tunnel opened into a stone room, with a smooth, blue-block floor, topped by inky glass. Glacier hued, the high ceiling was covered in complex rings of foreign letters that looped down to connect with an impressionistic wall profile of a hunched cat, with two enormous fangs. The taste of ocean salt mixed with other earth smells, chalk and lime, all suddenly cooler. Deeper into the room, people sat in irregular spots on the cavern floor, all facing away. Soupy black tendrils flowed out of them into the shadowy far wall, just like the boy upstairs. No more lights here, the electric glow was gone, and Josie heard murmuring. *The people* ... She stopped.

Grace knocked into Josie, and Angela said, "Shh—quiet."

Around them, the seated people whispered in an echoey, overlapping ripple. Josie couldn't see their faces without ducking closer, only their straight-back outlines and the shimmer-movement of their jaws.

"This way," Angela said. She tugged Josie toward the black outline of a woman painted on the back wall. It bulged free. The woman staggered out on black stalks. Below her knees, the flesh had been shaved down to flayed leg bones that ended in skeletal feet. She wore a frayed sweatshirt, etched with the words, *'Bob Dylan – Rolling Thunder Revue.'* The sleeves were rolled up to expose dark forearms.

She didn't have a face. The woman's head was a jagged hole, as if it had been scooped out, leaving burnt edges. Images of desperate faces swam in the curved opening. The blobby shapes of dozens of peoples' eyes, noses, and shouting lips swirled and faded, as if a film projector were running from inside her skull.

They stopped.

Angela said, "Hello, Sandra."

"Yes, we can use that name." A hoarse woman's voice rose around them, as if the other seated people were all speaking at once in the same tone.

Of course, they can't be. None of this is really happening. The thought helped to loosen Josie's shoulders, steady her.

Sandra stopped just out of reach, fingers flexing at either side, as if she wanted something to grip. Her hands were dark claws.

"Do you know why they brought you here?" Sandra—the murmur voices—asked Josie.

"Yes," Angela said. "The instrument ..."

"Not just that. This girl smells like fire." Sandra leaned toward Josie. "Dangerous."

Angela shifted, as if she needed to find her footing on a suddenly wobbly floor. "She isn't. She's here to trade that name for another."

What? No I'm not. What did Maureen say? 'Josie' is my name right now?

Still focused on Josie, faces surfacing and melting in the ruined husk of her head, Sandra said, "To trade?"

"Me," Grace said, voice shaky. "I'm not going back to him. You told me I could be me again. You promised ..."

"I understand," Angela said. "Nothing is changed. We need to use the instrument. Sandra, it's time. We have a schedule to keep, and a flight back ..."

"This?" Sandra held a white flute. A short, slender pole, lined with perfect grooves and holes. "What's your name?" Sandra asked Josie. "Tell me."

"Josie." Josie cleared her throat, and the sounded echoed. "Josephina, really."

"And what do you want, Josie-Josephina? Do you want me to give you a diamond that will make you the Queen of America? Do you want a ball of never-melting ice that will let you live long enough to watch New York City wash away? Tell him to give us back what he took. He made the world this way for you ..."

"Stop it. That's not why we're here," Angela said. "You know that."

"Yes." Grace stepped up, closer to Sandra. "We're here for me. Hurry up and do it. I'm ready. Put me back."

Run. Josie's legs tensed, and without thinking, she glanced back past Angela to the exit. *Beyond the seated, murmuring people, the tunnel is right there, maybe ten meters away.* It still glimmered faint blue. *I can make it, before they grab me.*

"What do you want, Josie-Josephina?" Sandra asked again.

When Josie looked back, screaming faces bubbled and dissipated in Sandra's head, swallowed by others.

I just want to make my family okay.

Angela gestured to the flute. "Please?"

Sandra raised it. "I can't restore the ashes behind you, Josie-Josephina, the heat you don't even remember, but I can give you a box of fire-wasps to show you which doors to open. Would you like that?"

Angela snatched the flute. Sandra didn't flinch or even seem to notice.

"Good," Grace said. "Thank you. Let's do this. Angela, where should I stand?"

"Stay there," Angela said and steadied the flute at her lips, closed her eyes.

"What's happening?" Josie asked.

"I'll finally be me again," Grace said, grinning. "You'll see. Well ..." Her smile wavered. "You will."

Will what?

Angela blew, and a trilling high note rose. She adjusted her fingers, until the sound quivered into a lower pulse that topped up again, then down to repeat.

"Pain," Sandra said.

Grace doubled over, screaming. Josie reached for her, then stopped: a wet, bloody mass pushed against the inside of Grace's shirt, out of her chest. It slipped up into the air, and Grace slumped to her knees, gasping. A heart. A beating heart, suspended in mid-air, the organ floated down toward Josie, and she stumbled back. "No ... wait ..." The flute music lilted up and tapered back down, and as Josie began to turn, the heart dove into her collar like a rabid animal, wet against her neck and slid down until pain lanced through her chest. So sudden and intense, she grabbed her shirt and collapsed. Eyes watering, Josie screamed, tearing to reach her skin—and felt the warm, wet mass pushing into her chest. Blinking through knife-point pressure, Josie watched the heart jam deeper, until it disappeared under her skin. *Grace's heart. Not mine.*

The knives were gone. No more pain.

Shaking, Josie couldn't breathe. The song stopped. Angela lowered the flute. Sandra hadn't moved, but Grace—no, a pigtailed Hispanic girl had fallen to her knees, clutching her chest. She wore Grace's clothes.

What the fuck is ...

When Josie tried to speak, she coughed, swallowed salty tears. Angela touched her arm, and Josie jerked away.

"You're okay," Angela said.

No.

The Hispanic girl in Grace's clothing smiled at Angela. "Thank you! Let's go, thank God! I am ready ..." Her face distorted, and she wheezed, shaking her head, as if the air had sucked away. Her lips gaped, like a fish, and she winced, still squeezing her chest hard. No blood, though. Josie checked herself, too. Nothing. Even in the dim, bluish shadows, she could tell that where there should have been a wet smear, her skin looked untouched.

"No. I didn't ..." The Hispanic girl turned in a panic, looking from Josie to Angela. "You fucking liar!"

Sandra opened a hand toward Angela, who set the flute back in her palm. Then Sandra pinched the air over the Hispanic girl.

"Stay away from me!" The Hispanic girl looked at Josie. "Don't listen to them!"

A swirl of black smoke grew over the Hispanic girl, as if it had been hiding in the empty space. Sandra tugged to stretch it.

"This is what *they* want!" The Hispanic girl shouted at Josie. The blurry line swam down toward the Hispanic girl's back. "Stop! Don't touch me with that ..."

The line sank into her back. She shivered and went slack.

"Are we done?" Angela asked.

Sandra's hands were empty again. The Hispanic girl silently crossed the room to sit with the others.

"Who is she? What just happened?" Josie asked. Her voice sounded gravely, strange.

Angela nodded back to the tunnel. "I'll explain. You trusted all this so far." Angela's voice was calm. "I'm impressed. Just give me five more minutes, until we're outside."

Sandra went back to the blank rear wall and sank into the stone, as if it were soft putty that folded around her outline, swelling to envelope her. The Hispanic girl's face screamed silently in Sandra's open head cavity, gone again.

Sandra said something in another language, then a murmur of almost-German words—Dutch—and then in English, "I am patient, Josie-Josephina. Grace."

She became an outline in the wall again.

Did that happen? Was that real?

Legs shaky and arms still trembling, Josie followed Angela back to the tunnel, where she ducked to track her in silence all the way to the steps that fed up to the cluttered wooden room. Applause sounded on the TV, and the sitcom episode froze to display end credits.

"Perfect timing," Tommy said, already up.

"We were going to watch another one," Samuel said. Unchanged, the black mist still trailed out of his back and down the steps.

Just like the Hispanic girl down there.

"Time to go," Angela said.

At the door, Tommy asked, "The other one?"

"Yes."

Through the door, loud rain still rattled outside.

"Wait," Josie said.

Tommy shoved open the door and held it, squinting in the storm. Rain lashed the cemetery in thick sheets, trees shuddering and swaying in the wind. *No umbrellas, really?*

"We can't just leave her," Josie said and rolled her jaw. *What is wrong with my voice?* "Whatever happened down there—Grace was with us. We can't ..." They all stared, even the blonde-haired demon boy, Samuel.

"Grace?" Samuel said. He laughed and shook his head, watching the TV again. A new episode started. "Silly. You're Grace now."

The Eburos Group
CODE OF CONDUCT

At Eburos, our dress code is business casual. However, an employee's role may also inform their dress. If you meet frequently with anchor clients, you will be expected to conform to context-specific dress codes, including formal wear, inflammable materials, butcher shop workwear and plastic sheeting, or traditional golf clubhouse attire.

COMPANY HANDBOOK

Chapter Twelve

Angela started outside, Tommy at Josie's back, but she didn't move.

What does that mean?

She raised both hands, turning over her palms to inspect the tops of her wrists and forearms. Cool, white flesh, with tiny freckles. Too tiny. *Not my skin.*

"Grace disappeared inside," Josie said, her voice still wrong. *More wrong.*

Angela paused by the low stone wall that led back into the cemetery, one arm up against the rain. "I'll explain on the drive back."

"Explain now," Josie said. "What is going on? Down there, I imagined a heart ... I hallucinated a fucking ..."

Tommy nudged against Josie, and she stumbled outside. The rain hit her in a steady warm spray.

"Sorry," he said. "We have to go."

They weren't going to tell her. Josie waved back at the blonde demon kid, Samuel.

"Do you know what this is? Why did you call me Grace?"

Still sitting in a folding chair, Samuel squinted at the TV remote and conch shell on his lap, not her. "Do you like my shell?" He traced his fingers along the groove in the shell, frowning. "She gave me this, so I can call *anyone*," he said. "Living cities, dead cities, doesn't matter. Pretty cool, huh?" He blinked back at Josie, as if for reassurance. "That was a good reason for me to stay, right?"

I don't want to know what you're talking about.

"You called me Grace," Josie repeated. "Why?"

"Um, because you *are*," Samuel said. "We can still be friends, can't we? Even if you're a new Grace, I mean."

"You want to be my friend?" Josie asked. The word didn't make sense here. "I don't ... aren't you like nine years old?"

Samuel cocked his head, concentrating. "No. I think I might be very old. Before he got wrinkly and died, my dad had a horse named Arnold and a ship with a real sails, orange and white ..."

"Josie, I promise this will make sense," Angela said.

"No," Josie said. Tommy blocked the doorway, but she gestured over his shoulder for Samuel's attention. "Down there, my heart ..."

"The last Grace was scared, too, at first," Samuel said. "I talked to her in her secret place, when she needed to be alone with the others."

Tommy levelled his arm, like a bouncer ready to escort her out of a bar. And would he? If Josie refused to follow Angela back, what was his plan? Carry her, kicking and shrieking, through a cemetery in a thunderstorm?

This is happening. Somehow.

Josie sagged and stepped away, like he wanted.

"I know this is disorienting," Angela said. "But—"

"How do you know? Because you've done this before? Because you tricked that girl we left with 'Sandra'? Did you bring her here, like me, so that anchor client *thing* could give you a flute to literally tear her fucking heart ..."

"Josie, stop." Water dripped down Angela's nose and chin, her hair already damp and clinging over both ears and into her eyes. "You did well back there. Don't spoil it now. Give me a chance to explain."

"At the car?"

"Yes, back at the car." Angela climbed over the stone wall again. "Okay?"

And if I don't dig the explanation? Do I get drugged the way that other girl, 'Grace,' was? A version of the situation hardened in Josie's mind, like a clay figurine heating in the oven. Once, as a kid back in Kentucky, she'd baked blobby figures, then watched them dry into tiny brittle people on a metal pan. The molding clay had been a birthday present from Dad. Josie had been shocked at first when she picked up a crude, brownish man with both arms posed straight out, as if directing traffic. He felt solid and strangely fragile at the same time. An hour earlier, the clay had been putty between her thumbs, now locked into this shape she'd formed, almost on a whim. And setting the clay traffic guard down, his left arm snapped off. So fragile.

This situation-shape, now, fumbling after Angela in silence along the same low path between the monuments ... this felt weak, too. *Because I don't know. But that girl wasn't Grace, was she? She was a Hispanic girl transformed into the pale woman on the plane.* Somehow Angela—someone—used magic to change her into Grace, maybe by plugging a foreign heart into her. *The same heart I'm carrying now.* Maybe in a pact with Sandra, who kept the flute in an agreement that the girl would be hers when the deal ended. When Angela found a new Grace. Someone who could see the Friendly Man and Angela's over-eager shadow. *And here I am. So there she went. They levitated out her heart for me, and I became her.*

Logic-ing this didn't help. *It's fucking nuts. But it's happening.*

As they neared the exit gate, the shape of this situation stiffened in Josie's mind, still squishy at the edges. Pieces she didn't want to know. *Angela is a liar.* She brought Josie here in a practiced choreography of paperwork and promises. Everything vague. Everything about to be explained if only Josie would suspend disbelief a little longer, trust these people until the next checkpoint. Just a little longer.

Back at the car, Tommy opened the back door. The driver was still there, his hands on the wheel, exactly as they'd left him.

"Go ahead," Angela said, and Josie climbed in, slid all the way across this time. Roomier with only two. No fogged windows or heavy condensation, the car was still running. Wiping her wet face, Angela sat beside Josie, and Tommy took his place up front.

"Airfield," Angela told the driver and then smiled at Josie, already reaching to take her hand.

Josie shifted away. "Just—explain. Go ahead."

"The Friendly Man likes you," Angela said. The car eased away from the cemetery, swaying back onto a parallel road. "Like Mr. Dean said, you wouldn't have seen him otherwise."

"And the other girl?"

"Yes, she saw the Friendly Man, too. You are our intermediary now, Josie. Think about what that means."

"No. Why don't you tell me what it means."

Angela's calm eyes and easy smile flickered, her jaw hardening. She glanced past Josie, as if a splash of water on the sideview caught her attention. "Hm." Angela tapped Tommy's seat in front of her, and he craned back. Past him, shimmery lines of rain swiped back-and-forth with the front windshield wipers. No other cars out, and in the darkening gray, long floodwater currents flanked the street. "Did it say anything to you?" Angela asked Tommy. "While you were watching that TV show?"

"About?"

Josie followed Angela's stare back out the rear window. Through the rain, she spotted a small figure on the left sidewalk. Not running or chasing them, just standing, with his small arms rigid at both sides—and gone, as they turned a corner, closer to the coastal path back.

"Why would that boy follow us?" Josie asked.

Angela met her eyes briefly—a flash of uncertainty, gone again—then nodded, patted Tommy's headrest. "Right. No, of course not."

"If you saw the kid ..." Tommy said.

"*If,*" Angela said and shifted to face Josie, with that steady smile again. "Do you know much about oracles, Josie? You probably read about ancient myths in school or saw them in a movie, maybe?"

"Fortune tellers?" Josie asked. She knew a little about oracles and their dancing riddles, mostly from long hours spent watching her high school girlfriend, Clara, rehearse an adaptation of *Antigone* years ago. Long-winded translations of ancient Greek that somehow still resonated in an auditorium near Columbus Circle. '*The fates, oh the fates...*'

"Yes, but not just the future," Angela said. "A traditional oracle is a vessel, a kind of conduit, like a fiber optic cable."

"Also a person," Josie said.

"Well, yes."

They swerved to avoid a line of orange cones blocking roadwork along the ocean-front street of Dutch colonials. No one out now, and the rain wasn't stopping. The sky darkened, midday or not. They banked into the center of the empty street, both sides flooded, tracking it away from the waterfront town and up to a steep incline that circled a hill clustered with windmills, closer to the small airstrip, where they'd landed.

"Will the plane take off in this weather?" Josie asked.

Tommy shifted, looked at Angela in the rearview, but Angela just nodded, still focused on Josie. "Yes. I'm trying to explain. You asked."

"Oracles."

"We all grow into a version of whatever we're meant to be," Angela said. "A pure form that exists before we're even alive."

Is she cribbing Plato now? Josie had vague memories of the heavy, pale book she'd lugged to a Freshman humanities seminar almost four years ago. *Shadows and forms. Uh huh.*

"Just tell me what happened back there. I'm meant to be what—an oracle?"

"It sounds silly when you say it like that," Angela said, leaning closer, as if they were both in on the secret. "Think of it however you need to. You tap into something other people don't, see colors that no one else can. Like an animal that can detect ultraviolet light, deeper spectrums of color."

The fenced perimeter of the airfield appeared ahead. Almost there.

"What do I look like?" Josie asked, reaching for her phone in her pocket—Angela caught her wrist to stop her.

"You look like—you are—Grace," Angela said. "If I had told you beforehand, really told you, would you have believed me? Would you have agreed to come? No. Of course not. No one would. But you'll see, Grace ..."

"My name ..."

"Your name is Grace now," Angela said. "You'll see just how important this is, when you help him weave."

They stopped at the perimeter fence, and Tommy jumped out, hunched against the rain to swipe a keycard at a post too flooded for the car to approach. The gate opened. There was the plane, right where they left it, with the stairs already down and waiting.

I shouldn't be here. This shouldn't be happening. It is, maybe. But it shouldn't be.

Crossing the airfield, the car skidded and stopped. They were close, maybe eight meters from the airplane. The car engine revved in a stuttering mechanical whine, and they slowly hydroplaned back across the mud toward the open gate behind them.

"We'll get out here," Angela said.

Tommy climbed out, then Angela, who stumbled, grimacing at the muck. Outside, a shallow flow of brown water rose to her shins, and Tommy waved Josie on, splashing over to hold the backdoor. But the car still drifted, caught in the muddy current. As Josie started to get out, the car lurched, and she grabbed the open doorframe. Water dragged the wheels, turned the sedan into a raft. She could jump free, push off the seat.

"What about him?" Josie nodded to the driver and called to him, "Are you okay?"

"He's fine," Angela said. "I'll explain more on the flight. We have a schedule. The last thing you should be worried about ..."

The car spun backwards in the water, and Josie fell onto the seat. The door still open, Tommy lost his grip, yelling and dragging his legs in the current. Josie slid into the opposite window, the door slammed, and the car spun into a sideways freefall through the open perimeter gate toward the steeper adjoining road.

"Shit," the driver said. He jerked the wheel, stomping the gas, then the brake, back-and-forth. The engine growled and pinched again and again. Not just water, they were caught in a mudslide. When the wheels spun, the car shivered, but floated sideways, seven meters from the edge of the road incline. If they hit it, the car would fall fast, straight back past the farms and trees toward the waterfront town. "Get out," the driver said. "Go on. Hurry up."

"Get out?" *He's right.* Josie grabbed the door handle, stopped. "You too—what are you doing? Let go of the wheel ..."

"I can't."

"Of course you can, it's just a car—"

"I *really* can't," he said again.

Wait. When the driver turned the wheel, his grip didn't change. It hadn't shifted once, not even at the cemetery. *He can't let go.* Leaning closer, she saw a circular black lump in the back of each of his hands. Metal screws, with flat-head indentations. *Jesus, he is literally nailed to the wheel.* Three meters from the top of the hill, the engine rumbled, and the car stuttered back to face the airfield. At the open gate, Tommy waved both arms, shouting. No sign of Angela.

"Go," the driver said. "You can't stay."

"Neither can you," Josie said. "Seatbelts."

What am I doing?

Directly behind him, Josie dragged the seatbelt across her chest and lap, clicked it in.

"What are you doing?" he said. "I can't control anything!"

"What are *you* doing? Somebody has to get you out of ..."

The car slid off the edge.

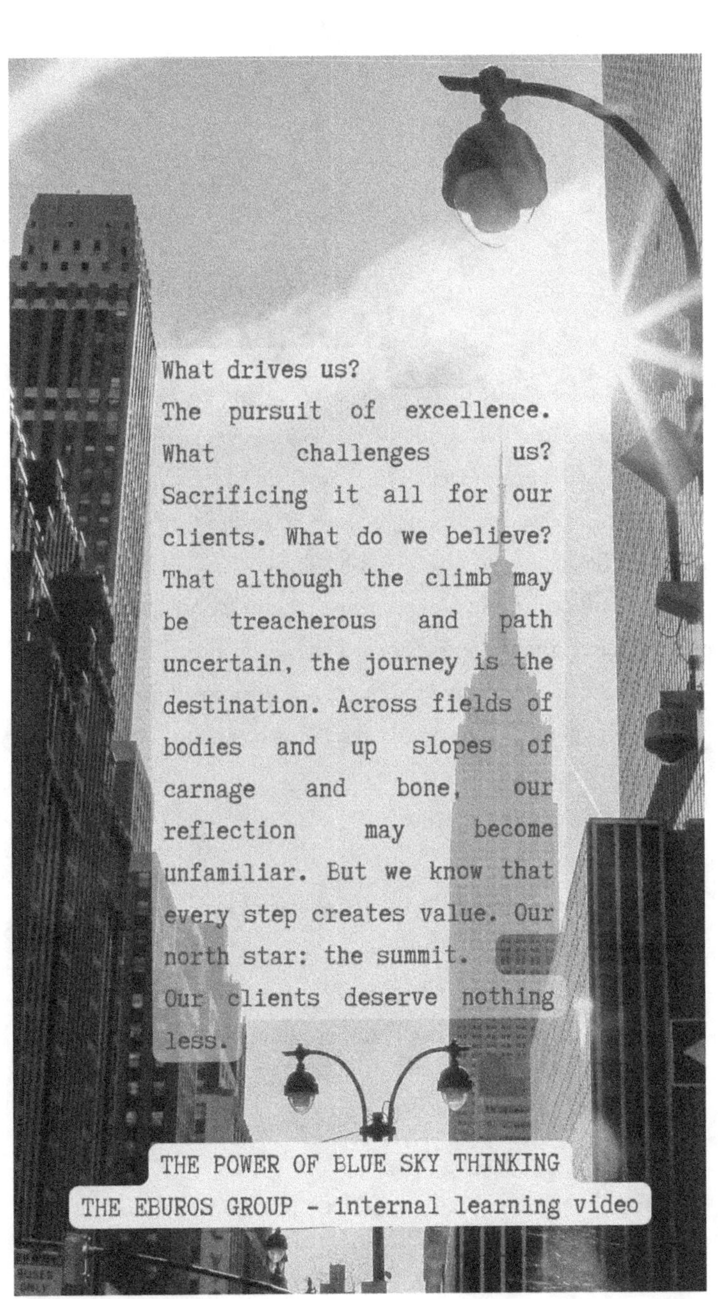

What drives us?
The pursuit of excellence.
What challenges us?
Sacrificing it all for our clients. What do we believe? That although the climb may be treacherous and path uncertain, the journey is the destination. Across fields of bodies and up slopes of carnage and bone, our reflection may become unfamiliar. But we know that every step creates value. Our north star: the summit. Our clients deserve nothing less.
THE POWER OF BLUE SKY THINKING
THE EBUROS GROUP - internal learning video

Chapter Thirteen

At the lip of the drop, the car jerked and roared, like a horse rearing up. Josie suddenly hung sideways against her seatbelt, a knot rising in her stomach. They spun into a freefall. Out the front windshield, the watery edge of the road rushed toward them. *Falling too fast.* The driver yelled back over his shoulder, eyes wide.

The roadside hit, and the car rocked back and forth against a deeper wall of water, then dipped forward to smash into a flooded pond. Warm water hit Josie's shoes. The back seat jumped up, the seatbelt still holding her in, as the hood tipped down, sinking. Water foamed into the front floor.

"Hurry!" the driver shouted.

Act. Move.

"Where's the—something for your hands?" Josie said.

"Get out of the fucking car!"

Josie grabbed the back of his seat. *He's right. We're sinking. Get out.* Water rose halfway up the hood, the car sliding in deeper, nose-first.

"No," she said. "Tell me how to help you."

"You can't ..."

Fuck it.

Josie unbuckled her seatbelt and scrambled into the flooding front seat. Water touched the seat cushions, above the driver's knees. She opened the glove compartment: a car manual, flashlight, tissues, *Altoids* mints, and there—a red Swiss army knife. The back of the car still rising, the water on the windshield and splashing warm around their waists, Josie fumbled with the knife extensions. A knife, can opener, scissors ... She lowered the knife to the top of the screw in his right hand, leveraging it into the groove and turning.

"Other way," he said. "Lefty loosey."

"What?" Josie pressed hard and switched directions, twisting counter-clockwise. It turned.

"Righty tighty, lefty loosey," he murmured, breathing fast. He smelled like mints and terror sweat. Water made Josie's shirt cling to her stomach. The waterline slid up the front glass, past the wipers.

"You never heard that?" he asked.

Focus on the water in front of you.

"No." Josie turned the bolt faster. "Clever."

"As a kid ..." The screw came out, and he yanked his hand off, shaking his wrist, then grabbing the knife. "Get out," he said, then smiled, eyes crinkling. "Please."

"You've got it?"

He did, was already twisting the left-hand screw up in fast half-twists. Josie climbed into the backseat, and the car lurched deeper, as if the weight of her movement had jammed it under. She grabbed the backdoor and shoved. It clicked and pushed, didn't open. The car was nearly vertical, water filling the front seat, over the driver's hands. He splashed and worked the knife, spitting at the surface.

"Don't wait," he said.

"The door's stuck—there's water on the other side!" *Not going to die here. Not drown like this.*

The driver's left hand came free, and he pulled himself back alongside Josie, both legs up. She did the same, bracing her shoes against the door, just like the exaggerated rowing form she used the first time on that Concept 2 at the gym, with her knees almost at her chest. Alice hadn't liked that. 'Rowing is a marathon, not a race. Steady and ...'

"... two, three," the driver said.

They pushed. The door bucked, and in a sudden gap of flooding water, it gave. Josie felt him catch her lower back to hold her against the flow. The car sank, and he held her wrist, as they swam out, surfacing on a muddy embankment.

Past the pond, the flooded street was empty, deep water still sluicing down from the empty fence-line of the airfield at the summit.

They left me.

"Should get back to the plane," Josie said, her voice too quiet in the rain. Unconvincing anyway. No way to storm that hill of water rushing down to this pond. She found her phone: dead and dripping beads of grimy water. *Maybe when it dries, if I can get some rice, try that social media life hack, or ...* "Do you have a phone?"

"They nailed my hands to the steering wheel," he said. "You really think they'd buy me an iPhone?"

Fair.

The car was a dark, rectangular shadow under the rippling surface. Wind knocked Josie back, almost flattened her. The driver took her hand, climbed up.

"But we should get inside," he said.

Josie let him help her up into an unsteady slog toward the trees. Drenched, she spat rainwater and snorted, squeezing both nostrils, as if she'd just been swimming. *I was.*

"I'm Josie." *Not Grace. Still Josie.* "What's your name?" she asked.

The trees muffled the beating rain, but wind still whipped them forward and back, as if testing their balance.

"You won't believe me," he said.

Josie steadied herself on a bare, rough tree trunk. Past this stand of evergreens, the road continued to the hazy outline of the town below.

"What?" She braced a hand against the rain. "Why wouldn't I believe you?"

"Noah." He grinned crooked, white teeth. "I never meant to drown a second time. You're the other one, aren't you? I don't think the last Grace would have done that for me."

Drown a second time?

"No," Josie said. "I told you, my name is Josie."

He looked away at the road. "Okay. Ready to walk?"

Josie fell into step beside him, following the curve of the rushing, shallow water on the pavement.

"You know about this?" she asked. "About me, I mean—what they did to me?"

He watched the road, not her. "A little, yes. You're not the first."

"Clearly."

"The other girl, she started with Angela, working for Mr. Dean in the city."

Just like me.

"And?" Josie asked.

"And I don't know. They took her down there, the same way they took you. She came back as someone else—Grace. The way you are now."

"And before her?"

"Yes, there was another one. I've only been here, with the company, for five years, since I ..." He hugged his arms tight, leaning into the rain.

The wet wind beat like static in Josie's mind. Fuzzy streaks loud in the background she tried to tune out. *Make sense of this. What is he saying? A long line of girls like me, transformed into Grace, so they could*

talk to the Friendly Man, that chalk figure in the walls of the Eburos
headquarters?

"Go on," Josie said. "You've been involved for five years ..?"

"Since I died," he said softly.

Josie shivered, felt a chill in her soaking shirt that tingled down her shoulders and arms. "What do you mean you died?"

"I was ..." His voice caught again. "Yes. My mother got sick, and my dad couldn't afford the hospital bills. We lost our house and moved into an apartment on the north side of the island, then into our car." He gestured at the colonial buildings ahead, still a few hundred meters away. "You'll never see it here, but Dutch Island isn't *just* for tourists. It's small, but we have struggles, too."

"I believe you."

"My mother never left the island. Can you believe that? Not once. But New Leiden Clinic couldn't help her."

"What happened?"

"She's gone." He leaned against the rain, strained to smile, as if to prove he could cope. "I only found out after."

"I'm sorry, I don't understand."

"Don't say that," he said, wagging a finger. "Didn't they tell you? Never admit you don't know something. But you haven't been with them long at all, have you?"

"This is basically my second day," Josie said. "Sort of."

Noah laughed, shaking his head. "You're joking. What a way to start!"

They reached the town, stepping up onto a narrow sidewalk to pass along a cobbled side street of shuttered art galleries, coffee and donut shops. All dark.

"I don't really remember what happened," he said. But the turn in his voice meant he was lying. *He does remember, can probably picture it—whatever it was—right now.* But Josie didn't interrupt. "I think it was a storm surge," he said, "kind of like today. Except then Angela happened. And Mr. Dean, I guess, although I've never met him. They bought me." He yawned to loosen his jaw and pointed to a narrow alley. "This way. We'll ask Aunt Evelyn for help."

Josie followed him into a tight, single-file passage between colonials. At the far end, Noah stopped at an unmarked white door, jiggled the handle, and it clicked open. Josie stepped after him into a long lobby hall, where a thin, big-eyed kid in a soccer jersey sat on a faded couch, playing a handheld video game.

"No school today?" Noah called, as he led Josie in.

"Teacher was sick," the boy said automatically, then looked up, blinking. "Noah? The police told us something happened to you ..." He shook his head. "Who is she?"

"I'm fine. She's a friend. Her name is Josie."

The kid scrambled up. A line of locked bicycles and top-heavy tropical plants lined the opposite wall all the way to a stairwell.

"You asshole," the boy said. "I can't believe you did that."

Noah paused, and Josie realized the boy was crying, the video game shaking in one hand, as if he wanted to throw it at them.

"It wasn't my fault," Noah said quietly and glanced at Josie. "This girl saved me."

"So what? I don't even like you," the boy said, swatting tears from his cheeks. "I don't care. But that wasn't right, to make her worry about you like that." When Noah reached for his shoulder, the boy jerked away. "Don't touch me."

The boy brushed past to the outer door.

"It's storming out there," Noah said. "Hey ..." The boy banged out, and before Josie could ask, Noah said, "Don't. Okay?"

She nodded, followed him to the stairwell and up, past a landing that swam with the smell of cooking chicken, and higher, to an apartment door in the third-floor hall. Noah knocked.

Inside, a woman said, "Coming, coming ..."

"I'm glad she's here," Noah said. "I don't have a key and was afraid ..."

The door opened to reveal a white-haired woman in a bulky gray robe. Her left eye was covered by an orange eyepatch, her jaw grizzled with stubble. She propped in the doorway, blocking a carpeted living room of cinderblock bookshelves and plastic-covered furniture.

"Well?" the woman said. "What do you want?"

"Aunt Evelyn, this is a friend," Noah said. "She's visiting from the city."

"Whose friend? I don't have any friends in New York."

"She needs your help," Noah said. "Mr. Dean ..."

"He sent her here? To my doorstep?"

"No," Noah said. "He doesn't know ..."

"Let her speak," Aunt Evelyn said, and more quietly to Josie, "Men are always doing that, aren't they? Narrating our lives for us. You look familiar. Have we met?"

Josie's pulse quickened. "No."

"Do you have a boyfriend?"

"Girlfriend, yes," Josie said. The words slipped out automatically, as if this were another interview. "I don't want to talk about that."

"No?" Aunt Evelyn said. "Well what then? Why do you need my help?"

"She met with Sandra today," Noah said. "I have to help get her off the island."

"Now?" Aunt Evelyn clucked her tongue and grinned yellowish teeth. "It's raining outside, boy. And why do you *have* to help her?" And to Josie, "Men are *so* observant, aren't they?"

"I'm serious," Noah said. "Please, Aunt Evelyn, can we come in? I'm here, standing here, because of her."

"Suit yourself." She stepped in, leaving the door open so they could follow. "Don't touch anything. We'll have coffee. Come on."

Aunt Evelyn walked them past a couch and side tables crowded away from the walls by heavy piles of E-Z Grow fertilizer bags. The bags were piled eight deep, rising like shitty insulation, so that the room stank of an animal, earthy smell. Like a primeval garden.

"What is all this?" Josie asked.

"Just full of questions," Aunt Evelyn said and glanced at Noah. "I don't know what Noah told you, but I work for the company, the same as everyone else."

They turned right, and in the kitchen doorway, Josie froze. Corpses crowded the room, watching her with black eye sockets. Their yellowed bones and pocked flesh was shrunken and spiraling with webs of mold. The dead people blocked the counters and refrigerator, some even sitting at a small wooden table, as if waiting for her to join. Their mouths moved, jaw bones rocking up and down in silence. Shouting on mute. Past them, a sliding door opened to a small balcony overlooking the narrow, rainy road of colonial buildings.

Aunt Evelyn went through the network of corpses without touching them to adjust a tin coffee pot on the stove and started the gas burner.

"Have a seat, while we talk," she said.

Josie didn't move. "I'm okay here."

Aunt Evelyn frowned, and Josie tried to focus only on her, not the dead people, whatever they were. *Getting out of hand.*

Behind her, Noah asked, "Wait. What is it, Josie? You see something?"

Yeah.

"Dead people," she said. The word 'ghosts' felt wrong. These were lingering corpses.

"Well?" Aunt Evelyn said. "What do they want?"

"*Want?*" Josie said. "How am I supposed to know? Looks like they're trying to talk, but I can't hear."

A low, overlapping murmur bubbled up around her. Not words, more like tree branches scratching in the wind or water siphoning down a sink, but louder now, it pitched higher, more frantic. Josie closed her eyes. *Like the people in Sandra's cave.* Her body wanted to go. *Turn and run.* She felt an animal tug in her legs. If she stopped thinking, her feet would move automatically. *Get out.*

"Do you hear them?" Josie asked. "Either of you?"

"This is bad luck," Aunt Evelyn said. "Tell your ghost friends that I want them out, unless they've got a good reason to be here. They'll draw attention."

The sound strained and click-popped, a weather scream trying to contort into the shapes of words. And there were syllables, actual language noises buried in it. Dutch and French and snatches of English and other languages, too, cadences Josie didn't recognize. The rush of sounds spilled together, making it impossible to sort one from another. Fifteen people shouting at once.

Steam began to rise from the stovetop coffee spout, and Aunt Evelyn asked, "Do you work for Mr. Dean? Did he give you something?"

"He gave me a job."

Aunt Evelyn rolled her eyes. "No, girl. An object. A *thing*. Did he give you anything, when you met him?"

The ball.

"Yes. A small toy, a rubber ball," Josie said. *A ball that Dani can't stop throwing, hitting off the walls and ceiling.* The memory brought a sudden sweat in her lower back. *Don't stress that now. Except she must be awake now, probably worried about me. Or not worried. Maybe she doesn't care at all.*

"Did you bring it?" Aunt Evelyn asked.

"No," Josie said. "My girlfriend ... it's not here."

"It sounds like a widow's eye. You know the story of how a trickster god gave a mortal man everything he ever wished for, because the god knew it would destroy him?"

"The ball grants wishes?"

"It's not a *ball.*" Aunt Evelyn shifted impatiently, watching the stove, not Josie or the corpses. "You smell like the cemetery, it's probably why all these dead folk are attracted to you. Which also means you met our local god already, right? A widow's eye is a rubber sphere around a piece of bone. *His* bone."

"Who?" Josie asked.

"This is all new to her," Noah said quietly.

"Doesn't matter," Aunt Evelyn said and glared back at Josie, half-smiling. "She needs to catch up. How did our little Dutch Island god seem to you? Did she seem happy and satisfied?"

Dark rain shook the glass of the balcony window.

"No," Josie said.

"If you gave your widow's eye to someone," Aunt Evelyn said, "it's probably already too late."

The corpse murmurs rolled around Josie in waves, dipping and ratcheting loud enough that she felt her gut tighten against the sudden spike of a sharp, high yell. Nonsense sounds, too low to understand.

"You said there's a bone inside it," Josie said. "Why would Mr. Dean ..."

Movement on the street below caught Josie's eye: the blonde boy, Samuel, approached from the opposite side of the street, and even in the blurry rain, she could still see the black shadow extending from his back.

"That kid is here," Josie said.

Noah stepped closer beside her, squinting. "Who?"

"See him?" Josie pointed. "From the graveyard—you weren't there, but he was. Samuel ..."

"Shit." Noah took her arm, easing them both back into the living room. "Aunt Evelyn, I'm sorry—we need your car. Is it on the street?"

"Absolutely not," Aunt Evelyn said. "I don't see you for months, and then you barge in with a mainlander asking to steal my car? You haven't even tried my coffee."

"One of Sandra's boys is coming—he probably wants to keep her with him ..." He waved at the limp corpses but missed half. *He really can't see. Neither of them can.* "The car, please Aunt Evelyn."

"There's a storm, you know," she said.

Out the balcony, Josie lost sight of Samuel, as he neared this side of the street.

Coming straight at me.

"He's close," Josie said.

"She has to get off the island," Noah said. "Please ..."

"Key is in the closet. No dings or scratches, or you're paying for the repairs, and the premium adjustment. My insurance ..."

"Thank you!" Noah said.

Josie squeezed her hand in quick thanks.

"You be careful," Aunt Evelyn said. "Don't let them plant you." And as Josie followed Noah out, Aunt Evelyn called, "That car is my baby, Noah! Four-hundred dollars a month for liability! The company deducts rent and fees direct deposit ..."

Noah grabbed a plastic key stub from a coat closet by the door, and then Josie went with him out into the hall, back to the stairs.

"Those bodies," Josie said. "I really saw dead people in her kitchen. Like a horror movie, but worse." *A lot fucking worse.*

"I believe you."

They hit the lobby, hurrying across, so he could check the narrow alley and then lead her in a dash through the rain to the closest main street. No sign of Samuel. But he couldn't be far. Noah pointed to a silver hatchback further up, and they got in.

"They probably followed you from the cemetery," he said, panting and dripping rainwater onto the steering wheel. "Other people she took."

"People who took?"

He gave her a 'don't bullshit me' look. "Who do you think?"

"The anchor client thing—Sandra?"

"All of the company's clients use people. Some of them infect a single person, others take busloads. Sandra is unique, because once upon a time she was human. That's why everybody can see her. Now, she has a whole colony of corpses here." He turned on the windshield wipers and adjusted the mirrors.

"A whole colony," Josie said, "all dead."

"Of course." He revved the engine, switched gears, and pulled out of the parking spot. "How else would it work? Why do you think I'm here?"

It should have been easy to shrug these stories away. Widow's eye. A demon god under a cemetery on a tourist island. A Children of the Corn kid stalking them in the rain. Folk nightmares. *Except the bodies I saw in Aunt Evelyn's kitchen were really there. And my skin still doesn't look right. My voice isn't my voice. I'm too tired to fight it now. I just want to go home.*

"What do you mean?" Josie asked.

Rain battered the car, as they rolled into the middle of the road.

"I told you," he said. "I died in a storm surge five years ago."

"You're not dead," Josie said, trying to smile. *No good.* "You're right here talking to me. Stop trying to scare me, this is fucked up enough ..."

"We've all got to serve somebody, right? Like the song." He checked to see if she got it. The lyrics were familiar, but she couldn't place them. *Fuck your lyrics, stop it, Noah. Stop saying you're dead.* "Currency flows up, not down," he said. "I signed a contract, that's why I'm here."

"No," she said. "I am not in the mood for—you are sitting right here," She wanted to slap him, knock him out the door and take the wheel herself. *Enough. No more bullshit, get me off this island.*

He leaned in, glaring at the street past the slash-slash of the wipers. "I know where we can find a boat."

To sail across the harbor in a thunderstorm? Is he insane? But she didn't answer back, just let him slow at a stop sign. And she noticed his hands. Where the screws had been removed, he should have ragged, bloody holes in his hands. In the frantic race from the drowned car, she'd missed it. Where there should have been blood, ooze glistened and congealed instead. Like sap. *Just like fucking tree sap.*

'Don't let them plant you.'

The Eburos Group
COMMUNICATIONS POLICY

Communication is essential to our work. You should use your firm email, phone number, social media, and skin primarily for work. When representing Eburos, we expect you to protect our firm's image and reputation. Specifically, you should be respectful, polite, and patient, wherever possible. When confronted with any misleading or negative content about Eburos, we ask that you follow a three step process: first, assess and 'stalk' the source; second, locate vulnerabilities or 'pain points'; and third, refer the source to your manager, who will coordinate with Brand Management. Typically, a resolution specialist can correct the situation so quickly that it will be as if it never happened.

COMPANY HANDBOOK

Chapter Fourteen

They drove away from the ocean, into a dense neighborhood of villas and overgrown sidewalks. Set back from the curb, columned mansions appeared in snatches through gaps in stone walls and evergreen hedges, Great Gatsby-style. Josie tried not to stare at Noah's hands on the wheel. *Just watch the houses.* The empty roads here became more and more muzzled with overhanging trees, as they rode further from the coast.

"Where are we going?" Josie asked.

"An Eburos property. They call it a satellite office, but it's more like a ..." He slowed at the corner, where a gate on the right opened to the front drive of a three-story, white-stone mansion. The entrance was blocked by a black bus, with tinted windows. Like something a band might tour in. Past the van, drooping trees glowed with soft white lights on the mansion lawn. Through the rain, something moved in the closest tree.

"What's wrong?" Josie asked. "Is that it?"

Noah stopped the car but didn't move. "Yes, that's it."

The faint shapes of people gathered on the long front porch of the mansion, lit in orange lamplight.

Noah hunched forward, hands tightening again. The sap splotch on his right hand smeared down toward his wrist. Josie forced herself to look away. "This was a mistake," he said. "I'm sorry. I thought the office would be empty. There's no way we'll be able to get the boat out, with everyone ..."

"We're here now," Josie said. "If it's owned by Eburos, let's go in."

"You don't understand."

"Then tell me." When he hesitated, she asked, "What happens if the kid from the cemetery finds me?"

Watching the windshield, not her, Noah said, "As long as you're on this island, she'll try to take you."

"Sandra?" He nodded. "Why?" Josie asked.

"It's what she does," Noah said.

"If you're alive, because you signed a contract ..."

"I'm alive, because a web of teeth in my brain keeps me alive."

What the fuck?

Josie opened the door. Rainy wind shook it almost out of her grip. "I don't want to ask ..."

"I'm me," he said. "And also not me. I am a host, Josie."

"Fine," Josie said. "Let's go, host. Bring your brain-teeth, leave the cannoli." She stepped out into the downpour, before he could react to her shit joke. *Not even a joke, what was that? I'm fucking losing it. Should have listened to Grace, before she stopped being Grace.* "Come on, Noah. You brought us here. Don't make me do this myself."

Faces in the trees.

When the rain stilled for a moment, Josie saw the shapes of people quivering in the nearest tree trunk, all the way up to the overhead branches. Lips moved below bulging noses and foreheads, all made of hard bark and wood. *People.*

"What the fuck is this?" Josie murmured.

Noah got out, circling the car to her. "I told you. We don't want to be here ..."

"After you brought us here." She approached, past the tinted van, for a better look. Not just the closest tree. Even as the storm pitched up again, she saw more faces in the trees further across the lawn, closer to the porch and along the side of the house: wooden people trapped inside the trees, struggling to get out. *Or carvings. That's all, just perverse, hyper-realistic art.*

A man dressed in black waved from the front porch, then ducked down into the rain and hustled toward them. Shit, Josie recognized that loping, professional run. Like a horse.

Tommy.

"Grace?" Tommy called. He shielded his face from the rain and gestured them closer. "I don't believe it. Noah, is that you? Well done!"

They met Tommy alongside the nearest tree. At the edge of her vision, Josie saw the desperate, rhythmic movement of jaws opening, tongues lapping, and eyes widening in the tree bark. *That's not real.*

"This is a surprise," Tommy said and shook Noah's hand, smiled at Josie. His cheeks were flushed, eyes a little misted. *He's been drinking.* "Come on in. Angela will be so relieved to know you're here. You did the right thing, Noah." Leading them up the soggy lawn, he said, "When I saw the car, I wasn't optimistic. Angela had to get back, but I stayed, just in case. And here you are."

"Here we are," Noah said, exchanging a quick 'bad idea' look with Josie.

Tommy walked them up to the wide front porch, where a crowd of around thirty people in damp suits and dresses watched the rain, all holding drinks. The porch went silent as Tommy approached.

"New arrivals," Tommy said. "Does everyone here remember Noah?" His voice slurred. "And this is our new Grace. Miss America."

A few glasses raised, murmurs, and Tommy pressed open the double door entrance. Inside, the space looked like a converted art gallery.

What had once been a formal entry hall and parlor leading to a broad wooden staircase, had been transformed into an open expanse of dangling glass constellations, like frozen, multicolored explosions. Half of an antique red convertible jutted out of the wooden floor in a blob of solid black, as if the car were sinking in oil. *Like us at the pond. Did they know about that, what the fuck is this?* Abstract, vaguely portrait-looking paintings decorated the walls, and low, electronic music pulsed from speakers, interspersed with bursts of saxophone and piano. The room smelled of citrus and tarry cigarette smoke. The entire place gave off art installation, demon sex-party vibes. And not in a good way.

"This is an office?" Josie asked.

Tommy led them to a bar stacked with open Havana Club rum bottles at the base of the staircase. "Eburos satellite office," Tommy said. "Between us, though, I don't see the ROI." He found three glasses and started working with an ice container, a jar of fresh mint, and limes.

"We're fine," Noah said. "We don't need drinks ..."

"Hurricanes? No?" Tommy said, still prepping the glasses. "It's a little *dark and stormy* outside, but I never learned to make those in the service either." He grinned back at Josie. "I wasn't a bartender. The navy taught me to drink, not blend. So mojitos, instead?"

"I need to talk to you," Noah said. "Outside, Josie saw ..."

The front door banged open, and Tommy jerked taller, his body tense. He glared at a pair of guys who had stepped in. "Business stays out there!" To Josie, "Give me one minute ..." And stomped off to intercept the front door guys.

"New plan," Noah said quietly. "I'll pull him away. You go upstairs. There are keys hanging on a hook in the top hallway, third floor. On a hook, shaped like a hand."

"Are you joking?" Josie watched Tommy meet the two guys at the door, ushering them back out to the front porch. *'Business stays out there?' Away from me?* Raining outside, and an empty party setup in here. "If you know where to find the keys," Josie asked, "why don't you go upstairs?"

"He doesn't trust me," Noah murmured. Across the room, Tommy shut the door behind the other two and turned back to them. Noah said, "It's got to be you, Josie."

"Sorry," Tommy said, returning to the bar. "You know how it is. When the cat's away …"

"We have a problem," Noah said.

"I'm fixing that now."

"Not the drinks," Noah said. "From the cemetery."

Tommy worked quickly, doling spoonfuls of sugar into each glass, crushing mint leaves in, then working lime wedges into quick squirts over the leafy-sugar mash. He found ice and clear rum, finishing the drinks from left to right. "What from the cemetery?"

Noah looked at her. "Tell him."

"The blonde boy, Samuel."

Tommy stopped, let out a slow breath, as if exhaling that idea. Finally, he nodded, crossed his arms. "Where?"

"Outside," Noah said. "Right outside the property."

Tommy frowned at him, then Josie. "On the street here? Is that true?"

No, back in the town. Josie nodded, met his stare. *Don't think.* "Yes. I don't understand why he's following me, but …"

"We'll deal with it." Tommy rolled his shoulders and shook out both arms, already starting toward the front door again. "Come with me."

"She shouldn't," Noah said.

Tommy stopped. "If Grace saw ..."

"He's looking for her." Noah stepped between them, almost protectively. *What does he think is going to happen?* "It's safer for her to stay in, until you deal with it."

Tommy shrugged, nodded to the door. "Good call. Show me where."

Noah met Josie's eyes. "Okay?"

Fucking great.

"Yes," Josie said. "I'll be here."

When Noah and Tommy stepped outside, the doors closed, and Josie was alone. *Look for keys on the third floor.* All three mojitos were still untouched on the bar, cool columns of opaque, green-flecked liquid and ice. Away from the bar, Josie followed the stairs up to a second floor landing, where a hall curled away into a network of dark rooms. The stairs continued up in too-yellow lamplight. One arm on the wooden banister, Josie followed them up to three.

At the summit, a small, black-and-white photo was mounted in an antique copper frame between a pair of swords. In the picture, a tired-looking man in a formal suit lounged on an expansive couch, with a round woman in a huge, bulbous dress on his left. A row of children fanned down the couch—three of them—with two more standing at the far end, holding a black dog. The room in the photo was dark and grainy gray, but Josie recognized the blurry staircase in the backdrop. *This house. That photo was taken downstairs in this place.*

A careful inscription in the frame read: *'New Leiden, 1862.'*

One of the kids holding the black dog was Samuel. *A hundred-something years ago. Of course it isn't. I shouldn't even be looking at this.*

At the end of the third-floor landing, Josie heard a sound from behind a heavy, closed door. The murmur of a woman's voice, definitely real. Solid and with medieval-looking iron strips and oversized bolts, the door looked like something from a theme park dungeon. *A torture room on the other side? Or something worse, even?*

Beside the door, an end table was stacked with unopened mail and an Amazon delivery box, and there, directly above: a skeletal hand stretched out of the wall, its fingers curled up, as if it had been holding a small globe. *Or keys. Gone now.*

Shit.

Another whimper from behind the door. Josie froze. A voice called for help. The stairs were right there. She could dash back down, yell to Noah—and then what? She wasn't trespassing, not really. Tommy invited her in. *I work here, for Eburos, too, right?*

Josie touched the heavy door latch. *This is the part where I'm supposed to run. Don't look back. Just go. I'm not a fucking hero. Except I'm here.* Maybe the keys were inside. Maybe someone needed help. *Maybe, maybe.* Josie turned the latch, and the door opened into gray shadows. Dust drifted in the light from the hall, and when Josie stepped closer, the sour smell of urine hit her. And something else. Sharper and acidic, the smell bit her nose, made her eyes water. Cleaning product, like industrial bleach.

Still in the doorway, Josie reached in, felt along the wall for a light switch. "Is someone there?" She tapped a plastic button, and white, phosphorescent lights buzzed on from both sides. The room came into focus.

The Eburos Group

THE EBUROS GROUP OPENS TOKYO OFFICE, EXPANDING ITS INTERNATIONAL REACH

The Eburos Group is proud to announce the opening of our first Tokyo office, boosting the presence of our teams in Asia. The office will bring Eburos closer to our clients and support our portfolio companies in this region. Under the leadership of Ichiro Tanaka, Director of Phanerotoxic Client Relations, the Tokyo office will strengthen our firm's foothold in Asia, which includes two existing offices in Japan; eight offices in Southeast Asia; six in Greater China; and as well as offices in India, Vietnam, and South Korea. At Eburos, we are committed to forging close relations with clients throughout the region by offering custom human donor solutions, as well as blood and soul harvesting at scale.

Chapter Fifteen

A human greenhouse. Shallow beds of dirt, fortified by wooden slats and tarps, were arranged in squares on either side, with nude people tethered in them. *No—trees.* Josie tried to make the image of the room rationalize, concentrating until the shapes made sense. They didn't. People stood motionless in the dirt squares in neat rows on both sides, supported by wooden beams and roped down by bungie cords, arms and legs tied to more support beams, as if they were ... *They are.* Leaves and fronds, flowers and sprouts of ivy grew from their heads, along their shoulders, chests, and groins. Their skin puckered brown, mottled black and crusty gray. *Like bark.* They were human plants. Four rows of six on the left, and five rows of five on the right. Josie's mind stuttered in a blank, frozen tumble. The bleach smell made her wipe her eyes again. There was another door back in the far right corner of the room, ordinary-looking. *I can run.*

"What is this?" Josie asked. Her voice was too quiet, weaker than she intended.

A woman moaned on her left. *People. People roped down in the dirt to grow like trees. They are trees.*

Josie stepped deeper into the center of the room. A tall man to her right watched with wide eyes that looked sculpted from oak. His gaping mouth stuffed with blooming leaves, his arms contorted down, stretched unnaturally long, with more leaves growing from his elbows and fingers.

He sees me.

The bark-flesh of his face strained, as if fighting to move. He groaned in a low rasp.

"What can I do?" Josie asked, her voice catching. "How can I help you?"

Behind her: "You can back up."

She spun. Tommy stood in the doorway, a blocky pistol in one hand.

"Why are you in here?" he asked. But it didn't sound like a question.

"I heard someone. I was ..." *What?* Looking for the bathroom, lost, trying to find a key? Josie sighed. "I don't know. Sorry. I'll leave. Downstairs ..."

"No." He pointed past Josie at the boxes along the far end of the room, by the other door. A post waited in one box, with a tangle of ropes, cords, and wooden blocks. "Stand over there."

"Over where—on the dirt?"

"Back up," he said slowly. "Grace, I'm serious." He pointed past the rows of plant people to the empty pole again.

"Why do you have that gun?" She started to say, half-joking, 'are you going to shoot me,' and caught herself. *Because what if he says yes?* Tommy's stupid, buzzed stare still looked all-business. Corralling her onto an indoor box garden of people-plants was his *job*. He thought it was, anyway. "What is this?" she asked.

When she moved down the walkway toward the back wall perimeter of the 'garden,' Tommy's shoulders relaxed a little.

"You shouldn't have seen this yet," he said. "We serve our clients. But there's nothing wrong with this place, however it looks."

It looks like fucking tree-people tied to poles in a murder room.

"What is it then?"

He extended a hand, as if she'd reminded him of something. "Give me your phone."

"It doesn't work." But she found it, handed it over. "I think the water from the pond ..."

Tommy snatched it fast and tapped the screen. It blinked white, starting up.

Great. Of course it works for him.

Tommy tapped again, asked, "How do I unlock it? Passcode?"

Josie told him, and the phone made a *'click'* as it unlocked.

He dialed and said, "Hi, yes. I'm calling for Angela from the Rose-cliff office."

This place is called 'Rosecliff'?

Tommy gestured her back toward the same wooden planter box, still empty except for a waiting pole, cords, and support beams. Past it, a wilty young woman—*girl, really, maybe even late teens, younger than me*—stared, helpless and frozen. Her ankles and calves were deep brown, twisted with wooden grooves, but the color faded up past her knees, running in veiny fissures through her waist into her stomach. More radiated down from her bound hands, lassoed to planks on either side, and small buds grew across her chest and along her lips. Almost beautiful. *Fucked up, surreal.*

"Go ahead," Tommy said. "Step up there."

"Why?"

"Because I told you to."

Josie had the wild urge to rush him. *'Because I told you to?' Fuck you.* She eased one foot back, almost to the edge of the box.

"Faster, faster," he said.

With the phone at one ear, Tommy stared past her, as if she were less interesting than the silence or on-hold tunes on the line. But he still held the pistol down in his other hand. And he was built like an athlete, with meaty arms and a broad chest, almost a head taller than her. *Because you told me to. Grab the gun—or dart past.* He wasn't really going to shoot her.

"No answer?" Josie asked.

"Not yet, no." He frowned, the phone still pressed to his cheek and ear. "It's not clear-cut, you understand. Your behavior. Coming up here, after your friend, *Noah* ..." He said the name like an insult, smirked. "That was a joke, right? The boy from the cemetery?"

"I did see him. I wasn't making that up."

"He's not outside this house," he said simply. "Not when I looked. And this room ..." He pointed the gun at the still-open door to the landing hall. "Alarmed. Silent, but you must have guessed that by now, right?"

"I didn't know what was in here."

"Well, you do now."

"No. I'm not ..."

"Get up on the dirt. Don't make me keep saying it." His cheeks darkened, splotches flushing down his neck. Alcohol and frustration. *Being on hold and catching a demon-heart girl in your people garden will do that. Run. Go to his right, duck under the gun. He can't grab you, if he's holding the gun.*

"Why?" Josie asked. "What happens if I do?"

"Look." Tommy's voice rose, slopping syllables together. He stepped closer, forcing her back. "This is your fault. I don't want to be in here. You made this happen."

"Made *what* happen?"

"I don't want to hurt you, Grace—"

"Don't call me Grace."

He reached for her, and Josie shoved both fists hard into his gut—an impact shock knocked her back. She fell, hands in the dirt, body twisted sideways. An echo cracked in Josie's eardrums that made her head ring, and then a hot bite of pain flared in her left shoulder. Her shoulder was on fire, amping up with her pulse in sudden spasms that made her stomach heave, eyes water, and Josie heard herself shout, grabbing the wound, fingers squeezing a lump of swelling heat, hurting.

Blood splattered the dirt down Josie's left arm. More dark red blood spasmed out of a small wet hole in her left shoulder, perfectly round. She felt the pressure of a foreign nugget inside. *A fucking bullet.*

"...why did you make me do that?" Tommy said. "Not my fault! I told you not to ..."

Josie heard the plastic slap of her phone hitting the ground. *He dropped it.* Josie's stomach lurched again. She tasted acid bile, blinked it down, and started to shift back to look up at him again—couldn't. Her right hand stuck to the dirt. Fingertips already numb, the fingernails and top joints of her fingers were darkening gray, as if the blood flow was stopping. Like frostbite. *Not fucking frostbite.* Josie shifted again, tried to pull her hand away, but it was trapped. The movement hurt, spotting her vision, and she cursed, almost a reflex. Twisting, Josie's left hand accidentally touched the dirt and sank flat against it, caught.

"Help me!" Josie shouted. She couldn't turn to see Tommy, her body still positioned awkwardly so that her legs splayed sideways across the floor, her torso over the dirt, both hands on it now. And her stomach. Josie looked down to the edge of the planter, where her shirt and a narrow gap of stomach skin darkened in a spiral wave of deep brown. A stream of blood flowed down Josie's left arm, and she heard Tommy walking back toward the door.

"I didn't do this," he said. "You did. This wasn't my fault …"

In the corner of her vision, Josie glimpsed Tommy rush out. The door slammed, and she heard another click. Locked. *This isn't happening.*

"Help!" Josie closed her eyes, the swell of pain in her shoulder brightening, worse. It throbbed up her collar and down her left arm in tingly sharp bursts. She screamed again.

The plant girl moaned.

Josie looked up to meet her sad eyes. The lights went out.

Perfect. Fuck.

In the blackness, Josie took a frantic breath, tried to slow it down. The pain in her shoulder flashed with her pulse, making her gasp, exhale in a sudden whimper. *I'm going to die.* She couldn't feel her right hand, and now the left was almost gone, too. Numbness all up her stomach, almost to her ribs. Everywhere she touched the dirt, it spread.

This is insane. Why did I come here? What did I want? Money? No—a future. Something to look forward to. Medicine, help for Uncle Don. That's all. Why is that too much? What did I do wrong?

A buzzing behind her.

Josie opened her eyes, tried to twist to look again. In the blackness, a blotch of white light flashed somewhere behind her. The phone was still there. *Still on the floor, he didn't take the phone.*

So?

Josie kicked one leg back blindly until she felt it with her foot, heard the plastic-glass rectangle slide closer across the floorboards.

And now what? I'm going to pick it up, unlock it with my teeth? Somehow type—shut up. Try. Focus on the water in front … shut up.

With one leg, Josie knocked the phone against the side of the planter at her waist. No more light, though. *Could someone be calling?*

How do I pick it up?

Straining and shouting in pain, Josie slid her thigh to jam the phone against the planter, raising it up into the dirt. Somehow, it worked. The phone was lying in the dark, right by her stomach. Even with the bark-ification or whatever the fuck was happening to her, she still felt the smooth phone edge.

Okay, now pick it up somehow.

She tried moving it with her body, catching it against her gut—no good. And then it stuck on the button of her shirt and dragged up. Even in the dark, Josie sensed it moving and angled lower to catch it with her elbow, closer, until—*there*—it was below her face. She flipped it over with her mouth, careful not to touch the dirt and used her nose to unlock it.

Insane.

The screen lit up with missed calls and text bubbles. The last missed call: The Eburos Group.

Angela calling Tommy back.

Josie tapped it with her nose to redial, pressed speaker. The screen changed, the line rang.

How is it working?

Josie watched the blank contact screen and phone number, heard it ring again. And again.

Answer. Please. For the love of God, please.

"Hello, The Eburos Group home office. How can I direct your call?"

"Can you hear me?" Josie's voice sputtered and dipped with the pain in her shoulder. "My name is Josie—Grace." *Whatever.* "I'm on

Dutch Island." *What did Tommy call this place?* "Rosecliff. At the Rosecliff. I need help."

"One moment."

A muffled click, and the line went quiet but didn't hang up. *Please, no. Please answer. Help me.*

Another click, and the brisk, half-smiling voice of Mr. Dean: "Grace, what a lovely surprise. Are you receiving this?"

"Yes, I can hear you," Josie said.

"I understand there were problems on the island, no surprise."

"I'm still there."

"On Dutch Island now?" Mr. Dean said, and she imagined him pausing to reach for a new cigarette. "That's unacceptable. How did this happen? Angela indicated you would return by now."

"I'm trapped," Josie said and winced at another flood of needles in her shoulder, down her numbing arm. *Fuck.* "I'm at a house. The Eburos office here. There are people as plants. I'm stuck in the dirt, because Tommy ..." *Rambling, slow down.* "I'm trapped."

"Is Thomas there with you now?" Mr. Dean asked, his voice sharper, more serious.

"Please, I need help," Josie said.

"I'm not sure I have all the information," Mr. Dean said. "You've been materially injured on Dutch Island somehow? You are needed here, Grace, as soon as possible. I'll get the full download when you're back in the city. Now, I have another call. See you soon."

The call ended.

"No."

The screen was still lit. *Don't quit.* Josie's hands and forearms were gone now. She hovered in the darkness, with half limbs. A voice coughed. *The tree people. They're all still here.* In her rush to call, Josie had wedged the reality of this room to the back of her mind for a frantic moment.

"Can you help me?" Josie said.

Nothing.

"Please? Can you hear me? You're all trapped in this ..."

This. What is this? Madness, an impossible, hellish greenhouse. Insanity, like the ghosts and cemetery demon. A harvest for the anchor clients, maybe. The company catered to *things* that weren't human, that used people.

The door lock clicked, and a rush of dim hall light appeared past rows of bound bodies. *Noah?*

The blinding white of the overhead lights made Josie recoil, shaking spots from her vision. Footsteps approached, and Josie craned sideways to see: not Noah.

Samuel.

He *was* here, still trailing a sinew of black fog from his back that looped out the open doorway.

THE EBUROS GROUP LEADS IN U.S. POLITICAL DONATIONS

STAY UPDATED!

Chapter Sixteen

"Noah, help!" Josie shouted.

Samuel paused by the path that led to Josie. "You're loud," he said. "Don't be so loud." And continued toward her.

"Stop," Josie said, then screamed again, "Noah!" This time, belting so hard it pinched her shoulder wound, and her yell twisted into a breathy animal noise. As Samuel neared, Josie panted, shaking over the dirt. "Please don't hurt me." Her left arm streaked bloody, the soil melting curdled brown around her left hand and along the angle of her shoulder, where red drops still fell. Josie felt a swirl of lightheadedness, gone again.

"Hurt you?" the boy said, as if he didn't understand. "What happened to your arm?"

"He shot me."

Samuel made an impatient sound. "He shouldn't have done that." He knelt beside Josie, close enough that she could see the splash of freckles around his nose and cheeks below his too-pale blue eyes. "Be my friend again, Grace?"

Again with this. "Your friend," Josie repeated. "Yes, okay. Please don't …"

He took Josie's right wrist and pulled. She felt the dirt loosen, and her skin came free. Feeling flooded back in blotchy lumps of hot, pleasant pain, as if she'd let the circulation get cut off. *My hand was asleep, that's all.* Samuel freed her bloody left hand, then guided her back until she slipped onto the floor, with her back to the planter.

Samuel jammed a finger through the hole in her shirt at the shoulder, directly into the bullet wound. Deep pain exploded, and she screamed, jerking away instinctively, but he held her. She felt cold, biting pressure, heard her own voice pitch high, and then it was gone, and Josie sagged, shivering. Tears streamed down her cheeks.

"I got it," Samuel said. "See?"

Josie wiped her face but didn't look. *Thank you. You saved my life, demon boy. Didn't see that coming.*

"Okay?" he asked.

Josie stared blankly at him. "Okay what?"

"I'll call you with my shell when you're in the secret place with the silver door and elephants."

"I don't ..." Josie pulled herself up. "I'm sorry, I don't understand."

"By the baseball stadium?" he said, as if it were obvious and she were playing dumb. "Where the others are. She didn't tell you? The last Grace didn't tell you where she goes when she's sad?"

Noah appeared at the open door, froze when he saw the tree people, then looked from Samuel to Josie.

"You're alive again," Samuel said, smiling at Noah. "Grace is my friend now, too."

Approaching, Noah saw Josie's bloody shoulder. "What ..?"

"Tommy shot me," she said.

Carefully, as if approaching a rabid dog, Noah stepped around the line of black-mist that still extended from Samuel's back, out the door. Noah kept his hands up, eyes on Samuel.

"We need to go," Noah said. "Josie ..?"

Samuel frowned, as if he didn't understand. "She's Grace." And to Josie, "Do you want me to call anyone for you? Your dad?"

A clammy chill made Josie shiver. She backed away from Samuel, closer to Noah, almost in reach. "No," she said. "My dad passed away, Samuel."

"Mine did, too," he said, with a shrug. "I talk to him sometimes anyway. He's usually just confused. I'll call you with my shell, okay?"

"Yes," Josie said. She took Noah's hand, wincing with the movement of her shoulder muscles. "Okay, Samuel. Thank you. We have to go now."

Noah walked her back to the door, and Samuel nodded, arms flat at his sides. "I know. It makes me sad, but I'll call you soon."

Noah hurried to the top of the staircase outside. The dark, frothy line hung in the air down the stairs to the second-floor landing and main level below. Probably all the way back to the cemetery.

"You have the keys to the boat?" Josie asked.

"Right here." He patted his pocket.

One hand braced on the railing, Josie walked with him down. *A secret place with a silver door and elephants by a baseball stadium. What kind of insanity is that? But he said he could talk to Dad. After tracking me here, he saved me. That kid saved me, then calmly let me leave. Dad is long gone, stop it.*

Halfway down the steps to the first floor, Josie spotted Tommy at the front entrance. Recognition clicked in his face when their eyes met, and he pushed off toward them.

"Grace ..." Tommy called.

"Back this way," Noah said, running around the side of the staircase into a narrow hall, with more abstract paintings that fed back to a noisy kitchen, where waitstaff were organizing trays of hors d'oeuvres and heavy coolers packed with ice. They parted when Noah led Josie through.

Through a back hall, a rear door opened onto a dark lawn, where a grassy hill sloped away, past a careful tree line, stone steps, a fountain, and globular statues to a sheet of glittery black. The shore. Rain thrashed the darkness, and even from here Josie heard the smash of waves below. They were back at the ocean, and as they stumbled closer, Josie picked out the dark outlines of boats arranged along a narrow dock and arched boathouse.

We can't sail in this. We'll drown.

Tommy called behind them, "Wait!"

"Don't stop," Noah said.

He pulled her harder into a stumbling run on the wet grass, Josie's legs pounding too fast on the slope. Any step could twist wrong in this near-dark, slip her ankle sideways, send her tumbling in bursts of pain, and they would be caught. They reached a low patio that fed to the boathouse and salt water crashing against the dock.

"That one." Noah pointed to a sleek, white-striped yacht at the end of the dock.

"Do you know how to ..."

"Not really, no."

Behind them, Tommy yelled, "Stop! Grace, don't do that!"

They stomped across the dock, and Noah helped Josie climb across to the yacht, then hunched to frantically uncoil the boat tethers and ropes from blocks. A flashlight beam waved on the back lawn. Three figures were dashing down fast, one fell on the slippery incline.

Tommy reached the patio first, aimed the streaking-rain light beam at Noah, then Josie. "Get off the boat!" he shouted.

Noah finished with the ropes and hopped on, ducked into the cabin. The boat bounced and tossed on the water. The engine rumbled through Josie's feet, and bright lights came on at the front, like headlights on a car. As the boat lurched away from the dock, Josie sagged to sit, a stiff support beam jabbed into her back. *We're about to die. Sailing into the storm.* When the yacht pitched, the lights of the house and spreading shore bobbed up in an uneven line on the darkness. She heard Noah ask if she was okay.

Josie couldn't lift her arms, felt the spray of warm salt water, when the yacht tipped down. It rocked harder, moving faster. The lights of the coast spread in a wide, irregular bend across the horizon, gone when the rain pitched louder, then back again.

"Let me help you up," Noah shouted over the storm. "You have to come inside."

Inside. He's right. I have to.

Josie closed her eyes and slumped sideways ...

... and woke under a warm blanket on a couch in the yacht cabin, with seagulls cawing and looping in the darkness outside. The rain had slowed to a drizzle-mist on the windows. Sitting up brought a lance of pain in her shoulder, and when Josie touched the wound, she felt a thick bandage. Through a doorway at the far end of the cabin, Noah stood with his back to her in a control room, steering them closer to an evening marina, crowded with fishing trawlers around weather-worn warehouses and boxy shipping depots. Inspecting her shoulder again, Josie found a tight net of gauze and what smelled like antibacterial cream underneath. *He patched me up.* Still hurt like a motherfucker, when she moved her arm or stretched to the right, but no more bleeding.

"You awake?" Noah called and smiled back at her. "Almost there."

"Almost where?"

As they sliced between the fishing boats toward an open network of births, Josie scanned for people. No one out. Somehow, they were arriving unseen in the wet mist. *Because no one else would be out in this.* They slowed closer to the dock, and Noah came into the cabin, smiling.

"We're somewhere on Long Island, I think," he said and dragged open the door to lead her out onto the deck. He knelt to work with a tangle of ropes and plastic-lined coils. "That crossing only took about ninety minutes."

Josie watched, still weak. As she raised her right arm to test the weight, Josie paused, her hand trembling in the air. Her shoulder throbbed, and Noah leapt to the dock, tied up the yacht, and then jumped back across, looking quickly up and down the line of quiet boats for any sign of people. No one, they were still unnoticed. Impossible, but they'd slipped ashore through the gale just like that. Already, the storm quieted.

Nodding and still grinning, Noah leaned in to help hoist Josie up. "I can do it," she started to say, realized that wasn't true, and let him lead her to the edge of the deck. It was a short, two-foot hop to the other side. *But if I slip, fall backwards, hit my head, go under ...*

Noah helped her across. At the end of the dock, they crossed between squat, utilitarian buildings, shuttered behind metal-plate sliding doors, and through a gravel parking lot to a road that fed into an industrial, seaside neighborhood. A long-haul truck idled in a lot further down, its lights blasting on the side of a brick building in the low fog of its exhaust, but otherwise, it was deserted. A steady rain beat down, but no wind now.

She turned in a slow circle to take in the concrete-brick-and-plaster warehouses, vacant lots, and working boats that crowded the shore. *Somewhere.* "I have to sit."

Noah helped her to the sharp front steps of the nearest closed warehouse, with *'BR Shipping Co.'* stenciled over the locked front glass door. "You should get your wound checked out," he said. "We can call an ambulance or ..."

Josie found her phone: 5:45 PM. *Have to get home. Fix things with Dani, see Mom and Uncle Don. Burn The Eburos Group to the ground. Or just run. Hide somewhere.* "Thank you. For helping me, bandaging my shoulder. I'm ..."

The phone rang: Angela.

"Don't answer," Noah said.

Josie hit the green 'Accept' button, almost a reflex, and before she could speak, Angela cut in: "I know what you're going to say, and we'll fix it. A car will be there in fifteen minutes. I am so sorry I had to leave you. I know you called Mr. Dean. I've spoken to Tommy, and ..."

"No."

A sudden pause, then Angela said, "Don't answer now. You've been through a lot, Grace ..."

"Don't call me Grace," Josie said. "That isn't my name."

"Okay," Angela said. "A car will be there."

"How does a car know where to pick us up?"

Another pause. "Us?"

Shit.

Noah shook his head, arms crossed, but Josie said, "Noah is with me."

"Noah left the island? That's ... okay. We have your phone's location, of course. I worried when you started to drift out on the Bight, but here you are."

Because they fucked with my phone, while I was in registration, didn't they?

"I'm not coming back," Josie said. "You put someone else's—"

"Josie, stop," Angela said, but she didn't sound angry. Just patient, confident, as if she'd had this conversation before. *She has.* "I know. I understand. I hear you. But yes, you are going to return to the office so we can patch up your arm."

"Tommy shot me in the shoulder."

"And you'll debrief Mr. Dean on everything that happened, before we introduce you to the Friendly Man. You're going to do that tonight, Josie. I can use whatever name you want, if it makes it easier."

Josie slid her thumb to the 'End Call' tab, but didn't press. "I don't have to," she said.

"You do actually," Angela said. "You signed a contract."

"Then I quit."

Josie heard a smile in Angela's voice, as she said, "Unfortunately, we don't accept your resignation. I'll see you here at the office ..."

"Don't talk to me like ..."

"... with your uncle."

The Eburos Group
COMPENSATION

Employees are typically paid bimonthly by check or bank transfer. If you are a full-time living employee, you may also be eligible for annual bonus in the form of monetary compensation, chattel interns, extended lifespan, or boutique gifts (e.g., past recognition awards have included Macallan 25-year single malt, an all-inclusive resort spa package, or bespoke cranial drinkware). Bonus is allocated on an individual basis, subject to both employee and firm performance.

COMPANY HANDBOOK

Chapter Seventeen

On the phone, Josie pressed for answers—"Is Uncle Don there? What are you doing to him?"—but Angela dodged and cleared her throat. "We'll see you soon, *Josie*." The call ended.

Call her back?

"Shit," Josie murmured.

From her slumped seat on the warehouse steps, she watched headlights appear at the end of the road. *The company car?* She tracked the lights in a steady beat, as they passed. *No. Not much time, though.*

"Is there someone else you can call?" Noah asked. "Before I go?"

Josie scrolled to find Mom's number, paused. "You're going to go?"

Still hugging his arms in a half-slouch over her, Noah watched the road. "I have to get back. I'll apologize. They might not believe me, but ..." He stopped, suddenly distracted by his left arm. Noah raised his arm, and beads of pale-pink skin slid down toward his elbow, like water on glass. A splotch dripped away, hit the pavement in a tiny white paint-shaped blob.

"What is that?" Josie asked.

Noah shook his head, reached a shaking hand to test his left forearm, and now Josie saw droplets forming on his right arm, too. And on his cheeks and chin. When Noah poked his arm, his forefinger slid in too far, as if the flesh were putty. A tiny hole opened around his finger, exposing dark red muscle and white tendon.

"What's happening to me?" Noah asked. He looked at Josie, eyes wide. The flesh began to slide away from his eyes, and a drop trickled down his nose like sweat, ready to fall. Not sweat.

"You're asking me?" The phone shook in Josie's hand. *Not a call, I'm trembling.* "I can call Angela back or ..."

"No. This is punishment, I think. For leaving the island. I'm supposed to stay on Dutch Island ..."

"I can call her back, Noah."

"And say what?"

Josie pressed one hand to her face, half-shielding her view of the blobs of watery skin forming on Noah. His shirt and pants were already clingy, as if he'd been jogging in a tunnel of pinkish mist. His body was soaking into the cotton, polyester, and denim. Dull pain still throbbed in Josie's shoulder with her heartbeat.

"Maybe you need to go back," she said. "You helped me, got me here. Thank you. But if this is some kind of voodoo tied to the island ..."

"It's my client. He's not supposed to leave." He looked back toward the boat. "Will you be okay?"

Josie started to say that the company didn't own him and maybe this was all just ... when she looked again, small rivulets of flesh, gelatinous and solid, ran down his cheeks, clinging to the ridge of his chin. *The thing inside him. Teeth in his brain, the anchor client, whatever the fuck is propping up his dead body ... He's melting.* Stepping away, Noah rubbed his chin, and a section of skin slopped onto the back of his hand, exposing wet muscle and bone.

"Go," Josie said.

Noah hesitated. "You'll be okay?"

A section of his left cheek folded down, opening the bottom of his eye socket in a bloody gap, like a slow, human mud slick. He didn't react.

No.

"Just—go!" she said.

Noah backed away flexing his dripping hands in front of him, as he started at a jog, then sprinted back to the dock. She didn't have a view of the boat but heard the engine. Its rumble quieted in a dip-slide-dip, probably riding the waves back out. *Is he going to die? Did I imagine that? Delirious from the bullet wound ...* But the thought folded back into a *'shut the fuck up, this is happening,'* answer.

A dark car banked away from the road and into the parking lot, slowing to a stop, the lights and engine still on. Josie hadn't seen it pull up.

Noah had answers. He knew about the tree people, and Sandra, and Eburos's business on Dutch Island—and I just told him to leave.

Because he was melting.

A young, uniformed driver stepped out of the car, called, "Miss Grace? Back door is open."

Josie didn't correct him. She shoved up, dragged open the rear car door, and fell into the seat, letting the door slam again on its own. Her shoulder pain felt more distant now. *Is that a good thing?*

"Just you?" the driver asked.

"Just me."

"They said—"

"It's just me."

They pulled away. Josie drew herself into a sitting position, buckled her lap belt. Tapping her phone to bring up Mom's contact, she called.

Three rings, and then Mom's muffled voice, "Hello? Josie? What's wrong—is everything okay?"

"I ..." Josie rolled her head back, the phone at her ear and cheek. *Is everything okay?* "Are you okay, Mom?"

"Am *I* okay?" Mom asked. "Josie, you sound strange. Your voice is different on this line ..."

Because I'm Grace. I'm using her vocal cords now, aren't I? Or she's using mine. Not a great thought.

"They told me that Uncle Don ..."

"Yes, that's right!" Mom said. "It's really wonderful what you've done. He wanted to thank you himself, left a message for you."

What I've done.

"What are you talking about?"

"His health care," Mom said. "And, I know it's happening fast, but I just can't believe the offers Eburos made. You must have pulled some real strings. Too good to be true, almost."

Mom's voice sounded so close. Like if Josie opened her eyes, looked across the car, Mom would smile back and take her hand. *Hold Grace's hand.*

"But it's happening," Mom said.

"What is?" Josie asked.

A pause, and Mom laughed. "They didn't give you the details? Eburos is offering me a part-time advisory position, Josie. Solomon decided to make me an offer in their legal department. For an ungodly amount of money, and they're going to let me work remotely, and ..." She laughed again, and Josie heard rustling in the background, then a metal click, probably the stove burner to heat water for tea. "Uncle Don has always wanted to visit Greece. Maybe I'll take him on a Mediterranean cruise, when he's feeling up for it."

The company car moved fast on a nearly empty highway, lined with overgrown walls and trees, following signs back to New York City. Josie didn't recognize the suburban neighborhoods that passed, but

Manhattan couldn't be far. Not much time to figure out what the fuck was happening.

"Mom, please tell me what's going on," Josie said slowly. "You said Mr. Dean offered you a job?"

"Yes." Now Mom sounded confused. "But really it was the chief legal counsel. I don't know her well, but she had heard of me. It's real, Josie. I didn't believe it myself at first, but it is."

"And they moved Uncle Don?"

"Right, to a private facility at the company office. What's wrong? You really don't sound like yourself."

I'm not myself.

"I'm okay," Josie said. "I'm just ..." *Just.* "You're still at home in Connecticut? Did you sign the papers already?"

"No, not yet,'" Mom said, a tug of evening frustration in her voice. "Are you worried about the documents? I *was* a lawyer for thirty years, let's remember. I'm not unfamiliar with how to make decisions."

"That's not what I meant."

"It's an amazing amount of money, Josie. I wasn't looking for it, but ... it's a very, *very* fair offer."

"Mom, don't."

"Things aren't easy," Mom said. "You know that. Even if I only go part-time for six months, it will make a real difference."

Words stuck, half-formed in Josie's head. *Why is my life suddenly a chain that I can't drop? Dani and now this job. And Everett, still missing. My friends—I don't have friends. They're all leaving me. What I have is a predatory contract with a company that bargains with demons. And changed me—literally, too on-the-nose changed me—into another person.*

"It's an unexpected opportunity," Mom said. "Anyway, we can talk about it the next time you visit."

"After you sign."

"Josie, please …"

"They took Uncle Don, and now you're going to work for them, too," Josie said.

"This doesn't sound like you. Are you feeling okay? Getting enough rest ..?"

"I have to go."

Josie ended the call, and before she could second-guess herself, tapped Dani's contact. The line rang, went to voicemail just like before.

"Hi. It's Josie. I need you to call me as soon as you get this." *I love you? I miss you? Where are you?* "Talk soon."

Josie swiped to hang up, and her screen went dark. *They want to own Mom, too, and Dani is AWOL.* Eburos took Uncle Don hostage. Josie steadied her breathing, as the car climbed a ramp through construction cones toward a wider highway. A wall of glass and steel buildings appeared on the horizon, surrounded by bridges and a dense mat of sprawling tower-house neighborhoods. A moment later, darker storm clouds turned the steady drizzle to hard rain again, and Manhattan disappeared behind a wet film, as they slowed into a crush of traffic.

"With the storm, there wasn't time to approve a chopper," the driver said. When Josie stared blankly back at him in the rearview, he pointed at the mass of cars blocking the highway. "Would have saved us at least an hour, I think, but they weren't positive where you would be for a landing."

They almost sent a helicopter to pick me up.

Forty-five minutes later, when they made the Eburos headquarters, Dani still hadn't called back, and Mom just texted: *'Talk later. I am so proud of you.'* Mom still composed texts like that, as if she were writing emails or formal letters, even, complete with punctuation and full-on pronoun spellings.

Inside, Angela waited in the lobby, holding a glass bottle of imported spring water. Above the outer windows, more grasping branches and ivy layered the walls than Josie remembered seeing before.

"Welcome back," Angela said. "Are you hungry?"

Yes. Fucking starving, but Josie said, "I'm fine." and accepted the water bottle, downed half. *Smash it over her head.* The icy water thrilled her mouth and throat going down. *God, I am tired.* "Where's my uncle?"

"He's probably asleep, Josie. We should ..."

"No—"

"Just." Angela touched Josie's arm, poised in a fresh, dark navy suit. All the muddy chaos of Dutch Island long gone. "Let me finish, okay? I was going to say that we should go wake him up."

Josie nodded and followed Angela through the security turnstiles to the elevator bank.

"Whatever you might think, I'm actually on your side," Angela said.

The second elevator arrived, and when they got on, Angela hit a bottom button for 'B3.' There were five sub-basements listed, along with six more unlabeled elevator buttons below those. *Are those new?* No, she just must not have noticed them before. Finance news anchors still laughed on elevator monitors above the floor buttons.

"I don't believe you," Josie said. "I'm taking my uncle out of here. That's the only reason I came back, after what happened."

"Yes, well, someone should see to your shoulder, too," Angela said, raising both hands, as if Josie were about to snap back. "Even if the wound is clean, you don't want it getting infected tomorrow, do you? How did that happen exactly?"

"I told you. Tommy fucking shot me. In a room full of ..."

The elevator dinged down to B3, and the doors opened to a carpeted hall set like a Scandinavian hotel, all minimalist furniture and tasteful plants. More ivy swarmed the walls here, too, in veiny streaks between white, spartan doors and uncomfortable-looking chairs. Midway down the hall, a bored woman in scrubs looked up from a workstation.

"Donald Morris?" Angela asked her.

"Room five," the scrubs-woman said, then straightened when she noticed Josie. "Oh wow, you're ... it's an honor to see you down here. Can I ask ..?"

Angela's shadow glided ahead of her down the hall toward room five, on the left, but Josie hesitated. "What?"

"Would you mind ..?" She slipped out of the workstation to stand beside Josie and held up her cellphone, the camera already on and reversed to take a selfie. "My husband won't believe me, unless I bring him proof."

Down the hall, Angela sighed. "Grace is very busy ..."

The scrubs-woman leaned close to Josie—*to Grace, not me; that's Grace on her phone screen, the woman from the plane and the cemetery*—and took the shot. "Thank you so much—this is wild!"

Shoulder aching and her mind numb with exhaustion, Josie joined Angela at the closed door of room five. *So I'm really her. This is still happening.*

"Have you thought about what you're going to say?" Angela asked.

Josie touched the doorknob, said, "What do you mean? I'm taking him out of here, I told you. Don't try to stop me."

"Yes, but will he go with you? Have you thought about whether he will want to go with you, like this?"

"What? Why wouldn't he ..." *Because of what I just saw. I'm not me. He won't see Josie standing in front of him either.*

"I am asking," Angela said, close behind her. "Not *telling* you. Will he?"

Josie squeezed the doorknob tighter, a knot of tension twisting under her ribs. *Below my heart. Her heart.*

Screw it.

She opened the door.

Contact Us

Thank you for your interest in The Eburos Group. Please complete the form below to inquire about our custom Client Services. We are proud to fuse state-of-the-art affliction mastery with distinctive corporeal vessels and extractive tools tailored to clients' specific needs. Please note: while we appreciate your questions, we are unable to respond to all inquiries.

NAME

EMAIL

ORGANIZATION

CURRENT HOST STAGE

SPECIAL REQUESTS

www.eburosgroup.com

Chapter Eighteen

Wedged between a crush of pillows, Uncle Don watched a home renovation show on a flatscreen television mounted on the opposite wall. Except for the washed out lumps around his eyes and gaunt pull in his cheeks, he looked better. No IV or cords, and he even wore a white, puffy luxury-hotel-looking robe, rather than a hospital gown.

He frowned at them, muted the television. "What's your name again, Angela?"

"You remembered. Bravo, first try," Angela said.

"Who is that with you?"

"Hi, Uncle Don," Josie said. She approached the bed. "How are you feeling?"

Uncle Don blinked at her, then asked Angela, "Who is this? I don't get it."

Josie slowed. Needle pain throbbed in her shoulder with her pulse. *Because I'm tensing. Stay calm.* "I know this is strange," she said, "but it's Josie. I'm your niece. I look different ..."

He focused on the TV again, as a big guy started talking loudly about drywall and the costs of cedar. "Stop bullshitting me. I appreciate what the company is doing for me, because of Josie, but whatever game this is, it's not funny. Is this some kind of test of my cognitive skills? Well, I know you're not Josie. My heart stopped working, not my eyes."

"I'm here," Josie said, her voice softer than she meant it to be. "It's me."

Still watching the TV, not her, Uncle Don said, "That's enough." And to Angela, "What did you say earlier, that Josie is busy with a super important company assignment? Traveling the world or something?"

Or something.

Josie glanced at Angela. "You told him that."

"It's true." Angela shrugged. "And we should get going."

"Uncle Don," Josie said and met his skeptical eye. "It's me. They still haven't taught me to lie ..."

A beat, and Uncle Don waved them away. "Go on, go on."

Returning to the hall felt like a retreat. *I lost. Grace's heart really did transform me. That fucking absurdity made me powerless.*

"He is doing well," Angela said, when she shut the door behind them. "Our doctors are world-class. Your uncle really is receiving the best treatment possible."

"Am I supposed to thank you for holding him hostage here?"

Angela walked them back to the elevator. On the phone at the work station, the scrubs-woman grinned up at Josie, as they passed. *Grinned up at Grace. Not me.*

"I'm not meeting with anyone or taking another nap or whatever you have planned," Josie said. "I'm leaving, Angela, going home. If my uncle won't come with me, then I'll go alone."

"I understand what you're saying," Angela said. "But you still don't understand. What I told your uncle is true: you are incredibly important to us, Josie. Not just because you see my shadow ..."

"You're infested by a demon," Josie said. "An anchor client, monster, whatever you want to call it. If I believe in all this, then that's true, isn't it?"

The elevator arrived, and when they got on, Angela tapped the 20th floor, and before Josie could object, said, "Give me five minutes. I want to show you something. I promise it's not a sinister trick to keep you here."

"What's on twenty?"

They ascended, already above the lobby, the numbers ticking up toward ten.

"Fresh air. Whatever you think of us, Eburos is not an evil cabal, and we honor our agreements. Check your bank account."

"I don't want to check my bank account, I want to go home," Josie said, but she didn't tap the emergency stop button or try to hit a lower floor to jump out. "Can my uncle leave if he wants to?"

"Of course."

"What about me?" Josie drummed her fingers—too cold and pale, with foreign, blue veins along her wrists—on her hips. *Not my hands. Grace's body, all of it.* She watched the numbers hit the teens, closer to twenty. *Because a part of me wants to see. And I can't just go, can I, not like this.* "How do I change back?"

On twenty, the elevator opened to an expanse of checkerboard carpet outside empty meeting rooms, like a mini convention center, with more wall aquariums that flickered with the bright movement of tropical, deep ocean fish. Angela took Josie to the back of a long room in the center, where glass doors opened onto a wet balcony overlooking the skyscrapers along the southern tip of Manhattan. The evening storm had lapsed into a steady, gray drizzle that gusted a line of international flags along the balcony railing: a U.S. flag, British flag, Canadian, Japanese, Chinese, and a dozen others.

"I asked you how I can change back," Josie said. "Why are we out here?"

"Do you see that?" Angela pointed at a craggy glass tower on the opposite side of the street. It leveled up into a narrow pincer, aimed at the sky, with garden terraces covered in tents.

"Am I supposed to recognize that building?" Josie asked.

"No, but I do. I come out here to look at it sometimes."

"Angela ..."

"That's where I died."

The anxious frustration in Josie's chest lapsed for an instant. *Joking right now?* No, Angela was serious.

"Well, not *there*," Angela said and frowned down, through the wraparound glass of the balcony barrier. It rose to about chest height. High enough to block someone from slipping over, but not to stop a climber. "I guess technically on the street pavement."

"You're standing right here," Josie said.

"I jumped," Angela said. Her eyes softened, as she watched the opposite tower. "Right off the twenty-third floor." She tapped the air at one of the terraces. "There."

"Why?" Josie asked.

Angela shook her head. "You wouldn't believe me." She said it thoughtfully, as if they were trying to solve a jigsaw puzzle together. Low stakes suicide. "I was working late. Not for Eburos, of course. Another firm. I was alone, and my laptop bricked. Just stopped working, and I lost it." She smiled. "That sounds funny now, doesn't it? I killed myself because my computer broke."

"That can't be why," Josie murmured.

"Well, it's what happened."

Josie waited, resisting the urge to press the obvious. *Why are you lying to me right now? If you died, how are you here? Like Noah. He said the same thing, didn't he? Drowned in a storm surge, only to be resurrected so he could work for the company. And he melted when he left the island.*

"The company brought me back, of course," Angela said. "Eburos scraped me up off the street down there. I don't remember that part, obviously, but when I woke up, they explained my options, and I signed. No one was tricked. They gave me a chance very few people get: to be part of meaningful change. To create real synergy." Josie shivered in a wet breeze. Warm out, but she felt a chill that coiled the queasy mess in her guts. *I signed too.*

"How?" Josie asked.

"Don't play dumb," Angela said, and she leaned on the terrace barrier between the Australian and French flags.

Josie felt a spasm of blood in her temple. *Don't jump. Jesus. What if she's telling the truth?*

"You know enough about how this works by now to recognize that we're not like other people," Angela said, wind gusting her hair in a wet billow. "This isn't an ordinary firm, and Mr. Dean isn't an ordinary CEO. Don't act surprised."

"I'm allowed to be surprised that you claim to have died."

"No," Angela said. "Not really. What do you think would happen if you leapt to your death right now?" She glanced back, face wet in a smear of mascara. "A tasteful burial and obituary?"

Am I lying to myself to make sense of this?

Angela leaned over the edge, closed her eyes.

"Stop that."

"Why?" Using both arms, Angela leveraged herself up to raise her waist to the top of the barrier. The metal top was slick and dripping.

"Please," Josie said. "Don't. Angela, seriously, stop ..."

"Seriously." Angela smiled. She eased back to watch Josie over her shoulder. "Because this wasn't serious before? I know you're upset. Believe me. But we are also part of something bigger than ourselves. It's our responsibility to add value."

"You put another girl's heart …"

"I know," Angela said. "Josie, Grace—whatever you want me to call you—would you like to know what happens next or not?" She stared, as if willing Josie to look away.

"What—I have to get with the program or you'll go over the side?"

"Yes," Angela said. "One of us will. How do you think this works? Do you think people create fortunes without making sacrifices? Real, blood-on-the-altar sacrifices? This is yours."

"Becoming someone else," Josie said. "Literally."

"Literally, yes."

This is fucked.

"Please get down," Josie said.

"Do you want to see why we've gone to all this trouble about you?"

"If you stop that."

Angela stepped back from the barrier. "Whatever you think, I don't actually have all the answers. I am only telling you my little tragedy, because it's important you appreciate the stakes before you meet him."

Meet him.

Josie felt the urge to rush inside and leave her out here alone. *She's bluffing, lying about her resurrection. Except Noah really did start melting, I saw that, too. And corpses standing in a kitchen and plant-people growing. And the anchor client demon-woman-thing at the cemetery. All of it—it is real. Whatever it is, it's happening.*

At the door, Josie asked, "You weren't really going to jump, were you?"

Angela glanced back at the edge, a hand on her hip. "You don't think so? Do we have a deal or no?"

See Mr. Dean again or be responsible for whatever she does next.

"You can't threaten me with your own life," Josie said.

"Of course I can," Angela said. "And? Do you want to test me? Say the word."

She's serious. Angela's jaw tightened a little too much around her usual, steady smile. Unpredictable. As if another person trapped inside her skin were eager to hurl herself over the side.

"I need you to tell me how to fix this," Josie said.

"Put you back into yourself?" Angela said and held the door. "Why? How was that working before?"

Josie stepped past her, back into the dry meeting room.

"Are you hungry?" Angela asked. "Because if you are ..."

"I'm not going to eat any more of the food here," Josie said quickly. "That other girl, before me, she was doped on the plane, right? No, I don't trust you that much. The last time I ate a meal in this building, I was unconscious a few minutes later."

"Fair enough." At the elevator, Angela hit the 'up' button. "Well? What about the previous version of you?"

"You're asking how it was *working* being me?"

The doors opened, and this time, when they got on, Angela pressed the top floor. They started up. *Back up to him.*

"Yes, I'm asking," Angela said.

"I was fine. I don't know what you're ..."

"Test scores say you were years smarter than your classmates in every school you ever attended—and you attended a lot. Not only that, you shook off the loss of your father and long-time girlfriend to sleepwalk through NYU, with honors courses out the wazoo."

Angela waited, but Josie didn't respond. *They did dissect my background, after all.*

"Do you think there's anything about you that we don't know?" Angela asked. "I'm not saying this to frighten you or make you uncomfortable. I'm simply asking: is struggling to pay the rent of a leaky one-bedroom apartment with a girl who cheats on you really where you'd rather be right now?"

A rush of adrenaline made Josie clench a fist, breathing fast. Her vision narrowed on Angela's smirk. Dull pain spasmed in Josie's shoulder. *Hit her.*

"You don't know that," Josie said.

"What—that your girlfriend cheats on you?" Angela crossed her arms, unfazed. The elevator ticked up, almost there. "You're missing the point. You can be so much more. That's what's relevant here. Not that you failed, but that you still have an opportunity to win. You don't have to be that person anymore. You *aren't.*"

The elevator opened back to the same wraparound glass waiting area and timeline-illustration hall that fed back to Mr. Dean's office, his voice loud and rambling from the open door. Even here, it smelled like faint cigarette smoke.

"Go ahead," Angela said and blocked the elevator doors from closing.

No. Josie could still shove Angela aside, jam the lobby button, and run. This might be her only chance. Unless they locked the elevator. And if Josie took the stairs, would uniformed security be waiting at the bottom? And even if she got out, somehow slipped the trap or maybe called the police, what about Uncle Don? What about Mom? *What about my own fucking skin? I need more information. I need to know what I'm up against.*

I need to meet the Friendly Man.

The Eburos Group
PROFESSIONAL DEVELOPMENT

At Eburos, you are assessed according to a 360-degree feedback process and the firm's proprietary five-point performance management appraisal system: Goals, Response, Initiative, Network, Determination. The firm is committed to investing in opportunities that will allow you to flower, while pruning challenges that could stunt your growth. Your manager will provide you with regular feedback and discipline (F&D) in these key areas. For full-time living employees, all F&D includes carefully calibrated verbal and noninvasive techniques. Interested employees should consult their health provider for post-F&D services (see 'Reconstructive Surgery: Dos and Don'ts' in 'Choosing a Health Plan').

COMPANY HANDBOOK

Chapter Nineteen

Josie saw Mr. Dean leaning on his desk, with two large dogs at his feet, talking to a line of three suited men. The first dog—a huge, spotted Great Dane—watched her, its cropped ears perking when she neared the door. The second, a large, fluffy white Great Pyrenees, just panted and drooled.

"Ah!" Mr. Dean said and waved Josie over. "Grace, meet Mr. Landon."

They don't all have names?

White-haired, with a prominent bandage on his nose, the oldest of the three men shook her hand, while the other two—*his sons, maybe, both in their 30s*—nodded, smiling. They all wore nearly identical striped suits, with heavy, expensive-looking cufflinks and embossed buttons.

"This is her?" Mr. Landon asked.

"In the flesh," Mr. Dean said, with a half-wink at Josie. He took a fast drag on a half-done cigarette and noticed Angela. "Come in, come in. No complications?"

"Nothing worth mentioning," Angela said.

"Good. We were just discussing cowrie shells," Mr. Dean said. "Angela, I know you know this, but Grace, are you familiar with cowrie and traditions of potlatch?" He pivoted to scoop a handle of small, multi-colored seashells off the center of his desk. Beautifully striated, the shells looked like polished bulbs or jewels.

"Josie," Josie said. "My name is Josie, not Grace."

Mr. Landon cleared his throat. "Thank you, Solomon, we'll send over for signatures this afternoon." He led the two younger men out of the room. "Nice to meet you both."

Angela shut the door behind them and exchanged a quick, coded look with Mr. Dean.

"For three-thousand years, maybe longer, cowrie shells just like these were global currency." Mr. Dean offered the handful of shells to Josie, as if nothing had changed. "Don't tell the goldbugs or bitcoin bros, but there has only ever been one real currency. And it doesn't come in shell form. Hazard a guess as to what it is?"

Josie shook her head. *This is a mistake. I shouldn't be here.*

"Angela?" Mr. Dean smiled.

Angela nodded to Josie. "You," she said. "Me. Us."

"People," Josie said.

"Correct," Mr. Dean said. "People are the first and last currency. Portable, replicable, malleable." He sucked the cigarette, then tapped it out into a desk ashtray.

"Are you kidding?"

"No," he said. "People *are* currency. Most cultures have viewed them through that lens, which makes the anchor client worldview relatively ordinary from a transactional perspective."

"That's what your last meeting was about?" Josie asked, somehow keeping her voice level through the charge in her pulse. "Transactions of *people*? Are you seriously saying that's why they were in here?"

"*They?*" Mr. Dean asked, and he swiveled to plant the shells back in the center of his desk.

The wall where the Friendly Man chalk illustration had been was empty now. Distracted by the dogs, suit men, and ominous shell-conversation, Josie hadn't noticed right away. Fatigue weighed her down, making her left eye twitch, until she closed her eyes, opened them again. *I do need sleep. And food. Even if I tried to avoid it with Angela, I can't keep going like this much longer.* Exhaustion cut her thoughts into impatient clicks. *Get through this word, that movement, so I can lie down.*

"Yes, *they*," Josie said. "Mr. Landon and the other two men you were just talking to."

"There, you see!" Mr. Dean said, clapping his hands loud enough that the white dog jumped. "What did I say?"

"That is impressive," Angela said, nodding.

"What?" Josie said.

"There was only one," she said. "Just Mr. Landon. But he is a host, too. You saw his anchor client."

"There were two other men." She hadn't gotten a good look, barely registered them. "They didn't seem ..."

"Yes, yes," Mr. Dean said. "Mr. Landon's companion is known as Mr. Echo, for obvious reasons." He leaned against his desk to finger-lick flip through a binder beside the shells, as if already bored by the conversation. "Did you happen to notice the mouth of the other two gentlemen, who was, of course, really one gentleman imaged twice?"

"Their mouths?" Josie asked.

"Yes," Mr. Dean said. "From what I understand, what your predecessor described when she met him several years ago, Mr. Echo has three layers of denticles. Generally, only the outer layer is functional, with the rest being held in reserve, if there are any issues ..." He paused when he saw Josie's confused stared. "Denticles, Grace," Mr. Dean repeated. "Shark teeth."

"Josie," Josie said. "Not Grace."

Mr. Dean closed the desk binder, frowning. "Let's try to avoid this unnecessary pushback on optics."

"Your name—what we call you," Angela said. "It's Grace."

Josie stiffened. "My name is Josie."

"Fine," Mr. Dean said and blew cigarette smoke. "Take her out." When no one moved, he raised his eyebrows at Angela. "If she doesn't want to be here, let her go."

"I'm standing right here," Josie said. "You can talk to me."

Mr. Dean shifted to face her, the binder flat at his waist. Both dogs watched her now, as if waiting for a command.

"I didn't see this clarity in you when we first met. You have three choices: go, stay, or resist. This is only interesting if you stay."

"We left a girl under a cemetery on Dutch Island, and they put a heart into my chest ..." Josie trailed off. "You already know all that."

"Yes, of course. And you called, when you were injured." He nodded to her shoulder. "You aren't other people. You're one of us. But if you want to go back to the rules out there—if you want to be *owned* by your struggle to survive—then by all means ..." He gestured to Angela. "Open the door." She did, and he squinted at Josie, patting the binder rhythmically on his stomach. "Go. We won't stop you. Find another job, if that's what you want to do. *I* can't change your appearance back. For that to happen, you'll need to trust us. You'll need to work with us and honor your contract. But you don't think we have been fair, now is the time. Climb out of your trench and abandon the battlefield."

"You haven't explained any of this to me," Josie said.

"Yes, we have. Is this clear enough for you? You aren't *them*. You aren't other people anymore, because we know how special you are. Do they? Out there, how many employers recognize what you can contribute? And what does that mean, that contribution? You'll find out. You'll learn. How many species of shark lecture their young on the rules of the deep ocean?" He took an impatient breath, then another cigarette drag. "I'm proud of you, Grace. And yes, that is your name now. It's a dealbreaker. Call yourself whatever you want alone at night, but here, on the Maginot Line, we serve. Or ..." He looked at the open door again.

Walk out in someone else's skin, alone. That's not an option. But through the obvious, arrogant bullshit, the curl of his lecture-speak made the room feel less constrictive. *He really believes.* Possibilities and living to higher ideals, even if it meant faking a name for just awhile.

"We are here for you," Angela said.

"Are you staying?" Mr. Dean asked Josie. "Grace?"

They have Uncle Don. And Mom plans to sign, too. If Josie left now, she'd be cut off, no chance to follow and mend whatever came next. *I'll never be me again.*

But part of her said those thoughts were practiced, too. Explanations to convince herself that she wasn't here for the real reason. The real reason: they told her she was smart and unique and important, and dangled 00's on a contract that could unlock secret, elite floors in her life. A part of her wanted to tap open the banking app on her phone to see her checking account. Money wasn't something she expected. All her life, Josie assumed she would somehow slide into a similar path behind Mom. A small, livable apartment, a slow-moving career. Never terrified of poverty, but always conscious of spending. No vacations or luxuries, because those were for other people. *Say whatever you need to say, you're here for greed and ego.*

I'm not. I want to be me again. Both things could be true, maybe. *I want to escape and peel this back just a little more, see where it leads.*

Josie nodded. "You can call me Grace. If that's ..."

"Good." Mr. Dean brightened, tossed the binder. "Then let's begin." He crossed to the blank wall, where Josie had seen the chalk figure the first time. "Anything now?" Josie shook her head, and Mr. Dean nodded, as if he'd known but hoped to be surprised. "We know where he is. Even if he isn't visiting us now, we can visit him." Mr. Dean knocked on the wall, watching Josie, and when she confirmed that it was still empty, he shoved off, back toward the elevators.

"In the basement," Angela told Josie, "there's a …" She hesitated, as they caught up with Mr. Dean at the closed elevator doors. He tapped the down button, waited.

"These should really be faster," he said, shifting his weight back and forth. "If there were something urgent … Look into a dedicated lift, Angela. Make that a priority."

"That's no problem," Angela said.

"The word is the same in Dutch," Mr. Dean said absently.

"What word?" Josie asked.

"'*Kript*' or sometimes '*krocht*.' A bit of a misnomer. As far as I know, no one is buried here. In our crypt."

Elevator doors opened, and he exhaled loudly, hurrying in.

Angela pressed the bottom button, and they started down. Mr. Dean looked briefly at the silent, split-screen financial news anchors on the elevator monitor above the floor-button panel, before turning back to Josie.

"You'll be happy to know there are no colonial graves or Leni Lenape burial grounds under our feet," he said. "But the word *kript*, as it was used 400 years ago, was sometimes more general. Shorthand for 'an important place underground.'"

Like where we found Sandra.

"What's in it?" Josie asked.

"Did you bring the ball I gave you?"

The widow's eye. Josie had tried not to think about it. "No."

"Good." He rocked back against the wall to rub his back, focused on the elevator monitor again. "It would be surprising for you to be here like this, if you had."

"What does that mean?"

"That part *was* a test," Angela said.

"'Test' is a lazy word," Mr. Dean said. "We really have to do something about elevator speeds. This is unacceptable."

"On it," Angela said.

The elevator was moving fast, already almost to the lobby.

"If it was a test …" Josie said.

"A *tool*," Mr. Dean said. "Think of it as a packet of seeds. I handed it to you, because I wanted to see where you would plant them."

And I gave it to Dani.

"What is it?" Josie asked.

"Besides a toy ball?" Mr. Dean asked, with a smile. They dipped by the lobby into sub-basements, descending fast. "Where is it now?"

"I'm not sure." *With Dani. Almost certainly in her hand. She couldn't let it go.*

"That's okay," Angela said. "Wherever you left it, the ball will find its way back."

They passed B3, where Uncle Don probably still watched his home reno show. Almost to the unmarked bottom.

"You didn't answer me," Josie said. "What is it?"

"It has a bone inside," Mr. Dean said. When Angela blinked, as if surprised he'd actually answered Josie, he shrugged. "What?" he said. "I'm prepared to trust her now. Grace has a right to know." And to Josie, "Inside, it stores a piece of *him*. Not a big one, but each fragment is intrinsic to the totality of the whole. He will pull it back here eventually. The ball will roll in off the sidewalk or show up in an employee's pocket or in a parcel of mail. It will want to return to him. Like a dog called by its owner, if the dog were a fingerbone or femur fragment."

The elevator stopped.

"But we won't let it," he said. "Because we love our Friendly Man too much."

The doors opened, and a blast of chlorinated air hit Josie, stinging her eyes, as she stepped into a circular room. The walls were dense with standing desks and monitors flashing red-and-green stock market lines and numbers, around a circle of glowing blue water in the center of the floor. Like a diving pool lit by submerged aquatic wall lights, the round waterhole was maybe three meters across and too deep to see the bottom. Past the computer displays, the walls and domed ceiling were old foundation stones, notched together without cement. The floor dipped in narrow grooves cut through with black minerals that shimmered like crystal.

At the edge of the pool, Mr. Dean folded his hands, rocking slowly, until Angela and Josie stepped beside him. "All right," he told Josie. "Climb in."

She studied the empty pool. Below the underwater lights, watery stone dropped away into darkness. The water was too clear, and this close, the swimming pool chemical wreak burned her sinuses. The perimeter of the room hummed with the low ambient drone of computers.

A blob of water bled into the stone at her feet, like perspiration seeping up through the rock. It mottled into a single word: *'Want'*

Josie felt her guts clench. "What's that?"

Mr. Dean knelt by the word, and Angela's shadow swayed backwards. She stepped away. Mr. Dean cleared his throat, said, "Hmm. This is interesting."

That last word, 'interesting,' didn't sound like interesting, though. No, he pronounced it like, 'this is fucked.'

The water-word changed into a new shape, with an extra letter: *'Bleed'*

Not good.

"I'm going to go," Angela said quietly. "Is that okay, sir? Can I go?"

Josie checked the empty pool, then turned in a slow circle. *No one else here, but someone is watching us. Something is.* She felt a new pressure in the air, as if the room were holding its breath.

"It's been quite some time since he's done this," Mr. Dean said. "Do you recall, Angela? I think it must have been twelve years ago? Maybe longer, since we were *graced* with his direct communication, free of an intermediary."

"I'm supposed to talk to him?" Josie asked.

"That's right." Mr. Dean frowned at the word, *'Bleed,'* which already drained away. He stood again, stretching both arms like a cat. "We will start with three requests. In exchange for your visit today, I'd like you to ask him to weave ..."

"Weave?"

"Yes, when you're down there, when you see him, we'd like him to weave three items. First, he should weave a major deposit of rhodium near Mokopane, South Africa. Can you remember that?"

The words didn't make sense, not in this chlorine-drenched crypt, with ominous syllables appearing and disappearing on the stone. *What is he talking about?*

"Rhodium?" Josie said. "That's ..."

"Yes, yes, a rare earth metal," Mr. Dean said quickly, as if she were focusing on the wrong part. "Can you remember? Rhodium near Mokopane?"

"Okay," Josie said.

"Second, I'd like him to weave a sixty-percent drop in the value of the Argentine peso against the U.S. dollar. And third ..."

Josie checked Angela: no change. Pale and unmoving, Angela just stared at the pool in the floor, one arm clasped across her body to hold her opposite elbow, as if she were trying not to be sick.

"Sir," Angela said again, "can I ..."

"One moment," Mr. Dean snapped. "Third, Grace ..." He nodded from Josie to the pool. "... when you are down there, my third request is that he weave a historic flood in the Indian state of Assam."

"He can do all of that?" Josie asked.

"If you ask him," Mr. Dean said and took out a cigarette. "Will you remember? Do we need to rehearse a pneumonic device or ..."

"She's smart," Angela said quietly. "She'll remember."

"Yes," Mr. Dean said and found his lighter, hesitated, glancing past Josie at the humming equipment along the walls. "Hmm. For a moment, I thought I smelled ..."

"Can I ..?" Angela gestured back at the elevator.

"Yes, of course," Mr. Dean said. "Go ahead. You shouldn't stay."

He lit the cigarette, and a spark exploded in the air between them. Josie jumped, almost slipped into the pool. The spark flashed to a nearby computer monitor that burst and rocked forward, ripping wires from the wall in a torrent of electrical smoke. Another short pop on the right, and another behind by Angela. She jolted away, lost her footing and swung in a circle, like a drunken dance, toward the pool, both arms waving to catch her balance—Mr. Dean shouted, "Grab her, Grace!"—but Angela slipped backwards. A striated red worm leapt away from her. The size of a small dog, it streaked across the room on four stumped legs, flashed a sucker-shaped mouth and eyeless head back at Josie, and disappeared into the shadows along the wall. Angela hit the water and slipped under.

"What the fuck was that?" Josie asked, pointing after the worm. *It happened so fast, but yes, I saw it. An insect-like thing sprang off Angela before she touched the pool.*

"Natural gas. Not uncommon down here." Mr. Dean knelt at the edge of the pool, with Josie crouched beside him. "And I imagine you saw her anchor client."

Josie stared at the shadows around the corners of the room. No movement, but it must be there. In the pool, the swirling shape of Angela sank past the underwater lights and was gone. The cavern flickered to black, then back again. Lights in the ceiling and walls that Josie hadn't noticed dimmed. Computers still sputtered gray, foul-smelling electrical smoke.

"Her client?" Josie asked. "It was a *worm*."

Mr. Dean broke into a startled laugh and clapped her on the back too hard. She caught the edge of the pool.

"No one told me about your attitude. Fantastic. That's apex, Grace. One of the top four elements I try to stay attuned to."

The lights stuttered again.

"What happened?" Josie asked.

"I told you, likely a minor gas leak," he said, as if it were obvious. "There's ongoing construction in the area, and we are approximately one-hundred meters underground, after all."

"No, I mean why did that thing run away from her? That thing was her shadow, has been pulling her around? Where is it?"

"Nearby, I expect," Mr. Dean said simply. "It will reattach when she surfaces."

"Where is she? She can't stay under this long," Josie said. "No one can hold their breath like this."

"Angela?" Mr. Dean said and pulled himself up again. "Oh, I wouldn't worry about her." He adjusted his cigarette, still smoking—nevermind the natural gas leak explosion—then paused at the way Josie stared at the pool. "Is something else ..?"

"Wrong? Yes," Josie said, "That thing I saw wasn't a *shadow*, it looked like a parasite."

"Well, yes," he said. "It would be, wouldn't it?" He paced alongside the pool, oblivious to the electrical smoke or the fact that Angela should have surfaced by now.

"How is she alive down there?" Josie asked. "Aren't you worried ..."

"She isn't," Mr. Dean said. "Obviously, Angela is not alive down there, no. Now are you ready? Do you recall our three asks for the Friendly Man today?"

"I remember what you said." And when he raised his eyebrows expectantly, she said, "Rare minerals in South Africa ..."

"Rhodium near Mokopane," he said. "Yes, go on."

"The Argentine peso ..."

"To drop sixty percent against the U.S. dollar. Yes, and number three? We ask that he weave a historic flood in the Indian state of Assam. Very good."

"So he grants wishes?" Josie asked. "Is that it?"

Mr. Dean shrugged impatiently. "That's not an incorrect characterization. But a more precise term of art is 'weaving.' He *weaves*."

"And each time I go in, you get three wishes? Three *weavings?*"

He sucked the cigarette, so the tip flared and smoked, burning down a layer of ash. "That's just for the sake of symmetry. Three is a powerful number to initiate a new relationship. Your relationship with him." Mr. Dean stepped closer. "I need you to get in the pool now, Grace. He won't hurt you. You'll need to swim down as deep as you can. Then, you deliver our three asks. Understand?"

Josie eased her legs over the side, until the warm water rose above her shoes to her calves.

"He can't come out?" she asked.

"No, he can't," Mr. Dean said, his voice clipped. "Go ahead."

"I don't know ..."

"You do," Mr. Dean said. "You're here. He wants to see you. You're safe, Grace. Into the pool, then out of the pool: a dance we'll rehearse again and again. One week from now, one month from now, one *year* from now you won't even think twice about dropping in to see him. That first step is always the hardest. That first million requires real sacrifice, otherwise everyone would be rich, wouldn't they? This is your opportunity."

He moved directly behind her, as if he might shove her in. Josie willed herself not to brace against him. *He won't push me. Unless I'm not supposed to come back. Unless it's a lie, and he doesn't need me after this.*

Mr. Dean rocked on his heels, his knees almost knocking against her back. "It's time. This is your hand, no one else's. Play your cards. This moment is what makes you exceptional."

What's down there? Josie slipped over the side and went under. *The water will be empty. There won't be ...*

She opened her eyes: there was.

Book Reviews

The Most Important Company You've Never Heard Of: The Eburos Group
by Jonathan McMannis

The Eburos Effect

For decades, The Eburos Group has flown under the radar for most people, despite its profound impact on global markets and governments. The firm is associated with professionalism and prestige, and, as the late author, Jonathan McMannis, writes, "no small degree of secrecy, as Eburos does not disclose information about its clients or activities." Through off-the-record interviews and a careful review of publicly available data, McMannis offers a snapshot of an organization that is as obsessed with quality as confidentiality. Although many of his insights are not new—such as arguing that "Eburos is aggressive about recruitment at top business schools, law schools, and across certain trades, such as meat science and blood banking and transfusion programs"—McMannis offers tantalizing hints at more: "Many research findings for this book, including from confidential interviews, were unfortunately rejected by its publisher. After publication, I will be speaking openly about these matters" ... a promise cut short by the author's untimely passing two days before publication.

295 PAGES

Chapter Twenty

Josie sank fast, and the water stopped. She dropped out of the pool onto a slick floor in a chamber that misted with yellow, green, orange, and peppery red clouds. The air tasted like harsh soot and char. Somehow, the pool suspended overhead now. That circular funnel of blue liquid hung in the ceiling above her, linking this room with the basement cavern, where it had been in the floor. Around the edges of the water, sinewy wood clung to the overhead stone, too thick to be vines and wrong-way-up for tree roots. Even through the colorful, frothy air, it looked organic. *Like the lobby.* The color of the wood resembled the new snarled branches that ringed the main corporate lobby. *And the tree people on Dutch Island.*

Movement on her right: Josie spun, waving away the colorful fog, and in a sudden clearing saw Angela, slumped and holding her head. Her body was rotten. Eyes gone in shriveled sockets, nose missing in gaping skull-holes, and her lips peeled away, Angela's face had sunken into decaying flesh. Her hair remained, but everything else wasted away. Dripping from the pool, her suit coat, blouse, skirt, and shoes, every inch of her outfit still looked spot-on. A corpse in the latest fall fashion.

Angela stirred, started to sit up. *Shit, she's alive. Like the others.*

Behind Josie, a soft male voice said, "You're here."

The water in the ceiling hung two meters up. *How am I supposed to climb back out?*

Across the chamber, a figure approached through the spooling air. With stuttered clanking and scraping movements, colors swirled and parted around it. *Him.* It was a man ... no, the *shape* of a man created by a confusion of cobbled-together sections. Above feet of bristling, broken glass, seashells wrapped in overlapping layers to create legs that connected to knees made of multicolored plastic. More shells and shiny coins made thighs, and his groin and gut swarmed with uneven rings of silver and gold. Above that, his chest swelled with the domes of jawless skulls, and more bones layered in patterns to shape shoulders and arms. Shriveled eyeballs encircled his neck like a mass of jewels below a black bag, tied down with wire to hide his face. The bag sucked and pulled with heavy breathing.

As the figure approached, a hive of wooden stalks flexed on his back. Tree trunks curled up and out of him, flowing into the walls and ceiling, where they melded with root systems in viny constellations. *As if he's a plant.* The absurd seed-heart infecting this entire building. Through all the pieces of bone and gold and shells, it was impossible to see whether there was anyone under it. Any*thing*, creature—whatever the fuck this was. *The Friendly Man.*

"I think about you all the time," he said.

"You're him," Josie said. She heard a tremor in her voice but wasn't as afraid as she should have been. Terror hunkered somewhere deep in her mind and veins, ready to burst. She might panic, but now she kept her breathing level, stared back at him. No running or screaming or trying to climb out. "You're the Friendly Man?"

"I try to be," he said. "Do you ever miss me?"

Josie couldn't look away from the thing. *Do I ..? How could I? What the fuck are you ..?*

Angela's voice rasped, "Say 'yes,'"

Josie looked back at her corpse, half-propped against the wall, with one gnarled, skeletal hand holding her up. "You're alive."

"No."

"What happened to you? You fell through the water and …"

"Do you ever miss me, Grace?" the Friendly Man asked again. The black bag around his head sucked and inflated again in the shape of a mouth. "I think about you all the time."

"Say you miss him," Angela said softly.

"I miss you," Josie told the Friendly Man. "Okay? There are three things Mr. Dean told me to ask you …"

"Of course," he said. "Anything."

"He wants you to weave," Josie said.

He stepped closer, shells, bone, and metal rattling and whining up-and-down his body.

When Josie started to back away, Angela said, "No. Stay there."

Let him approach? Stand here and talk to this thing about the price of the fucking Argentine peso?

"You're not the same," he said and lifted his left arm, then sagged, shoulders drooping, as if disappointed. "I wish I could hold you. Tell me something true and good about this new you. Tell me who Grace is now."

"I met the other girl," Josie said. "The one who looked like this before." *Whose heart I'm carrying now.* "We left her on Dutch Island. I don't know her name."

"Tell me about *this* life," he said. "*This* girl."

Something true and good about my life.

From the floor, Angela said, "This only works … because he loves you."

This monster, whatever the fuck it is, 'loves' me? What did I expect? A chalk figure on the wall that mutates into something terrible. Not this ruined thing asking about my life, as if it's nothing but lonely.

And my life? My life is ... my life derailed, flew into a sideways pitch off the side of the road before this. I don't fucking know.

"I have people who care for me," Josie said. "I have ..."

What? Friends? Is that even true now? What friends? Everett disappeared, and Dani? She might not even be in the apartment anymore. No texts or calls. Mom and Uncle Don, though. They love me. That's not at risk, except ... except they love Josie. Not Grace. They don't know Grace. Josie felt nervous tears in her eyes. Surprised, she reached to wipe them, and he stepped closer, his right hand up to her shoulder. She smelled buttery meat under the burnt stink of the room.

"I love you," he said. "I told you. As long as you live."

Josie tried to blink the tears away, sniffed more charcoal-smelling air and the blood scent of him. "I'm okay, just confused. I don't know why ..."

"Cry. I accept your tears. You don't have to hide from me."

Josie wanted to lean into him, relax and just stop struggling. *Insane. Close your eyes against the moldy skull bones covering this monster's chest ...* but she did. Josie slumped forward, and as he put his one arm around her, she shook, tears welling up. She cried. *I failed. I have no friends. My family doesn't know me. I grew up—everything Mom and Dad did for me—so I could have promise. So much I was supposed to do and become. I was their hope. They sacrificed and believed in me, and I've done nothing. I've barely survived, so I can be abused by this company. And I said 'yes.' I agreed to this.* Her back shaking with sobs, Josie cried harder. Bones pressed against her cheek and forehead, but it didn't matter.

Finally, he slid his hand away, and Josie pulled back, still wiping her face. She knew her eyes and nose were probably swollen red, tasted snot on her lips.

"What shall I weave?" he asked.

"I can't believe I did that," Josie said. "You asked one question, and I lost it. I don't believe this is happening. That I'm here, like this ..."

"It's okay. You and I are more than they'll ever understand." He breathed in a rhythmic huff-pull through the bag. "I know how they think. I know what they believe in. The Red Warrior, Maggie Powers, Solomon Dean—I know. But my love doesn't care. Ask me to weave, but before you do, what can I have?"

Still off-balance from that jut of emotion—*who are my friends*—Josie didn't register his question. "What?"

"We usually start with a part of her childhood." He tapped Josie's right pinky finger. "Like an extremity she doesn't use. She won't miss those early years. That's an easy place to begin. What is her name?"

Josie couldn't move. Both legs stiff, arms slack, she heard water hitting stone from the ceiling. *He wants to take my childhood. Is that what he said?*

"I'm not upset," the Friendly Man said. "I know you have to change each time. Find a new person with a different story."

He's talking to me as if I'm Grace, strangling the real me. No, I'm still me. Still Josie.

"She feels strong," he said. "Does she have scars she's hiding? Experiences she doesn't want? Her father, maybe? Most girls have fathers they can forget. Is that true for this new girl?"

"You want to take a part of me?" Josie asked. "Part of Josie?"

His head-bag sucked violently, as if he were gasping inside. "Josie. That's a nice name," he said. "Yes. I'll cut out a piece today. And each time you return, I'll take more. Not all at once. Until you are Grace again."

Cut out parts of me, memories trimmed like flowers—or fingers—until I stop being Josie. Is that it? Little by little, take me apart, until I'm the person he wants me to be.

Josie dragged her left foot back, then her right, and he tracked her, mimicking the movement, with a scrape of shells along his legs. His glass feet crinkled and snapped.

From the floor, Angela flexed her jaw, thin sinews and muscle stretching through flaps in her skin. "Do what he says."

"No," Josie said. "I don't want to forget my life. Just because ..."

"Does Josie remember her life?" the Friendly Man asked. "Are there things she's hiding, wants to forget? Let me cut them out of her brain. She won't miss them."

He's right. I don't remember everything. Don't want to. But those hollowed out parts of my past, they're still me, aren't they?

"I need to go," Josie said.

"Not yet," the Friendly Man said. "What will you give me? You decide on the part. But an exchange, I must have an exchange ..."

"No," Josie said again. "I don't want to. You're not taking part of Josie—part of me. I'm leaving."

He stopped, slouching again in a ruined stance, like a prisoner. *And that's what he is, isn't it? Trapped down here.* "If you don't, I won't weave. Nothing for him." Josie started to answer back that she didn't care, and he lurched forward. She staggered into the wall, knocking a foot against Angela, who scratched with the backs of her boney arms to slowly pull upright, leaning on the wall.

"I'll *tear*," the Friendly Man said, voice rising. "Not weave. I will *rend* and *rip*. Is that what you want? Where did they leave the last girl? Dutch Island? Those were your words. I'll *tear* it."

"Don't do this, Grace," Angela said. "Please, you have to."

Josie watched Angela stagger to her feet on the wall beside her. "Don't threaten me, Angela."

"Not threatening," Angela said. "Look at me. How could I? I'm warning you …"

"Will you let me cut?" the Friendly Man asked. "Will you make an exchange?"

"No," Josie said again. "I'm not trading anything with you. No part of Josie. None."

She breathed fast in the granular, multicolored air, just three steps from the dripping ceiling. *Climb and swim out. How?* This wasn't possible, none of it. *If I jump, grab the stone along the inside bottom of the pool … What? Pull myself up somehow?* No, even with her rowing routine, no way could she leverage her body up with a grasp on that almost-flat wall. But the water, if she reached the water, couldn't she use the tension of the suspended pool to swim *up* and through it?

Two meters up, with her shoulder still weak from the gunshot wound. *No … wait.* Her shoulder didn't … She pressed the top of her shirt aside to check the bandage and—no bandage. Just blank, clear skin.

"My wound is gone," Josie murmured.

Angela's corpse quivered against the wall, like it couldn't quite stand but was managing somehow. "What?"

"The gunshot wound, from Tommy—I told you, he shot me."

"No," Angela said. "I don't know what you mean. Stop this, Grace. Give him what he wants."

Think about the wound later. Magically healed. No, not just 'healed,' gone. As if it was never there. No bandage or gauze or scar. Nothing. Did the water do something? Is it this room?

The Friendly Man drew a sliver of glass from his back, as if it had been lodged in his flesh. Cutting and tearing, not a metaphor at all.

"Stop," Josie said.

Angela shuffled away from the wall toward the pool, her skeletal left foot bending backwards on a snapped ankle bone. Her head lolled to the side, thin ribbons of flesh along her neck struggling to keep it aimed back at Josie. *Signaling. Signaling what?*

"It won't hurt," he said. "And when your head closes again, you'll see." He leveled the blade at Josie's face. Too close, if he jabbed, she might not be able to dodge. "I'll find something she doesn't want. A tiny piece of meat she won't even miss. Did Josie see the shadow creatures before coming here? The ones he calls 'clients.' She must have, all her life, or she wouldn't be here. She wouldn't want to remember them, would she?"

And suddenly Josie did remember. Snatches and bursts of frozen images: a burning fleshless man by a gas pump, a misshapen fish person with a mean-looking blade in her kitchen, a larva woman with drooping features inside a restaurant. *Anchor clients.* Breathing hard, Josie knocked the back of her head against the wall, away from the Friendly Man. He kept his blade poised, level with her vision. *He's right, I've seen them all my life.* Now, even as the horror show images faded, the after-outlines lingered when she closed her eyes. Memories of memories. *This madness isn't just happening now. This isn't the first time. Angela's worm-shadow and Noah, a boy who fell apart in front of me, and Sandra and her demon kid, Samuel. A kitchen full of living corpses. I've seen these things my whole life, blocked them out. Look away from the dead person who shouldn't be there. Don't notice the monster at the end of the hall. So automatic, I don't even realize I'm doing it, but I am. I did.*

Those are the memories he wants. Things I've blocked out, walled over. Trauma. A lifetime of seeing things that shouldn't be there, that aren't *there.*

Except they are.

"Meat believes it matters," the Friendly Man said. "And that's what Josie is, isn't she? Meat. Does she want me to show her the folds inside her skull? Would she like to cup her own brain fluid in her palms?"

A cold knot spread in Josie's chest, making it harder to breathe. *Fucking move.* But she couldn't.

"She cried because she is alone." A hoarse chuckle shook his face bag. "Does she want to feel connected? That's what she wants, isn't it? Meaning and purpose. When I chew and digest parts of Josie, her meat will have purpose. To reveal Grace."

Josie eased slowly to the side, toward Angela and the ceiling pool.

"Some meat is stubborn," he said. "Does she think she is the first to say 'no'?" Another ugly, rasping laugh, and Josie took another slow step away from the wall, circling him. Slowly. "The last girl said 'no,' too. She was already half-gone, when she refused. Couldn't even remember the sound of her sister's voice."

The last girl, the Hispanic girl from the cemetery. She did what I'm doing right now, is that it? She stopped placating this thing, and they left her with a cemetery monster. We left her.

"Josie is meat with a face," the Friendly Man said. "Does she really believe she is different? Stronger? Does she see these?" He patted the shrunken eyeballs netted around his throat and then traced down to the skulls. "And this?" He gestured to the coins, rings, plastic, and shells. "Everything the others tried. Every time they say 'no' and ask for a different exchange, I take something from them. But really they all want the same thing Josie does. Even if they won't admit it, and I have to teach them. They *want* me to cut them open. They *want* me to wear them." He circled a finger around a layer of joints at his shoulder. "Doesn't Josie *want* to be a part of me, too, so she can be Grace?"

"You're a prisoner here," Josie murmured.

"Said the mouse to the snake."

Almost to the edge of the overhead pool, Josie could spring up, grab a notch or something, and climb. *Into the water. Insane, but I have to fucking try.*

"After I take my piece of Josie," the Friendly Man said. "When we smile at each other across the bloody nubs, then I will weave. You can tell me what he wants this time. And then, when you return tomorrow, we will do it *again* ..." He knocked the glass against the gold on his stomach in time with the word. "... and again ..."

Go. Now.

Josie tensed her legs, arms steady, fingers open.

"... and again ..."

Angela fell to a shaky kneel, ruined arms crossed at her waist directly below the pool. *What is she ... a perch. She wants me to jump.* Angela propped both hands upright, ready to boost Josie up into the water hole.

The Friendly Man sucked through his face bag. "What are you doing?" But he didn't move, the blade still steady in one hand. "Grace, I love you. I only want you back. We have to cut away the other meat around you. Like a statue in marble. Find your face inside her pieces."

"Josie pieces," Josie murmured. "Right? That's what you want to cut out."

"I gave you everything," he said. "All of it up there. My love, Grace, I ..."

"I'm not coming back here," Josie said. "Maybe I'll find a way to kill this fake person, Grace, too. Would you like that?" The words slipped out. Reflexive anger.

"Don't say that," Angela whispered.

"You will *not*," he said, huffing through the bag. The blade trembled, and he shuffled, almost like a child on the verge of a tantrum. "If you harm my love, I will sever every cord ..."

Josie planted a foot on Angela's hands and leapt up, driving Angela's corpse to the ground with the momentum. The Friendly Man shouted—"...back the way it was!"—and Josie's hands, arms, now her head and shoulders hit the water in a shock. She extended both arms up, blinking in the blurry swell for anything along the edge—*there.* She reached for a round, white light fixture in the underwater wall, and as she grabbed it and pulled, the rest of her body rose into the water. *The water in front of you. Only focus on this. Pull. Higher.* Suddenly buoyant, Josie leveraged herself up along the wall, kicking hard with both legs, as if she were in the deep end of a pool.

She surfaced in the same chamber, with Mr. Dean still smoking over her. An alarm blared, lights flashing behind him. A small fire spread along the computer equipment by the wall, spurting white, chemical smoke. Somehow, he focused only on her. "What did you do?" Mr. Dean shouted over the noise. "What in the blazes happened down there?"

Josie hauled herself up, dripping. She panted, but the swim had been quick, almost easy. The chlorinated water stilled below. No sign of Angela or the Friendly Man.

"Did you ask him to weave?" Mr. Dean asked louder, body tense, eyes hard on her. "Did you remember what we talked about? A rhodium deposit and the Argentine peso and ..."

"And a flood in India," Josie said. "I remembered."

"And?"

"He wanted to cut me apart." She started to stand, but he stood too close, blocking her. "He wanted ..."

"You didn't reach an agreement?" Mr. Dean said quickly. "Unacceptable. Go back in. Now."

The high-pitched alarm blared in a one-two-one sequence, repeating fast, and a section of black stone to the right of the elevators clicked and swayed open to reveal a blue-painted concrete stairwell. A security guard shouted from the stairs, "Sir, we need you upstairs!"

Still focused on Josie, Mr. Dean flicked the cigarette at him off-handedly, as if he were a gnat. "Get back down there, Grace. If he wants to trim Josie back, that's fine. That's what we're here for."

'Trim Josie back?' Are you fucking serious?

"Sir!" The security guard jogged closer. "Sir, the fire department has asked us to clear the building. We can't ..."

"Tell them to fine me," Mr. Dean snapped, and to Josie, "Go back in!"

Josie shook her head, still out of breath. "If it's a gas leak ..."

"Get in the water, Grace." Mr. Dean finished his cigarette, glared briefly at the security guard. "What is the danger exactly?"

"We've been advised," the security guard said slowly, with a tense glance from Mr. Dean to the burning equipment. "There is a nontrivial risk of deflagration, sir. If you don't meet with them now, they're threatening to call the mayor's office about the company's licenses ..."

Because you were smoking. Because you couldn't help bringing a cigarette down here.

Mr. Dean glared at her, as if she'd said that out loud. "*He* did this." And stomped away with the security guard, waving Josie on after them. "We'll be brief. Eight minutes up to the lobby, fifteen minutes to solve for the incendiaries, twelve minutes to restart the HVAC, and then eight minutes back down here. Do you understand? I want you in that pool in no more than forty-three minutes."

In the stairwell, the alarm echoed even louder, and wall mounted lights flashed white and red above the landings. A pre-recorded voice said, *"Fire. Fire. Proceed to the nearest exit immediately. Fire. Fire…"*

Josie followed Mr. Dean and the security guard up to the first landing, then another. Passing the third landing, Mr. Dean asked her, "What happened down there?"

"I saw Angela," Josie said. "She wasn't…"

The alarm voice swallowed her words.

Josie closed both ears with her hands and shouted, "She looked dead. But she wasn't…"

Mr. Dean nodded impatiently, and the security guard gestured that they should continue up. "Yes, yes. But the Friendly Man," he said. "Did you tell him what we agreed to?"

Get out. Get out of the building and run. That thing under the water won't turn me back, he wants to slice out my memories. Get as far away from this place as possible.

"It happened fast," Josie said.

"Grace, if your conversation was not productive, it is imperative I know the details, so the company can plan accordingly."

They stomped up more flights. Josie lost track of how far, none of the doors were marked, but they must be close. More than eight minutes already.

Josie shook her head. "Not super productive, no."

Also, fuck you.

"It's very important that you tell me the truth about everything that happened," Mr. Dean said. "Not just for the company, but for your own safety…" The alarm cut him off again, and the security guard opened an ordinary-looking wooden door labeled, *'Main Level.'* Beyond, lines of people crowded the lobby, filing out the front doors under more flashing red-and-white lights and the same blaring alarm.

Uniformed guards waved people out the security turnstiles, ushering them through the outer doors onto the rainy nighttime sidewalk. A group of firemen in heavy outfits, complete with helmets, oxygen tanks, and axes chatted with staff at the front desk.

"Stay here," Mr. Dean said. He ran for the desk, already waving at them.

Josie slipped away from the security guard to the outer rim of people clustered by the front windows. Men and women in collared shirts and suits chatted casually, in no hurry to rush out, unaffected by the ringing alarm.

"... and I just said, 'well gosh darn it, Jim, that's no way to treat a mannequin!'" Through the crowd, Josie tracked the familiar voice to Maureen, as a small crowd burst into laughter around her. Maureen wore a bright yellow Easter sweater, with a stitched poodle in a bunny costume, and now, when Josie made eye contact, Maureen blinked with confused recognition. "Well, look at you. Grace, you look positively radiant. Did they make another change ..?"

Get out of here. Somehow slip past all of them.

Behind her, someone shouted, "Josie!"

And Maureen lit up, hurrying over. "Ah ha! I knew it, you workaholic rascal!"

This is it. Run? Sprint—try to get out. Josie turned back to find whoever had called her ... Uncle Don limped over quickly, still in a plush robe and slippers. Smiling, he caught her elbow and pressed her toward the exit.

"So glad I bumped into you, dear." Maureen grabbed Josie's other arm to pull her to a stop. "I was just bragging about your registration time, and wouldn't you know it, guess what we found on the floor of Beth's office?"

"Maureen, I've got to ..."

But Maureen's grip tightened, and she smiled harder, one hand into her pocket—*to stab me, who knows*—and she slapped a metal key into Josie's palm. *My apartment key. It must have ...* "You see?" Maureen said and let go. "Talk about making a good first impression! That's dedication. You haven't even gone home yet, have you? And I bet you didn't even know you dropped it?"

"No, I ..."

"Well, scoot, scoot." Maureen said, shooing Josie away, with a wink. "Don't let me stop you, *Grace*."

Uncle Don guided Josie to the exit doors.

Don't look back.

"Uncle Don?" she murmured. "How did you know it was me ..?"

"My heart is broken," he said, "not my brain."

A beefy security guard watched by the doors, and Josie met his stare, smiled back.

"Just a drill, right?" she said.

The guard nodded, forced an uneasy smile back. "Never know. Too many flammable assets to risk it." He glanced up, and she followed his stare. Directly above the main doors and windows, what had been lush greenery just hours ago now browned and withered, as if the entire plant system needed water. *Suddenly dying.* In new gaps between the collapsing leaves, Josie saw human shapes imprinted in the bark: the curl of an arm, the crease of a stomach and chest, and there, frozen in the wooden branches, almost close enough to touch, a grimacing, familiar face: Everett.

The Eburos Group
BENEFITS & PERKS

Employee health is vital to firm health. All full-time living employees are eligible for a comprehensive benefits package that includes health, dental, and vision coverage, as well as life and afterlife insurance; disability, possession, and reanimation insurance; and paid family leave. After six months of service, employees in good standing will have the option to enroll in the firm 401(k) retirement plan and soul forfeiture schedule. At six months, the employee's soul will be 25 percent harvested and employee equity grant will be vested by a corresponding 25 percent. The soul forfeiture and equity vesting schedule then continues at a rate of 15 percent every six months. Termination prior to total vesting and forfeiture results in all equity returned to the company, with soul forfeiture continuing in perpetuity. The 401(k) retirement plan is managed by Charles Schwab.

COMPANY HANDBOOK

Chapter Twenty-One

Outside, Uncle Don led her around a corner, shrouded by scaffolding. No sign of Mr. Dean behind them, but any second he would step out. They had to keep moving. *Don't think about Everett. The shock of his face in the wood didn't seem real. Because it wasn't real. It wasn't him. You're projecting. Mr. Dean will come for me. That is real, focus on that.*

Josie flagged a yellow cab that stopped in the rainy street, so the driver could roll down his window. "I'm off," he called. "Going far?"

"Brooklyn," Josie said. "Flatbush."

She started to give him her address when he waved them in. "Fine—going that way anyway."

In the taxi, Josie watched out the rear window for any sign of security or Mr. Dean. Still nothing, and they sped through two green-light intersections, logging more and more distance. *Good.*

"Are you okay?" Josie asked Uncle Don. "The surgery ..."

"It hurts, but yes, I'm fine," he said. "They wanted me to sign all kinds of papers. I didn't."

"They want Mom to sign up, too," Josie said.

"I know. She told me. An amazing amount of money ..." He shook his head and watched storefronts flash by in the cloudy light outside. "If something seems too good to be true ... I don't have to tell you."

"No." Josie rubbed her face, tried to fight the pull of the backseat cushions. The cab was lumpy with springs and stank like pizza grease, but her back and shoulder muscles relaxed into it. "It's been a really long day."

"Was it surgery?" Uncle Don asked. "Is that what they did to make you look like this?"

"No." Josie's mind fogged, thoughts stuttering, as adrenaline sapped into exhaustion. She didn't have a plan, not really. Get home, and then?

"Can you tell me what happened?"

Josie felt another slow tug of tension in her belly. *A demon woman under a cemetery on Dutch Island traded my heart for another, with a mystical bone flute. So I could be a sacrifice to the Friendly Man. Pretend to be a girl he's in love with, so he can manipulate reality for the company. Or something.* "Not really," she said. "It doesn't make sense. I don't want to say 'magic,' but it feels like magic." *And not in a good way.*

"Yeah," he said at last.

Crossing the Brooklyn Bridge, Josie traced the lights of the city through the dark rain on her window. Since moving to New York at the start of high school, Josie had seen a constant series of construction cranes ever-changing the skyline, like insects reimagining the shape of their hive. It was the same city, but recent buildings on both sides of the East River might have jarred someone visiting for the first time after several years.

No, it is the same. I know this town.

Color streaked over the river, cross-trails of chalky light, like ethereal suspension lines. Gone, then back again. Maybe the movement of the taxi shifted her perspective, so the light strands reflected tiny snatches of rain. She rubbed her eyes, and as the cab switched lanes, closer to the Brooklyn exit, the air looked empty again. *Because they weren't there.* The taxi banked into a turn off the bridge, merging with traffic in a roundabout, surrounded by new glass condo towers. *Those colors were the same shimmery, bright tones from below the water. The misty light surrounding the Friendly Man.*

Mr. Dean wanted him to 'weave,' didn't he? *That's what all this is about.* And those lines could have been 'string' over the East River. Invisible, hallucinogenic fabric. She closed her eyes and took a slow breath. Steady in, then back out. *I need to sleep.* There were no magic 'strings' across the river. *If anything, my brain is still scrambled from running, without pause. Maybe Dani will be better. Even if she's gone, that means I can rest in our apartment. Regroup.*

The taxi wound through low, residential Brooklyn neighborhoods to finally stop outside Josie's apartment building. Uncle Don handed the driver a wad of cash—"I wouldn't let them take my wallet," he said—and they went up to the stoop. *What will Dani say? What should I say? She hasn't sent me one word since all this started.*

Inside, they stopped outside Josie's door. *Here goes.* She pressed in her key, but it wouldn't turn. *Something wrong with the lock.* Josie tried again. *Maureen gave me the wrong key, that's all.*

"Are you okay?" Uncle Don asked. He was breathing hard from the walk up to Josie and Dani's second-floor door. "We don't have to stop here, if you don't want to."

"No, I brought us here ..."

"I know. Just with the accusations in the news about her followers—sorry, I know she doesn't call them that," Uncle Don said. "The 'movement' or 'family'? I can't remember the terms ..."

Josie started to smile. *Absurd: what the hell is he talking about?* "Do you feel okay, Uncle Don?"

"Me?" He shrugged. "Of course—I told you. But your 'prophet' might not recognize you looking like this. And you know I wasn't exactly welcomed with open arms the last time."

"Last time what?" Josie heard movement inside, the leaning creak of the kitchen floor on the other side of the door. So Dani *was* home. "Honestly, I have no idea what you're talking about, but I have to knock, because my key isn't ..."

The door opened on a skinny guy and girl, dressed in matching black robes. Past them, fake electric candlelight cast lumpy, bulging shadows up the too-dark kitchen wall, as if the whole place had been replastered or covered in amateur wallpapering.

"Who's this?" the guy asked.

"Who are you?" Josie said and stepped closer. They closed to block the doorway.

"Oh no you don't," the girl said. "It's vespers."

"Let me in," Josie said. "I live here."

They looked at each other, smirking.

"Live here?" the guy said, his arm shaking as he held the door. "No, I don't think so." He nodded to Uncle Don. "What about him—he live here, too? Nice robe, guy. No press, no police. Both of you, turn around and walk back where you came from."

She couldn't get through without shoving them. They weren't going to make a path. Josie heard noises on either side. A grunt from the right-hand living room, and a woman called, "Shut the door."

"A girl and another cop dressed in a weird bathrobe," the door-guy leaned back in to answer. "We'll shove them back to the wild."

"You'll let me into my fucking apartment," Josie said.

"*Your* apartment?" the door-guy said. "I already told you the prophet is asleep ..."

"Wait." The girl approached, raising a flashlight. The beam blinded Josie, until she flinched away, blinking white spots. The girl aimed the light at Uncle Don. "I've seen him before."

"Where?" the door guy said.

"Social media. He knows the prophet."

"Of course I know her," Uncle Don said and sighed. "Can we ..?"

The girl backed away, and the door guy followed, shaking his head. They whispered in the empty kitchen, as Josie stepped in. *What happened to the table and chairs?* Their furniture and counter-top appliances were all gone, replaced by random electric candles that flickered along all the walls into the living room—except it wasn't the living room anymore. The floor crowded with sleeping bags in three crammed rows, like cloth sausages, and no sign of the couch, bookcases, or TV.

What the fuck?

Josie counted fifteen people, most asleep. On Josie's left, the hall to the bedroom and bath was empty, but here, too, all the walls were darker than they should have been, with chunky paint streaks beneath unfamiliar picture frames.

"What is this?" Josie murmured. Voices from the living room, and people shifted on the floor. "Who are you?"

"Servants of the truth," the girl said quietly.

"This isn't a good idea," Uncle Don said. "They don't recognize you."

"How *could* they recognize me, even if I was the old me?" Josie said, and to the girl and door guy, "Why are you two here—who are all these people? Where's Dani?"

They traded a quick look.

"The prophet is asleep," the door guy said.

Josie started down the hall, paused at the closed bedroom door. "Is she in here?" Silence beyond.

"Maybe this isn't the best thing right now," Uncle Don said.

What am I supposed to do? Leave? Yes. Get out, don't go deeper into this. These people aren't supposed to be here. And Uncle Don is acting like I should understand.

A photo beside the bedroom showed Dani smiling, as she shook the President's hand, a semi-circle of Middle Eastern men in traditional white robes and headpieces around them. There was a date: September of last year.

Bullshit. I was with Dani here in college then. She never met the President. We prepped senior year every minute of every day that year. She barely left my sight.

Another photo a little further down showed Dani on a stage, shaking an old guy's hand, receiving some kind of oversized, globe-shaped award. It was dated December of last year. *Another forgery.* And across from that, Dani at an outdoor table surrounded by grinning celebrities with a palm tree, blue ocean, and jungle-mountain backdrop. The date: last February. *Except.* In the photo, Josie grinned, mid-laugh, wearing an Eburos-logo bikini and frilly white sun shawl on Dani's right. *Cute shawl, though.*

Josie stared at herself. *Not me. Photoshopped. Someone framed a bunch of fakes.* The surreal assembly of actors and corporate executives around Dani and Josie at the tropical table looked like a joke. *What if it isn't?* Whoever made these images wanted them to feel plausible. *The guy and girl in the kitchen ... the sleeping bag people in the living room ..?*

Josie swallowed and glanced back at Uncle Don. He was right, they could still walk out. She didn't have to open the bedroom door, no need to push this, whatever it was. Her stomach bubbled with nausea, but too empty to make her sick. She felt drained. *This isn't real.* But that was even less convincing. Whatever this was, it was here, now.

Leave.

"Do you understand this?" Josie asked Uncle Don.

He looked from her to the wall-photos, then back. "I'm not sure what you're asking."

Josie knocked on the bedroom door. A still silence. The wall was moving. Not a lot, but as she stood here, the bumpy dark plaster drifted in a slow clot around the Dani-President photo, like mud or clay. *This is not okay.*

Josie banged again and tried the doorknob. It turned.

THE EBUROS GROUP
Saint Madeira Corporate Retreat

All week: Breakfast at Leisure; Lunch at Villa; Dinner offsite TBD

MONDAY | Morning: State of the Union; Afternoon: Overview of New HR Policies and Procedures and coworking time; Evening: Icebreaker Game: "Greatest Fears"

TUESDAY | Morning: Intro to Ops Process Documentation; Afternoon: Company Values Exercise and Bloodletting; Evening: Surf and Turf Catamaran Day

WEDNESDAY | Morning: Intro to Role Scorecards; Afternoon: Scavenger Hunt Briefing and Scavenger / Low Performer Hunt; Evening: Leisure

THURSDAY | Morning: History of Eburos; Afternoon: Optional Activities: Spa, Kitesurfing, Crucifixion; Evening: Team Cooking Fiesta

FRIDAY | Morning: Business Strategy and Roadmap; Afternoon: Mindfulness Class with open skinning, case skinning, and filleting methods; Evening: Trivia Electrocution Extravaganza

SATURDAY | Morning: Headshots and coworking time; Eburos Olympics (weather permitting); Evening: Bone sculpture FAQs

SUNDAY | Closing Ceremony, Prizegiving, and Discipline; Afternoon: Scattered Departures; Evening: Conflagration of premises

Chapter Twenty-Two

A wave of incense-pot stink hit Josie, when she opened the door. She coughed, covered her nose and mouth with the back of one arm, eyes already watering. *Pungent.* Breathing sounds in the blackness inside. The bedroom wasn't large, just a short line of dressers and the closet to the right, with their queen bed off to the left. That's what it should have been, but as the edges of the wall and floor took shape, the floor looked too empty, the right-hand wall blank where the wardrobe should have been. Her dresser was gone, too. *Dani junked everything.*

Josie felt along the inside wall for the light switch, and her fingers squished sticky film. She recoiled, wiping it away. The walls were wet, slimy. In the darkness where the bed should have been, a mass came into slow focus, like a heap of clothing. Mattresses. They were stacked in a tiered pyramid, overflowing with sleeping bags, all occupied. People crowded the network of beds in tight, overlapping rows, all the way up to a black top, rimmed with round, pale shapes and more sleeping forms.

Josie searched for the light again—*there*—and flipped it on.

In the sudden glare, the air drifted with brown smoke from a pair of engraved copper lamps on the floor. Some kind of marijuana mix. Past that, robed people stirred on five shelves of mattresses, blinking in the overhead light. Around them, the walls and ceiling swam with gray-brown putty that puckered in pink rivulets, like flesh. It glistened and dripped, forming meaty stalactites overhead. A row of jawless skulls with clinging bits of hair were lined up along the top mattress on a black sheet, where more people sat up under furry blankets. A bronze-skinned woman with frazzled hair lay with Dani, whose head was half-shaved. She looked ten years older, and when she sat up, Josie saw a flash of emaciated ribs through her open black robe.

What the fuck is this?

Josie froze, while Dani squinted down at her and someone else asked why the light was on. Josie started to speak—an insane smile jerked up from her belly. She burst into laughter. Josie shook, her head already tingling from the pot smoke. *The fucking U.S. President. A mattress monument, with skulls and a cult model sleeping beside her.*

"I ..." Josie tugged her hand away from the wall in a clingy bulb of goo. She scraped it off on her leg. "Uncle Don ..."

"Let's go," he said.

"Wait!" Dani called.

"... awake?" someone said.

"... who is she?"

Past the other two in the kitchen, Josie followed Uncle Don out the front door again, back to the stairs.

Dani banged out behind them.

"Wait," she said, tapping Uncle Don's shoulder. "What are you doing here? I thought this was a fucking joke to you. A 'Ponzi,' 'cult'—isn't that what you said? Hey: I'm talking to you!"

When Dani tried to spin Uncle Don around, Josie shoved between them, knocking down Dani's arm. Dani's black robe hung open to expose a pale, too-thin body, with heaving ribs, sunken stomach and gray hair around her pubis, legs veined and lumpy with joint bones.

Her feet looked cold, toenails discolored purple. Even with the wild eyes and this tucked, distended face, it was still her, though, still Dani. *This isn't possible.*

"What happened to you?" Josie asked. "It's only been a few days. This couldn't ... I don't understand."

Dani stared back at her. "Who the fuck are you?"

"You don't know me," Josie said.

"No. So get the fuck out." And to Uncle Don, "And it's his fault we have police here, reporters camped out until last Thursday. Now they're all singing the same tune. Paid off by the fucking Eburos goons."

Leaning hard on the railing, Uncle Don shuffled down the steps. "Come on, Josie."

"Josie?" Dani clenched Josie's arm too hard. "Why did he call you that?"

There it was: in Dani's other hand, she'd been half-hiding it at her side, but was squeezing it hard now in a steady pulse: the ball. *Widow's eye. The ball did this. The madness inside, whatever is happening to Dani—it's because of me. This is impossible.*

"He called me Josie, because I see things other people miss, remember?" Josie said. "Like that ball. You should give me that back."

"What?" Dani seemed not to notice her staring at the ball. "What are you talking about?"

Carefully, Josie slipped her arm out of Dani's grip and backed away to the top of the stairs. "I don't know what to say to this. The ball ..." She hesitated, as Dani stiffened, the ball gone behind her back. "I think it's like poison."

"You're not Josie," Dani said, but she didn't sound sure.

"I'm not your Josie anymore, no."

"I can make them stop you," Dani said, her voice distant, just like before, when she'd laughed coming home drunk from Columbia. Except with a new dangerous curl at the ends of words. "My pilgrims will bring you both inside with me, if I ask. I can help you understand what I'm doing here. My purpose. Even you, Don."

Uncle Don slowed at the first landing below. "Don't threaten us, Dani."

"I'm not threatening," Dani said. "Just explaining. I have that power."

Josie stepped lower, one step, then more, until she was halfway to Uncle Don. Maybe that wasn't bullshit. Those cultists inside might be able to stop them. If Josie screamed, would neighbors react, or would Dani's people drag her in, maybe cut off her head, smear her guts onto the walls of that horror-house one-bedroom?

"Who are you really?" Dani asked Josie.

"You don't know."

"No, I don't. That's why ..." She hesitated, as Josie descended to the next landing. One more flight of steps down and they'd reach the first floor hall and exit. "You can't be her." Josie walked with Uncle Don around a turn in the stairs, almost out of Dani's line of sight, when Dani said, "We were in love. Josie made me a better person."

A prickle of doubt. Josie clenched her fingers on the banister. *It wasn't all bad. Before whatever the fuck in our apartment, our relationship wasn't broken completely.* Uncle Don squeezed Josie's hand, met her eyes, with an 'it's okay, keep moving' look. *Yeah.*

"Wait ..." Dani called.

They didn't. Walking up Myrtle Avenue, the night rain thinned to mist, as if clouds were settling low on the city. "Can you believe that?" Josie asked Uncle Don.

"She seems worse," Uncle Don said.

Josie started to laugh, then saw that he was serious. *What kind of fucking joke is that? 'Seems worse?'* "Yeah, just a little. I think maybe I need to get out of the city, as far away from Eburos, from Mr. Dean, as I can." *That's not a plan, just a reaction.* "The train, maybe? Should we go to Penn Station or will they be looking for us there?" *What—casing the transportation depots? And so what they are.* She didn't *belong* to Eburos, contract or no contract. But the further they walked by these familiar neighborhood storefronts—a laundromat, a discount phone store, a bodega—the cold knot in Josie's torso stretched tighter. *We can't get away. The company is everywhere.* They stopped for sandwiches and water, and Josie downed hers before Uncle Don had even finished paying.

Back on the street, he said, "I didn't count how many followers she has now. It seemed like more than I remember ..."

Which made no sense, but through another intersection, Josie slowed to stare at a wall of industrial buildings on the block ahead ... with a still-open car rental lot midway down. "There. I'm being paranoid," she said. "But I'd feel better with a car. Just getting out of here now, before any more time passes."

Uncle Don caught her hand to steady himself, limping alongside Josie closer to the rental car entrance. "You are so much like Mark."

Dad. Uncle Don did that sometimes—compared Josie to her father—when he didn't know what else to say. *It's how he processes my impulses. But I'm not Dad. His alcoholism and schizophrenia, snatches of those memories from before. Before high school and college, a mini-lifetime ago. The things I see aren't swimming in my bloodstream, they're real. Whatever is happening, I am in it now.*

Maybe they were real for him, too. Maybe that's why he and Mr. Dean didn't get along.

They crossed a puddled lot of cars to approach a squat, well-lit car rental office, with a line of people waiting at the desk inside. The storm slagged into a humid veil, and when Josie checked the sky, a bright line shimmered overhead. Another one. The same colors as that chamber at the bottom of the pool. A thin filament, like a spiderweb strand, it dipped and swayed, maybe a hundred meters overhead. Red, blue, and orange light slashed along its side in chalky bursts.

He's doing this, whatever it is.

The strand was gone.

"What's wrong?" Uncle Don asked.

Josie stared for another long moment. *Tell him? What? I saw lines in the sky, because the Friendly Man is 'weaving' chalk colors? What does that even mean? Maybe a trick of light from the storm, and it wasn't there at all.*

The sky drifted with dark blankets of thin rain.

"Nothing," she said. "What did you mean a minute ago? About Dani and the people in the apartment? You said she was worse, and something about her followers?"

They stepped into the car rental office, with a bell door dinger. At the desk, a guy in a green uniform polo apologized to an elderly couple at the front of the line for how slow 'the system' was today.

"Just that there were more," Uncle Don said.

"More than what?" Josie asked.

At the desk, the polo-shirt guy tapped in frustration on his computer, apologizing again.

"Than before," Uncle Don said at last. "I mean more than when I saw you both last. She had only a half dozen people—'pilgrims,' whatever she calls them."

"I don't understand," Josie said. "Why do you think I know about this?"

Uncle Don started to smile. "Are you kidding? Her anti-capitalist cult, anarchist, whatever it is, you were ... If you *are* Josie, the Josie I know—and I believe you are—then you should know about it."

"Why?"

"You were part of it, before you were recruited by Eburos. You don't remember?"

The room felt unsteady for a moment, as if they were on a boat. Not rocking, but ready to tip sideways. *No, I don't remember. Not so much.*

"Folks," the polo-shirt guy called and gestured to everyone in line. "I apologize, but our system is completely down. If you want to leave your names and contact info, I can be sure they process a refund for any reservations you might have had."

People cursed, and the elderly couple started talking about alternatives and wasn't there *anything* they could do, how was this possible?

Maybe this isn't random. Maybe Mr. Dean, The Eburos Group, is shutting it all down, so I can't get away. Like we're mice in a trap. But not the catch-and-release plastic tubes that Mom used to hide behind the oven in their old apartment—no, this was a sophisticated electric box, like the ones the exterminator used. *Or a snake, like the Friendly Man said.*

"Come on," Uncle Don said. "It's not a big deal. I'm sure we can ..." But he stopped when he saw the way Josie shuffled, watching the street through the front glass.

Nothing unusual. Just people hustling by: a woman with two plastic grocery bags, a line of three teenage kids laughing and swinging backpacks, and a pair of men smoking in the doorway of an Ethiopian restaurant across the street. Beside that: a hardware store and corner McDonald's—*no, I'm missing something. He knows I'm here.* Mr.

Dean couldn't switch off all the rental car company computer systems just in case they stopped in.

"What is it?" Uncle Don asked, and he followed Josie's frantic stare outside. "The rain let up at least …"

Behind them, a few people from the line still pleaded with the polo guy, but he repeated an apology.

There: a dark sedan slowed at the sidewalk, stopped. The driver's door opened, and a thick guy in a too-tight suit—Tommy—got out. *Impossible, but there he is.* Tommy looked directly at Josie and glanced down at a phone in his left hand, then started up the lot, totally unhurried.

"You see him, right?" Josie asked. "I'm not imagining this."

"I see a man," Uncle Don said, his voice low. "Looks like security."

"His name is Tommy."

"You know him?"

Tommy crossed the front lot with an even, level step, still keeping his phone half-raised, watching something on it at the same time. *How did he find me? How did he get here so fast?* Josie stepped to the office front door and twisted the deadbolt to lock it. Nobody inside noticed. She caught Uncle Don's hand. *Doesn't matter how he's here. Figure it out later.* She pulled them both back, sidestepping the people at the desk as Tommy reached the locked front door. Josie ran with Uncle Don for an unmarked door on the rear wall.

"That's for employees only!" the polo guy called.

Josie didn't look back. One hand on Uncle Don, she led them through a narrow, maintenance hall to a heavier *'Emergency Exit'* door at the back. She shoved open a metal bar marked *'Warning: Alarmed!'* No alarm sounded, as they stepped out into a wet alley bordered by a fenced lot filled with more rental cars. Turning left would take them around the front of the building; right led to more brick apartments and a walled-off construction block.

"Who was that?" Uncle Don asked, already panting again.

Shit, they couldn't just try to outrun Tommy, could they? *We need a plan.*

"He works for Mr. Dean," Josie said. "I saw him—he was on Dutch Island with me." They went right, Uncle Don limp-jogging beside her.

"What's that?" Uncle Don asked.

Josie checked the empty apartment stoops and a quiet construction site: all clear. At the far end of the block, she spotted the familiar storefronts of Knickerbocker Avenue, still just a couple blocks from her apartment. *Dani's cult headquarters.*

"What's what?" Josie said. "Tommy works for Eburos. We took a plane, and he ..." She glanced back. They were halfway down the block, and no sign of him yet. Maybe he stalled at the locked door. *But he was looking at his phone.* Josie found her cellphone. "I haven't checked my messages or called anyone since ..." *Since Angela told me they tracked my phone at the Long Island docks, so she could send a car. Of course.*

Uncle Don watched the empty street behind them. "You think they're tracking your phone?"

"They are," Josie said. "I don't know why I didn't think of it before. Too tired." She flicked the phone over the ledge of a walk-down stairwell and heard it ding into a trashcan. "Hole in one." Uncle Don frowned, but he didn't argue, and Josie took his arm again, said, "Let's keep moving." *But where? We can't just run. Even if somehow we slip out of the city, what then? Hide from them in this Grace skin forever? Eburos has people all over the country, the world. That's not a solution.*

As they neared the end of the block, Uncle Don touched an iron fence to slow for a shaky breath.

"I need to think," Josie said. *Sandra can fix this. That anchor client Bob Dylan fan under the cemetery on Dutch Island. If she drove Grace's heart into my chest the first time, she can use her Mapuche flute to levitate it back out again, until I'm me.*

Across the street, Josie spotted the black-glass front of *'E&W Health and Fitness.'* Her 24-hour gym. Behind them, a woman walked a beagle, and there were two guys in hoodies further back, but still no Tommy. *Good. Get off the street and find a way back to Dutch Island.*

"We can stop for a second," Josie said. "I think I know where we need to go." *Not in a private jet this time.* And when Uncle Don let her guide him toward a crosswalk, she said, "We'll take a bus or taxi to one of the ferry terminals to New Leiden."

Wincing as he strained with each step, Uncle Don gave her a 'thumbs up' and said, "Perfect. Where's that?"

"Dutch Island," she said, without stopping. "That's where ... look, it will sound ridiculous if I explain why, but I think I have to go back there. That's where they did this to me."

"Okay, I trust you," he said. "But what's Dutch Island?"

The Eburos Group
WORKING HOURS, PTO & VACATION

Eburos offices are accessible to employees 24 hours / day throughout the year, with all support staff available onsite during professional hours (7 a.m. to 10 p.m.) and afterhours remotely via Microsoft Teams / blood summoning. Employees receive 20 days of Paid Time Off (PTO) per year, with accrual beginning the day you join the firm (1.7 days per month). You cannot transfer any remaining PTO to the next year, and the firm encourages you to use your time off throughout the year. Subject to your manager's discretion, your unused PTO will be allocated to anchor clients who will make use of your bodily PTO on your behalf (see 'Organ Puppetry' in 'Professional Development').

COMPANY HANDBOOK

CHAPTER TWENTY-THREE

Crossing the street, Josie held up a hand, smiling at the cars that stopped to let them pass. Through rain-streaked windshields, she couldn't see the drivers, but no one honked. On the opposite sidewalk, Josie walked Uncle Don into the throb of drum machine music and metal-mat-sweat smells. Alice looked up from the front desk, but when Josie smiled, started to say, "Thank God, can we sit in your office, just until we figure out the ferry schedule ..." Alice's expression flicked from Josie to Uncle Don, didn't soften. *Because she doesn't know me like this.*

"Help you?" Alice asked.

A trio of women in yoga outfits talked loudly at the lockers, just behind the desk. From here, Josie could see most of the open gym was empty. She checked outside again: still no Tommy.

"Excuse me," Alice said. "Is everything all right? Are you interested in a new membership?"

"I need to sit down," Uncle Don said, his face flushed, and he patted his chest. "I think I'm having a heart attack."

"What? Oh shit." Alice rushed around the desk.

Josie tightened her grip on Uncle Don's hand, met his eye. He half-winked, not noticeable unless she knew what to look for.

"This way," Alice said. "You can rest in the back. Are you—have you called an ambulance?"

"Yes," Josie said. "They're on the way."

Careful with Uncle Don's arm, Alice led them around the perimeter of the gym to a door that opened to a simple office, complete with desk, sofa, and transparent mini-fridge packed with energy drinks.

"Did they say how long?" Alice asked.

"Not long," Josie said, and she sat with Uncle Don on the sofa. "Thank you. I've got it from here."

"Are you ..." Alice stared at Josie. "Have we met? Sorry, you seem ..."

Uncle Don leaned back, theatrically closing his eyes and holding his chest. "Water?"

"Yes!" Alice said, and she ran back into the gym.

Josie kicked the door shut. "You're not really ..."

"No."

"That wasn't nice. You're freaking her out with this act, and we won't have long."

"We shouldn't stay long anyway," Uncle Don said. "Keep moving, right?" He took out his phone, started swiping to find the contacts.

"Can you look up the ferries to Dutch Island?" Josie asked. "I want to make sure we can get tickets. I don't know the schedule, and if we have to wait ..."

"I think we should warn your mother."

The door opened. Alice hurried back to Uncle Don with two large, plastic cups of water. He sipped one. Josie took the other, and Alice said, "Anything else? What can I do? No one out there is a doctor—I did ask, like you see on TV. 'Is there a doctor on the plane?' Or in the gym, I guess. Health club." She paced, watching Uncle Don. "How do you feel?"

"He'll be okay," Josie said. "Thank you. Maybe just give us a minute?"

"Can you help us out?" Uncle Don asked her, eyes closed again. "My niece here is asking about a place called 'Dutch Island.'"

Josie checked to see if he were joking. *Why poke Alice with this? As if he doesn't believe me.* "No, I was just ..." Josie sighed. "I think I need to go there, so I asked you, Uncle Don, to look up the ferry schedule and see if there are tickets available."

Alice stopped pacing, and Uncle Don murmured, "See?"

"I don't get it," Alice said.

"What?" Josie said. "I know it's late, but maybe there's a ferry ..."

"No, I mean I don't get 'Dutch Island.' What is it, some kind of resort?"

Not her, too. Are they in on this together somehow? A bizarre practical shenanigan conspiracy?

"Dutch Island," Josie said. "The little island off the coast of Long Island, just outside the city ..?" And when Alice stared back blankly, Josie turned to Uncle Don. "Do you both really not know what I'm talking about?"

"No," Alice said. "Are you okay?"

"I'm fine," Josie said. "But I feel like ..." *Like I'm losing my mind again. Like my memories aren't my memories.* The neat lines of coastal New Leiden turned to scruffy chalk outlines in her mind, already muddy. *No, stop that. It's real.* "Dutch Island," she said again, as if repeating it would shake them awake. "The tourist island, with Dutch colonial buildings and farms, windmills: none of that means anything to you? Every single person in New York and probably the East Coast has heard of it. The last Dutch outpost in North America."

Alice shrugged. "Sorry."

"I don't recognize it," Uncle Don said. "But it sounds nice."

Sounds nice.

"No, this doesn't make sense," Josie said, a manic snap of tension jumping from her gut up to her throat. "I need to go back there. Everyone knows about Dutch Island. Just like they know about Long Island or the name of the five boroughs or Martha's Vineyard or whatever. Alice, you grew up on Staten Island. You can probably see Dutch Island from your old neighborhood on a clear day."

Alice backed to the door, one hand in her pocket, probably ready to hit a panic button on her phone. "We *have* met, haven't we?" she said quietly. "But I don't remember where."

I used her name and mentioned Staten Island. Damn it, just slipped out. I need to sleep.

"Yes, maybe," Josie said. "I'm sorry. I'm mixed up." She touched Uncle Don's shoulder. "We should go. Come on."

"How? There's no car," Uncle Don said. "And he might still be outside, watching for you."

"Who?" Alice asked, then tensed. "You're not really having a heart attack, are you?"

He swallowed, forced a tight smile. "False alarm. I got overly enthusiastic. I did have an attack recently, so I'm at increased risk."

"Whatever this is, whatever you're talking about—I don't care. I need you both to leave," Alice's voice rose louder, more confident, and two guys using nearby weight machines looked over. They didn't stop their sweaty workouts, but both looked primed to jump in. "This is my private office, and I need you out right now," Alice said. She raised a cellphone from her pocket. "I *will* dial 9-1-1."

Uncle Don pulled himself up, leaning hard on Josie. "I believe you," he said, then to Josie, "If you say there was a Dutch island, there was."

"Is," Josie said.

One of the workout dudes lowered himself out of a butterfly weight-lifting machine to approach. "Everything all good in here?"

Josie stood. "Okay, we're going." And to Uncle Don, "Focus on the water in front of us."

Alice held up an arm to stop her, staring hard. "Wait." She shivered. "Who told you to say that?"

"No one. It's just something ... Josie says," Josie said, too fast. The workout dude hovered behind Alice, as if curious to see how this played out. "She's a friend." *Keep talking.* "Josie told me to come here, if I needed help. She mentioned you."

"Why didn't you say so?" Alice said, and her shoulders loosened a little.

"I should have, I'm sorry."

Half-convinced, but this helps. She wants an explanation that doesn't blow up the world, even if it's a lie. So why was she still blocking the doorway?

"We're fine," Alice told the workout dude. "Thanks." Then, closer, she asked, "You're a friend of Josie's? How is she? The other day, she was in and said her uncle was in the hospital ..." Alice blinked at Uncle Don. "Is that you?"

"That's me," he said.

"I'm actually glad you're here. I need to talk to her," Alice said, hesitating. "About her membership."

That embarrassed pause in that sentence meant 'money.' Josie's subsidized gym membership had ended, hadn't it? *Of all the fucking things to worry about now.* Now that Josie had graduated, with student loans ready to dig into her dwindling checking account, she couldn't come back here, could she?

No, 'Josie' couldn't come back here. But I'm not her. Not completely, anyway. I can be here any time I want. And what does my bank account look like?

Stop it.

"Can I grab some paperwork for Josie the next time you see her?" Alice asked and started out of the room. "Two seconds."

Before Josie could respond, Uncle Don's phone rattled with an incoming call. Onscreen: *'Unknown number.'*

Josie shut the door behind Alice, said, "Wait. It could be ..."

He said, "Could be Caitlyn," and answered.

It wasn't.

Remember
these
quick tips!

Disciplinary Room
Reservation Guidelines

All staff are reminded that reservation guidelines for private
disciplinary rooms on floors 20-25 are available online.

• Book early. Reservations can be made up to two weeks in
advance and recurring reservations require manager
approval.

• Cancel and update promptly. If you no longer need a
disciplinary room or less time is required than anticipated,
please free up the room for others.

• Check availability. Do not assume a room is free or interrupt
another member of staff. Check the system or digital
signage panel by the door.

• Familiarize yourself with the system. Integrate the
reservation system with your Outlook calendar and
consider downloading the reservation app, 'CRY' in your
mobile device.

• Good neighbor policy. Please be respectful and tidy in your
use of disciplinary rooms, including, but not limited to,
cleaning meat processing tools, washing and sanitizing
drains, and following best practices in composting,
anaerobic digestion, alkaline hydrolysis, rendering,
incineration and burning.

www.eburosgroup.com

Chapter Twenty-Four

Uncle Don tapped to turn on the speaker phone, said, "Hello?"

Silence. Josie glanced at Uncle Don's phone, one hand on the doorknob, as if she needed it to stay level. A solid escape hatch.

"Hello ..?" Uncle Don said again.

"Grace?" A young, high voice, it was a child.

The demon boy from the cemetery, Samuel. The cemetery on an island that doesn't exist anymore.

"Who's calling?" Uncle Don asked.

On his fucking conch shell. That's real, too.

"I want to talk to Grace. Has she found the secret place yet? The others are waiting for her, they told me."

Uncle Don reached for the red 'End Call' button, but Josie caught his wrist and met his eyes: *'Not yet.'*

"Hi Samuel," Josie said.

He laughed with a rough scratch, as if he were holding his phone too close. *Not a phone, a shell.* "There you are!" Samuel sounded relieved, and she imagined him rocking back-and-forth in a folding chair, with the conch shell to one ear. "I told Sandra you're still my friend! She didn't believe me. Even now that everything is different, we're still friends. But he's going to find you if you don't go to the secret place soon, and that would be bad. You're not very good at hiding."

Uncle Don whispered, "Do you understand this?"

No. Maybe a little, almost. She shook her head and asked, "Where are you? Samuel, are you still on Dutch Island?"

"What's that?"

Goddamn it. Josie swallowed. "You're not there anymore?"

"Not where anymore?" he asked. "I'm with Sandra. You know that."

"Where?" Josie asked. "Does she still have the flute? Can she use it to ..."

Uncle Don stared hard at Josie, jaw tightening, as if fighting to restrain his questions, and Samuel sighed loudly into the speaker.

"I am in the under place, below the vegetables," he said simply. "Like always."

"Vegetables?" Josie asked. *Make this make sense.* "Samuel, are you in New York?"

"Well, yeah!" He laughed. "This is boring. You need to go to the secret place if you want to be the other you again."

The other me again.

"Okay, what's the secret place, Samuel?"

"I told you already. The silver door?" he said slowly, as if she were being dense. "By the baseball?"

"Near a baseball stadium?" Josie asked. "There's a silver door by a baseball stadium that leads to a place where ..." *What? What does this mean?*

"It's not for baseball *anymore*," Samuel said, with another sigh. "That was the old-old Grace." And then a sing-song, *"Tip-top!"*

"Tip-top? Samuel, what does that mean?"

"That's from old-old Grace," he said simply. *"Tip-top, tip-top!"*

Push through. Try to understand. "What does 'old-old Grace' mean? Are you talking about someone else? Were there were other girls before me?" Josie said. "Like the last Hispanic girl, the one I met ... She was Grace. There were others before her?"

"Uh huh."

"And they all went to this secret place? Why?"

"Because he doesn't know about it," Samuel said. "He's lonely now. You can't let him find you, or he'll open you up."

Open me up to snip out the Josie parts.

Samuel asked, "Do you want to talk to your dad?"

Without thinking, Josie ended the call.

"What the hell was that?" Uncle Don asked.

"I don't know." *Tip-top. Because I don't actually. A demon kid in a cemetery on an apparently imaginary island. An island I've also known existed my whole life. And now he's under 'the vegetables.' What the hell am I supposed to do with this?* "Someone ... something I met on Dutch Island," Josie said. "That kid was there."

Uncle Don stared at his phone, as if he expected it to ring again. "What was he talking about? A silver door and ..?"

"A place we can hide, maybe," Josie said. Her thoughts numbed together, like tape caught on a strand. *Too tired, I need to rest.* "You heard him, it's near a baseball stadium that isn't a baseball stadium ..."

"Before we do anything else, I'm going to warn your mom," Uncle Don said.

He tapped to call, and after two rings Mom's voice snapped on: "Don? I wasn't expecting to hear from you. How are ..."

"Caitlyn, don't sign the contract. Whatever agreement they gave you, don't sign it." A pause, and Uncle Don said, "Your daughter is here with me."

"Don't sign?" Mom said. "Did you put him up to this, Josie? Are you two in cahoots?"

She said it like an off-hand joke, as if they'd switched a dinner reservation or were planning a surprise party.

"Whatever is happening, Mom, you can't trust Mr. Dean," Josie said. "The company ..." *What? Has a tree demon trapped in its basement and my friend-as-a-plant on their lobby wall? And more. Every moment it gets worse.*

"You sound strange," Mom said. "Josie, is everything ..."

"I have a cold. But this is important," Josie said. "Whatever deal they're offering you ..."

"Listen," Mom said. "Just stop. I hear you."

"You don't. It's not just a job offer."

"Josie, listen to me," Mom said, "I'm your mother—I'm not an idiot. This isn't the first time I've ..." A stutter pause. *The first time what?* "Anyway, you can rest easy. I won't sign without talking to them. There are things in the agreement I want clarity on, sure. Is everything else okay? Where are you?"

"We're in Brooklyn," Uncle Don said.

Is everything else okay.

Alice knocked and came back in, smiling. "Hi, you're Don and Grace, is that right? There's a man here who says he's a friend of yours ..."

"A man?" Josie asked.

"Yes." Alice looked back toward the entrance, waving someone on. "He said you work together."

"Close the door," Josie said, and before Alice could react, Josie yanked it shut, forcing Alice in. "Not a friend."

Footsteps on the other side of the door, and the knob started to turn. Josie caught it with both hands, bracing to hold it closed.

Alice started to smile. "What are you doing?"

"Don't open it," Josie said. "That man is dangerous."

The doorknob turned inside Josie's fingers, and she squeezed harder to hold it—no good, the brass circle still moved.

"Don?" Mom said on the phone. "Is something wrong?"

"Yes," Uncle Don said. "We'll call you back."

The door shuddered open against Josie, knocking Alice a step into the room, but Josie rammed it shut again, her right shoulder planted against the wood. *For like two more seconds. We have to get out of here.*

Rubbing her arm, Alice said, "Who the hell is—"

The door burst open, knocking Josie onto the floor beside Uncle Don. Both hands raised and tense, Tommy half-crouched in the doorway, as if he expected to catch a piece of furniture. *We should have thrown a chair, something.* His arms bulging, veins visible in his neck and forehead, he looked like he belonged here, backed by shiny exercise equipment, pads, and weights, as if he'd just finished an elaborate cardio routine in that suit.

"Hello again, Grace." Tommy stood taller, blocking the doorway. He pointed at her, his expression already flattening. It was over. They were cornered, no other way out of this room. Tommy was a cat, ready to flick the mice around with one paw, just because he could. *Or a snake, maybe.* "It's time to go." Uncle Don helped Josie up beside him. *How the fuck do we escape? Walk out with him, and it's over. They won't let me free a second time. Not until the Friendly Man gets what he wants.* Whatever was about to happen, after Tommy dragged them to his car, they wouldn't get another chance to run. Once Josie was trapped, the noose wouldn't loosen. *No secret place, no way to find Sandra to change back. Stop it. Think.*

When Tommy stepped in, Alice moved between them. "No, I don't think so," she said. "This office is private."

"You need to move," Tommy said quietly, still watching Josie, no change in his stare.

"*I* need to move?" Alice swiveled to take in Josie and Uncle Don. "Are any of you police? No? Then turn around and walk out."

"Come here, Grace," Tommy said slowly, and he extended a hand.

Fucking gentleman.

Alice turned to her. "Do you want to go with this man?"

Josie gave her a *'really?'* look, breathing fast, and Alice started to pivot back, said, "Sir, I told you—"

Tommy shoved her aside. Alice hit the wall hard and went down, with a surprised grunt, but somehow landed on one knee, like she'd trained for this. Maybe she had.

"Grace ..."

"Asshole," Alice said and sucked a deep breath, then belted, "Help! Someone! Please—he attacked me!"

Tommy froze. The workout dude appeared at the door again, saw Alice, then took in Tommy, Josie, and Uncle Don in one quick scan.

"Him!" Alice shouted and pointed at Tommy. "Get him out of here!"

"That's enough," Tommy said. He lowered his arms to either side, palms open, as he faced the gym dude. "We're fine."

"Don't look fine," the gym dude said. He stepped in, already pulling himself up taller, chest puffed out. He and Tommy were both big, Tommy's shoulders maybe a little broader, but thick muscles flexed on the gym dude's arms. His cheeks reddened. "Come on," he told Tommy. "You don't want to be in here."

"I do," Tommy said, still calm. The folds of his suitcoat shifted, as his back tensed. "This has nothing to do with you."

Alice pulled herself up. "Seriously—get him the fuck out of my office. I'm calling the police."

The gym dude reached for Tommy's arm, and Tommy twisted free in one motion. When he started to tell the gym dude to "Back off, don't touch me," the gym dude answered back, reached again, and this time, Tommy couldn't twist free. The gym dude held Tommy's arm, and they swiveled into the wall, banging a framed promotional shot of New York City to the floor. Like wrestlers, they rocked with locked arms, then twirled, and the gym dude shoved Tommy back into the wall.

Uncle Don grabbed Josie's arm. "Now," he said.

When Josie started for the door, Tommy lunged, and the gym dude yanked his arm hard, pinning Tommy's second arm down.

"Bro, I did two tours in Afghanistan," the gym dude said. "Stop."

"Go," Alice said, ushering Uncle Don and Josie out into the gym.

"Where?" Josie asked.

They reached the entrance, and something crashed in Alice's office. Now two more gym guys ran to investigate, shouting. Someone screamed, and Tommy appeared in the office doorway, slumped against the frame. Breathing hard, the shoulder of his suit gashed, one sleeve hanging loose like an old doll, he dripped blood. *Not his.* His entire forearm was slick with blood from a shard of broken wood gripped in his right hand.

Tommy raised the blade at Josie. He staggered closer, wincing when he put pressure on his left foot. So the gym dude hurt him, but not enough. Josie yanked open the outer door to loud street noise, and Uncle Don and Alice followed.

"That one," Alice said. She pointed to a red hatchback further up the block and tapped on her phone.

"9-1-1 emergency response," a voice said over Alice's speaker. "Are you in immediate danger?"

"Yes," Alice said. She found her keys and circled to the driver's door. The car trilled and unlocked. "I'm outside E and W Fitness. A man just attacked me. He's there now with a knife."

"Okay, ma'am, is anyone injured?"

"Yes, I just told you."

I guess we're doing this.

They climbed in, Josie up front with Alice, and Uncle Don in back. Behind them, the gym door flew open, and Tommy limped out, his cheeks and chin smeared red, too, as if he'd accidentally wiped his bloody hand. He still held the wet wooden shard.

"Shit," Josie said. "Go."

Alice adjusted the rearview mirror, started the car, and they lurched into traffic. A delivery truck swerved and honked. Alice's phone spun across the front seat and hit the floor by Josie's feet. When she picked it up, the call had ended. Still watching the mirrors, Alice sped into a fast right turn that bounced them past row apartments and a school, approaching the long, tree-lined walk of a park. Josie couldn't remember the name.

"Thank you," Josie said.

"You really helped us back there," Uncle Don said, leaning closer behind them.

"That fucking guy," Alice said. She rubbed her right arm and grimaced, when she rolled it. "Damn, look at me, I'm shaking. Are you both okay, where can I drop you?"

"Good question," Josie said and leaned back. "Uncle Don, can I borrow your phone?"

He handed it up to her, and Josie tapped fast into an internet search bar: *'New York City baseball stadiums.'* Two obvious stadiums, of course, for the Yankees in the Bronx and the Mets in Queens, but those felt wrong. *Because didn't Samuel say the place isn't for baseball anymore? It was for 'old-old Grace.' A version of me from a long time ago created a safe house. A secret place to hide from the company. Am I thinking clearly?*

"Do either of you know about baseball?" Josie asked, swiping up through random results.

"You mean like the kid on the phone was talking about?" Uncle Don asked. "Josie, are you sure we should be worrying about that? It didn't make sense."

It does. Almost.

Alice watched Josie, as they slowed in a line of cars at a red light. "I know about baseball ... but why did he call you that? Your name is Grace, right?"

"It's complicated," Josie said. She checked the side mirror. No Tommy chasing them yet. On the phone, she flipped through the *'Top 10 Ballpark Deals,'* ads for discount tickets, and links to buzzy social media feeds with reviews of hotdogs and nachos at Yankee Stadium.

"Complicated how?" Alice asked. The light changed, and she took a left, as if she already had a route in mind. "I know Josie, and you're not her."

"I misspoke," Uncle Don said.

"No you didn't," Alice said quickly. "You called her 'Josie,' and she answered right away, like she wasn't even surprised."

The internet search was useless. Worse than useless, it distracted Josie, until she looked up to watch them pass the car rental store, headed back toward Myrtle. *Because when I invited Alice out for my birthday last year, I gave her my address. She knows where I live.*

"Stop," Josie said.

"What—why?" Alice said. "I'm taking to see your friend Josie. You said you know her, right?"

"Just stop the car, please." *Not back to Dani, not now.*

Alice swerved into an illegal parking space and jerked to a halt. In the backseat, Uncle Don stiffened, one hand on the backseat door. To do what? Leap out onto the curb and start running again? A jittery bulge of emotion spasmed in Josie's gut, like boiling water ready to froth up around a lid. She clamped it down, let a focused numb feeling take over. *We need a plan. I can't keep running.*

Arms crossed, Alice turned to Josie, ready to lay into her, throw her out, probably, when Josie said, "Tip-top."

In the back, Uncle Don said, "Are you serious?"

"What are you talking about?" Alice asked.

Holding the phone up so they could all see, Josie tapped to activate a voice search and said, "Tip-top, New York City, baseball."

An automated, search-result voice said, *"The Ward Baking Company gave the name of its product, Tip Top Bread, to the Brooklyn Tip-Top baseball team. Also known as the Brooklyn Fed or BrookFeds, the team was part of the Federal League from 1914 to 1915."*

Josie released a breath that made her grin. *You see. Right here. Somewhere in Brooklyn.*

"I don't believe it," Uncle Don said.

Me neither.

"An old baseball team?" Alice said. "That's what this is about?"

Josie asked the phone, "Where did the team play?"

It answered: *"The Brooklyn Tip-Tops played at Washington Park, which had been in use by the Brooklyn Dodgers, until 1912. When it was rebuilt in 1914, Washington Park was virtually identical to the Chicago baseball stadium that would become Wrigley Field."*

"Where is the Washington Park baseball stadium located?" Josie asked the phone.

"Washington Park was demolished in 1922. It was located on 3rd Avenue, between 1st and 3rd Streets."

Josie looked up to meet Uncle Don's skeptical stare. Alice just frowned back. "Explain this," Alice said. "I'm sorry, make it make sense. Or get out of my car."

"I wish I could," Josie said. "Believe me."

She helped Uncle Don out to the sidewalk and hailed a taxi. Ten minutes later, they found the wall.

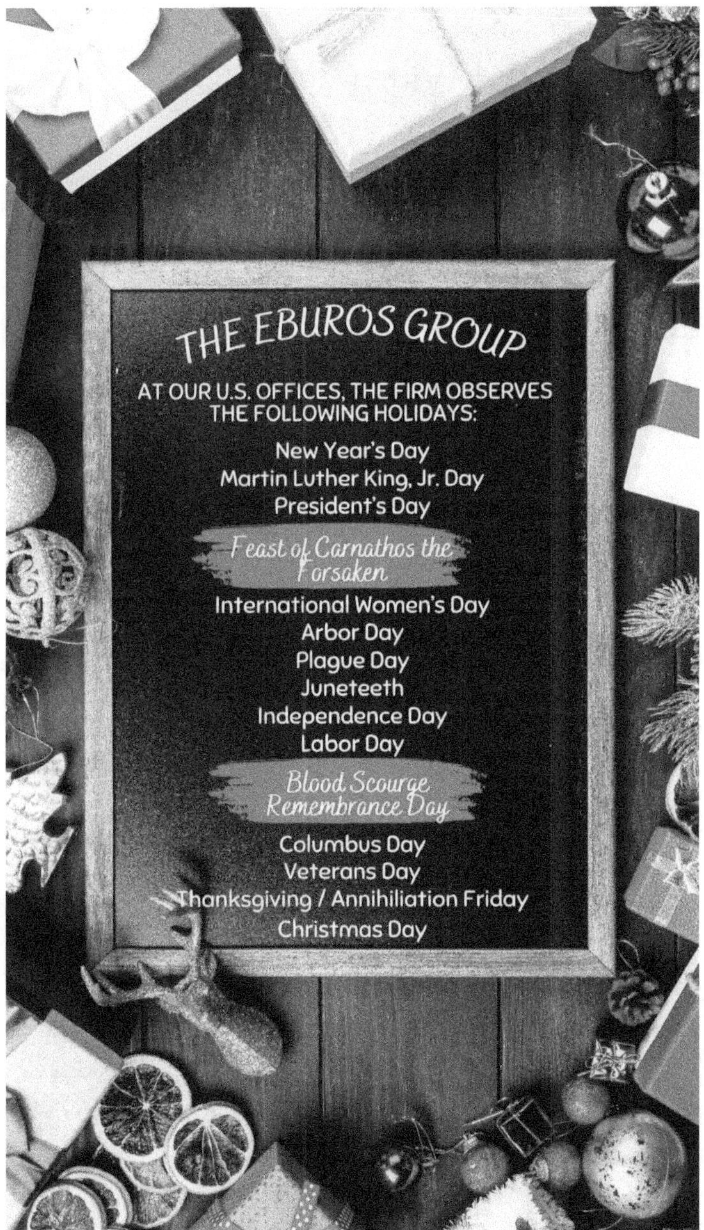
THE EBUROS GROUP
AT OUR U.S. OFFICES, THE FIRM OBSERVES
THE FOLLOWING HOLIDAYS:
New Year's Day
Martin Luther King, Jr. Day
President's Day
Feast of Carnathos the Forsaken
International Women's Day
Arbor Day
Plague Day
Juneteeth
Independence Day
Labor Day
Blood Scourge Remembrance Day
Columbus Day
Veterans Day
Thanksgiving / Annihiliation Friday
Christmas Day

Chapter Twenty-Five

Directly across the street from a blue utilitarian self-storage warehouse and a corner veterinary office, the remaining wall of Washington Park didn't scream secret hideout or even historical landmark. No, approaching with Uncle Don, all Josie saw was a white-gray slab, about half as tall as the thin sidewalk trees, with old boxy indentations along the side and covered arched spaces for what might have been windows once upon a time. Blotchy white paint covered random sections of the block-long wall, probably patching over graffiti. Past the wall and storage warehouse in one direction: barbed wire lots and rundown old-brick warehouses. They followed the wall to the opposite corner to face another intersection of self-storage buildings, the vet office, and there, directly adjacent to the corner vet office and car repair shop, with a nondescript gray building wedged between them, half-hidden behind the regular pavement trees, she found the silver door.

Closer, Josie spotted windchimes hanging from a tree branch in front of the solid-looking entry door of the gray, two-story building. They jingled and *tocked* in the wind: elephants. Three wooden elephants, with metal discs spaced on the dangling wires between them. All the building windows were dark and covered from inside. Josie stepped up to the entrance, looking directly at a black bulb-camera overhead. *Whoever is here is watching right now. He said 'elephants' at the cemetery. And I found the Tip-top baseball stadium, what's left of it. This has to be it.* No doorbell, but to her right, a metal plate with a depressed handprint contour—like a spy movie security check—was fixed just beside the doorknob, above the words: *'Who are you?'*

Josie stared at the blocky letters, checked Uncle Don. "What do you think?" she asked.

"I was going to ask you the same thing." He tried to smile. "What do you want to do?"

Go away. Run back down to the street and ... what? Dutch Island literally vanished, and I'm not me. If I run, what then? Whatever this is, I have to fix it.

Josie's legs felt soft, and she caught her balance on the door with her left forearm, bowing her head against the wood, eyes closed. *Just for a minute.* Her pulse ratcheted too fast. *Just until it slows down.*

'Who are you?'

Sandra said that, too. The person-thing, whatever she is, who took the other girl. The other version of Grace, after changing me. She can do it again. If there's any logic to this, even a little, my heart—my real, tissue and blood heart—still exists underneath the flesh she forced into my ribcage. She can make me whole, Josie again. She has to. Samuel told me to come here, and I listened. He helped me on the island, even pulled the bullet from my shoulder. He wants to help me.

Unless it's a trap.

Josie forced her vision to steady on the words and black hand-print pad again. *If this is the secret place, it will know me.* She opened her right hand and planted her palm and fingers carefully on the metal: a perfect fit.

Nothing happened.

'Who are you?'

"I am Grace," Josie murmured.

The door clicked open. *Shit, did that happen?* She caught the door-knob and stepped into a quiet entry hall with Uncle Don right behind. All black-and-white marble tiles with a thick Persian rug that fed back to some kind of living room area, just to the right of a wide staircase that rose to a landing, and continued in a curl, out of sight. Mechanical ticking deeper inside, but otherwise no sound. The air tasted like dust and faint woodsmoke.

Josie called, "Hello?"

Nothing, so she and Uncle Don followed the hall back to a wide ovular room, with recessed bookshelves and intricate wooden window blinds along the back wall, all closed. A triangulated configuration of four couches and three chairs surrounded a low, central table, backed by a deep fireplace, and on the left, dead women crowded a long dining table.

Josie jumped, jostling the wall. All young, early twenties or late teens, but with slack skin and sunken, desperate eyes, their too-dark lips opened and shut frantically. *Just like the island.* Shouting and screaming in near-silence, with just the clicks of their jaws and dry-mouth chatter of teeth. Except for their age, nothing was the same about these girls, all … Josie squeezed the corner of the hall doorway with one hand, counting. All thirty-three of them. All different races, two with hair so short it was almost shaved bald, and five others with damp, stringy-looking mats of hair past their waists. An Indian girl beside the front left corner of the long table wore a pastel dress decorated with sunflowers; and beside her, a freckled girl, who stood a head taller, dressed in tight leather; and another, a Black girl beside her with teeth streaked bloody, who wore a simple frock and linen dress, like something from a storybook or … or the past.

"What's wrong?" Uncle Don asked. "Josie, do you see something?" He stepped toward the dead girls, one arm up and waving blindly.

A whisper behind her: "Josie?"

She whirled around: the Hispanic girl. The one from Sandra's cave, the girl who was Grace just before ...

"I thought that was your name," the Hispanic girl said quickly.

She looked faded but not as washed out as the others. Like a spotted apple in a room full of decaying fruit, she still flushed in both cheeks, just a little, even if her lips purpled and hollows surrounded both of her dark brown eyes. And still in the same young professional uniform from that day, wearing a whitish button-up blouse and smart pants, both dusty now, streaked at the joints.

"Josie?" Uncle Don asked.

"Yes, I see something," she murmured. "You're not going to believe me."

"I believe you," he said quickly. "I remember how it was with Mark. What is it?"

Dad again. Uncle Don knows, because Dad saw them, too.

"There are dead people here," Josie said. "Women."

From the dining table, the low chatter-rasp of the others continued, but no words.

"My name was Maya," the dead Hispanic girl said. "Before they made me Grace. Why are you here?"

Why am I here? Why are these dead women all ...

"I don't know," Josie said. "Samuel told me to come. I panicked, I didn't know where else to ..."

Uncle Don came back over, lowering himself silently to the couch to watch the air where Maya stood. "Someone's right there?" he asked quietly.

Josie nodded.

"This place is safe," Maya said and sighed, as if disappointed. "But you probably don't have a lot of time left."

"What is going on—what is this place?"

"This?" Maya turned in a slow circle to stagger into the circular living room area. "This is our home, one of them. Where I hid, when I needed to be alone with the only other people who understand. Look, you see?"

The walls: between the shuttered windows, the inlaid shelving might be old and grand, but it wasn't packed with encyclopedia volumes or the complete works of William Shakespeare. No, as Josie approached, she could make out an eclectic collection of weathered paperbacks, slim comic books, folio notebooks, and brightly-colored romance novels in a long line to a mash of folded newspapers ... and more, all the way up five long shelves to the ceiling.

"Those were mine," Maya said, stepping beside Josie to nod to the romance novels. "If you read Spanish, you're welcome to them."

Further up, the shelves of novels and comics were replaced by hardbound leather volumes and rigid envelopes spaced out by small boxes and chests.

"I don't know much Spanish," Josie said. "Sorry." She glanced back at the dead girls, still struggling to be heard in the dining room.

"Most of them read English," Maya said. "I'm sure you'll find something to pass the time."

"What is this?" Josie asked again.

"You don't like to read? The theater is on the second floor, but no internet. That wouldn't be safe. You got rid of your phone?"

"Yes," Josie said and heard the shake in her—Grace's—voice. *Not mine.* "Can you tell me what's going on. All of you were ..?"

"Yes," Maya said. "Isn't that obvious? We came before. And when they're done with you, you'll be here, too."

"I watched that woman, demon-thing, Sandra—I watched her take you ..."

Maya looked away, blinking fast. She started to raise a hand, but stopped with a shake in her arm, like she didn't have the strength, dropped it again. "She only kept me for a little while. She ate ... parts of me. So I'm not whole anymore. I'm losing myself, the same as the others." Maya forced a smile. Meant to be cheerful, calming, but the blackness of her tongue and the decaying insides of her cheeks made Josie's gut clench. "But I haven't forgotten you, Josie. I warned you, didn't I? But here you are."

"Why are you here?" Josie asked. "Like this?"

"I broke my contract."

"How? You were Grace, I saw you."

"I hurt the company," she said. "Everything we do is meant to add *shareholder value.*" Those last words sounded like an insult, as if the words were an obscenity. "All this feels unnatural, doesn't it? Being Grace. But that's only because you're alone with it and can't share it with other people. That's why we all come here, I think. We know exactly what you're feeling."

Maybe. "All of you who are already dead," Josie said.

"Yes. But do you want to know the truth? Being Grace, being this other person so you can talk to the Friendly Man, that's not unnatural. It's their *numbers* that are unnatural."

"Numbers?" Josie asked.

"Out in the *normal* world, when you pay for something, isn't there a part of you, in the moment when you hand over your printed paper notes or coins or plastic square or phone, that knows it's wrong? Like the world was molded into a shape it doesn't fit?" Josie's legs felt weak, and she slipped down to the couch beside Uncle Don, but let Maya go on. "I bet part of you, Josie, part of you flinches in that split second the way you would flinch if you smelled smoke in your bed at night or noticed a black beetle crawling up your bare forearm. Because money is fucking wrong."

"Money," Josie repeated, and Uncle Don frowned, but still didn't interrupt, just listened. *Meaning what? Something to do with Grace and the Friendly Man. If he can change anything, so that it never was* … "They made it this way?" she asked. "Is that what you're saying?"

"Not 'they,' *him.*"

"Do they know?" Josie asked, nodding to the dead girls.

"Maybe." Maya frowned across the room. "Some of them can still speak. But the longer you're dead, the worse it gets. Some aren't doing great. Some are completely fucked. I saw all of them, too, when I was you. We all did, when we were Grace."

"Who is she?" Josie asked. "Or who was she—Grace? Was she a real person, whoever I am right now?"

Still smiling, but now her expression dimmed. "No idea."

"I'm tired," Josie said and let her eyes close for a long moment, willed them open again. "Maya, you said I don't have time …"

"They know you," she said simply. "If you threaten the company, they'll hurt you. They know exactly what matters to you. You know how they say dogs can tell if we're sick or sad, before we're even aware of it? This is like that. You gave them your soul. They don't own you yet, not completely—that happens over time—but every part of you, things you don't even know about … they do." She started to snap her fingers, couldn't, and frowned at her limp hands. "I thought I could outsmart them. I convinced myself I would get away in the cemetery, even though I knew none of us do. I just wanted to be me again. Why is that too much to ask?"

"I know," Josie said and rolled onto her side. "Is it all right if I …"

Uncle Don rose to let her stretch across the entire couch, crossed to inspect the bookshelves. "I'll keep an eye out," he said.

Josie smiled at him. "Thank you, Uncle Don. I wasn't talking to you."

"Oh." He swallowed, checking the room again, staring straight past Maya.

"You shouldn't for long," Maya said. "But yes. One other thing, though, Josie. Something I wish I had known. This is really fucking important: the Friendly Man isn't dangerous like the company. He's different. He wants to cut you, I know. Carve Josie into Grace. But that's not why you should be afraid of him. The Friendly Man is dangerous because *all this* ..." Maya threw up both arms. *Meaning what? The room, the city, the entire world?* "... this is only one version of the world, okay? And the others, the ones he can *weave*, they can be much worse."

When Josie woke, another dead girl was waiting.

The Eburos Group
INTRODUCTION

For The Eburos Group, the yew tree is a symbol of resilience, longevity, and wisdom. The yew may be beautiful in itself, but it also embodies traditions of death and rebirth that span millennia. Yew trees can be found in cemeteries and ancient sacred sites across the world, with root systems that dig deep into the soil and tombs. Some of the oldest trees in the world, today yews form the cornerstone of the Eburos corporate culture. Innovation, honesty, respect, teamwork, and commitment: we demonstrate these values to our clients with the same dedication as the mighty yew tree. Our company is only as strong as its weakest branch—and we are always growing.

COMPANY HANDBOOK

Chapter Twenty-Six

Bleary-eyed on the couch, with her back aching from the awkward way she'd slept, Josie registered the moldy face of a dead girl, perched too close. The girl knelt at her side and spoke in a catching whisper, with lips and jaw rotted back to expose ruined teeth and black gums. She stared at Josie with empty eye sockets.

"My name is Barbara. It wasn't called The Eburos Group then," the girl, Barbara, said. "The building was shorter, all stone with arches and steeped carvings of lions and winged horses, like something you imagine in Europe."

Josie eased up to a sitting position, and the girl moved with her, keeping her face level. Most of the other women still lingered in the dining room, and new light cut through the dusty air in slanty bright slivers of early-morning sun, through the blinds. Uncle Don dozed on a nearby chair. No sign of Maya.

"Magdalene Powers chaired the partnership, no one called it a company," Barbara continued. "A tall, ginger Irish, she once horse-whipped a banker on the street outside for whistling after her. She built the pool. You must have wondered, it was her."

"Why are you telling me this?" Josie asked.

"This was my house," Barbara said, looking around the room and nodding to herself, as if trying to remember where everything went. "I used the money she paid me to buy it. So I could be alone with myself. Then the other girls found it."

"You worked for a woman called Magdalene Powers?" Josie asked. "Back in ... when was that?"

"A long time ago. When I was alive, I first worked in service for Miss Powers's brother, until the day she stopped by for tea and I saw her reflection in the dining room mirror. Huge and gold-trimmed, that mirror showed the whole room, with a straight view of the adjoining serving halls, so guests could check on the arrival of new courses without turning backwards in their seats to look."

"Her reflection?" Josie asked. "She didn't have one—like a vampire or ..."

"No, nothing like that. But the mirror let me see a purple ... *halo*, I guess you would say. Around Miss Powers, almost angelic, like from a painting, except it had a face. In the room with us, I saw nothing, you understand. But in that mirror, that cloud of light watched me, whispering. Sharp teeth and two tongues and ..."

"An anchor client," Josie said. *Like Angela's worm-thing and Noah's brain-teeth. One of the monsters that puppets the dead.*

"Yes, it wasn't human," Barbara said. "I dropped my serving tray, you can imagine. Not the first time I saw one. I know that now. But back then, I was young and tried to stay out of trouble. People forget how mean the world was in those days. Go watch the films and pictures I saved upstairs. Women like Miss Powers talked about the places they came from in Europe like a furnace. A fiery funnel they were lucky to have escaped, before their bones burned up. And she knew what I saw the moment I lost my grip on that tray."

Just like Angela's shadow. "That's why you became Grace," Josie said. "Why you're here, because they—because Miss Powers hired you?"

"Yes, but not right away. No, she made me sweat for it, because she already had a Grace. A girl named Antonia ..." Barbara looked sadly across at the silent dead girls. "She can't talk anymore. I don't know why I can. Others younger than me lost it, too. I think maybe it's because I didn't let him cut out too much, before ..."

"What can I do?" Josie asked.

"Samuel remembered the Tip-Tops, didn't he?" Barbara's ruined face lit up, muscles tugging up into a bare-jaw-bone grin that made Josie look away.

"Yes."

"The Tip-Tops," Barbara said again. "Oh yes. I never had much time for games or sports, but one spring an Italian boy took me to a game. He asked me to marry him there, if you can believe it. Our first date, and he told me—I'll never forget—he said, 'Barb, you are the prettiest girl I've ever seen. I will love you until the day I die, whether you like it or not. You don't love me yet,' he said, 'but you will. I'm going to make you my wife, so why don't you say yes today, and let's save ourselves a world of hassle.' It sounds stupid saying it now, doesn't it?"

"No," Josie murmured. "Not stupid at all."

She felt hollow inside, tension twisting again in her stomach, up to her chest, so she had to concentrate and measure out her breathing. *I don't want to hear this. No more.*

"He was sweet," Barbara said. "Maybe the sweetest boy I ever met. I don't know if he meant it. I never found out, but I wanted to keep that memory. I didn't let him cut that out. Not even after I accidentally gave the boy the widow's eye."

Josie guts lurched, and the air went out of the room. "Widow's eye?"

"A ball with a piece of the devil inside," Barbara said. "Miss Powers gave it to me, and I tossed it to him during the baseball game. It made him ..." She released a quick, ragged gasp. "More himself. But not the same."

"Did he ..."

"I don't want to talk about that. He changed. And the world changed around him, like it had always been that way."

"How do I fix this?" Josie asked. "How do I change back?"

"Back to the real you?" Barbara's flesh drooped even lower around her eye sockets, as if she pitied Josie. *She feels sorry for me.* "Oh dear, you can't. Not until they take that heart out of you again, but then you'll be claimed by one of the devils. They'll kill you, try to make you their slave."

"No." Josie pulled up from the couch, spotted Maya in the entry hall, staring at the front door. "Maya, you didn't die when the heart came out of you. You were alive at first. It wasn't until Sandra ... and you're here right now, even if you're dead, you're not with Sandra anymore ..."

"Eburos has a contract with Sandra," Maya said, without turning. "Everyone has a contract."

Even Mom.

"Sandra stopped my pulse, when she put her black poison in me," Maya said. "The only way I'm here is because she got tired of me. Maybe she's not as strong as she used to be, who knows? My guess: Sandra can only hold so many puppets in her stupid demon head at once. She's flesh and blood, too. Easy to forget, but even though they make no fucking sense, the *anchor clients* are actual living things."

"Devils," Barbara said simply.

Maya sighed. "Not devils, Barb. Animals that escaped from the zoo."

"Uncle Don ..." Josie went to him, shaking his sleeve. "Hey, wake up. What time is it?"

He stirred, checked his phone: 6:55 AM. *I slept all night. Mom might have already ...* "Call my mom. Please, we need to ..."

He paused to hold up the screen for her: a missed call from Mom and a voicemail. Just an hour ago. Uncle Don tapped 'Play,' and Mom's voice said, "Hi Don, sorry we got cut off yesterday. I thought about what you said, and I agree. I won't sign anything, until I see him in person. I already called, and I'm heading in now to beat rush hour. I'll give you an update, as soon as I know more. Also, Josie's not answering her phone. Can you let her know to call me? Thanks, Don!"

When the message ended, he tried to call her back, left a voice-mail—"Call me, Caitlyn. Don't go into the Eburos office ..."—and texted. No response.

"Shit." Josie paced past Barbara and Maya toward the women in the dining area. "I can't understand what you're saying. Can any of you help me? I need to change back, stop my mom ..."

"They can't," Maya said behind her.

Maya watched from the doorway, Barbara from the center of the room, still half-kneeling by the couch.

"What can we do?" Barbara asked. "We're dead, Josie. Almost gone."

Uncle Don asked, "What did they say?"

"Stay here with us," Barbara said. "Don't go back."

"Don't listen to her," Maya said. "You don't have a choice. You have to work for them. Do what they say for as long as you can, and when you're hurt and think you can't take it anymore—*that's* when you come here. We'll be here for you."

"A room full of dead people," Josie said. *Ghosts will be here with me on days when it's too much. As the Friendly Man carves me up.* "Is that what you did?"

"What I did?" Maya said. "Sometimes I hid here, yes. But mostly, for years, I did the work."

"You did the work," Josie repeated. "Meaning you told the Friendly Man what to weave, so Eburos could make money."

"Yes," Maya said. "Josie, I created entire countries and industries that didn't exist before. Places you think have always been there: Panama, Switzerland, the Cayman Islands. Places like Haiti, Chad, Myanmar, Singapore—none of those were real, before I told the Friendly Man we needed them."

"Your mother is heading into the office right now," Uncle Don said.

"I know," Josie said. *Mom is probably on the train right now, maybe almost to Penn Station. How long after that until she walks into the lobby and Mr. Dean convinces her to sign?* "I have to go back."

"What?" Uncle Don sat up. "No. Josie ..."

"Uncle Don, I have to. My mom is probably almost there, and that little demon boy, Samuel, he is still out there, too. Which means Sandra and the flute are still real and can change me back." *So she kills me, and I join this room of ghosts.* "There's a way through this. I don't know what it is, but there's something I haven't thought of that will make this work." Josie started for the door.

"Josie, stop!" Uncle Don came after her, with Maya and Barbara still watching from the living room. "What if they do something to you? Hurt you or ... Josie, you escaped, and if they're angry enough ..."

"They need me," she said. "Without me, they can't talk to the Friendly Man. He is in love with Grace, and right now, I'm her."

"Yes," Maya called. "Be Grace as long as you can."

"I don't..." Uncle Don's shoulders slackened, as if he were too tired to argue. "I don't understand this. Let me help you."

"Uncle Don, I love you." She hugged him, head pressed to his neck to take a deep breath of his deodorant-sweat smell. Panic sweat. *He smells like terror.* "Okay." She let go, backed away. "I'm going."

"Anytime you want to meet back here," Uncle Don said. "Or somewhere else, with fewer ..."

Fewer dead people.

There is a way to survive this, there has to be. Josie walked outside, braced against the rustling wind, and pulled the door shut. *What if there isn't?* She walked for a long twenty minutes, wandering past graffitied walls, auto repair garages, and a tract of boarded up apartments, until it felt far enough to duck into the reception office of a car parts shop and ask to use the phone. No one argued, barely noticed her, even when she asked them to look up the Eburos main number and was finally routed by a receptionist through to Angela. *Maybe she's still at the bottom of the pool. Maybe ...*

Angela answered with a curt, "This is Angela."

"Hi," Josie said.

A quick smile in Angela's voice, "Grace? Oh my goodness, where are you? You know what—nevermind, I see the number and location on my screen. Still in Brooklyn, fantastic. We can be there in thirty minutes. Stay put. Is everything all right? Are you safe?"

"Yes," Josie said. "Perfect."

Twenty minutes later, Angela—perfectly put together, not-dead Angela—stepped out of a black town car to meet Josie on the sidewalk, with Tommy's blocky, almost refrigerator-shape up front with the driver. Angela's shadow slithered closer up the pavement, and she followed, checking the car repair shop, as if to be ready to dodge whatever trap Josie had set.

"Thank God," Angela said. This time, she wore a spicy yellow-and-red jacket over a blue top and matching skirt—all designer-demon sheik, as she stepped in for a quick handshake. "You had us worried, you know. Genuinely worried, Grace. But here you are, safe as houses. What are you doing here?" A hand still clasped with Josie's, Angela guided Josie around to the back door of the car, asked, "Why did you leave?"

"The Eburos office ..."

"Yes, the office. What were you thinking? You made poor Tommy trek halfway across the city and back."

Climbing in, Josie saw fresh bruises around Tommy's cheeks and right eye in the front passenger seat with the driver: Noah. Right there, with both hands on the wheel, but this time he didn't meet Josie's stare in the rearview.

Trying to meet Noah's eye, Josie said, "I panicked."

Angela got in, slammed the door. "Panicked? Well yes, but *why*—do you have any idea ..." A finger up to her lips, fresh red-and-yellow flame nail polish, too, a perfect match. "No," she said, "of course you don't. Let's go."

They pulled away from the curb, and Noah adjusted his grip with the turn, fingers rising and falling in the air. No screws, of course not. *But it's him. In this version of the world, without Dutch Island, he's right here. Alive again.*

And so what?

"No one has explained anything," Josie said. "In that place, with that thing, the Friendly Man, whatever we're calling it ..."

Up front, Tommy cleared his throat, and Angela made a sour face. "Hmm," she said. "We don't speak about him that way. With that tone. The Friendly Man. We speak of him with respect, deference, when we speak of him at all. Are we clear on that, Grace?"

Driving up the block, Noah glanced back at Josie with a slow frown. *I'm staring.*

"You don't know me, do you?" Josie called to him.

Angela tracked Josie's attention to Noah, as if to be sure she hadn't missed anything. Tommy turned, too, to trade a quick 'what the hell' look with Angela.

"Sorry?" Noah asked. "You mean me?"

"Yes," Josie said. "We've never met, have we?"

"I don't ..." Noah glanced at Tommy, as if for instructions.

"What is this about?" Angela asked Josie. "Our driver has been with the company for ... how long has it been now, Noah?"

Five years.

"Five years," he said.

Except not on Dutch Island. Here. When the Friendly Man erased that place, he didn't scratch out the people, just dumped the pieces out on a new board. Right here in the city. Like a law of conservation of demon energy. And you'll probably melt if you leave, won't you, Noah? You helped me once. Saved me.

She forced herself to look away, focus on Angela. *A different you.* "I just want to make sure ..."

"Go ahead," Angela said.

Fine.

"What was that thing on you?" Josie asked. "The animal attached to you, it was ..."

"We don't speak of that either," Angela said, with a tight smile, her shadow perfectly still, as the car accelerated into the neighborhood. "Not like that. You see, whatever you may think right now, and I get it—it's okay to be confused at this stage. To a point. Whatever you think, we have an agreement. You signed a contract."

"Right," Josie said and sat back. "Are you serious?"

"Eburos is very serious about honoring its commitments, and we expect our team to behave accordingly."

"A contract to change me into someone else, so I can meet with a demon-monster-thing," Josie said. "Are you sure that contract will hold up in court? What would you tell a judge, just out of curiosity? 'Nope, sorry, she signed away her soul to negotiate with a creature buried under our corporate headquarters in downtown Manhattan ..?'"

"Yes."

Josie's mouth went dry. She should laugh, but her jaw tightened at the empty way Angela stared through her. *Like I don't matter. Like anyone could be sitting in this chair—and will be. Was Uncle Don right? Will she hurt me? Did Tommy tense just now, and he's still wearing a heavy jacket, too bulky—why? To hide whatever weapons he's carrying, right? Will they ... what will they do?*

"Your contract is binding," Angela said slowly. Her shadow bent to the left, and finally she adjusted her skirt, crossed a leg to poise back, as if in interview mode again. "But that works both ways, Grace. You have received your signing bonus," Angela continued. "Would you like to see?" She pulled up her phone, swiping to bring up a crowded spreadsheet program and turned it around, so Josie could get a closer look. "See, right here? This is our HR payroll administrator, and this ..." She tapped an entry labelled, *'G09: New contract, signing bonus: $50,000 USD.'* "This is you."

The dollar amount made Josie cross her arms, one hand tight on her opposite elbow, as if to steady her posture. But before that ...

"G-9?" Josie asked. "Does that mean ..?"

"Yes," Angela said, with a shrug and moved the phone in again. "You're the ninth Grace to work for this iteration of the company."

Nine of us. And how many before that? Before this Eburos? "The figure is correct," Angela continued. "Check your bank account."

Tell her what she wants to hear. Say the wrong thing, and it's over? Ask too much, without the right words and ..?

"I'm trying to understand," Josie said at last.

"Yes, I know." Angela took a patient breath. "So there are pieces of the world only you can see, the way some animals perceive other forms of light and energy. Just like that. The living, the dead—they're real, and that's a gift. Grace. Your gift, to help build shareholder value."

For a company that serves husks of people animated by demons.

"The last girl," Josie said, "the last version of Grace, what did she do to cause so much trouble?"

"You don't need to worry about that." A pause, as Angela's phone shook with another text. She silenced it, looked up. "Let me put it this way: have you ever heard of New Venice on the Balmara Peninsula off the east coast of Florida? No? What about the last Prime Minister of New France, who died in a Louisiana prison in 1968? He ceded the entire territory west of the Mississippi River to the Confederation of American States or CSA."

Angela said the words so fluidly, without a flicker of hesitation. No sign she was inventing this or searching for a punchline.

"No," Josie said. "Of course not."

Angela nodded, eyes on her phone again, swiping and scrolling. "Neither had I, except from that little whippersnap*tress*. The girl before you, the girl you met on her way out, who upset our friend even more than you did, much more."

Out the window, Josie watched the Brooklyn neighborhoods expand and become more gentrified, as they neared the East River. "Those things you just mentioned," Josie said, "New Venice and all that, they're not real ..."

"Well, no. Not here. But they were—or the last Grace claimed they were, in the world *before*."

"Before," Josie repeated.

Angela sighed and lowered her phone, as if Josie were being deliberately dense. "I'm sure it happened again, as a result of what you did."

"What did I do?"

"You left abruptly, upset our friend."

And you helped me climb out. No ... not this you—this version of Angela's corpse is being run by a worm, isn't she?

"What was I supposed to ..."

"You panicked," Angela said. Her shadow swung forward, and Angela patted Josie's knee awkwardly, then shook her head. "And whatever you said to him ... if you said the names of people or places ..."

I did, didn't I? In that chamber with the Friendly Man, I mentioned Dutch Island.

"Like Dutch Island," Josie said. *Thinking out loud, I didn't mean to say that.* "We flew there yesterday morning, you and me—all three of us, actually, to see Sandra ..."

Up front, Tommy swiveled around to check Angela's reaction, but she just flashed one hand up—the universal 'just chill for a second' signal—and nodded to Josie. "Go on."

"It's a colonial Dutch town, island resort for tourists ..."

"Where is it?" Angela asked softly.

"Not far, a few miles offshore from the city."

"Uh huh. Okay." Angela tapped on her phone, then showed Josie a satellite map image, zoomed in to the five boroughs. She reverse-pinched to zoom out and out ... and no Dutch Island. "See it? Our friend sees the world like a medieval tapestry," Angela said. "Can you visualize that? Knights on horseback, etcetera? Think of all time and places—everything, always—existing at once in a single scene. The future, the past … all of it."

Like the timeline outside Mr. Dean's wall.

"If he doesn't like something," Angela continued, "if he tears out a thread to spite you, like your Dutch Island, for example, then that thread disappears forever and always. Snip-snip."

"Like it never existed," Josie murmured. "I've been there, and it never existed."

Angela swatted her phone at Josie, smiling. "Exactly."

The Friendly Man can bend the entire world, any of it, into anything he wants? It can't be that simple. And if so, why is he trapped in the Eburos sub-basement?

Outside, apartments bled into offices and new steel-glass towers. Josie watched the street curve and rise ahead into a press of stopped traffic on the bulky metal of the Manhattan Bridge. Past that, walls of office towers, all those familiar skyscrapers of lower Manhattan, looked like a maw of teeth, snapping up for her.

Suddenly, sitting here, felt beyond naïve. The future didn't have to work out. *They'll force me back down there, until he rips me apart. No way out now.*

"So he grants wishes," Josie said at last.

Angela sighed, as if Josie were missing the point. "I'm not sure that's a helpful comparison."

But it is. That's what he is. A genie bottled under a fucking skyscraper.

"And he loves me," Josie said. "Loves Grace."

In the front seat, Tommy pointed at the wall of traffic on the bridge ahead, murmuring to Noah and working with his phone's navigation app.

"Grace and the Friendly Man have a long relationship," Angela said. "The place he lives, the room you saw, that was created for him. This entire city, in some ways the whole world, was built around him."

"Like a cage," Josie said.

"A *cage?*" Angela smiled, shaking her head. "No, Grace. You're smarter than this, surely."

All the monsters and the dead, none of them can do what the Friendly Man does.

Still no movement in the traffic ahead, and Tommy's phone rang loudly up front. "Sorry," he said. "Emergency line." He answered in a hushed tone, then craned back to face Angela. "There's a situation at the office. Outside. There's a ... well, you should see."

He handed back his phone. Onscreen: an ariel shot of the city street and sidewalk outside the Eburos building crowded with people, the entire block cordoned off by flashing police cars.

Angela said quietly, "The water, Grace. You, all of it, it's not to keep him in. It's to keep *us* out."

Us.

'Us' not as in 'people,' 'us' as in 'anchor clients.' 'Us' as in the puppet version of Angela I'm speaking to right now that isn't Angela. That's why the worm bolted away and let her corpse sink. Eburos found a way to keep its clients from meeting the Friendly Man.

Tommy's iPhone video came into focus: a mob wearing black robes, with a hooded female figure in front, who raised a burning torch at the Eburos entrance, like an absurd prophet of fire and ...

"Oh shit."

Dani.

The Eburos Group

EMPLOYEE RESIGNATION
& TERMINATION

Eburos believes in giving employees a chance to correct their behavior when possible and assisting them in doing so. The firm's progressive discipline process has six steps of increasing severity: verbal warning, informal consultation with manager, formal reprimand and peripheral digit amputation, formal disciplinary meeting, psychic penalties, and termination. The severity of offenses will correspond to different steps in the disciplinary process (e.g., a breach of our dress code policy may trigger Step 1; whereas disclosing confidential firm information will trigger Step 5, with immediate soul flaying).

COMPANY HANDBOOK

Chapter Twenty-Seven

"Oh shit indeed," Angela said, started to hand Tommy back the phone, then noticed Josie's locked stare. "Grace ..?" Another quick trace of Josie's line of sight, and a slow smile formed that made Angela look meaner somehow. No, *hungry*. Like the realization that Josie knew something quickened Angela's pulse.

Or maybe it's the other thing reacting, her shadow. I should've looked away, shouldn't just stare, except it's Dani. What is she doing?

"You *recognize* her, don't you?" Angela asked. She let Tommy take his phone. He looked confused, only mildly interested, as he flicked out of the video feed. "Explain this to me, Grace."

Josie nodded, as Angela texted two contacts in a fast one-two-three, done; one-two-three ... Over and over, answering messages on autopilot, as if she didn't even need to read them. *Because she doesn't. Because it's doing that, right? The human Angela is maybe only sort of alive.*

"She was a girl I knew, Josie knew. My—*her* girlfriend."

"The traffic isn't moving," Tommy said.

"Yes, thank you," Angela snapped, eyes fixed to Josie, still with that cold smile. "What is she doing?"

"I don't ..." *No, don't say that.* "I think maybe she's a cult leader now." *After I gave her that bouncy ball, the widow's eye.*

Tommy said, "There's no way through this traffic." He raised his phone to show Angela a mass of red grid lines. Everything stopped.

"Great, terrific," Angela said. "How long?"

"Hours, probably. The police ..."

Angela jerked around to glare back at the crush of cars boxing them in from behind. "Tommy, Grace—come on. We're going." She shoved out of the car without waiting, and Tommy sprang after her.

What is she doing? Josie didn't move, until Tommy opened the door, and then, as she ducked out, glimpsed a pistol holstered at his side. *The same gun you shot me with? Or did that disappear on Dutch Island, too?*

Angela stalked away from the bridge against the flow of traffic toward a street of scaffolding below. "There. Plan B." As they walked faster, Angela asked Josie, "This girl, Dani, was she always this way? No? You acted surprised when you described the cult."

"I was—am. I think it's the ball," Josie said. "The widow's eye, whatever it's called."

Angela stomped on, leading them through a crowd of students outside a busy college building. "Who told you that?"

"A woman on Dutch Island, after you left me in a car ..."

"Okay—stop. Remember: none of that happened. You think it happened—it didn't. I have no memory of a place called Dutch Island, because it doesn't exist, right?"

They crossed an intersection, just as the light changed, Angela totally oblivious to the traffic.

"Right," Josie said.

This is insane.

Angela waved Josie on to hurry them into a network of scaffolding and construction tarps. "Who gave you the widow's eye, Mr. Dean?"

"Yes, when I interviewed." *After I insulted his art.* "I gave it to Dani."

"*Josie* gave it to her girlfriend," Angela repeated, shaking her head, as if that were absurd. "So *Dani* could cause havoc?"

"What are you talking about? I thought it was just a ball, I didn't ..."

"It's part of *him*, Grace. Our friend. It contains a piece—there aren't many, and when they get out, all they want to do is return home. Like a magnet. A polarized joint encased in rubber, understand?"

No.

At the next light, Angela swiped her hair back, beads of sweat along her forehead and under her eyes. *Not just from the rushed walk, that's anxiety sweat. She's afraid. Whatever is happening, she's scared.* "That's why Josie's girlfriend is there. The widow's eye brought her in, so it can return."

"But the cult," Josie said. "I have no idea how that ..."

"Everything our friend does, *it* does, only different," Angela said, and when they got the signal, she hustled them through a crosswalk, faster. "It's part of him." She paused, as if Josie were meant to clap and agree. 'Oh, of *him!* Of course!' But she just stared back. *Tell me.* "It latched onto a part of Josie's girlfriend somewhere inside her, a desire to be this cult leader ... whatever she is now, and made it real. *Always* real, the same as he does with the rest of the world."

"Dani never wanted to be in a cult."

"She did," Angela said. "Whether Josie knew it or not—whether *she* knew it—she did. And now she is and has been." On the opposite block, Angela gestured to a green subway entrance for the R train. "Here we go."

"The subway?" Josie asked, as they approached the stairs down. "That's it? You made it sound like Plan B would be ..."

"Grace, listen to me." Angela stopped her at the top, people rushing past. "You are known to them."

"Known to who?"

Angela held Josie's arm a little too hard. "To *us.*"

'Us' again. Angela's shadow rocked sideways, and she released Josie. *To the monsters and the dead. To the other anchor clients, like the worm in her shadow.*

"They know me," Josie said.

"Yes, they know Grace very well. They know you can speak with our friend. And they want very much for you to lobby him on their behalf." Another pause, as Angela measured Josie's reaction.

What am I meant to say to that? Demons and ghosts are coming for me, and that's why the subway is Plan B?

"The subway?" Josie asked again.

"It's not safe," Angela said quickly. Behind her, Tommy held his waist, checking the sidewalk crowd and oncoming rush of people from below. "A lot of people have died down there, and others are ... well, other things live along these routes, even if most of us never see them. But we'll be quick, yes?" She started down, paused for Josie to follow, with Tommy in the rear. "Who knows?" Angela called back. "Next time, maybe he'll weave it so the subway never even exists. Oh, and Tommy: when we get to the platform, I need you to grab a sacrifice."

EBUROS LIMITS WORKDAY TO AVOID BURNOUT

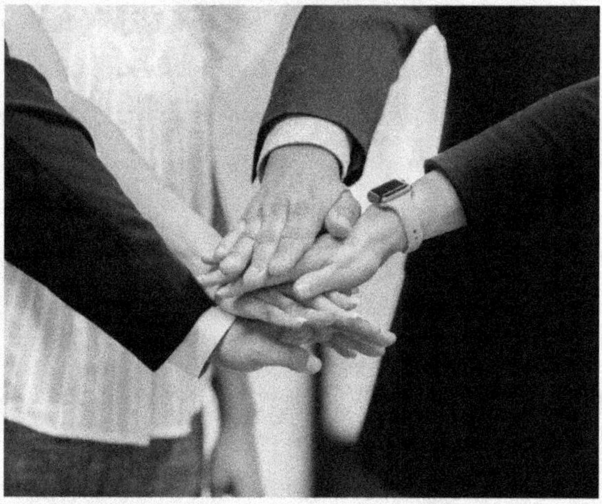

Work hard, but safely. This is the message The Eburos Group, one of the world's premier finance and consulting firms, has given its new employees. New rules for interns and recent hires have been introduced "to strengthen overall work experience and performance."

This shift to caring capitalism comes after unconfirmed reports of Eburos staff reported missing by concerned family and friends, as well as a spate of recent medical emergencies that have included three deaths in the past year. An Eburos spokesperson notes that these "regrettable deaths were all due to natural causes, such as epileptic seizure, heart attack, and fatal familial insomnia" and "the firm has not been accused of any wrongdoing."

Chapter Twenty-Eight

Through the subway turnstiles and up a connecting bridge that fed over the tracks to the Manhattan-bound side, Josie ran after Angela. "Sacrifice?"

A rooster on the plane when we hit turbulence, like that? The clouds darken, and it's time to chop up more birds?

"Well, yes," Angela said. They stopped between two supporting posts on the other side. A broken display sign scrolled gibberish words where the train times should have been. Across the tracks, someone coughed and a baby wailed, but otherwise, just the subdued hush of commuter's voices and that specific electrical-cement and sewer water smell of the subway tunnels. Tommy lingered behind them, near the stairs, frowning at the thin platform crowd.

"All of the things that you see," Angela said, "they affect the rest of us, too, even if we don't know why. A punch in the dark still hurts, doesn't it?"

A bloated dead man stood at the end of the platform, the entire left side of his head and arm missing. Bone and shiny flesh caught the light, when he perked up to look back at her. Josie turned away, eyes on the tracks. A rat dashed across, hunkering in a pile of plastic trash. *A rat, that's what Tommy will sacrifice. If he has to.*

Don't look.

"What happens if we don't?" Josie asked. "Don't sacrifice, I mean?"

"Going under the East River?" Angela said it as if Josie had suggested they travel to the Moon without a spaceship. "We have to. With you here, we don't have a choice."

Josie glanced up: the dead man loped closer, still three columns away, and now his dangling half-jaw curled into a desperate grimace. Totally silent, he lurched past a woman listening to earbuds holding a grocery bag, right between a couple in a hushed argument. No one saw.

"Can we move that way?" Josie asked and looked for Tommy. He leaned against the wall at the opposite end, directly behind—too close to—a thin, balding guy in a *'John Jay University'* polo and dark-rim glasses. This grad student guy was on his phone, everyone was.

The broken overhead display read: *'Grace…'*

The word scrolled across slowly, surrounded by jumbled letters and numbers, then more: *'Save us. Please Grace.'*

"Do you see something?" Angela asked.

"Yes," Josie said and stiff-walked away toward Tommy, with Angela close behind. She passed under the sign without looking up. "Just a dead man. Back there. But it's ugly."

"Oh," Angela said and didn't even look. Not that she could see, but still. Josie's explanation actually seemed to relax her.

Lights on the track and the near-distant rumble of wheels approached fast, almost here.

"That's okay then," Angela said. "That happens. The dead may be attracted to you, too."

Because the Friendly Man can bring them back, can't he? The Friendly Man can do anything. But if that's true, why isn't Mr. Dean king of the world?

The train rushed in, and Tommy grabbed the grad student from behind in a neat headlock, with the guy's other arm twisted back and pinned. The train stopped, and as the doors opened, Angela shoved in first, waving people off, shouting, "Emergency, can we please have the car! Thank you! Move that way!"

People cleared to the other side but stared, murmuring when Tommy got in with his hostage. The grad student's face reddened, and he swung one arm wildly, chortling and kicking uselessly at the seats.

Josie counted ten people in the subway car, with two men already up, ready to move on Tommy, as the doors shut. The two guys wore brown uniforms with neon vests, like construction workers. The first guy sported a retro mustache, and the second one's cheeks streaked black, like he'd had tattoos removed—and not well.

"What the fuck, man! Let him go!" mustache-guy called.

"Tommy," Angela said slowly and checked her phone: the tracking map was on, with a night-sight display that showed their blue location dot arcing for the edge of the East River. "Almost ..."

"Right," Tommy said. Ignoring the two guys, he swiveled so Angela could reach into his side holster and hold up the pistol.

"Oh shit!" someone shouted.

People ducked and banged out the opposite end, hurrying through the gap connecting them to the next train car. Her phone display still up, Angela lowered the pistol to the grad student's forehead, careful, oh so careful, as if she were about to signal an Olympic race and needed the timing *just right*.

Still, the two construction guys stood their ground in the aisle. "Don't!" mustache-guy shouted. "Come on, please!"

"Angela ..." Josie said.

"Stop it," Angela said. "I have to concentrate."

"What happens if you don't?"

"If I don't ..?" Angela shot Josie a frustrated look. "I told you. To cross under the East River with you onboard, we need a sacrifice, something to distract the Red Buffalo ..."

The train jostled, and Tommy's grip slipped. Angela lost her footing, and her gun aimed past the grad student's face to point at the windows—in that opening, the aisle guys charged. Mustache-guy tackled Angela from behind, hands scrambling for the gun, and the former-tattoo guy dove at Tommy. Tommy threw the grad student like a doll to topple him backwards, then drove his elbow down hard into the mustache-guy's neck. The pistol spun away, and as Angela pawed backwards across the floor, hair wild and jacket torn sideways, Tommy kicked the mustache-guy with a steel-toe-tooth crack that rolled the guy into the other two.

Josie went for the gun.

She had it on them, aimed at Tommy, then Angela, back to Tommy, as the train rocked and sped through flashing darkness. "Go!" she shouted. "All of you—out of here!"

The two guys and the grad student crawled back, bloody and shaken, while the other passengers continued out onto the next train car.

"Stupid," Angela said. "Stupid and stubborn ..."

"No," Josie said. "I can't let you just kill people like this."

"Shut up." Angela climbed into a seat, panting.

Tommy raised his hands, tense, as if he were ready to spring on Josie. She kept the gun on the center of his face. *Maybe I'll miss. Maybe not.*

Angela pointed at the ceiling. "Do you hear anything?"

"No," Josie said. "What?"

Angela watched her, searching for any sign of a lie. "You don't?"

The train banged, wheels screeching around a turn, but nothing else.

"No, just the train. That's it."

"Okay." Angela sighed, shook her head at Tommy. "Stand down. It's okay."

But Tommy didn't lower his arms or unclench, still like a cat hunkered in high grass, ready for a distraction to catch her eye or an itch or …

They slowed into the next station. The lights of the platform and crowds waiting in front of movie posters and fast-food banners came into view.

"We got lucky today," Angela said and gestured to Josie. "*You* got lucky. Give me the gun."

"Why? Are you going to …"

"No. We're through. It wasn't necessary. The Red Buffalo sleeps a little longer. Now, Grace. The gun."

The doors chimed to open, and Josie handed her the pistol. *Stupid, but what can I do? Shoot them both? Run and hope that Tommy doesn't drag me down?*

On the platform, Josie told him, "I should have shot you, you know. To make us even."

"Even?" He followed a few steps behind Angela and Josie, up the stairs, back through the turnstiles. "I didn't shoot you—"

The ceiling collapsed on top of him.

THE EBUROS GROUP

01
COLLABORATE

The ProVista team are here to help Eburos shine. It is essential that you work with them before and during the shoot to discuss logistics and their vision and any concerns you may have. This is particularly important for staff who may not be fully visible on camera.

02
DRESS THE PART

Consider your role at Eburos carefully, when planning your outfit. While most staff will wear formal attire (be sure it has been ironed!), in some instances client-specific clothing may be appropriate. If you are wearing plastic sheeting or plan to wield tools (e.g., clippers, knives, drills), we recommend accompanying with neutral colored clothing to avoid distracting the eye.

03
GROOMING MATTERS

Keep in mind that professional photos are intended to stand the test of time, and so take extra time with the little things: hair, makeup, nails, tumors and abrasions to present yourself in the best way possible. These details can make all the difference!

Don't be afraid to smile! Being photographed can be stressful and scary, but we hope you can relax and enjoy the experience.

Chapter Twenty-Nine

Through a gray cloud, Josie shaky-stepped up and out of the subway stop, realized she was gripping Angela's hand, her other fingers pinched to hide her nose and mouth under the top of her shirt, like a make-shift mask. A turret of demolition smoke rose from the subway entrance. Shadows of people struggled up to the street, coughing and gasping. Up here at the edge of Manhattan, cars and trucks honked on the street, and past that, Josie saw the perimeter lanes of the FDR highway that traced the eastern flank of Manhattan island, with just a sliver of a walking path and basketball courts on the other side, between the deadlocked highway cars and the expanse of the East River and crystalline condo towers of downtown Brooklyn beyond.

"Where's Tommy?" Josie turned in a slow circle, scanning the dirt-streaked faces of people around them. No one else emerged from the tunnel, but still immense spools of dust rose from it, swallowing the stairs. Impossible to see further in. *He shot me in that other reality. Did he deserve to be buried? Happened so fast.*

A loose crowd—some layered in grimy debris, others pausing to gawk or help—clustered around the subway entrance. A woman collapsed, crying, and another man yelled instructions to a 9-1-1 dispatcher into his phone. Chaotic voices: "Sounded like a bomb!" "People down there?" "What did you see?"

Josie slipped her hand away from Angela and tried to see back down through the wall of dust. *Maybe, maybe because of what he did on the train—what he* planned *to do, maybe he deserved ...*

"Is he still down there?" Josie asked.

But Angela stepped up onto the base of a streetlight on the sidewalk to climb onto an adjacent garbage can to see over the street traffic and crowd. Probably looking for the police perimeter at the Eburos building ... no. No, Angela turned the wrong way, looking back at the river toward Brooklyn.

Because something is moving closer, just under the surface. Even at street level, without Angela's trashcan perch, Josie spotted it. An approaching lump on the water. A large form that swelled toward them, leaving a foamy wake on either side.

"You see?" Angela called to Josie and karate chopped the air toward the river. "Here he comes."

"Who?"

"The Red Buffalo, who do you think?" Angela said and climbed back down. She grabbed Josie's hand again and jerked her out directly through stalled traffic toward the pedestrian bridge over FDR Drive and the river.

Josie's ears rang from the sudden subway collapse. They were alive, should slump to the pavement and reach for a water bottle like everyone else. Not march into the path of whatever this was. When a taxi started to cut them off halfway across the street, Angela hop-stepped into its path and pointed the gun at the driver. He raised both hands, eyes wide. "Stop!" Angela shouted and pulled Josie on. "Hurry up. Grace, this anchor client circles the island, like a territorial shark or killer whale or ... whatever."

"A demon shark swims in circles around Manhattan," Josie said.

"Not a shark, but yes." Angela aimed the pistol at another mail truck that started to accelerate into their path, and the driver stomped on the brakes, calling out his window, "Jesus, what are you ..." and they continued to the opposite sidewalk, where Angela pulled Josie through a packed open-air parking lot, through a gap in the rear fence and to a narrow slope of grass looking down on the traffic of the FDR. "There." She pointed to a pedestrian overpass about twenty meters away.

The bulge in the river still neared, but not moving any faster. *How long until it hits? Five minutes? Less?*

"You can see it, too," Josie said.

"I can see that, yes," Angela said. "The water, I see the water moving. Just like everyone else can see me, but not everyone else can see ..." She paused at the short stairwell up to the overpass to let Josie watch her shadow jump ahead. Angela followed an instant later, her grip still hard on Josie's wrist, the pistol ready in her other hand.

"What are we doing?" Josie asked. "Why are we going toward this thing, whatever it ..."

"Him," Angela said. "Going toward *him*. Because you created this mess, Grace." She hustled them over the highway and down two flights of concrete stairs onto a walking path along the low seawall. The East River lapped against rocks and garbage just five meters down. It stank of fish.

Looking up from the shore, the swell of water closed on them with a dark shape just visible beneath, like a whale or slow-moving submarine.

"We're just going to stand here?" Josie asked too loudly, but she didn't pull away. "Where is Tommy?"

"Tommy is dead. What do you think? You killed him." Angela glared from the water to Josie, shaking her head. "Your arrogance on the train …"

"You were going to shoot that man."

The water shape was thirty meters away, twenty-five …

"Yes, to stop this!" Angela aimed the gun at the water, without breaking Josie's stare. She tossed down Josie's hand in disgust. "You did this—*you*!"

Twenty meters, and now the water splashed harder against the rocks, picking up. Fifteen meters.

"What are we supposed to do when this thing gets here, the buffalo …"

"Do? You are going to apologize."

"Apologize?"

Ten meters, and now the water bulbed back around the top of an immense shape, beginning to emerge.

"Yes," Angela shouted over the crash of waves below. "And if you don't, I am going to shoot you in the head." She jammed the gun into Josie's hair, just above her right ear, and the hard metal press—that feeling—froze Josie's legs and arms, all of her, in a moment of surreal quiet as an animal form climbed up onto the shallows of the East River.

Skeletal, with long, white beams and jointed limbs, it looked like an oversized connector set covered in garbage bags. A child's toy in an enormous mold of a buffalo. Josie could make out small horns and the curl of a hunched torso and legs. At least fifteen meters tall and twice as long, its shoulders hunkered over an impressionistic head. Like a giant art project, the buffalo was lined with lumpy black garbage bags over what looked like PVC piping in its frame.

Not red, why isn't it red? The garbage bags swelled and jostled, like something was trapped inside, trying to get out. The lumpy bags were tied to all four of its stalk legs and in horizontal lines along the thin slots of its torso. The creature looked like a cheap joke, a slapdash garbage-carrying buffalo, waiting for fur.

"What the fuck is this?" Josie murmured. Water sloshed around the buffalo's PVC knees as it waded closer, towering over them. "Do you see this? Angela, do you ..?"

"No," Angela said quickly. "I see air and displaced water. Whatever you see ..."

"I see a fucking pipe buffalo covered in ..."

"Stop it," Angela hissed. "Just stop. Focus. Do your job."

Small, liquid pillars rose from the river around the buffalo's legs, growing into human figures and animals. The shapes—people dancing, sitting and running, large birds, a lion, a horse, and a mass of smaller animals—froze and shimmered as suspended water sculptures. Then, when the buffalo took another step, they splashed down, gone. Another pause, only five meters from shore, close enough that Josie heard voices calling from the garbage bags. *People. People trapped in there. Or a trick. Another delusion.* Angela shifted the barrel of the gun against Josie's head. For an instant, just that instant, Josie almost forgot it was there. Almost.

"Grace," the buffalo rasped, its voice low and rumbly in Josie's chest. "Give us back what he took."

"I apologize," Josie said, both hands up, as if she were under arrest. *Held at gunpoint, but not by this thing.* "Please, I'm sorry. You can go back to ..."

"No." More shapes grew from the river water. Josie watched rivulets of dirty water harden into the specific beads of an intricate, smiling woman. "You will speak to him, broken girl. We want what he took."

"Who?" Josie asked.

Beside her, Angela tensed, adjusting the gun. "What did he say?"

"I apologized," Josie told Angela. "You heard me."

"The last king of America," the buffalo said. "Your owner."

"My what?" *The Friendly Man or Mr. Dean, must be. Or both.* "What am I supposed to ..."

"Smash it open." The world flashed—lightning struck the buffalo's front legs, igniting them in a stream of white-yellow light with a piercing blue corona. Up the legs, the garbage bags shrieked and melted in a wave of flame.

"Oh my God." Josie staggered and fell, her hands slapping the pavement hard on either side.

Angela tracked her stare to the spreading fire on the buffalo—the *red* buffalo—but she just frowned, as if ... *as if, as if.* Josie ducked to look away, shaking. Chemical burn and meat smells, hair roasting. The scent coated her nostrils, down her throat.

"What he took," the buffalo roared.

"What?" Josie asked. Heat tinged her face, when she looked again, tears streaked her vision. The buffalo's entire frame swelled with fire, smoking into the blue sky. The garbage bag cries and screams pitched higher. "*What?*" she shouted again.

"The world."

The screaming stopped, and the buffalo slowly sloshed back, away from the shore. *What world, what the fuck?* It sank under the waves.

Angela stared down at Josie, the gun at her side. "You aren't up for this," she said quietly. "Are you?" Not an insult, she just sounded tired, ready to move on.

Josie covered her face, until the smells dissipated and she could look again at the empty water of the river. Behind her, gridlock traffic on the FDR still honked, moving in stutter-starts, and just a little further down, a group of teenagers played basketball, hooting and calling to one another.

None of them saw. Of course they didn't. None of them, except ...

Except when Josie took Angela's hand to pull herself up again and finally turned away from the East River, looking back at Manhattan, a young teenage girl had stopped at the base of the pedestrian overpass, clutching the railing and staring hard at the water. Totally pale, her cheeks looked almost green, as if she were ready to vomit. She couldn't have been much older than thirteen and wore a school uniform: white shirt, blue skirt, with shiny shoes and a backpack she'd dropped, along with her phone.

Angela saw her, too, and stepped away from Josie, hiding the pistol in the back of her pants under her coat. "Hi," Angela said. "Are you all right?"

The girl's eyes snapped on Josie, then to Angela. "Did you ... what was that?"

Angela motioned Josie over fast, and as Josie approached, Angela smiled, voice in animal-control mode. *Just like with me. Just like our impromptu coffee date at the hotel lobby.* "It's okay, sweetheart," Angela said. "What did you see?"

"What did I see?" The girl blinked at them, then released a nervous, shaky breath and wiped hair from her eyes. "Oh my God, I must be losing my mind, right? Shit."

"What was it?" Angela asked again, all practiced patience. "It's okay. You saw ..?"

"A pipe animal. A buffalo?" the girl said and looked at Josie. "Didn't you? I mean it was right there. It talked to you."

"Yes," Josie said. "I did."

"See!" The girl shook her head, laughing nervously. "Oh my God, some kind of movie special effects, right?"

"Yes," Angela said. "Exactly. What's your name?"

"Tamara."

"Tamara, it's nice to meet you. I'd like to talk to you about an opportunity."

"Opportunity?"

"A job, Tamara," Angela said and flashed Josie a 'follow my lead or else' look, with a flicker glance back to her concealed gun. *Play along or you'll what—shoot her? Shoot both of us?*

Yes. You will.

Josie started up the stairs first, as Angela kept talking, and by the time she reached the bridge, Angela walked in-step with Tamara, carrying her backpack again.

"This is amazing!" Tamara called to Josie. "You really work for this company, too, The Eburos Group? I've heard of it. You're like rich, right?"

Josie met Angela's stare. Still with an easy smile, but Angela's eyes were sharp, almost angry.

"Yes," Josie said. "That's right."

"We want to give you that chance, too," Angela said. "It's a very selective scholarship. You'll need to sign a few papers, of course—and definitely talk to your parents, but do you mind, Tamara, I don't want to delay anything, and in the interests of transparency, Grace and I have an errand to run. Do you mind if we continue our conversation on the way?"

"On the way?" Tamara's pace wavered, but she didn't stop. "Yeah, but I'm not sure I want to drive anywhere ..."

"Oh no, it's just a short walk," Angela said, as if it were the most ordinary thing in the world. She gestured through the office-building canyons of Manhattan ahead. "It won't take long. We just need to make a quick pitstop. Grace is starving."

What is this? What is she doing?

"To your office?" Tamara asked, walking fast again. "Yes, I have time."

Following us. Following me. Stop this. Warn her, tell her to run. Now—go.

"Oh no," Angela said. "Not the office. Just the grocery store." And when Josie frowned back, Angela shrugged. "Let's grab a bite."

Chapter Thirty

A grocery store?

Under the vegetables. That's what Samuel said, must be.

In a steady stream of professional pleasantries—"Yes, tell me more about your parents, what will they think?"—Angela convinced Tamara that she'd been selected for a corporate scholarship, which carried abundant perks and an outsized salary. "It's how we give back," Angela said. "Eburos believes in community and equality of opportunity. So often, people are grouped unfairly: what school you attended, how much money your parents make, what kind of car you drive ..." Walking side-by-side, directly in front of Josie, Angela held Tamara's arm. "You and I both know, Tamara, those are just excuses to keep the world the way it is."

"I have good grades," Tamara said quickly. "Last year, I screwed up math, but this year Mr. Peters told me I can be a B, maybe even an A, if my final ..."

"There will be plenty of time to talk about that," Angela said. A quick check back to Josie, and she pointed to a Whole Foods at the opposite corner ahead. "That look good?"

Josie didn't answer, and Angela reassured Tamara that her academic performance would be acceptable. Eburos understood the challenges facing young people today, and as soon as Tamara called her parents ...

"Oh no," Tamara froze, and a pair of women in suits knocked into them from behind, muttering as they walked around. "I forgot my phone. I dropped it back there by the water." Her eyes wide, whole body shaking, Tamara started to pull away. "My dad will kill me. That's a new phone, I can't ..."

"Tamara." Angela caught her shoulder, faux-friendly, but she didn't let go. "We'll get you a new phone."

"What?" Tamara hesitated, as if she genuinely didn't understand. "What do you mean?"

"A new phone," Angela repeated. "We'll have one for you today."

"No," Tamara said. "My phone, I need mine ..."

"And that's no problem either. I can send someone to pick it up right now." Angela whipped out her own phone, texting fast, then showed Tamara the message. "You see? One of our interns will retrieve it in five minutes, faster than we could walk back. I guarantee you they will hustle."

"Really?" Tamara turned to Josie. "They'll get my phone?"

Behind her, Angela stared hard at Josie, but Josie tried not to look, keeping her attention on the girl.

"If you're worried about it," Josie said. "Maybe you should ..."

"No, it's fine." Angela's shadow flicked sideways, and she leaned in to turn Tamara back around toward the grocery store.

"Wait." Tamara pointed at the cracked pavement by Angela's shoes. "What just happened, did you see that?"

This girl has all of it, too. Get her away.

"Yes," Angela said, and her shadow blotched forward an instant before she did.

Still pointing, the movement startled Tamara, walking again, all the way to the corner. "How did you do that?" She grinned back at Josie. "Are you seeing this?"

"She sees it," Angela said. "It's fun, isn't it? I'll explain this trick to you, while we grab something to eat, how's that?"

"Okay," Tamara said and continued across when the light changed, almost to the grocery store entrance, lined with flowers for sale. A man in a green apron handed out coupon books. "But my phone …"

"You'll have it back in five," Angela said, one hand raised. "Promise. If not, we'll all go back to find it. Deal?"

"Yeah …" Tamara checked Josie again, as they neared the doors. "Do you like working there?"

Josie stopped, eyes on Angela. "What is this? Why are we here?"

Angela slowed, her hand still resting on Tamara's shoulders, as people bustled in and out of the automatic store doors behind her. The faint smell of citrus wafted out. "This? This is clearly an ordinary grocery store." She said it as if Josie had lost her mind. What a strange question. "Grace is feeling light headed, because she needs to eat," Angela told Tamara. "Low blood sugar. Once we get in …"

"No," Josie said and caught Tamara's attention. "Don't do this. Don't listen to her. Walk away right now."

"What?" Tamara wavered, like she didn't understand. "Why are you …"

"I don't know why she brought us here," Josie said. "But whatever it is …"

"It's to settle your bad vibes," Angela said, with an eye roll, and she spun Tamara back around, starting in. "Come in or don't, Grace. Tamara and I are hungry."

Josie watched them pass through a rush of people grabbing push carts and baskets, heading back, past a pyramid of oranges, along a display with seven different varieties of apples.

"Everything all right?" The green apron guy smiled and offered her a newsprint-coupon book. "If you're a carnivore, there are some great deals."

Inside, Angela walked Tamara further back, around the bananas and along a rear shelf of broccoli, carrots, and cabbage. "This is just a store, right?"

"What?" The green apron guy backed off, offering coupon books to other people. "Just a store?"

"There's nothing, I don't know—*wrong* about this place, is there?"

"Maybe the prices," he said and laughed to himself. "Sorry, you didn't hear that from me." He grinned at a couple pushing a stroller.

What do I do? Storm the office with Dani protesting outside? Throw myself into that chaos or try to call Mom again—and then? Call Mom with Grace's voice, Grace's entire body, so she won't know me, even if she sees me or ... what? The police? And say what?

At the far end of the fruit-produce area, almost out of Josie's line of sight, Angela turned back to meet her stare. *Still holding that girl like a hostage. Maybe Angela is actually hungry. What can she do to us in this place? Under the vegetables. Is Samuel here? Is Sandra?*

Tell someone she has a gun. Scream. Run.

Instead Josie stepped inside, straight back to where Angela finally released Tamara's shoulder to cross her arms, eyebrows raised. "Are we done being difficult?"

Before Josie could answer, Tamara said, "It's okay. She told me. A kid in my class has anxiety, too. Like serious."

"She told you I have anxiety?" Josie asked.

"Yes," Angela said. "Now we need to find a place for Tamara to review her scholarship contract. But darn it, wouldn't you know ..." She gestured past the produce and adjoining nuts-and-coffee section to a salad bar and cluster of circular tables, all filled. "No place to sit."

"It's okay," Tamara said. "I'm okay to wait. Maybe that way your intern will be back with my phone."

"Uh huh." Angela frowned at a nondescript door with an *'Employees Only'* sign. "You know what? They have a staff break room here that's pretty amazing. Free drinks, cereal, candy bars ... should we?" But Angela didn't wait, a hand still on Tamara again to keep her close.

"Are you sure we're supposed to ..?"

"No," Josie said. "Whatever you're doing ..."

"It's simple." Angela typed a code fast into a keypad by the door, and it opened. "See? How would I know that password, if we weren't allowed?"

She stepped in with Tamara, holding the door so Josie could follow. Still explaining how lucky Tamara must feel that she'd been selected, Angela led them down a bare hall of bulletin boards and adjoining supply rooms, past a bathroom and lockers to a simple black door. No security panel, and the rusted hinges and doorknob looked old, unused.

"The thing is, we really don't have as much time as I would like ..." Angela was saying. She opened the door to water-stained wooden steps that descended into some kind of cellar. Angela tapped the wall, and bright yellow light flooded the walk down to a concrete floor piled with boxes and huge empty bottles. "You see, if we don't settle this quickly," Angela continued, ducking to lead them deeper, as if they'd expected this, "I'll get questions from *my* boss, Mr. Dean."

At the bottom of the stairs, Tamara stopped, Josie right behind her. Angela paused between the stacks of boxes.

"What are we doing down here?" Tamara asked. "I appreciate everything you're saying, but this is weird, right?"

"No, it's back this way," Angela said, pointing. "You can look at the agreement in private. Here, I'll show you." She raised her phone, swiping to bring up dense, miniature writing. "See? You'll want to look this over."

"But why down here?"

"The break room," Angela said. "I told you. It's right back there, so ordinary people don't find it."

"No," Josie said and reached for Tamara. "Come on. Back up with me."

Angela stepped in fast to take Tamara's arm, her phone right at Tamara's eye level. "Check the document for yourself, Tamara." Tamara stepped in after Angela. "Really, we just need one signature."

"I thought you said my parents ..."

"Yes, your parents should see it, of course," Angela said, and Josie followed through the boxes. Here, the air tasted of mildew and sweet rot.

"Oh my God," Tamara said and stopped midway down the walkway between the boxes. She swung the phone back to show Josie. "Did you see this! Two-hundred *thousand* dollars!"

"That's right," Angela said. "And your signature locks it in. If you want to talk to your parents, I completely understand. You should. But if you wait, we'll need to open this up for other applicants."

"Other applicants?" Tamara swiped fast down the document on Angela's phone. "But if I sign, I get ..?"

"Grace!" a boy's voice called, and Samuel came bounding around the corner of the boxes. "You came back!" A waving black stream of mist still attached to Samuel's back, as he ran in for a hug.

Josie knelt to let him wrap a thin, cold arm over her shoulder, then followed Samuel to a makeshift entertainment center, positioned by a stone doorway that led deeper. Like a low-budget guard post, complete with two Batman folding chairs and a boxy television on a perch, Samuel showed Josie a new-looking video game console and nest of wires that split off into the far wall.

"Do you want to watch my movie with me now?" he asked. "It has robots."

Samuel's tether of mist extended through the doorway, where a short flight of stone steps dropped deeper into near darkness.

Stall. Think of a way out. Tamara won't listen, but I have to stop this.

"Samuel, it's good to see you," Josie said. "Sure, I'll watch with you."

"No," Angela said. "I'm sorry. Grace doesn't have time to stay."

"She's my friend," Samuel said, already sitting in one chair, with the conch shell between his simple brown shoes. "I want her to watch with me."

On the TV, a trio of animated, brightly-colored robots shot lasers at a mass of hairy, red-eyed giants. Clearly, the robots were the good guys, but they looked hopelessly outnumbered.

"Really," Angela said. "We need to see Sandra. That's why we're here."

"Shh," Samuel said and pointed excitedly for Josie. "This is the best part!"

The attacking giants smashed one of the robots, and then a volley of flaming arrows knocked down a second robot, too.

"I don't understand," Tamara said. "Who is he? Why are we down here?"

Angela told Samuel that she'd been patient, but honestly now they really needed to go in. *There is no way out of this, is there? Not without abandoning this girl or trying to drag her away.* Josie watched one of the wounded robots shouting to a third robot, who retreated onto a cliff. The third robot popped open a hidden panel to reveal a golden disc, like the retro imagining of a futuristic CD, and hurled it frisbee-like over the giants to the smoldering chunk of the first robot. Rainbow light exploded, the giants recoiled, and when the glare cleared, a new, stronger-looking robot stood where the disc had been.

"See?" Samuel asked Josie, with a huge smile. "You see? They did it!"

He isn't just showing me this. This is a message. Something to do with the Sandra?

"No more," Angela said and started for the doorway. "Let's go. With or without your permission ..."

Samuel shooed her away. "*Fine.* You can go in now."

Or he's just the ghost-corpse of a dead child, who wanted to share his movie with me.

Through the doorway, a line of dead people stood along the opposite stone wall. A man whose head ended at a hedge of meat above his nose and cheeks, a short-haired woman missing both arms, a lanky girl with wet holes in her chest, and more, whose outlines were too faint to see all the way back into the darkness of the room. The floor was uneven stone, different than everything above it.

Angela spotted Josie's reaction to the dead people and eased Tamara around to face her, not the wall of corpses. Inscriptions, plaques, and symbols lined the wall, too. Impossible to make out from here.

"Here is where you sign," Angela told Tamara and tapped a space at the bottom of her phone screen.

"That's it?" Tamara asked.

"That's it."

"For ..."

"Yes, for all of it," Angela said.

Josie forced herself to look away from the dead. Their mouths moved, but no sound. She took a swallow of basement damp. *The smell of death. That's what it is, isn't it?* An obese woman shuffled out of the dark, with burst veins in her neck. She flexed her black jaw, teeth scraping.

"Don't sign, Tamara," Josie said. She reached for Tamara but Angela pivoted between them, one arm over the girl's shoulder to lock her in position.

"You promise?" Tamara asked Angela, and looked up at Josie, as if she felt sorry for her. "Is she lying about the money?"

"Not about the money," Josie said. "The rest of it ..."

"But the money?" Tamara asked.

"The money is real," Angela said and raised her eyebrows at Josie. "Isn't it?"

"That's not the point ..."

"It is," Angela snapped. "The point is there are 1,200 other applicants. If you *don't* sign, Tamara ..."

"You're jealous," Tamara said, blinking at Josie, as if she'd solved a puzzle.

"No," Josie said. "Look: turn around and *look*."

"Honestly," Angela said, reaching to take back her phone, "if you're not sure, maybe we should rethink ..."

"I'm here *with* you," Josie told Tamara. "Not against you. Do not ..."

Tamara signed. A quick loop-di-loop with one finger, and she let Angela take back the phone.

A shriveled boy stepped along the wall, closer.

"Congratulations," Angela told Tamara. "Welcome to the Eburos family."

"Look," Josie said again, and now Tamara finally followed her stare, pitching back, almost out of Angela's grasp, when she saw them.

"This is another joke, right? Hey!" Tamara called to the dead people. "Hey, you hear me? Scary AF, but that's enough, you got me."

Angela moved to block the doorway and tapped on her phone.

"You see this, too?" Tamara asked her.

"No," Angela said.

"But you do?" Tamara tried to smile at Josie, paling. "It's not funny. I don't know why you brought me down here for this."

A video call started on Angela's phone: Mr. Dean's smiling face appeared, sucking a cigarette.

"I am sorry not to call sooner, sir," Angela said. "It couldn't be helped."

"Right," Mr. Dean growled, and when Angela raised the phone so he could see Josie and Tamara, he snorted smoke out both nostrils, a dragon CEO. "Grace, salutations. And you, young lady ..."

Angela said, "Tamara."

"Tamara, welcome. How familiar are you with the meaning of the bull and bear markets?"

"Shut up," Josie said.

Another cigarette drag, and Mr. Dean nodded, as if he'd expected that. "Yes. Unfortunate to see you in this duality, Grace. And in that location."

"What location? We're in the basement of a grocery store ..."

"You are on holy ground," Mr. Dean said simply. "There are twenty-three undocumented burying grounds on Manhattan south of Central Park. Some are now parks. Washington Square Park, Union Square: what were these sites before? Why is the grass so green? Because the soil is rich with mass graves. Nineteenth-century potters' fields and pits of cholera victims, bodies that were never reinterred. Other sites, such as your current location, were well-used much longer ago, even before *you* arrived, Grace, on a Dutch merchant man."

Tamara asked softly, "What is he talking about? I want to leave."

"We're going," Josie said.

"You're not," Angela said, and, the phone still raised so Mr. Dean could watch—Josie heard him typing in the background, fucking *multitasking* during this—Angela took out the gun.

Tamara grabbed Josie's sleeve, a half-step behind her, as if to hide. "I'm sorry. Please don't shoot me. Whatever I did ..."

"You haven't done anything wrong," Angela said. "Not at all. Grace here, on the other hand ..."

"Are you going to shoot me?" Josie asked. "If I try to run?"

"Yes," Angela said. "I told you. I will shoot you."

"Then her heart stops." Josie patted her chest. *They need this heart, don't they? To keep their little world running. The blood that changed me into this, they can't just let it die.* "If you kill me ..."

"Is she there yet?" Mr. Dean asked, clipped, as if he were bored.

"Almost," Angela said, and called, "Sandra? Can you hear us?"

"Sandra?" Josie said. "No, she was on Dutch Island, that thing lived in a cave under ..."

"Sandra lives here," Angela said, her phone and gun both trembling a little, as if her arms were starting to tire. "She always has."

"Whatever you experienced the last time," Mr. Dean said, still distracted. "It has clearly been woven into a new shape."

A woman's dark outline coalesced on the stone wall, and the dead people shuffled to either side, parting for her. It just looked like a human-ish mold stain, but now, as Josie stared, the edges sharpened and a lumpy left arm bulged out. Then, a leg that was shaved down to wet bone at the ankles, where it fit into a fashionable high-heeled shoe.

"Listen to me," Josie told Tamara. "This is real, what's happening right now."

"No." Tamara shook her head, shivering. "No, I don't want to be here."

"She can't shoot both of us. When I move, you run," Josie said. "Don't look back, just ..."

"Grace, stop tormenting the girl," Angela said, with a tired pull in her voice. Done explaining. "She's part of the team now, just like you."

"There are a few externalities to be addressed," Mr. Dean said. "When this current situation is resolved."

Another misshapen leg emerged from the wall, followed by a dark torso and second arm, and the concave, reflective hollow of Sandra's head. She wore the same Bob Dylan t-shirt as before. *Once a Dylan fan, always a ...*

"Don't listen to them," Josie told Tamara, talking fast. "When I move ..."

"Hello Sandra," Angela called past them. "We're honored to see you again. You have the instrument?"

Past the line of corpses, Sandra approached. Faces screamed silently in her black, open skull, shimmering away and back again, like swirls at the bottom of dirty dishwater.

"Did not last long, this one," Sandra said and raised both hands. She held the bone flute.

Slowly, Angela set her phone in a nook on the floor, so it rested up for Mr. Dean to keep watching. Her gun aimed at Josie, she stepped in to take the flute.

"It is sad what he takes," Sandra said quietly.

Angela angled the flute up to her lips, twisting one arm, but she couldn't quite get the angle to cover the holes, while holding the gun.

"The Mapuche Indians boiled conquistadors alive," Mr. Dean said on the phone, in lecture-mode again. "This instrument is very specific. It can do many things. It wasn't even originally designed for this, but the combination of protein, collagen, calcium, and other minerals, with specific fluctuations in the airflow can be customized like a brilliant algo to pierce through the ambient noise of markets ...”

"Fuck." Angela dropped the flute in a clatter, breathing hard and stabbing the gun at Josie. "Stay there. If you die, we still own you."

There's no way out.

"Tamara, listen to me: before you run from him, tell the Friendly Man about Eburos's investments," Josie said.

Total silence on the phone. Carefully, Angela crouched to pick up the flute again, but she didn't try to play, just held it over the gun. Josie felt Tamara still trembling beside her.

Only Sandra clicked her fingers down to clasp her claws together. "I eat," Sandra said. "That is our deal."

"I swear to God," Josie said and looked into Tamara's eyes, holding their heads close. "When you see him under the basement water, the Friendly Man—I know you don't understand yet, but you will—and when you do, tell him all about every location where Eburos is invested." *What were the names? What did Maya say?* "Panama, Switzerland, the Cayman Islands. You'll be afraid when you see the Friendly Man. You should be. And when you're afraid, talk about all of those places. Make sure he hears you, before you run." *The same way he heard me mention Dutch Island.*

"Before I run," Tamara repeated, in a daze. *No idea what this means. But she'll remember. They hear it now, they'll remember, too.*

"No," Mr. Dean said and cleared his throat. "She won't do that. Angela ..."

"Haiti, Chad, Myanmar, Singapore," Josie said quickly. "Say those words to him, Tamara."

Angela raised the flute again, fingers awkwardly positioned, with the gun somehow still trained on Josie. *But she can play. In that position, she can play.*

"Tell him about the company's money," Josie told Tamara. "Talk about where the money is—nothing else."

Erase it. Erase it all.

"No," Mr. Dean said, with a new tightness. "Stop. Bring them back here."

Angela wavered. "Bring them both?"

"Yes, back to the office now."

Sandra crinkled toward Angela, faces blotting faster in her skull, shrieking and panicking in silence. "You can't. You do it here, so she is mine."

"Temporary adjustment," Mr. Dean said. "Post-haste, Angela."

Angela lowered the flute but didn't drop it. She flicked the pistol at the doorway: the way out.

"You *cannot*," Sandra said. "Your investment allows me to eat."

"It will be made right," Mr. Dean said. "We will honor ..."

"If you take her away with the instrument, you are in breach," Sandra said, voice scratching. The corpses behind her staggered closer, and more from the darkness. "She ..." A crooked finger jabbed at Josie. "She is mine. To eat. To fill the hole. In my ..."

"Not yet," Mr. Dean said again. "Not until we have this sorted. I *will* honor the terms of our investment."

"No honor in this," Sandra said.

With Tamara clinging to her back, Josie stumbled back through the doorway. Samuel leapt up from his chair, the robot movie still playing behind him.

"Grace, what's wrong?" He blinked from Josie to Tamara, then back to Angela, who kept the gun on them, with the flute in one hand. "No," Samuel said. "You're not allowed to do that." A shock of wide-eyed fear in his eyes, as Sandra stepped out behind them. Samuel ran into Josie's path, blocking the aisle between the boxes. "Don't! She'll hurt me! You're my best friend, please!"

"Go," Angela said and jabbed the pistol, almost touching Josie.

At the doorway, Sandra fingered the air above Samuel's black-mist trail. "Only admit the right ones," she said and clucked her tongue. "I am disappointed, child."

"No, I didn't know." Shaking, he went back to Sandra, hands clasped. "Please. Grace is my friend ..."

Sandra pinched, and the black mist severed. Samuel choked, turning in a slow circle to watch Josie with wide, desperate eyes.

No. Oh God, what am I doing?

He collapsed into a pile of dark bones and dirt.

"Move!" Angela knocked them forward. "Now, Grace—now!"

Up the stairs, back in the employee hallway of Whole Foods, Angela held up her phone—the video call still on—to say, "Sir, I am so sorry ..."

"Counter-battery fire across the board," Mr. Dean said quickly. "It is an eleven-minute walk from your location. I expect to see you in ten."

 —————THE EBUROS GROUP

FEAST OF
CARNATHOS THE FORSAKEN
POTLUCK!

START 12PM

25th Floor   **Next Thurs**

It is that time of year again for a celebration of community and good friends. In recognition of the Feast of Carnathos the Forsaken next Thursday, Eburos will be holding our annual all-hands firm potluck luncheon.

We encourage you to bring your favorite dish, family recipe, or live specimen/prey to share with the group. If you have trouble deciding on what to bring, we suggest bringing an appetizer (e.g. fresh cartilage, deviled eggs, spinach dip) or dessert—for those of us who use Carnathos as a cheat day!

Please don't forget to label your dish for any allergens or special diets. We can't wait to see you.

Attendance is mandatory!

Chapter Thirty-One

"The problem, as I see it," Josie said, with Angela's gun jammed in the center of Tamara's back, concealed from the busy sidewalk crowd under Tamara's backpack, "is we are all going to die."

"Not my first time, remember?" Angela said. "Keep moving, Tamara."

Her eyes swollen, almost bloodshot but not crying—like the stress of this situation swelled up to flood her tear ducts—Tamara shuffled forward, then tilted back to Angela. "Wait, what did you say? You died?"

"She left that part out of her pitch," Josie said. "Angela jumped off the roof of a building not far from here, right across the street from the Eburos building."

"Not the roof, the twentieth-floor terrace," Angela said. "Tamara, head down. No eye contact with anyone." She still carried the Mapuche flute at her side, like a baton.

"Your boss sounded mad," Josie said.

"Mr. Dean doesn't get mad."

"Angry then."

"No," Angela said. "Just stop. Stop trying to provoke me or whatever you think you're accomplishing right now ..."

"So he won't kill you again, you're saying?" Josie said. Nervous energy. Back there, underground, in the moment between Sandra stepping out of the wall and Angela dropping the flute, it had been over. Done. The skin of Josie's chest already prickled in anticipation of wet-hot pain, bracing for the tug of her heart to push out through her ribcage until ... until I slumped and became a dead girl in a Brooklyn hideout by the ruins of a baseball stadium, uselessly gnashing my teeth at the Grace version of Tamara.

That almost happened. I almost died. In another version of the world, I did. Except here we are, marching south to see Mr. Dean so he can ... what? What happens now?

"And if I die," Josie said, still talking fast, wired, "does that mean you would *plant* me? Grow me, until one of those things, an anchor client, like your shadow, comes along looking for a host?"

Tamara murmured, "What are you talking about?"

Angela said, "Walk."

They crossed another street. Josie didn't know these blocks well, but they couldn't be far. Still, no sign of Dani's cult protest, or ... She heard sirens and distant shouting off to the right. *Nevermind.*

"That's how this works, isn't it? You don't waste the dead, do you ? You don't bury them. I saw it, Tamara. It's where I got shot ..."

"You got shot?"

"Oh yeah," Josie said. "I took a bullet in the shoulder."

"Seriously?" Tamara asked.

"My wound ceased to exist, when the island disappeared," Josie said. "But still."

They turned at the next corner, and there, three blocks down, a line of police cars parked diagonally to block off the street, lights flashing, with cops pushing back a small crowd. Right outside the glass entrance of the Eburos lobby. Josie craned up to take it in, all forty-five shiny-dark stories of it. *Is he watching us right now from the top, or do we rate that highly?*

Closer, through a gap in the crowd and police cars: a ring of about thirty people filled the street, lassoed together and surrounded by trails of barbed wire. Smoke rose from a bonfire in the center of the group, as if they planned to hold this fortified spot and celebrate with a bar-b-que. *What is Dani doing?* Even this far—now, two blocks away—Josie spotted her at the front, waving a torch, her hood pulled back to expose wild hair and her thin, veined jawline and neck. *Like she hasn't eaten in a year.*

"*Could* he kill you?" Josie asked Angela.

They kept going, straight through another cross-street and past a line of food trucks, the air thick with the smell of sizzling meat. People in suits and finance bro vests called for their orders, laughing and eating, as if there were no police barricade a block away, no sirens or shouting. *This city …*

"Why would you ask that?" Angela asked.

"I'm curious. We're all probably about to die, so you can tell me."

"Grace …"

"My name is Josie." And when Tamara frowned at her again, lost, Josie shook her head: *'Don't worry about it.'* Angela just kept them going. *I still need a plan.*

Tamara said, "Why does she call you …"

"Because her name is Grace," Angela said quickly. "Right now, her name is Grace. Soon, that may change."

"Then you'll get to be me," Josie told Tamara, and to Angela, "I'm asking the other you, you realize. Not human Angela, the other thing. Can Mr. Dean kill your anchor client?"

"I know what you're asking," Angela said and pushed Tamara into the street toward the watching crowd and line of police. "We're almost there."

"Because if he can kill you," Josie said, "I bet he will. You fucked up pretty badly choosing me. You're the one who recruited me. That's HR 101, right? Don't hire people who will delete the company's offshore accounts."

"You have an agreement, the same as everyone," Angela said, and shouted at the crowd, "Move! Let us through!" She waved to the police at the front, offering her phone. "Call the CEO. We're expected."

"Ma'am, no one ..."

"Let us through," Angela said. "Or call. Do you need me to get our security out here?"

"She'll do it," Josie said, still with that off-kilter rush. Adrenaline, fear. *The realization that I'm alive. We have a chance, I don't know how, but we do.* "Don't test her!"

"Ma'am, no," the cop said again.

Inside the perimeter, Dani saw Josie, mouthed something and pointed her torch. The cop's radio crackled. Someone shouted for Dani to drop her weapon.

And she did. Slowly, Dani tossed the torch and picked her way over the barbed wire, away from the others. A helicopter stuttered and roared overhead, the noise swallowing the street sounds, until Angela pushed Tamara and Josie through the police line, closer to the protest—whatever this was—and the steps up to the Eburos doors. *Where Everett pissed on them a million years ago. Just days ago. Is it really that new, all of this?*

Dani stared at Josie, frozen at the edge of the wire. The circle of roped people chanted and swayed, arms up. Angela forced Tamara up to the entrance. On the other side of the glass, security guards worked an elaborate door lock, ready to shuttle them in.

Angela paused to look back. "Grace!"

"That's not her name," Dani said.

She's here, she's right here. Insane that she knows who I am. She can't. Didn't he change the world? Didn't Grace's heart swallow that other me under this skin?

Dani came closer, and even fifteen meters away, Josie smelled the raw charcoal-lighter fluid stench of their bonfire. In one hand, Dani squeezed a fist.

On the ball. She still has it.

"You know me?" Josie called.

"Josie," Dani said. "I don't know why you look like that, whatever they did to you ..."

The ball, somehow the mashed up reality of the ball keeps Dani pinned to me. Must be.

"... we weren't doing well, were we?" Dani asked.

From the now-open office doors, Angela shouted, "Grace, come inside!"

"Don't," Dani said.

Josie tried to keep Angela out of her field of vision, even as one of the security guards pulled Tamara into the building. Josie let the flashing lights and screaming sirens blur behind Dani. "We were happy before that," Josie said. "Maybe not perfect, but we were good. What are you doing here?"

"We came to burn it down. Our friend, Everett, I think they have him here, too."

"You remember," Josie said. *They planted Everett in the wooden wall, right on the other side of that door. A corpse, germinating, waiting for a shadow to infect him. To pull his skin on, like a suit hanging on the line at the dry cleaners.* "But you can't, Dani. What can you possibly do here? They'll arrest you or worse. All these people with you ..?"

"They believe," Dani said. "We all do."

"Believe in what? What are you talking about?"

Dani approached. Shouting behind them—"Stop!" "Do not move!" "Freeze or we will open fire!"—as Dani slowed, close enough for Josie to see the lines of muddy tears on her cheeks, the emaciated folds of her forearms and the joints of her wrists and fingers.

"I believe The Eburos Group is evil," Dani said. "This building is evil." She waved her fist at the office tower, where Angela still poised in the open entrance, watching. *Listening? Trying to gauge how to leverage this to force me inside?* "Their money isn't natural," Dani said. "It feels wrong to you, too, doesn't it? I don't think the world was always like this. I think the rules were changed for them."

"You're right," Josie said. "It sounds insane, but you're right."

"I know."

"You were going to be a lawyer."

The words jolted Dani, and she smiled with sudden shock, opening both hands to touch her face, as if she couldn't remember the feeling of her mouth in a grin. The rubber ball hit the pavement, bouncing sideways toward the building. "No!" Dani shrieked and lunged after it. The police shouted—a *crack*, like fireworks behind Josie—and Dani spun and went down, blood on her chest. *Just like that. Oh my God, just like that.*

The circle of people in the street wailed, rocking like a human wave. Angela rushed out, arms up—"Don't shoot! She's with me! She works here!"—and snatched Josie's wrist, yanking her toward the door.

Josie opened her other hand and caught the rubber ball on the third bounce, before they hustled inside. *I watched Dani get gunned down and did nothing.* Security guards slammed the outer door again, and

Josie looked up without thinking, an instinct to remind herself that she wasn't insane and Everett ... wasn't there. *They took him down.* Above the door, the wood paneling wilted with dying vines and leaves.

In the street outside, Dani wasn't moving. A pair of cops rushed in, guns on the other protestors.

"They shot her," Josie said. Her voice sounded hoarse, more unfamiliar than usual even. *And some version of that is about to happen to me. Think. Don't just follow her orders.*

"Of course they did," Angela said and turned Josie around to join Tamara at the elevator bank with an armed security guard. "Let's go."

Halfway across the lobby, Josie's knees locked, when the security guard's face registered: Everett. The same stupid shock of blonde hair and square, muscley jawline, he posted beside Tamara, dressed in a bulky suit with a gun holster. *Bulky because it's armored. Bulky so he can knock me down, without taking a hit.*

"We're almost done, Grace," Angela said. "You're doing great."

Josie forced herself on. "Everett," she said.

He squinted at her the way he always did during a pub quiz, when he was convinced the announcer got the answer wrong.

"Yes?" he said. "Have we met?"

All four of them boarded an elevator, and Angela hit the top floor.

"Where are we going?" Tamara asked softly. The doors closed.

"Where do you think, honey?" Angela said. "To see Mr. Dean."

A lump moved under the skin of Everett's left cheek, with tiny crawling legs and flexing pincers. Like a crab, the shape pushed against his jawline, then bulged down under the skin of his throat and was gone into his shirt collar.

"No," Josie told Everett. "I don't think we've met." She pointed to his nametag: *'E. Fisher.'* "I'm good with names."

"Lucky guess!" he said. "Very intuitive!"

"Yes, she's a whip, this one," Angela said.

The elevator screens still displayed a serious-looking market news show, with a running stock ticker along the bottom and people working at open-office desks in the background. But now the captions registered: '... *suffered the largest one-day drop in its history today.' 'That's right. Eburos is down 52 percent since the opening bell and showing no signs of stopping. Investors are spooked ...*'

A graph showed the plummeting value of The Eburos Group stock. *And that's what all this is about. That's all it's always been. Nothing profound. Just money.*

The elevator ticked up through the 20s.

Angela stiffened when she saw the screen, but didn't speak.

"What does Eburos do?" Josie asked.

Everett checked his reflection in the doors to fix his hair, with the half-listening expression Josie knew from the psyche class they took sophomore year. Tamara still looked dazed, in shock. But the question pricked Angela.

She frowned. "You are just being provocative now. It's a challenging day, that's all."

"No, seriously," Josie said. "What does the company do? What do *we* do?"

Angela sighed, as if Josie were a child screaming for attention. "We serve our clients, Grace, what do you think ..."

"What does that mean, though?"

They hit 30, 31 ... continuing up. Onscreen, the commentators shook their heads seriously, and the captions read: '... *have to think the shareholders may call for an emergency meeting ... now down 60 percent. It really is a bloodbath ...*'

"I don't know what 'serving clients' means," Josie said. "I pretended like I did. I didn't ask questions, but I really didn't. We don't build anything or create, we just …"

The elevator dinged and opened at 45.

"Thank God," Angela said and soft-pushed Tamara out into the wraparound glass lobby, with the same bull skeleton facing off against a taxidermy grizzly bear, and … Josie's mom sat on a couch at the back wall, flicking her phone, with a heavy folder on her lap, as if this were a doctor's office waiting room and she'd just finished all the forms.

The forms. Her signatures—they want to make her sign. Even with Mom's training as a lawyer, she would miss the fine print. Eburos would own her.

"Ah!" At the end of the hall of timeline wall art, Mr. Dean saluted from his open doorway. "The orchestra is assembled! Come in, come in!"

Mom sprang up, noticed Angela and paused, the folder clutched in front of her. "Sorry," she said. "I thought he meant me …"

"He does," Angela said and flashed a knowing glare at Josie. "Come with us. We'll get everything taken care of."

Mom nodded, still wary, but she fell into step beside Josie and frowned at Everett in the elevator, just before it shut again. "Huh. I could have sworn I knew him," Mom said. "A friend of my daughter."

"Josie," Josie said.

Mom brightened, distracted by the wall mural, halfway to the office. *Just like me the first time I came here.* "That's right," she said. "Do you work with her?"

"I did," Josie said. "Do."

"I don't know where she is," Mom said. "I worry, but I'm sure she's fine."

"Busy, maybe," Josie said.

At the end of the hall, they entered Mr. Dean's office, unchanged except for three long rows of hanging plants along the windows, filling the glass in a swarm of fronds, ivy, and tiny fern sprouts. The circular wooden planters suspended on ropes that rose to the vents and flying pigs along the ceiling. On the opposite wall, by an overstuffed bookshelf, the white chalk, stick-figure outline of the Friendly Man watched from the same shadowy blue column ruins Josie saw the first time.

Mr. Dean followed her stare and clapped. "Ah ha! I thought so."

Mom raised the folder in one hand. "Solomon, it's good to see you. You're busy, but I have the paperwork here."

"Of course you do." He crossed to hug her, with a quick kiss on each cheek, then swiped a cigarette toward the door. "Angela, would you ..?" And lit it, pacing back to the center for a quick puff, like a stage actor prepping the audience.

Angela shut the door, Tamara stiff and unmoving just inside. "Can I go?" Tamara asked.

"Yes, of course," Mr. Dean said and nodded elaborately at each of them. "No one is here who doesn't want to be."

"I'll be quick," Mom said. "On the paperwork, I just have a few technical questions. On page seven, the third paragraph ..."

She started to open the folder, and Mr. Dean swung a trail of cigarette smoke in a Z formation between them. "Caitlyn, we're pals, aren't we? Let's let the lawyers earn their fees, and you and I can relax a bit?"

"Yes," Mom said, but she didn't close the folder. "You know I'm an attorney, too, Solomon."

He smiled from her to Josie. "Of course. We both are. Are we locked and loaded on the signatures?"

"Not yet," Mom said. "That's what I wanted to ask you about. A few of these clauses seem a little strange and expansive ..."

"Strange and expansive," Mr. Dean said and drew a line in the air from Josie's eyes to the chalk drawing of the Friendly Man behind him. "You see him, don't you, Grace? Right now on this wall?"

Josie swallowed. *Don't give him any information, let him talk. Grab Tamara and Mom, and get out—after he makes this right somehow.*

"I want you to let Everett go," Josie said.

"That was his name," Mom sad. "Everett. Unique—you know him, too? If you're friends with my daughter ..."

"I am your daughter," Josie said and nodded at Mr. Dean. "He changed me. This company literally gave me another body to wear."

Mom closed the folder. "What are you talking about? He just said your name is Grace."

Josie stared at Mr. Dean and the chalk drawing. "My name is Josie."

"Well," Mr. Dean said. "That answers that. But I am willing to counter. Just once. Let's think about your life. About *her* life." He tapped the air toward Mom. "Unremarkable. Not bad, not desperate, but aimless wasted potential. Lost and sinking. A privateer without an astrolabe in rising water. Fair?"

Mom's eyes narrowed on Mr. Dean. "If this is some kind of game ... Solomon, do you know what this reminds me of?"

"Of me," Mr. Dean said. "Me and your late husband? Mark could never see past the end of the month. The next rent check. We both know that. His gift was wasted."

"What gift?" Josie asked. "Don't talk about my dad like that."

Mom turned to Josie again, caught in this sudden back-and-forth, as if she'd walked into a burning room with no exit.

"He saw them," Mr. Dean said. "Very rare. You don't remember, of course. Dissociative amnesia can be a powerful fortification."

"The things I don't remember," Josie said quietly. "How do you know about that?"

"Background," Mr. Dean said. He sighed, as if this were suddenly tedious. "You exhibited a history of emotional trauma, particularly at a younger age. You have the ability to encode new memories, and all of your physical and neurological exams ..."

"My *exams*?"

"We're all adults here," Mr. Dean said, then shrugged at Tamara. "We can *behave* as adults anyway. Yes, your exams. Eburos investigated your prior history, as we would any investment, to gauge risk against potential upside. Everyone comes from somewhere. You came from Mark."

Now Mom said softly, "Don't talk about him."

"Noted." Mr. Dean shrugged, waved Angela in, and when she stepped past Mom to shuffle Tamara closer, he kept Josie's stare. "I told you: one more counter. Keep this life. Keep your mother safe. Donate to charity, whatever fuel your mental engine needs to achieve optimal performance—we can give you the resources to do that. You know we can. This girl, Tamara? Nice to see you, Tamara. Tamara returns home with a story, a check, and an NDA. We keep an eye on her, yes, but she expands her life, as well. Your mother ..."

Again, Mom looked hard from Mr. Dean to Josie, shaking her head. "It isn't ..." Mom said. "Josie? It can't be ..."

"She'll make peace with this eventually," Mr. Dean continued, "and you retain your comp and role."

Angela stiffened. "Sir, she caused the Red Buffalo to ..."

"I know what she did."

"She is not stable," Angela said.

Mr. Dean started to respond, then paused to study Angela, flicking ash on the carpet. He paced back to the chalk drawing and adjacent windows. Still, the Friendly Man hadn't moved. Mr. Dean raised a hand to twirl the lowest row of hanging plants, and as they turned, Tamara gasped, tried to stagger back—Angela caught her. Not pots, heads. Human heads made of wood, with their skulls opened like planters, but alive, with wild eyes and flexing lips and tongues.

Josie looked away. *Think.*

"Sir," Angela said. "She is not a team player."

"Angela," Mr. Dean said, pausing for another long smoke, as if to work out the exact phrasing he wanted. "Fuck. What else can I say? I am disappointed."

"Sir ..."

"I was hands-off your unorthodox recruitment tactic, but the selection of a hotel lobby adjacent to the uncle's medical facility for a meeting—I should have identified that as scope creep. The right road, wrong direction. This situation and her response to it ..." When Josie looked again, he aimed a cigarette at her. On the wall, the Friendly Man was standing now, like they'd gotten his attention. *Good.* "We are experiencing degraded information on the reliability of our investments. Which causes? Volatility. This is sub-par project management," Mr. Dean said.

Flushing, Angela bit her lip. The flute trembled in a fist at her side. "Yes, sir."

"I see this as a host issue," he said and stepped away from the head-plants., with two of them still twirling slowly against the glass. A hand to a black nugget in his right ear—Josie hadn't noticed before—and he said, "It's Solomon. We require an HR interface at the top. Yes, now." Another quick ear tap, and Mr. Dean shrugged at Angela. "It's time for your exit interview."

Angela lowered her head, eyes closed. "Sir, I apologize."

"Yes, well." Mr. Dean smiled at Josie again, hands clasped. "What is your current reality with respect to version 2.0?"

"My current reality is ..." Josie stopped herself. *Push back, and they'll levitate your heart out.*

Beside her, Mom murmured, "You can't be Josie ..." and reached for her hand. Josie started to take it, realized she still held the rubber ball. The widow's eye that destroyed Dani, because it melts reality around whoever holds it. *Throw it back at Mr. Dean? Try to use it on the Friendly Man himself?*

No. Mr. Dean gave it to me, probably expected it to kill me—or just curious what I would do.

What if I could ...

The image of a surreal potential movement formed in Josie's mind. Not a plan, a specific pull of sinews and muscle in her arm, followed by the timed release of the ball. Still, she held it down, unmoving.

"Grace?" Mr. Dean asked her. "Is that still your name or is it time for a change?"

What will happen?

"My name ..." *Don't look at the plants or the stick figure on the wall, just concentrate. One action, one movement. Not aimed at him or any of them. What will happen?* "I'm Josie," she said.

The Eburos Group
EMPLOYEE RESIGNATION
& TERMINATION

All terminated employees are required to meet with HR for an exit interview to prepare for their post-life role. The firm typically asks that employees give at least two weeks' notice, if possible, to allow HR to accommodate employees' preferred method of termination. During busy times of the year, exit interviews will be held on a first come, first served basis, with some in-demand termination methods unavailable (e.g., drowning, lethal injection, nitrogren hypoxia) in favor of more traditional methods (e.g., boiling, impalement, Persian Scaphism or insect nesting). All terminated employees are compensated for accrued vacation and sick leave, according to local law.

COMPANY HANDBOOK

Chapter Thirty-Two

"No," Mr. Dean said and flicked a hand at Angela. "You are not Josie yet. But you will be. Go ahead."

Angela straightened, wiped her face. Tears in her eyes, but she blinked them back, sniffed and nodded. "Good. Yes, sir. I agree with this decision."

"Irrelevant," Mr. Dean said, watching Josie closely, as his cigarette burned down to the nub. "Play." And then to Tamara, "Congratulations, and welcome aboard."

As Angela raised the Mapuche flute, Tamara asked questions, confused, and Mom stepped closer to Josie, as if maybe looking deep enough into the pores of her skin would reveal her daughter hidden underneath. The music started.

Hot pressure pushed out from Josie's chest, and she screamed, tried to grab the edge of Mr. Dean's desk and fell. *So sudden.* Vision spotting white, Josie heard herself shout. Mom's voice. *Doesn't work, if I don't try. Look past the pain. See the room.*

Squinting through a blur of tears, Josie watched a bleeding heart levitate up and out of her shirt—Grace's heart—while Angela played the Mapuche flute with her eyes closed. Mr. Dean tossed his cigarette, pulling a new one from his suit pocket, and Tamara pointed, scrunching her own chest with one hand.

Now. Do it now.

Muscle movement: Josie's right arm lurched up, heavy, directly at the heart, as it floated away. She jammed her hand into the organ's open valve and released the ball, whipped her arm back.

Mr. Dean bolted forward. "What did you do?"

Angela lowered the flute—silence—and the heart hit the floor with a wet thud, before Mr. Dean could catch it.

Josie's bloody hand and arm had freckles in all the right places, and when she touched her cheeks, feeling the familiar ridges and depressions of her skull, Mom grabbed her tight. "Josie!" Mom said. "It's okay."

Standing over the heart, Mr. Dean sucked hard on a cigarette, breathing out a smoke snarl. "It's not. That was not intended to happen."

On the floor, red tubes grew out of the bloody organ in thin tendrils, already blotching over with white and pink flesh.

Mr. Dean staggered back, murmured, "Off script ..."

He dropped his cigarette, and Mom yanked Josie toward the door. Loops of blood vessels puffed out into wet pouches of organs, then two frizzy white nets that sealed up and disappeared under a ribcage. *Lungs. Organs and lungs.*

"Sir ..." Angela said.

"Play," he said, then rushed to her, shaking Angela's flute arm. "Music now!"

But her hands shook, eyes wide, and she blew an off-kilter hoot, like someone whistling along the top of an empty bottle. On the floor, the torso—that's what it was—began to close with another layer of muscle, and two arms sprouted, a pelvis, the tops of thigh bones, and now a neck crumbled up from protruding vertebrae.

It's her. The ball is making a person.

Tamara gasped from the stop-motion anatomy on the floor to Josie, expression locked in panic. *We have to take her.* Josie slipped away from Mom, around the growing body, and snatched Tamara's elbow—Angela fumbled again with the flute—and Mr. Dean stepped behind her to draw the pistol out of Angela's back in a smooth motion. He aimed it at Josie.

"Did you know this would happen?" he asked. "Who told you to do that? The Marquis? One of the RNI Group? Who talked to you? What's their offer?"

On the floor, pinkish skin punctuated the muscley torso and pelvis in patches, like mold. The arms ended at bloody finger joints now. A skull grew pale eyes, and the leg-meat flowed down to ankles, with foot bones blooming.

Angela piped off-key into the flute again, her arms still knocking in the air, eyes fixed to the thing on the floor.

"It's all right," Mr. Dean said, totally calm again, with the gun in Josie's face. "We can solve for this. Your agreement with us supersedes anything others may have convinced you to do."

"Nobody told me," Josie said.

Another ugly whistle on the flute, and Mr. Dean whirled around to knock Angela sideways with the gun. She stumbled and lost the flute, a hand to her forehead. "I'm sorry," she managed, hair in her face. "Sir, I'm so ..."

A rap at the door, and when Mr. Dean called, "Enter!" Maureen slipped inside with a friendly smile.

"Knock, knock," she said and gave the scene a quick once-over, her attention hesitating on Josie. Maureen wore a new black-and-red Poodle sweater embroidered with a sinewy Halloween spider. No, not a spider, because the legs had suckers and were tipped with forked talons. "Well hello, you," Maureen said to Josie. "Back to your classic look, I see." Then she smiled at Mr. Dean, totally oblivious to the body forming on the floor or the gun in his hand. "Rumor has it," Maureen continued, "someone up here won't be joining us for Friday happy hour?"

"Please," Angela said to Mr. Dean, and when she reached for him, he sidestepped out of her grasp.

"Come on now, dear." Maureen took Angela's arm, spinning her in a slow circle to the door. "On a scale of one to five, how would you rate your overall experience at the company?"

Angela still watched Mr. Dean. "Please, no ..."

Still aiming the gun at Josie, Mr. Dean said, "I've told you where we are and what the situation calls for. Your services are no longer required, Angela."

Angela's shoulder slumped, and she slow walked with Maureen into the hall, as Maureen said, "We'll scoot on down to take in some fresh air on twenty." *Heading for the balcony.* "How does that sound?" A mumbled response. They continued out of view toward the elevators, and Maureen asked, "Would you recommend a friend or family member work here? Why or why not?"

Josie heard the elevator ding and the doors open and shut. On the office floor: the shape of a woman in a fetal position, like a newborn, with only one bloody foot and a mat of fast-growing dark hair still forming. Rough fabric flowered over her into the shape of a simple dress and beaver-fur shawl. *She'll jump. Angela will die again, won't she?*

"Our people are obviously our most valuable assets," Mr. Dean said, looking from Josie to Mom and Tamara. "True capital. That's why I need you all here. Now, let's evaluate our revised circumstances."

The woman on the floor opened her eyes, shifted to sit up. She said something in another German-sounding language—Dutch, must be—and then asked, "English?"

"Yes," Mr. Dean said. "English works well here."

She stood to face Josie, pressed a hand to Josie's chest. Exactly the same height, the woman smelled like the cold, open meat of a deli counter. But clean somehow. "You carried me."

"Grace," Josie said.

"Thank you." Grace kissed her quickly, then scanned from Josie to Mom, and the door. "I'll go now."

"No," Mr. Dean said, but already Grace left the office, headed down the hall. "Grace, my name is Solomon Dean ..." He ushered Josie, Mom, and Tamara out, running after Grace.

Josie glanced back: the wall was empty. No Friendly Man.

Back in the forty-fifth floor lobby, the windows shone clear sunlight from the balcony all around. Facing the elevator, as if she knew exactly what this was, Grace hit the down arrow. *She does. She watched it through me. And all of the women before, didn't she?*

Mr. Dean pointed the gun at the back of her head. "We need to discuss this development."

"Men like you always say that," Grace said, without turning. "'Sit down, let's think.' 'Wait until I've had time to process.'" Still, Grace didn't turn, ignoring the gun. "Or my favorite: 'don't go in the cave.'"

"Explain that," Mr. Dean said. "You're recounting your memory from the first time, the beginning? You expect me to believe that your brain, *this* brain here, right now ..."

"No," Grace said, and the elevator arrived. She knocked her head backwards into the gun—it spun out of Mr. Dean's hand to the floor—and Grace hop-stepped into the elevator, hit a button. "I don't care what you believe. *De sigaar zijn.*"

As the doors closed, Mr. Dean crouched to grab the gun, said, "The other one." And tapped the button down. "I told her to fix this. I told Angela we need prompt elevators on call."

"Where is she?" Josie asked.

"She went down, you saw."

"No, I meant Angela ..."

"Yes," Mr. Dean said. "She went down, too." A long pause, and when the second elevator arrived, he hustled all three of them in with the pistol, slapped the bottom button, and then found his phone, with a quick look at the news monitors. The elevator started down. Onscreen, a serious-looking trio of men in suits debated the Eburos stock drop. The captions: '... *wiping out more than $250 billion in a matter of hours* ...' Mr. Dean tensed, then took a practiced, meditative breath, like he'd trained for this, said, "We create efficiencies at every node in the value chain. Our clients depend on us for that." Almost as if he were talking to the financial show, not them. "But," Mr. Dean continued, "misallocations have consequences." '... *rumors that a shareholder vote of "no confidence" could be coming as soon as this evening* ...'

"You're in trouble," Josie said slowly. "Aren't you?"

Focused on the screen, not her, Mr. Dean touched his ear nugget again, as the elevator descended. "Security on our friend. Everyone, now. Thank you." Mr. Dean took another breath that made him cough. "We'll have the ship level soon."

"Will you?" Josie asked.

He pointed the gun at her. "You don't agree?"

"No. If you can't control the Friendly Man ..."

"This is fog of war," he said simply. "Unknowns. If our relationship is truly degraded, none of you will leave."

Mom shook her head. "You can't keep us here, Solomon."

"Your daughter and Tamara are both employees with post-lifetime contracts."

Tamara murmured, "I want to go."

Staring back at Mom, Mr. Dean said, "You understand consequences, Caitlyn. I know *you* do. It's hard to walk with a hole in your head, isn't it? *I* can't keep you here. But the reality of a corporate accident, recorded as an major insurance event on our P&L? That can."

They dropped past the 30s and 20s, into the 10s. The screen captions continued, '*... I have to think the market is shocked, and it may be time to pull the plug, bring in fresh blood ...*' The lowest sub-basement wouldn't take long to reach. Minutes, less even. He sounded meaner than upstairs.

Desperate. That's panic in Mr. Dean's voice.

Below the 10s, the floors ticked down to one, and they continued without stopping, until the elevator opened back into a black-rock cavern lit by the willowy glow of water in the floor at the center. All the computers and equipment around the walls looked new, replaced after the last time. Grace hovered at the edge of the pool, watching her reflection.

"Step back, please," Mr. Dean said.

"Why am I afraid?" Grace asked.

Mr. Dean walked them out, closer, the gun on Grace now. He shoved Josie, Mom ,and Tamara to the back wall, said, "Security will be two minutes. Should be down here already. Any second."

"What if he doesn't remember me?" Grace asked quietly. "This me?"

"Away from there," Mr. Dean said and tried to pull her—she twisted free, frowning back at him.

"What will he do if you shoot me here?" she asked, with a slow smile. "What will happen to you?"

"Nothing," Mr. Dean said. "His barrier will hold, and you will be dead. He won't know."

"But you," Grace said, inspecting him again, as if she couldn't understand Mr. Dean's face. Like his reaction was wrong. "What about you? All of those lives, I thought you must be part of him. Maybe even a host for an anchor client yourself. I really believed you had a pact, something old and secret and important that tied you to him. You never leave the building. Ever. Just like him. But you aren't special, are you? You aren't a demon?"

Mr. Dean sighed, the gun aimed out of her reach. "No."

"You're just a man, here because you worship money."

"Because our shareholders put me here," Mr. Dean said.

"Not a god or a demon or even a host for one of them. You never leave this office," Grace said, "not because you're trapped, but ..." She shook her head, as if waiting for the words to align. "Because you're *working*."

"It's called achieving impact," Mr. Dean said. "Producing high-quality deliverables. Now please step away." When she still didn't move, he hesitated, noticed the elevator displays: both were back up on the first floor. "Security is unacceptably slow, no doubt caught up in the streetside distraction, but they're on their way." The first elevator ticked back down toward them. "You see?"

Josie pushed away from the wall. *Do something. Distract him.* "Why didn't you just make yourself king of the world?" she asked. "Of the universe?"

Mr. Dean glanced at her, the gun level on Grace. "Your question presupposes ..."

"If The Friendly Man can do anything, why all this currency trading and floods and ..."

"It's important to acknowledge what we have and what we want," Mr. Dean said quickly. Still the elevator hadn't arrived. "What we want is not what we should have. In the caricature you describe, do you imagine the world would be stable? *'The happiness of your life depends on the quality of your thoughts.'"*

"It wasn't always that way," Grace said distantly, as if trying to remember. "People *did* use my voice to make radical changes to the world."

"Yes," Mr. Dean said. "In the past, some of my predecessors were not so stoic in their management practices. Excessive growth for its own sake is not ..."

The elevator dinged and opened, and three security guards stepped out, Everett in front ... all with black-mist talons extending from their backs. Sandra came out last, her fingers wet with blood, splatters of gore on her t-shirt.

"No," Mr. Dean said and trained the gun on them. "Sandra ..."

The guards approached in a stilted puppet-walk, arms limp. Sandra hobbled closer behind them, new faces screaming silently in her dark head. Everett's face pleaded, gone again. This dead, puppet-Everett neared Mr. Dean, but Mr. Dean aimed the gun past the security guards, at Sandra.

"Give it back," she rasped.

Mr. Dean nodded. "It's in my office. Absolutely. I'll have it brought down."

"No." Sandra staggered closer, one hand curled toward Grace, holding all three smoke tendrils. "Her. Give it back."

The heart? The flute, what is this? Mom took Josie's hand, and Tamara ducked against Josie on the other side. *Wait for a gap and run.*

Out of this room, he can't shoot all of us. Reach the elevator, then the lobby, then …

"Sandra, I apologize," Mr. Dean said slowly, a step back, closer to the pool and Grace. Grace just frowned, as if trying to interpret this, as the security guards formed a semi-circle around her, almost in reach. "I am at a loss," Mr. Dean said. "We left the instrument on the floor of my office. An oversight."

"No," Sandra said again, the black mist trails twisting in the air with the movement of her clawed hand toward Grace again. *"You."*

"Sandra, you're confused." Mr. Dean shook his head. "She doesn't …"

"No, Sandra," Grace said.

She does. Whatever this is, she does.

"I will swallow you into me, child," Sandra said. "With or without …"

"No," Grace said again, staring down the dead security guards. "You will not. You will return to the mud. My love believes in *us*, not you."

A guttural moan from Sandra, and the security guards came in, their dangly arms ready to swing.

"Sandra, stop," Mr. Dean said. "Whatever you think this girl has done, she doesn't know …"

"This *girl* was food in our world," Sandra snarled.

The second elevator started down. *Security, must be. More security.*

"This *girl* erased us. Convinced your god to bring you—hairless monkeys with gold coins and shells—into the light."

At the wall, Josie whispered, "On three. We run on three. Mom? Tamara, you hear me?" They nodded, and the elevator dinged closer. "When the guards come, we'll follow the wall …"

Mr. Dean broke into a grin and shoved between two of the dead security guards, toward Sandra. Their bodies swayed, pawing the air too slowly to catch him. "*She* did all that?" He pointed back at Grace. "Amazing! Humanity—we were *animals!* Remarkable." The elevator dinged, and he whipped the gun up into Sandra's face. "This is breach of contract. Like dear old Catuvolcus ..." And shot her, again and again in flash-snaps that exploded wet clouds of blood across the floor, until the black clouds dissolved. The security guards collapsed, and Sandra whimpered to the floor.

"One ..." Josie said, eyes on the elevators. Just one dark outline in the second elevator, one last security guard. "Two ..."

"No," Mr. Dean said and aimed the gun back at Josie. "Don't think I don't see you. No heroics. Know when your action plan is kaput. That's the lesson here. You remember our friend Catuvolcus, Josie? He betrayed Julius Caesar. He missed a prime generational so-what: the critical path of Rome. And today, Sandra made a similar error here at Eburos. You all saw it." Then to Grace, "This is a Sig Sauer P365, one of the most popular, reliable modern handguns in America. The grip accepts four magazine varieties: ten-round, twelve-round, fifteen-round, and seventeen-round."

"You fired ten times," Mom said quietly.

"Very good," Mr. Dean said, turning the gun on Grace. "But do you know which magazine variety is optimal?"

"No more," Grace said. "You bargained with pieces of me. I believe that when my love sees me, we will find a way out of this prison. We will be happy. And you will be alone. Because we will take away all of your money. All of *you.*"

This Grace, maybe it's her. Or a version hot-fired into solid form by the widow's eye to mimic a specific, hard part of who she was. Not the whole person, just like Dani in the street. An iron version of what she could have been.

"You'll ask him to do that?" Mr. Dean said, with a half-smile. "If I let you jump in the pool, you will erase everything we built together?" He stepped closer.

Grace didn't move. "Never me. You did this."

"Is it true, what she said?" He meant Sandra. "About our clients, that they used to run the world? They were apex predators, and we were—what, rodents?—until you found the Friendly Man and reimagined the timeline."

"He'll put it back that way," Grace said. "If you make him angry enough. He won't just take away your bank accounts, he will take your entire world. Turn you into food again. All of you ..." She blinked at Josie, Mom, and Tamara. "I don't want that. I won't let him. But if you make him angry, well and truly angry ..."

"Enough," Mr. Dean said and steadied his grip on the gun with both hands. "A new agreement. You will be under contract to The Eburos Group, and on behalf of the firm ..."

"No."

"... you will promote synergy between our core competencies and our friend here. You will ..."

"No," Grace said again. "I am going to step into the water." She smiled at Josie. "Goodbye."

Mr. Dean shot her in the head. The force snapped Grace backwards. She slipped, and he rushed to catch her fall, rolling her away from the pool. Blood and bits of brain and bone floated at the top. "Fifteen," he said. "Fifteen is optimal." Then looked up at Josie. "I can't let any of you go. You understand that, don't you? The Friendly Man won't know that Grace is dead. None of us will go down there ever again. It's very unfortunate." Mr. Dean rose from the body.

"You are so much worse than I remember," Mom murmured.

"We will move on," Mr. Dean said and reached for another cigarette. "This is solvable. Until we locate a new solution, we will have a difficult shareholder meeting, but I believe ..."

A woman in a black robe charged out of the second elevator, and before Mr. Dean could shoot—his cigarette hand up reflexively to stop her—she shoved him back into the pool. He flipped, cracking his head, and went under.

Dani.

Josie rushed to her, and they spun together, arms tight. "I can't believe you," Josie said. "They shot you. I saw ..."

"Yeah," Dani said, nodding weakly at Mom over Josie's shoulder. "Caitlyn, it's good to see you. What was all that?" Dani eased back to look at Josie, inspecting her face.

Color had returned to Dani's cheeks, and her whole body looked fuller, healthy again somehow. *Yes, it's me. We're here. My God, somehow we're here.*

Josie said, "I don't know if I understand it all. I can say that now."

"Me neither," Tamara said, approaching with Mom.

On the floor, none of them were moving: Everett and the other two security guards, Sandra's bloody body, and Grace, flat on her back alongside the bloody pool. Water dripped somewhere, and computers whirred and hummed along the walls.

"Something down there can rewrite history—and the present," Mom said distantly, watching the water. "Is that what he meant? There's a thing down there, something that loved Grace, that would put the monsters in charge again, turn people back into rodents, if it knew Grace is dead." Mom looked up, with a nervous smile. "Listen to me. I can't believe any of this. But that's what he said, isn't it?"

"I want to go," Tamara said. "Can we go?"

"Yes," Josie said.

Mom went first with Tamara, headed back to the elevators, and Josie stumbled over Everett's body, missing a step.

"Josie?" Dani paused to help her balance. "Do you need a hand?"

"I'm okay," Josie said.

"I wonder if it's true, though," Dani said. She let go, stepping back toward the water.

"Mr. Dean is gone," Josie said. "Whatever this is—Eburos is over. All of this ... it doesn't matter. Does it?"

At the elevator Tamara stopped and pointed at Dani. "Hey ... she ..."

On the wall beside the elevator door, a white chalk figure stood with its arms raised high, as if summoning a storm.

"Well, yes," Dani said. "It kind of does." She kicked Grace's body into the pool. It splashed and went under, sinking fast. *Rage. He'll feel nothing but rage when the body drops into his pit. Rage for all of us.*

Why would she ..?

"Hey," Tamara said again. "Look!"

And when Dani stepped close again, Josie saw it, too, should have earlier. *Should have right away: the flicker-movement on the floor, an instant too early.*

Something was wrong with her shadow.

Market News

Chief Executive Solomon Dean has been replaced by The Eburos Group shareholders during an extraordinary session that was held to address the firm's recent under-performance. Dean was unavailable for comment, but provided a statement via a company spokesperson: 'I want to thank the Eburos shareholders and board for this opportunity. For the past 35 years, it has been my privilege to execute the firm's multi-pronged strategy to make Eburos the global market leader in human facsimiles of SAAS revenue models, psychic capture, and nociceptive pain on behalf of our clients.' A new member of the firm's legal team, Deputy General Counsel Caitlyn Morris, will serve as interim CEO.

Eburos stock was up 42 percent on the news.

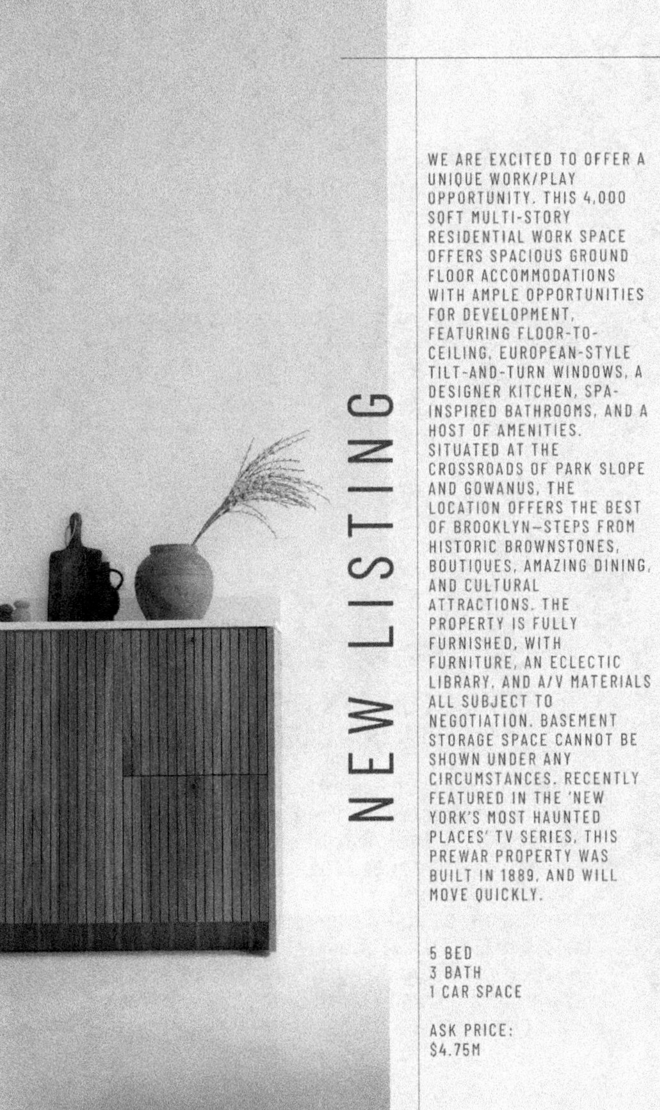

WE ARE EXCITED TO OFFER A UNIQUE WORK/PLAY OPPORTUNITY. THIS 4,000 SQFT MULTI-STORY RESIDENTIAL WORK SPACE OFFERS SPACIOUS GROUND FLOOR ACCOMMODATIONS WITH AMPLE OPPORTUNITIES FOR DEVELOPMENT, FEATURING FLOOR-TO-CEILING, EUROPEAN-STYLE TILT-AND-TURN WINDOWS, A DESIGNER KITCHEN, SPA-INSPIRED BATHROOMS, AND A HOST OF AMENITIES. SITUATED AT THE CROSSROADS OF PARK SLOPE AND GOWANUS, THE LOCATION OFFERS THE BEST OF BROOKLYN—STEPS FROM HISTORIC BROWNSTONES, BOUTIQUES, AMAZING DINING, AND CULTURAL ATTRACTIONS. THE PROPERTY IS FULLY FURNISHED, WITH FURNITURE, AN ECLECTIC LIBRARY, AND A/V MATERIALS ALL SUBJECT TO NEGOTIATION. BASEMENT STORAGE SPACE CANNOT BE SHOWN UNDER ANY CIRCUMSTANCES. RECENTLY FEATURED IN THE 'NEW YORK'S MOST HAUNTED PLACES' TV SERIES, THIS PREWAR PROPERTY WAS BUILT IN 1889, AND WILL MOVE QUICKLY.

5 BED
3 BATH
1 CAR SPACE

ASK PRICE:
$4.75M

The Eburos Group

EBUROS COMMITS TO DELIVERING FOR OUR CLIENTS

At The Eburos Group, we are proud of our core values and mission. The firm's recent settlement of a matter associated with alleged discriminatory conduct was determined to be in the best interest of our clients, allowing us to reduce distractions and focus on results. We are pleased that Josephina Morris has publicly withdrawn all allegations of wrongdoing and wish her well in her travels abroad. As an Eburos alum, she will always have a place waiting for her here.